Rid of a Pest

A M MANTHORPE

Also by:
A M Manthorpe

The Fifth Bullet

My sincere thanks to
Trevor Hampel (http://trevorsbirding.com)
for permission to use his great photograph for the front cover.

ACKNOWLEDGMENTS

To Diane Hester, Kathy Blacker, and Mary Gudzenovs, the three other members of my critiquing group, once again many, many thanks for their help, support, and encouragement. They have critiqued and proof read every draft of this story. As well as that, Diane Hester has kept us focussed and enthusiastic for over twenty years, Kathy Blacker has offered 'just a thought' suggestions and kept us laughing, and Mary Gudzenovs has done all the work in getting this book printed. Without those three this story would still be a file on my computer.

And many thanks to Kathy and Terry for rootling through their sheds to find the cord I wanted for the back cover

CAST OF CHARACTERS

Mounted Constable Bowler Brown
Joan, his wife
Tom and Rose, their children
DC Hugh Morgan, detective from Adelaide
MC Clarrie Palamountain, stationed at Edgerton

Em and Trotter Musgrave, licensees of the Kularook pub
Johnson, their new housemaid
Durwin Harris, their handyman

Silas Beadnall, playboy
Horry Beadnall, his son, and Brenda, his wife, farmers
Leon Beadnall, his second son, and Fran, his wife, farmers
Lilian Beadnall, his daughter
Ada and Joss Beadnall, his sisters
Margot Jennings, his girl friend

Diggory Kenrick, farmer
Muir Kenrick, his uncle, and Sheba, his wife, farmers
Lyall, their son; Stella White, their daughter
baby Andrew, Stella's son
Phemie Borthwick, Sheba's mother

Gwenny and Ralph Wilson, farmers
Maurice, their elder son
Ron Wilson, their nephew
Jack Pedler, farmer
Vince, his second son; Alan, his third son
Juliet and Archie Davidson, farmers
Aleck Fielding, Billy Miller, Bob Norman, farmers and old diggers
Clive Wishart, farmer
Bub Gregory and Ross Lawson, his shearers

Aubrey Venables, would-be farmer
Niels Petersen, carpenter
Jack Pitts, bank manager
Tip Tillerman, commercial traveller
George Pollock, remittance man
Gladys and Pen Parry, concert party owners
Robert McBain, member of the party
Gerard Talbot, Rector at Edgerton
John Shapcott, GP at Edgerton

*

Old James, Young James, and Helen
Diggory's deceased grandfather and parents

1

In the cupboard-sized office of the Kularook Hotel Em Musgrave, frowning over a column of figures in her ledger, heard the rumble of a powerful car engine outside in the street. A second later came a feminine scream, a loud crash, and the screech of metal clawing metal. She slapped shut her ledger. That sounded as though Silas Beadnall had arrived.

After a moment she heard his voice, one of two strong men's voices swearing antiphonally. She didn't recognise the other voice: who had he run into this time?

Her curiosity wasn't strong enough to take her outside. She grabbed a couple of room keys from the pigeonholes behind her, lifted the hinged end of the desk, and went into the bar to tell her husband Trotter they were now on the final run-up to Silas's dinner party and he'd better bring in the luggage.

Silas had arranged the dinner by telephone from Adelaide a fortnight before. 'Oysters and lobsters and chickens, things like that, Em. Nothing but the best. And a birthday cake, I'd better have a cake. But don't stick candles on it, I don't want sixty-six damn candles dripping grease everywhere.'

'Yes Silas.' Em hooked her scratch pad from under a drift of bills and scrawled a few notes. 'How many guests?'

'Ten. A slap-up dinner for ten. And get Trotter to order in some decent champagne. We're celebrating more than my birthday.' He added hastily, 'You don't have to tell the boys that, Em. I want to surprise them.'

'I won't say a word.' Ten of them? His two sons and their wives, his unmarried daughter — who else? 'But champagne? What about my policeman friend across the road? He'll do us for trading after hours.'

'I'll take care of a licence.'

'Good. We can manage the rest of it. What do you want for pudding, Silas? I could make you fruit salad and ice cream, or a trifle, or rum babas. What? Apple pie? Bavarian cream? Plum pudding?'

'Slow down, dammit. Make it a trifle. My grandmother used to make one so full of sherry that all of us small fry got tipsy every Christmas. Make me one like that.'

'All right.'

'And send the bill to Horry; he's paying for this.'

'Does he know that, Silas?'

'Well, not Horry, the farm accounts. It's all right, Em, you'll get your money.'

'Horry is crying poor.'

'Horry is always crying poor. He grudges his poor old dad every penny he has to fork out. But after all, whose farm is it? I could kick the lot of them off tomorrow if I wanted to. And they'd better not forget it. Oh and Em, I need to book a couple of rooms too — we'll be staying with you, not out on the farm. Two rooms.'

'Yes, Silas,' Em said. Though he'd probably only use one, the lecherous old goat: he must be bringing whichever young woman was the current recipient of his volatile affections. And, if he was arranging the party for her, she must be a bit more important than usual. Silas didn't usually return to the scenes of his youth to celebrate his birthdays.

Em pencilled two rooms into the guest book and turned to a fresh page of her pad, to begin making lists.

2

Silas's two sons, Horry and Leon, worked the family farm fourteen miles out of Kularook and lived on the place with their wives. Because neither wanted more of their father's company than was absolutely unavoidable, they didn't drive in to Kularook until late on the afternoon of the party.

They made a slow journey, a cold journey. Icy winds whistled through gaps in the side-curtains of the tourer car. Heavy rain had left sheets of water across the track and laid bare new reefs of limestone; Horry had to take care that he didn't drive into deep mud and get them bogged. They arrived just before six, their red faces tingling, and trooped into the pub lounge to greet their sire before they went to change for dinner.

They were unprepared to find a young woman, a well-groomed blonde in her twenties, sitting beside him at one of the half-dozen small tables in the room. Silas leapt up, nearly upsetting the sherry glasses.

Like his sons, Silas was of middling height, though where farming kept them lean, good living was beginning to thicken his waist and bulge a little pot into his shirtfront. In spite of this, his grizzled hair, and his developing jowls, he was still a strong and active man.

He surveyed his sons with the eyes of a predatory animal —

greedy, alert, and totally devoid of sentiment. His strong features wore a slight smile, partly self-satisfied, partly malicious, as though congratulating himself on the unpleasant surprise he was springing on his nearest and dearest.

'Horry! Leon! Here you are at last. My sons, Margot. This is Miss Jennings, a dear friend of mine.' Smiling blandly, his gaze going from one to other of them, he was obviously relishing the consternation he could read in their faces. 'And Brenda and Fran. Their wives, you know.'

Margot Jennings rose. She was dressed with impeccable good taste in a grey coat and skirt, cream silk blouse, and black pumps; a small grey felt hat was perched on the side of her head. Extending a small hand in an expensive kid glove she said pleasantly, 'How do you do. I am so pleased to meet you at last.'

With gritted teeth both Horry and Leon managed to shake the hand.

Their wives could not. Horry's wife Brenda, affronted beyond words, gave a frosty nod and then wished she hadn't.

How dare the old pest foist his latest tart on them! They'd known for years what he got up to in the city — known, and bitterly resented the way he squandered more than his share of the farm's profits on a succession of gold-digging floozies — but they had never been faced with one of the shameless creatures before. Stiff with offended rectitude, Brenda stalked from the room. She wished she had kept her distance like Fran.

For Leon's wife hadn't even entered the room. Dark and slender, she leant at ease in the door frame, arms folded, eyebrows raised, unimpressed by Miss Jennings's charms and obviously amused at the dramatic potential of the scene before her.

As she passed her Brenda muttered, 'Are you coming, Fran? I want a word with Lilian — if she's known about this — this — this hussy and hasn't warned us, she's as bad as he is.' From the thin, bespectacled housemaid carrying an armful of towels up the passage, she demanded, 'Where is my sister-in-law? Miss Beadnall — which is her room?'

Fran followed. 'I'm quite sure Lilian knows nothing. When has she ever done anything as intelligent as keeping an eye on her father?'

When they went into her room Lilian Beadnall, in a black silk kimono with a vivid gold chrysanthemum embroidered on the back, was sitting before a mirror arranging thick, glossy brown plaits in a coronet around her head. She smiled faintly at their reflections at her shoulder yet didn't look round.

'Good afternoon, Brenda. Fran. I didn't hear you knock. How are you both?'

Her sister-in-law's ponderous manner had always annoyed Brenda. She exclaimed, 'Lilian! Have you seen the Old Pest's latest? Did you come down with them?'

'I did not. I came by train. I never go anywhere with Father, since he usually embarrasses me in public — intentionally, I might add. Yes, I met Miss Jennings a few minutes ago. Did you knock, by the way?'

Brenda flipped her hand at such trivia. All right, she should have knocked, but the disaster confronting them demanded an immediate conference, one too important to be derailed by trifles.

Fran, however, smiled and said, 'No, dear. Brenda is a little upset.'

Damn Fran, always ready with her pinpricks. 'You should be too. Both of you.' Brenda shrugged out of her overcoat and hurled it on the bed. 'What on *earth* are we going to do? Good God!' Lilian's hair! She leant to inspect her sister-in-law's coiffure more closely. 'That isn't your hair.'

'No,' Lilian agreed, placing another pin. 'As you yourself have remarked more than once, my hair isn't much of an advertisement for a hairdressing salon.'

'Well, those plaits look lovely.' Did they? Brenda wasn't sure, yet she might as well try to mend her fences. They'd need Lilian's help and support if they were going to defeat the machinations of that blonde whore. And the coronet of plaited hair, she supposed, did add a certain distinction to Lilian's stout, well-corseted figure. 'Not at all false.'

Unmoved, Lilian thrust in the last hairpin. 'What you have never understood, Brenda, is that my salon is not some poky little shop in the suburbs giving cut-price perms and uneven haircuts and reeking of cheap cosmetics. It is an exclusive salon where I employ only the most skilled girls, and if my hair looked false I would sack the girl involved.' In the mirror she raised her glance to the woman behind her. 'You should let her try what she could do with yours.'

Brenda, whose bobbed hair was set in artificially regular waves with the aid of curling tongs, could recognise tit-for-tat when she met it. Instead of the fiery response she would have liked to make she restrained herself.

She said, 'I have neither the time nor the money to spend on fancy hairdressing. And if Silas squanders as much on that young whore as he did on the last one I'll be lucky if I have the money to feed my family, let alone for hair styling.'

She was irritated to see Fran, detached and amused, lounging against the pillows on the bed; she had kicked off her high-heeled shoes and stretched one long silk-clad leg along the counterpane. Fran always pretended that the money squabbles were beneath her, yet she made damn sure Leon was there with his hand out when cash was to be had from the farm. *And* she spent it fast enough when she got it.

Anyway, perhaps Fran was coming to her senses, for at this she nodded lazy agreement and said to Lilian, 'You at least have an income the old pest can't get his hands on. We don't — whatever he spends comes straight out of our pockets.'

Lilian raised her brows. 'I hope you are not suggesting that I give up my share in the farm? I am at present setting up my second salon and I need every penny.'

Brenda said passionately, 'Why can't you borrow what you need? Why do you have to rob my children just to make your business bigger?'

'I am not robbing anyone. Part of that farm's income is mine, and I have just as much right to it as Father and my brothers have to their much larger shares. Though I have sometimes suspected,' Lilian added, spacing her words judiciously, 'that some of the profit never finds its way to the bank, to be shared with the rest of us.'

Brenda felt her face flush its familiar blotchy red. 'That's a lie! A shocking unjust lie!'

Lilian turned, the better to see her. 'Is it? You would know.'

'Lilian! That's an outrageous accusation. I have never been so insulted in my life, and I'll tell Horry. We would *never* do such a thing. He'll make you apologise.' She was almost stuttering in her fury. How dared Lilian!

Smiling, as though amused by the acrimony, Fran drawled, 'Girls, girls.' She made a patting, keep-it-down motion with one hand. 'You're straying from the point. Have your fight later if fight you must. Now we have to decide what we should do about Little Miss Muffet out there. Do we cut her dead, or wriggle ourselves into her good graces so that she can put in a kind word for us with Silas?'

'I doubt if she would do that,' Lilian said. 'I for one intend to treat her with common courtesy.'

'Never!' Brenda glared at her imperturbable sister-in-law. 'You do realise he has arranged this fancy dinner in her honour, don't you? It's nothing to do with his damn birthday. He's planning to marry her. He must be! We'll have to get rid of the hussy.'

Lilian had finished with her hair. She threw a towel round her shoulders to protect the kimono and dusted a swansdown powderpuff across her nose.

'If you know of some way to get my father to change his mind I wish you would impart it to me. I have known him longer than either of you and I have never seen him take notice of anything but his own selfish wishes.' She lifted her head and met Brenda's gaze in the mirror. 'If, on the other hand, you know some method of detaching blood-sucking little leeches like Miss Jennings when they know they are on to a good thing, I wish you had employed it before, on some of his previous fancies. Then we would all be better off.'

Fran laughed, and clapped gently. 'Admirably put. In other words, no matter how outrageously the Old Pest is behaving we'll just have to lump it. As we always do.' She bared her teeth, a restrained vixen snarl. 'And you're right of course, Lilian. Putting Little Miss Muffet's back up won't help us at all. Nothing will, that I can see.' She stretched her arms above her head and got off the bed. 'Who else is invited to these dire jollifications, do you know, Lilian?'

'Father informed me the Aunts have come down for the occasion. And he has invited Colly Gordon as well.'

Fran groaned. 'That old reprobate! And Silas's ghastly sisters. What a merry evening this promises to be.'

'You shouldn't say that about Ada and Jocelyn. They are very good-hearted women.' Lilian tucked the puff into the top and carefully replaced the lid on her box of face-powder.

Brenda beat her hands together in frustration. 'Stick to the *point*,' she beseeched. 'We've got to do *some*thing. It's criminal what that man is doing. I wish I could get you two to see that this isn't funny.' Despairing, she looked from one to the other. 'Isn't there *any*thing you can think of?'

Lilian said, 'Would you like to borrow this room to change in?'

'Thanks, but Horry's booked a room here in the pub for the night and Brenda says I can change there.' Fran bent over to pull on her shoes. With her face hidden she added, 'Leon and I are going to stay with Aubrey. We can't afford hotel rooms. Brenda and Horry get more of the farm's profits than we do.'

'Horry takes all the responsibility, and does most of the work,' Brenda said, her voice tight with anger. What was the matter with them? Just as they should be presenting a united front they were ganging up on her. 'You light a fire under your damn Leon, and perhaps the farm would earn a few more quid for you to spend.'

Fran made a wry face and raised her brows at Lilian in the mirror. Brenda saw it, and thought Fran intended her to. The bitch.

3

Miss Margot Jennings, in her own bedroom across the passage, leant towards the dressing-table mirror and studied her reflection. Satisfied her make-up was still flawless, she sat back and took stock.

Her well-tailored coat and skirt now hung in the wardrobe after they had done their work at that first meeting with Silas's family, though the effect hadn't been quite what she had intended. She'd known Silas's snooty daughters-in-law, expecting another of his peroxide blondes, all flashy clothes and crimson nails, would be ready to despise her utterly. Well, she wasn't going to have them looking down their damn noses at her. She was a natural blonde, and with a plain hairstyle and a plain yet elegant suit she had meant to jolt them out of their prejudices by an appearance of quiet good taste.

Yet, instead of making them despise her less, all she had done was make them hate her more. They had been deeply resentful and, if she was any judge of their expressions, almost sick with envy. Her expensive, stylish outfit had been so much newer and smarter than the utilitarian overcoats they had been wearing — of necessity, to protect themselves from wintry weather for slow miles in a tourer car — that they had been infuriated, not appeased. Margot had read the signs. She sighed.

Silas had said, 'Put on a bold face, Sugarplum, they can't touch you. Enjoy your triumph over that frowsty lot.' His eyes had gleamed. 'You know I will.'

Which was all very well for him, but if looks could kill his Sugarplum would be dead by now. That Mrs Horry had looked murderous, absolutely murderous. And Leon's wife had seemed to think she was a bit of a joke, which wasn't much better. I'm no joke, sister, Margot thought, and you'd better believe it. The red bow of her mouth hardened. If they wanted war she had all the ammunition. She had old daddy Silas right where she wanted him.

Someone knocked on the door and the housemaid came in, towels over one arm and with the other holding high a long sky-blue dress on a hanger, which she hitched to the face of the wardrobe. 'The creases pressed out well, Miss. Would you like me to run you a bath now? I can fire up the chip heater.'

Margot turned in her chair to watch the girl hang the towels over the horse. Now she had crossed the great divide she still enjoyed having servants address her deferentially. She had the power to make serving girls jump if she wanted to. Not so long ago she, Margot, had been the deferential one — behind a counter, which was a step or two up from housemaids, yet still not one of the elite who snapped their fingers to make others jump to wait on them.

'What's your name, girl?' The kid couldn't be much more than twenty, and didn't look as though she'd been around much. No makeup, dark beetling brows — someone should show her how to pluck her eyebrows to a decent shape, the poor downtrodden country mouse. And to get different glasses, not those owlish things with heavy tortoise-shell rims. Margot felt herself swelling with pleasantly condescending sympathy.

'Name?' The girl seemed surprised. 'Johnson, Miss. You call Johnson if you want me to get you anything.'

'Well, Johnson, I don't think I have time for a bath but I would like a drink. You can bring me a port and lemon from the bar.'

'I suppose that's all right. I'll ask the boss. Anything else?'

'And bring it to Mr Silas Beadnall's room,' Margot said. 'The one next door to this.'

And how was that for a bold front? You might even say brazen. A single girl drinking with a man in his hotel bedroom — what would the locals think!

They could think the worst, and be damned to them. Silas was right. They couldn't touch her.

4

That Silas's two sisters had, like his daughter, remained unmarried was no coincidence, seeing that in disposition Silas took after his father. All three women had grown up bullied by an ill-natured, bad-tempered, often violent father who was oblivious of any needs but his own. The experience had left them with a deep distrust of men and no confidence that any man could ever show normal consideration towards women.

They had reacted to this upbringing in different ways. Ada, Silas's elder sister, had grown into a fluttery old maid, with a battery of ingratiating smiles and a fund of inane chatter guaranteed to glaze the eyes of any male within a range of ten feet. She was tall and thin, and dressed to match her dithery manner in frills and flounces of pastel-coloured chiffon and similar draperies, usually in shades of grey and lilac; her figure was all wispy outlines without definition.

Jocelin — 'Call me Joss' — was six years younger than her brother and had chosen the other extreme. She was shorter and sturdier than her sister, and became what was known as a 'good sort', with a robust manner, a hearty laugh, and a severe rather mannish style of dressing. She told mildly risqué stories and rolled her own cigarettes, a habit so unheard of for a woman, so horrifyingly uncouth, she got away with it because of its astonishing novelty.

Neither of these personas was a natural one: they had been adopted to deflect condescension and to conceal not only the sisters' considerable intelligence but also the fact that they despised most men, their brother and their long deceased father in particular. They lived contentedly together in a boarding house in North Adelaide, on a meagre income which they augmented by inventing chess problems and selling them to an interstate monthly magazine.

When they had received Silas's telephone call inviting them to his party, they hadn't accepted at once. 'Call you back,' said Joss. 'Have to see if we can afford a trip to Kularook.'

'Of course you can. You've nothing else to spend your money on,' said Silas. 'Pair of dried up old girls like you.'

Joss replaced the earpiece in the bracket. To Ada, at her elbow, she remarked, 'All these years and I've thought my dislike for our brother could go no higher. Now it seems not. There is no end to his boorishness.'

'All the same, Joss, let's go. Phemie is always asking us to stay with her. We can have a few days' holiday in Kularook, see a few old friends at the same time. Anyway, can you remember when we last attended a dinner-party?'

So they had travelled down the day before by train, to be greeted by their childhood friend Phemie Phillips, now the widowed Phemie Borthwick, and driven to her small terrace house on the edge of town behind the pub. It lay in the middle of a row of three, known locally as Widows' Row.

Joss surveyed the paddocks stretching away into the distance beside and beyond it and wondered, not for the first time, why anybody had believed it necessary to build three conjoined dwellings squashed together on one block of land in the middle of all that space.

5

Em cast a last searching look round the pub dining-room, carefully set up for the party. The rest of Kularook might be satisfied with masses of looped coloured streamers and swathes of crepe paper to create a festive mood, but not Em — she had decked the room in flowers she had scrounged from every garden in town, augmented them with branches of glossy leaves, and set the table with the silver dishes and candelabra she had borrowed from her friend Joan Brown across the road. Snowy damask, gleaming silver, soft candlelight — a big city hotel couldn't have done it better.

Satisfied, she returned to the kitchen, now full of canisters of dry ice and mixing bowls and saucepans and stacks of plates, to keep an eye on her pots on the stove.

Her new housemaid came in. The girl looked nothing but skin and bone though Em had discovered, in the weeks since she'd been there, that she was strong as a horse and a tireless worker. The pub hadn't always been so lucky when they'd been forced to advertise in the city papers for help.

'The fires are alight,' the girl said. 'In the lounge and in the dining-room. And it's raining buckets. What time are they eating?'

'Seven. Could you set out the plates for the oysters? Trotter's opening them now. Along with his thumb, poor dear.'

'I heard him.'

'I hope you didn't learn any new words, Johnson.'

Johnson smiled and shook her head. 'Some of the boys where I went to school had pretty comprehensive vocabularies. We heard most words in our playground.'

And that was what bothered Em about her. She was too full of contradictions. She could believe the girl came from a poor and struggling family, as she claimed, but not that she had been in domestic service ever since she left school. Although she might know the correct way to lay a table without being shown, this could be because she came from a family which knew these details as a matter of course. Her language wasn't that of an uneducated girl. And she was too self-contained, too careful to keep her distance from those around her.

All the same, whatever her background and whatever her reasons for taking a housemaid's job, Em liked the girl and had to admire her sturdy independence.

Over the clatter of plates on the table Johnson asked, 'How many of this Beadnall family are staying the night here, Mrs Musgrave? I've only made up four rooms.'

'That's right. Leon and his wife are going to stay in town with friends. Old Silas wants to see them in the morning before he goes back, and so they're all staying in. The farm's fourteen miles out and the track's an axle-breaker at this time of year.'

Johnson laid down her last plate and circled a finger over them to count them. 'Which one is Leon?'

'The dark one. The fair one is Horry, the eldest, he takes after his mother. He and Brenda — she's the stocky one, on the short side — do most of the work on the farm, according to them, though Leon and his Fran insist they do just as much to make the farm pay. All the same, they are certainly more easy-going. Everything seems a bit of a joke to Fran. She's quite a dish.'

'Haven't they any children to bring too?' Johnson thought she might as well keep asking questions while she had the chance. She suspected Em prided herself on knowing most of what went on in and around Kularook; she took all a dedicated gossip's pleasure in telling what she knew of her neighbours affairs to anyone who might ask — and even to those who didn't.

'Not Fran. Brenda has four, but cranky old Silas told them specifically no children at his party so they've left them with a neighbour.' Em glanced at the alarm clock beside the kerosene lamp on the mantelpiece over the stove. 'It's six twenty-five. Silas wants canapes and cocktails in the lounge at six thirty. There are a couple of plates under those tea towels on the dresser. You can take them up any minute now.'

Time for the fancy dress, Johnson thought. She took off her large kitchen apron of floral cotton and tied a small, frilly white muslin rectangle over the skirt of her black dress. With bobby pins she fastened a starched white muslin band in her short dark hair and turned for Em's approval.

'You look fine.' Em grinned. 'Isn't the old Kularook pub putting on dog. If Silas thinks he can intimidate me with all his fancy orders he can think again. I'll trump his ace any time.'

Johnson took the platters and walked sedately up the passage. She waited outside the pub's small lounge for Trotter with the cocktails.

A hissing pressure lamp suspended from the ceiling revealed surely the most ostentatiously formal scene those kalsomined walls had ever seen. Silas must have issued a few instructions to his family as well as to Em, since the women wore elbow length gloves and long dresses, the men black dinner jackets and boiled shirts. Three of the six women were grouped round the fire as though posing for a photograph for the society pages of a magazine.

After Em's descriptions Johnson had no difficulty deciding their identities. Miss Jennings and Miss Beadnall she had already met when she attended them in their rooms; of the other two Fran held a long black cigarette holder elegantly poised in one hand and gazed serenely into the middle distance, Brenda chatted determinedly with Lilian. Across the room Margot, stunning in the blue satin dress Johnson had pressed, every line of her excellent figure displayed, had a possessive hand on Silas's sleeve. He gazed raptly into her eyes.

In a corner two older women were listening with spurious attention to a white-headed man, stooped and gaunt, who was doing his best to flirt with them. Those must be the elderly Miss Beadnalls and old Colly Gordon. He was local; she'd heard a bit about him.

'An old crony of Silas's,' Em had said. 'Pretty wild when they were young, according to local legend.'

The two Beadnall brothers, just inside the door, were muttering together. Johnson thought they were arguing. Horry and Leon, she thought, looking from one to the other and testing the names in her head.

Then Trotter Musgrave — who had drawn a very hostile line at boiled shirts for himself, and was dressed only in a dark suit — emerged from the bar with the cocktails. As he offered his tray to the guests in turn Johnson followed with a plate in either hand. She was facing the door, lifting a plate towards Margot, when the young man who had come out of the bar after Trotter strolled into the room.

One of the women gasped, although Johnson could see nothing startling about him. Just an ordinary young man with a thin face and untidy, overlong hair. Ignoring everyone else in the room he walked directly to Lilian, took both her hands, and bent to kiss her cheek.

'How very good to see you, Lilian. And looking so well.'

A smile of great sweetness lit her heavy face and she patted his shoulder. 'My dear boy, what a lovely surprise.'

'Can you spare me some time tomorrow? I'd like to show you the place.'

'Certainly, Diggory. I will look forward to it.'

'I'll pick you up. Early.' He smiled at her, then turned his head to survey the others. With calm dispassion his gaze rested on each for several seconds before moving on. His mouth twitched. 'I'll tell you all about it then, dear Lilian. Now isn't quite the time. I'll see you in the morning. Good evening.' He made her a courtly half-bow, and turned away. He came face to face with Johnson and her platters.

Her uniform perhaps surprised him; he raised an eyebrow. Then he helped himself to a canapé from her plate, stuffed it in his mouth, winked at her, and strolled out as unhurriedly as he had entered. He had been with them for less than a minute.

Silas's normal high colour was heightened by rage. 'That was the illegitimate brat? Lilian, do you mean to tell me you are on speaking terms with him? I will not have that scum weaselling his way into the family. This is not his family. I won't have it, do you hear? The arrogant bastard, I'll — I'll — I will not put up with it. Lilian, if you planned this —'

'No of course I didn't. Diggory must have heard I would be here, though I didn't tell him. I don't know why you are so angry, Father. Obviously he is not proposing to gate-crash your party.'

'Hush, Silas.' Margot raised her eyes to his face. 'Please. Surely it doesn't matter. He's gone now, don't let him spoil everything, whoever he is.' And she intended to find that out pretty soon. Stray members of the family she hadn't heard of could be unsettling. Though it didn't look as though she need fear much competition for Silas's affections from that one.

What was more worrying was Silas's disregard for this sensible advice. She saw for the first time that he wasn't completely under her spell. When anger possessed him her powers diminished.

He barked at his daughter, 'I forbid you to have anything more to do with him. You will not meet him tomorrow. Do you understand? Horry! Did you know the bastard was in Kularook?'

'Yes, Father. He's been living here for nearly two years. Mostly he keeps out of our way. His grandfather — his other grandfather, I should say — bought Gosling's old place out west of town some years ago and left it to him when he died.'

'I'm no grandfather of his, and I'll sue the next man who says it,' Silas roared, thrusting his head forward from his shoulders like an irate bull. 'He's a bastard, an illegitimate nobody.'

'Technically, no,' Lilian corrected him. 'His father married your daughter before he was born.'

'I have only one daughter.' He glared at her. 'Unsatisfactory though she is.'

'And that one will see whom she pleases when and where she pleases.' Supremely indifferent to his rage, as the sky might be to a bit of volcanic smoke down in one corner, Lilian helped herself to another angel-on-horseback — she didn't often get a chance at those — and said, 'Do be your age, Father. I'm over forty. How do you propose stopping me doing whatever in the world I like?'

'I might decide I have no daughters,' he muttered. 'I'll talk to my lawyers. That'll bring you to heel.'

'Like a dog? You're getting senile if you imagine you can control my actions by threats or any other means.' Lilian turned to Margot. 'Of course Diggory's mother is dead. She died years ago. She was Silas's daughter by his first wife, my half-sister, and he disinherited her when she was nineteen. This must be the first time he has ever laid eyes on her son.'

'Don't listen.' Silas grabbed Margot's arm and turned her to face him. 'This is nothing to do with me. Nothing to do with you. Forget it ever happened.'

'And you must too.' Margot lifted a hand to his cheek, as though to stroke some of the dangerous colour from his face. 'Dear Silas, you must forget it too. This is your birthday, and we are celebrating.'

His expression softened as he looked down into her eyes. His former slyly triumphant manner returned. 'So we are, Sugarplum. So we are. We'll show 'm yet.'

Brenda took a sip of her cocktail and kept her expression blank. She wished she knew of some way to encourage this breach between Silas and Lilian. If only the old pest *would* disinherit her.

Sotto voce to her sister Joss said, 'Old Sy better watch that temper of his. He'll give himself a stroke if he's not careful.'

'So that was Helen's boy.' Ada looked across at her niece Lilian. 'The journalist. Good for Lil for standing up to Silas.'

Colly Gordon wagged his white head. 'You young things, you're getting too independent for an old man these days.'

'Colly, not even you can get away with calling me a young thing,' Joss said. She didn't add what she was pretty sure he wanted to hear, *And you're not an old man.* 'How's that grandson of yours getting on in the Navy?'

That set him off. They could stop listening and entertain themselves watching the rest of the party.

6

Silas sat in state at the head of the table, in a heavy oak carving chair. On his right sat Margot, Leon and Brenda; on his left Fran, Horry and Lilian. Colly Gordon sat at the foot, with one of the Misses Beadnall on either hand.

The women were carrying the burden of the conversation. The brothers, early in the meal, had tried to bring up some details of the farm's management and had been told sternly by Silas to stop, he wasn't going to listen. This was a party. They mustn't talk shop.

So Horry had relapsed into an angry silence. Fran had nobody to talk to but her father-in-law and he, since Margot was cross-examining Leon about the farm, was free to entertain her. Apparently he saw no need. Not that she had anything to say to the old pest — except abuse. Would he agree to sign a settlement, a legally binding document sharing out the farm's income equitably between the four of them? His sons had the facts and figures ready to present to him in the morning, a lawyer's opinion written out, all their best arguments marshalled in order to persuade him. Somehow he had to be forced to share with the rest of them. Their situation was becoming desperate.

Though how persuadable was Silas? Fran glanced at him, caught his eye and smiled, as flirtatiously as she dared. Leon had told her years ago that Silas admired her — 'a high-stepping filly, and a few brains in her handsome head too' — so perhaps she could make use of a few feminine wiles. Though probably now wasn't the time, when he was so taken up with Little Miss Muffet.

Wherever had he found her? And why, this time, was he insisting on introducing his bit of fluff to his ever-loving family? Fran had grave forebodings: she agreed with Brenda that this time it looked serious. Little Miss Muffet looked smug as the cat that swallowed the canary and if she was pleased about Silas's intentions Fran would bet his family would not be.

Yet what could they do? Lilian was right. If Silas was influenced by any member of his family in their discussions tomorrow it would be for the first time.

And that had been an odd incident with his black sheep grandson. Horry and Leon never spoke about their elder sister, so Fran knew only the bare bones of her tragic story. Now it appeared that Lilian had kept in touch with the boy ever since his childhood. She had seemed surprised that her family were interested — as far as she was concerned the matter was between her and Diggory and nobody else.

'I was fond of his mother,' Lilian explained, after the young man had gone. 'Helen was five years older than I, but we were friends as well as sisters, seeing how isolated we were out there on the farm. I was fourteen when Father threw her out, and I never saw her again. By the time I was old enough to defy Silas and leave home myself she was dead. I have never forgiven Father. And I never will. I thought you understood.' She hadn't appeared to care whether Silas heard her or not. Luckily for the peace of the evening, he had been too engrossed with his bit of fluff.

So dignified, pompous old Lilian had harboured fierce resentments under that imperturbable exterior for all those years. Astonishing.

This was a cockeyed party. The four who lived on the farm knew one another too well to have much conversation left over for social occasions. Still, it had been fun getting out her glad rags for a change, and she liked the novelty of eating a meal she hadn't cooked, and in such elegant surroundings too. Mrs Musgrave had worked wonders on the dull pub dining-room.

The best thing about this strange evening was the food. Fran was surprised at the sophistication of the menu and the standard of the dishes brought to the table. She wasn't greedy, but she had an educated palate and these days never saw food like this, since she was an indifferent cook herself. So she had made the most of the meal, consciously enjoying every bite and remembering regretfully the last time she had ever eaten such feasts regularly, when Leon was courting her.

In those heady days he frequently took her to the dining-room of the best hotel in Adelaide in his efforts to impress her. The old duffer: she'd made up her mind to marry him the second time he had invited her out. All the same, it had been pleasant being wined and dined and fussed over for a long enough period for him to believe he had won her heart.

She looked across the table at her husband, caught his eye, and smiled. Dear old Leon. She was fond of him, her big, well-meaning old boy, even if now and then she did wish she could ginger him up a bit. And she had to admit he was coping well with Little Miss Muffet, answering her questions politely without responding to the smirks and fluttering eyelashes. I'd flutter you, my girl, if I had my way, Fran thought. You slimy little chiseller.

7

On Brenda's right hand Ada was pretending to listen to old Colly Gordon, and on her left Leon seemed engrossed with that little whore beside him. Why couldn't he cut her dead? Even exchanging two words with her made Brenda feel contaminated. Bloody Silas.

He had slighted her deliberately. As though it wasn't enough that he had his whore seated on his right hand, he had placed Fran on his left, letting her, Brenda, the senior in rank and certainly the senior in importance, sit at the bottom half of the table. He could at least have let her have the chair at the foot instead of that unpleasant old goat Colly. She was married to Horry, the older brother, the manager of the farm — she and Horry ran that farm, whatever Fran might think. Leon worked there, but he was too unreliable to take any responsibility.

And his wife was seated above Horry's. Silas had done it on purpose to insult her, she had no doubt.

Him and his whore. Prim and proper Brenda found herself wondering why someone hadn't gelded him when he was younger. Although she would have died of embarrassment if anyone suspected she had such vulgar, disgusting thoughts, she had discovered years ago that inside her head was private — nobody could guess what went on in there — and she could let her imagination run wild.

Sometimes it ran so wildly she surprised herself.

She glanced round the table as though to reassure herself no one suspected her awful thoughts. Nobody was watching her. A dreadful man, Silas. None of them could control him. They called him an old pest, yet he was worse than that. He was evil. A licentious, debauched old man who collected expensive whores and lavished on them money she needed for her children. Hatred of Silas gnawed at her soul like a hungry rat. He ought to be locked up.

If only they could make him see sense in the morning. Making him sign an agreement was the only way to guarantee fair shares for them all. Not that Lilian was fair, still drawing an income from the farm when she was also making money in her hairdressing shop. Oh yes, it wasn't a shop, was it, it was a 'salon'. Huh. Pretentious woman. And fancy her keeping in touch with the unknown grandson all these years. A bit underhand, really. If Silas had known he'd have pretty smartly cut her out of her share in the farm, so she'd really been getting her money under false pretences too.

She'd never pay it back, though, selfish bitch. Perhaps if her father was angry enough about her association with young Diggory he would insist she got cut out of the farm now — that might be one bright spot. Though perhaps her brothers wouldn't agree. They were absurdly protective of their sister.

Brenda's eyes filled with tears. She couldn't imagine how she was going to give her children the advantages they deserved. She fought, and struggled, and scrimped, and saved, and she never got ahead; and if she complained Silas called her a snivelling little fool and told her to stop whingeing when all it took was a bit of proper management to make the money go round.

Silas was impossible. Her tears threatened to overflow. Then she saw that Lilian was watching her from across the table so she pretended to cough, to give herself an excuse to bring out her handkerchief.

8

Silas was enjoying himself. The food had surpassed his expectations and he knew a bit about fancy cooking. Good old Em, she had done all he asked and more. She had created a setting worthy of his Sugarplum, and a memorable meal suitable for the announcement he was planning. He must remember to tell Horry to add a bit to the cheque, as a bonus.

And the champagne had been really good. He suppressed a twinge of guilt, because they had got through a few bottles by now, and perhaps he could have economised — but no. Nothing was too good for his Sugarplum. What a little beauty she was.

He'd better not have any more champagne. Except for the toast, of course, when he proposed it after he'd made his announcement. But Sugarplum had promised to come to his room later, after they'd all gone to bed and the pub was quiet, and so he must keep all his faculties alert for her. He grinned. She'd wake them up soon enough, though, even if he was a bit sleepy, his lovely little tease. What a lucky man he was. He put out his hand to cover hers, where it lay on the cloth beside her plate.

Margot turned to smile at him. He whispered, 'Are you ready? Any time now. I'm buggered if I can wait any longer. I know we said after the dessert, but I want to tell them now. Surprise them all.'

'I doubt if you'll surprise them, Silas,' she replied softly, with a ravishing, intimate smile. 'You haven't exactly hidden your feelings.'

'Haven't tried to,' he responded. 'You know how I feel, that's the main thing.'

He patted her hand, pushed back his chair, and stood up. What desultory conversation was going on between his guests was instantly silenced. He wished he had time to read their faces but he couldn't wait.

'My beautiful girl tells me that this announcement will come as no surprise to you. All the same, I wish to announce to you and to the whole wide world that Miss Margot Jennings has done me the great honour to agree to become my wife.'

Surprised or not, the members of his family sat staring at him in a stunned silence.

Silas's formidable brows descended. 'So charge your glasses,' he growled, lifting his own glass, 'and drink to my bride to be. To Margot!' He threw the wine down his throat with a flourish.

'Margot!' echoed Colly, with a leer.

The only other at the table to drink the toast with any semblance of meaning was Lilian. 'I wish you well, Miss Jennings.' She sounded dubious, as though she believed the young woman was going to need all the good wishes she could get. She gave a lead, however, to the others who were dithering, unable to bring themselves to use the hussy's first name. 'Miss Jennings,' the brothers said, grudgingly. Fran sipped and nodded without uttering a word. Brenda sat with her hands in her lap and her gaze fixed firmly on the tablecloth.

Silas swelled, on the brink of an explosion of rage; then he saw the expressions on the faces round the table and the situation seemed to him inexpressibly comic. As he had said to his Sugarplum, they couldn't touch him no matter how sour they looked. He let out a huge roar of laughter.

'If you could see yourselves! Here's your dear old Dad just told

29

you the happiest news of his life, and you look as though you're at a funeral, not a party to celebrate my engagement. Margot, my dear — may I?'

He leaned for her hand and pulled her to her feet beside him. From his breast pocket he fumbled a small red velvet box, snapped it open, and slid a ring on her finger. He lifted her hand and kissed the finger and then, as though affixing a seal, her lips.

'So now it's official,' he said. 'Are you happy, my Sugarplum?'

'Yes,' she whispered. She tilted her hand so the diamond flashed. 'You know how much.' He laughed, patted her haunch, and sat down.

So that was that. Brenda almost felt relieved now that their worst fears had been confirmed. So much for their schemes for a legal settlement of the farm's affairs. Now another player had entered the game, and she had no confidence that the future Mrs Silas would be reasonable in her demands.

For the first time a heavy chill settled in Brenda's heart and she wondered if the worst was really coming to the worst and she and Horry would have to leave the farm to make their living elsewhere. They couldn't! Horry wasn't trained for any career except farming. And they had put their whole lives into the place, so much time and money and heartbreak — they could not walk away from all that. They could not.

9

The clock on the kitchen mantelpiece showed five past eleven by the time Em and Johnson finished washing up and clearing away the mess. The rest of the pub was dark and silent. Fran and Leon had driven off to their friend's house on the other side of town — all of two streets away: anyone standing at the pub's front door could hear the car engine all the way until it stopped — and the other guests had retired to their rooms.

A gust of rain was sweeping over the iron roof, sounding like a wire brush on steel. Em slid the shutter across the vents on the stove front; she straightened her back, stretching the tired kinks.

She said, 'Off to bed with you, you're out on your feet. Goodnight, Johnson.'

The girl pushed up her glasses and rubbed her eyes. 'Goodnight, Mrs Musgrave.'

She took her candlestick from the shelf, lit the candle, and crossed the passage to the little room where she slept. In the weak light she stripped off her uniform and hung it on a hanger. She'd felt rather an idiot in it, almost as though she'd been wearing a fool's cap and bells; she hoped Mrs Musgrave didn't want her to wear that regalia too often.

In pyjamas and dressing-gown she stumbled half asleep to the washhouse at the back door, where she sluiced her face with cold water and cleaned her teeth. Then she collapsed, a rag doll, into her bed and drowned immediately in the depths of sleep.

Some time later a sharp noise woke her. After listening drowsily for a few moments she thought she heard stealthy footsteps in the passage outside her door. The click of the back door closing must have woken her. She rolled out of bed and cracked open her door.

The doorway on the opposite side of the passage glowed softly. Em had turned low the wick of the big kitchen lamp and left it on the table in the middle of the room, for the benefit of one of the guests. A farmer from an outlying property was sleeping at the pub until three in the morning, when he would catch the express train for Adelaide. A thermos of tea and some wrapped sandwiches had been set out for him under the lamp.

Against this light Johnson saw the bulky shape of a man in an overcoat moving cautiously up the passage. He looked furtive and rather sinister. Her heart thudded. She must warn Musgraves. But he was between her and the rest of the pub — should she run out the back door and scratch on their window? Or run round and in through the front door? That was probably better. She hoped she could do it without Overcoat hearing her, in case he turned nasty and tried to stop her. Silently she unhooked her dressing-gown from the door and dragged it on, then peered out, readying herself for a dash to the back door.

While she hesitated she saw him again, in the reflected glow of the still burning fire in the dining-room, and realised she knew Overcoat's identity. Some of the tension left her shoulders. What on earth was Silas's disowned grandson doing sneaking in the back door of the pub at this hour? Anyway, that decided her. Setting her bare feet noiselessly on the cold linoleum she followed him towards the front rooms.

At the junction with the cross passage he stopped. Before he could turn and discover her Johnson extended a finger and prodded him in the back.

'Sheesh!' The young man jumped a foot in the air. He spun round, grabbing for her.

'What are you doing here?' she hissed.

Holding her by the shoulders he demanded, 'Who the hell are you?'

'Keep your voice down, you'll wake everybody. I'm Johnson. I saw you sneaking past my door.'

'Well brought up girls shouldn't go creeping after strange men in the dark,' he said indignantly, letting go of her. 'You scared the life out of me. For all you know I could be highly dangerous, a murderer on the prowl. When they hear intruders skulking up the passage well brought up girls should hide their heads under the blankets in maidenly trepidation and stay put.'

Entering into the spirit of this Johnson asked, 'And let you carry on with whatever nefarious enterprise you have in hand?'

He gave a grunt of amusement. 'As it turns out you're in luck. I am not in the least dangerous nor is my enterprise nefarious. I am merely looking for a dry spot to spend the night.'

'Why not go home, wherever that is?'

'I would, only the flivver had other ideas. She conked out on me. And as her side curtains haven't been sighted since the year dot, if I spend the night in her it will be not only draughty but damn wet. Rain squalls are still coming through, and the rain is not only heavy it's horizontal.'

'Anyway, you aren't strange, I knew who you were. I saw you last night, when you came to visit Miss Beadnall. You're Diggory somebody.'

'Diggory Kenrick, at your service.' He inclined his head in a half bow. 'Oh yes, the demure parlourmaid. You've left your glasses off.' He shook his head, took her elbow, and started steering her back towards the faint glow of light in the kitchen. 'I knew you were too good to be true. Who are you really?'

'Really — of course I'm Johnson,' she said, flustered. 'Who else would I be?'

'Johnson you might be, but you're no parlourmaid. What's your dark secret?'

She stopped in the doorway and dragged her arm free. 'I have no dark secret, none, you're making things up. You don't know — what are you hinting?'

10

Diggory Kenrick leaned across the big kitchen table, his back to Johnson, and turned up the wick in the lamp that had been left burning there. The cupboards along the walls, the cooling stove, the open box of short logs beside it, grew solid as the light reached them.

He said, 'All right, no dark secret. I'm sorry, I didn't mean to frighten you.' He stripped off his overcoat, the shoulders dark with rain, and hung it over the back of a chair which he dragged close to the still-warm stove. 'Come and sit down. Some kind soul has left us some supper.'

'That's not for you, that's for Mr Wishart. He's staying here until he has to catch the train.' She glanced at the alarm clock that lived on the kitchen mantelpiece. Twenty-three minutes to one. Mr Wishart wouldn't be stirring yet.

'There's stacks here, Clive won't miss a sandwich. I've been dancing all evening and I'm starving.' He pulled out a chair and waved an invitation before he seated himself in another and began unwrapping the waxed paper from the packet of sandwiches. 'Chicken sandwiches too. We are doing well.' He broke one and held half out to her.

She hesitated, and then took the sandwich and sat down. She had been so busy that evening she hadn't eaten much; she now discovered she was hungry. 'The chicken was left over from the party.'

With his mouth full he said, 'They're excellent. Tell Em from me.'

'I made them.'

'My congratulations, then.' He bowed from his chair. 'Good girl, you made plenty. Have another. Now I have introduced myself you should do the same.'

Stolidly she said, 'I did. I'm Johnson.'

'Yes, but what Johnson? Or, Johnson what?'

'Johnson full stop. Mind your own damn business.'

He looked at her through his lashes. 'All right I'll change the subject. I'll bet Silas doesn't know Clive Wishart is under the same roof.'

'Why not?'

'He'd have a fit. They fell out years ago and neither is of a forgiving disposition.'

'Fell out over what?'

'How would I know? Ask your boss, Em Musgrave. She makes it her business to know all the dirt in Kularook. But Silas and Clive's farms share a boundary, so they were neighbours, thus giving them plenty of scope for quarrelling. Silas likes quarrelling. It's rather a pastime of his.'

She nodded. 'We heard him roaring at someone at bedtime tonight.'

'There you are then.'

'Is Silas — I mean Mr Beadnall — really your grandfather?'

'I should tell you to mind your own damn business, shouldn't I. On the other hand, my life is an open book, and I freely acknowledge the truth however much I would wish it otherwise. He is not a nice man, Silas.' He shut his mouth hard. Wherever his thoughts had taken him was not a pleasant place.

To break his mood she said, 'I heard your aunt say you had never met him before.'

'What?' He looked at her as though to reposition himself. 'Oh, tonight. If you can call an encounter with that horror-stricken glare of loathing a meeting, yes, that was the very first time.' He paused, considering. 'And the last, seeing I will take damn good care to keep out of his way in future. I never want to lay eyes on him again. Once was more than enough.' He pushed the last of his sandwich into his mouth, pulled out a handkerchief, and wiped his fingers. 'I have my reasons, though I won't burden you with them at this present.'

'Meaning you will some other time?'

He laughed. 'Who knows? You look like a wench who can bear burdens.'

She didn't much like the sound of that. 'Do I?'

'Don't sound so doubtful, I meant it as a compliment. I detect certain strengths in you.'

'How kind of you.'

'Do you have grandfathers, young Full Stop? I suppose yours are lovable old gentlemen, the sort who pat you on the head and top up your pocket-money from time to time.'

'No.'

'No? You should arrange matters better. They're the sort to cultivate, not the Silases of this world.'

'Why should I be better than you at arranging grandfathers?'

'Because I think you'd be very good at arranging your life.' He leaned back in his chair, studying her. 'What's more, I like you better without the glasses. You seem to be managing perfectly well without them. I'd give them up if I were you.'

'Stop it! You're hinting again, of course I need glasses, I —'

'Don't worry, I'm not going to tell anyone what a fraud you are.'

In spite of herself she smiled, believing him, though protested automatically, 'I'm not a fraud.'

'Liar,' he said amiably.

'And you can't have any more sandwiches.' She reached across and pulled the packet away from him. While she re-wrapped them she asked, 'What are you going to do now?'

He got up from his chair, stretching his arms widely. 'What I intended doing before you scared me half to death — park myself in a chair in the lounge and endeavour to sleep. To set your suspicious little mind at rest, I've done it before and Trotter doesn't mind.'

She reached across the table and turned down the lamp. 'I must get some sleep too.'

At the door he stood for a moment looking down at her. 'Good night Johnson Full Stop.'

'Good night.' She watched him walk away up the passage.

11

The lamp was out and the sandwiches gone when Johnson went into the kitchen to light the stove next morning, so presumably Clive Wishart had caught his train. The overcoat draped over the chair was in her way; she hung it on one of the hooks in the passage and knelt to rake out the ashes of yesterday's fire. Later, wheeling her traymobile loaded with teacups up the passage, she looked in the lounge to see if Diggory was still sleeping. The room was empty.

At the first bedroom door she tapped, and waited a second before she opened it. 'Mrs Beadnall? Would you like early tea?'

'What bliss! Yes I would.' Brenda pushed herself up in bed and stretched, arching her back voluptuously, like a cat. One thin strap of her pink swami nightdress slipped down her shoulder yet she made no attempt to retrieve it. Then, realising Johnson had turned from raising the blind and was watching her, she snatched a pink knitted hug-me-tight from under her pillow and struggled into it. 'Horry?' She poked the blankets beside her.

Horry surfaced with a grunt. 'Eh? Tea? Yes, of course. What time is it?'

'Just on eight,' Johnson said, putting a couple of marie biscuits in each saucer before she set the cups on the night table. 'You said to call you at eight.'

Horry, in pyjamas so faded the stripes barely showed, wriggled up to a sitting position. 'That's right.' To his wife he added, 'I must have a word with Leon before —' He rubbed his hand across his bristly cheek. 'Hell! Father! I was forgetting — Have you woken my father yet?'

'No, sir. I'll get to him in a minute or two.'

'I'll walk round to see Leon before breakfast,' Horry decided. His cup rattled in the saucer. 'Though heaven knows if Father will listen to us now.'

Johnson closed the door and rapped on the next. Lilian, plaits removed and her own wispy hair round her shoulders, was sitting up in bed reading; she peered over her glasses.

'Thank you, yes. A luxury I don't enjoy at home. I live alone, you see.' She smiled at the girl, inviting her to share her pleasure. 'I'm a little peckish — could you spare another biscuit, do you think? Thank you so much.' She frowned, as though at an unpleasant memory. 'Is my father stirring yet?'

'No, miss.'

'I don't suppose — no, never mind. Thank you, Johnson.'

A commercial traveller had been staying in the room on the end but he was gone now; she had served him an early breakfast over an hour before. The next door was Silas Beadnall's. Johnson, reluctant to beard the lion, pushed her traymobile past it. She would leave him until last.

Miss Jennings, wearing an eau de Nil satin negligee over matching satin pyjamas, opened the door herself. She looked past Johnson into the corridor, glancing about as though expecting someone else. Her movements were nervous and jerky; she looked almost frightened, and so heavy-eyed she couldn't have slept well.

She brought her gaze back to the housemaid. 'Tea? Yes of course I want tea.' She scrambled into the tumbled bed. 'You haven't — I mean, has Silas had his tea?'

'No, miss. He's next.' Johnson saw the young woman's eyes were rimmed with red, almost as though she'd been crying. 'Are you all right?'

'Of course I'm all right. What are you staring at? That's all, damn you. Go away.'

What could have happened to upset Miss Jennings this morning? At the dinner party the evening before she had looked like a girl whose every dream had come true. While waiting at table, Johnson had heard Silas announce the engagement and seen Margot Jennings relishing her triumph, had seen her almost purring with satisfaction. She'd been savouring every moment, enjoying the other women's discomfiture, flashing her diamond ring, revelling in her power over Silas, a woman on top of the world.

She didn't look that now.

Johnson knocked on the next door. No answer. She put her head round the door and asked, 'Tea, sir?'

The figure on the bed didn't move. Yet he too had asked to be called at eight, so she crossed the room and pulled up the holland blind. The showers had stopped though dense white clouds still raced across a pale sky. Cloudy reflections slid over sheets of water lying in depressions in the trodden earth of the pub yard; in front of the old stone stables Silas's powerful sports car gleamed wetly. Johnson turned to the bed.

'Sir?'

She stepped closer. Her breath stilled. After a few moments she stepped back. Stiffly she walked into the passage, carefully she closed the door behind her. Then, leaving the traymobile where it stood, she ran along the passage, round the corner, and back to the kitchen.

Em turned from making toast at the open door of the stove. 'What's up?'

'It's Silas Beadnall. He's —' She snatched a breath, released it. 'I think he's dead.' She pulled a chair from the table, collapsed onto it, and covered her mouth with her hands. She closed her eyes. 'He is dead. He has to be. There's something round his neck.'

'What!' Em stared. Then she whipped off her apron and dashed out. More slowly, Johnson followed.

12

Em was holding about six feet of electrical flex between her hands when Johnson entered the room. It was a standard electrical connection, three insulated wires bound together by a layer of brown cotton sheathing and fastened into a round Bakelite three-pin plug at one end, a flat rectangular plug to fit an electric jug or toaster at the other. In two places the cord had been forced into tight spirals.

'He's been dead some hours,' Em said. 'I was a nurse, you know; he's not the first I've seen.' She turned the flex in her hands and examined it closely, as if it could give her information on how the man on the bed had died. Johnson thought her movements automatic while her mind was busy with a problem.

'Yes, Mrs Musgrave.'

In the short time she had worked there Johnson had already discovered that Em-at-the-pub was, as well as an efficient disseminator of local gossip, the first stop for medical advice for most of the Kularook population before they undertook a drive of forty miles to a doctor. She watched the older woman reach for a dangling corner of the sheet and flip it over the face of the man on the bed.

Johnson had seen that face when she found the body and had been careful not to look at it since. The appalling distortions, the starting eyes and gaping mouth, not only horrified her they disgusted her, and she believed this was wrong. She should have been more compassionate; she should have been moved by pity for the tragedy of a man killed before his time, when all she wanted to do was keep out of range of those staring eyes.

The man had died horribly. Now the figure on the bed was no longer a man. That thing was a body. A corpse. A lump of unmeaning clay. Not an object to be afraid of.

'Johnson.' Em was back to her brisk, everyday self. 'Run and wake Trotter and send him here. Then go over and tell Bowler Brown. I know it's Sunday, he might be sleeping in or he might be working his horses — he might be anywhere, but make sure he knows as soon as possible. I'm going to stay here.'

'Yes, Mrs Musgrave.'

'And come back straight away. You'll have to get the breakfasts for the guests if I'm busy.'

'Yes, Mrs Musgrave.'

Once Trotter Musgrave had been told the shocking news Johnson ran out the back door of the pub into the side street.

The elms in front of the petrol pumps on the corner were thrashing in the stiff breeze. A gleam of sunlight pierced the tumbled clouds, flashed over them, and was lost. Racing across the unsealed road Johnson had to watch her feet to avoid the ruts of puddled slush, the shining wet mosaic of dots and dashes gouged by the Model T's tyres when Trotter drove to the railway to pick up supplies for the bar. The gate in the police station front fence, embedded in weeds, stood open permanently as though in welcome. She jumped up the step to the half veranda of the bungalow that housed the Kularook Police Station as well as the policeman and his family.

The office would be unattended on a Sunday. She banged loudly on the front door beside it. She heard footsteps, and then the door was yanked abruptly open by a scowling man in shirtsleeves and braces. His cheeks were dark with a weekend beard and he looked so ferocious she fell back a step.

Mounted Constable William Brown's expression softened when he saw her. 'Oh, hullo, Johnson. I thought you were some hardhearted beggar with work for me on my day off. What does Em want now?'

'I am,' Johnson said. 'I mean, it is work for you, it's Silas Beadnall. He's dead. We just found him.'

'Party too much for him, was it?' Bowler reached behind him and hooked a jacket off a peg on the wall. As he waved for her to precede him he shrugged himself into it. 'All right I'd better see for myself.'

'No, you don't understand. There's a cord round his neck.'

'Bloody hell.' Bowler stopped dead. 'He was strangled?'

She nodded, feeling the weight of her head heavy on her neck.

Bowler said, 'Look, you go on. I must get a couple of things and warn my wife I might be a while.'

He watched her go, trying to remember what he knew of Silas Beadnall. He knew the sons better, though that wasn't saying much. One of them had an attractive wife; Bowler knew all the attractive women among those he called his 'parishioners'.

Not that he'd swap his Joan for any of them. Not even now, when the infuriating woman was making his life damn difficult. And if that wasn't enough, here was a messy murder to sort out.

He sighed. He'd been happily looking forward to a full day off, with nothing to do except school his horses and hope the weather was clearing.

13

'Hullo, Bowler,' Em said. 'Here's a pretty kettle of fish.'

'That's not showing much respect for a man's life cut short.' Bowler bent over the bed. The room smelled of some kind of hair oil, too strong to be pleasant. 'Where's the cord? Your girl said he had a cord round his neck.'

'Respect for Silas Beadnall? Come on Bowler, you knew him too.' Em handed him the electrical cord. 'He was a spiteful man who positively enjoyed stirring up trouble, and it's a wonder somebody didn't knock him off before this.'

'I didn't know him, I only met him once. The rest was hearsay.' Bowler extended the cord between his hands, careful not to stretch the crimped sections. 'You took this away?'

'Don't tell me I was tampering with the evidence, damn you,' Em said irritably. 'I was so shocked I hardly knew what I was doing. As for evidence, you can see what happened more clearly with the cord removed. And there's been a lot of force exerted to make those marks on his neck.'

'Yes.' Corrugations in the cord showed where they had been twisted tightly together. Someone had run the cord round Silas's neck, taken the two parts in one hand, pushed a lever — something strong and short — between the parts, and wound the cord up like a tourniquet. Patiently he said, 'Show me how the cord was lying. Were these sections still twisted together?'

'Oh all right, all right, I'm sorry I touched the damn thing. Yes, I think they were. Behind his neck.'

Bowler turned himself in a full circle and saw nothing which could have been used as a lever from where he stood. A fountain pen? A shoehorn? A piece of stick? A fly was crawling up inside one of two empty glasses which stood on the washstand beside the china basin and ewer.

He said, 'Which side of his neck?'

'To his left. Does it matter?'

'Probably not. But detectives like their i's dotted, and you can bet Adelaide will send one like a shot as soon as I tell them about this.'

And if Em had had the bollocking Bowler had endured from the head sleuth, when he hadn't reported all the bloody details the man had wanted, she'd probably start counting Silas's eyelashes as well, in case some of them had gone missing.

'Unless of course in the meantime someone puts his hand up,' said Em, 'and admits he'd finally had enough of dear old Silas. Have you rung John Shapcott?'

'He's as delighted as I am to be called out on a Sunday, but yes, he's coming.' Not that Bowler expected him to be able to tell him any useful information, like time of death, but at least he could make out the damn certificate.

'He'll have a slow drive. The road will be half under water.'

'That's his problem. He shouldn't be a country GP if he can't cope with bad roads.'

And if Bowler had overcome his scruples and retired to live on his wife's money he wouldn't be confronted by murdered corpses on a peaceful Sunday morning either. Though if that was what she wanted, as he kept telling Joan, she should have married some other man.

Silas lay on his back, arms and legs straight, with the bedclothes pulled roughly over him. Ignoring his swollen face Bowler pulled the sheet back further to look at the position of the limbs. 'Someone arranged him tidily when it was all over,' he said. 'Thoughtful of the bastard. I don't suppose you have any idea who did this?'

'Fat chance. The place is crawling with people who detested him. After last night Horry and Leon were properly steamed up, and Silas has never been short of enemies. He was always trampling over someone.'

'Do you know where this cord came from? Can't be many lying about in Kularook when we have no electricity.'

'No idea. A useless thing. It isn't mine.'

Bowler straightened his back and flexed his shoulders. 'Well, I'd better let my bosses in Adelaide know, and then start asking questions. Who have you got staying, Em?'

'Horry and Brenda and the daughter Lilian,' Em said. 'You wouldn't know her. And the cause of the rumpus, Miss Margot Jennings.'

'What rumpus?'

'Silas announced his engagement last night, that's the reason he arranged the dinner party. The family were horrified. She's less than half his age and he's been carrying on as though he wanted to rub his family's noses in it to annoy them as much as possible.' She nodded towards the bed. 'Looks like he succeeded. Better than he intended.'

Bowler ran his fingers through his hair and stood, hand on head, gazing past his upraised arm at the terrible, livid face of the dead man. He had seen enough of death in the Great War to be familiar with most of its guises, yet this was a new one. Bullets — No, he didn't want to think about bullets.

14

With his gaze on the corpse, Bowler said, 'One of the family, you think, Em?'

Hastily she said, 'I'm not telling you your job.'

'Not mine. I told you, they'll send some detective. All the same, I'd better get statements from everybody concerned before they have time to invent too many lies.'

'I haven't told any of them yet. And Trotter's made sure they stay in their rooms until you can see them. No swapping notes. But there's only one other room between this and the side door to the dunny — anyone could have come in that way without disturbing the rest of us.'

'Who slept in the next rooms? They might have heard something.'

'Miss Jennings on that side. Lilian Beadnall's room is across the passage opposite this, with Horry and Brenda next to her.'

'And the room next to this, on that side?' He tilted his thumb.

'Mr Tillerman, a commercial traveller, but he's gone, ordered an early breakfast and was away before seven. I've got his home address in the book if you need it, though he could be back in a couple of days. Sometimes he stays again when he's heading home.'

'We'll see. Who found him?' Bowler nodded at the bed.

'Johnson. The housemaid.'

'A nasty shock for her, poor kid. It's a wonder she isn't having hysterics.'

'She's tougher than that.'

'How is she doing? You must miss Agatha.'

'Of course I do, though that's because Agatha was a friend as well. This kid is all right.'

'Has she opened up enough to tell you her first name?'

'No, and I'm not going to ask. But I don't think she's hiding from any of your mob, if that's what's worrying you. You leave her alone, Bowler.'

'Curious, that's all.' And he was curious. The girl was so self-contained she was almost secretive; she put all his policemanly reactions on the alert.

Bowler prowled the bedroom where Silas Beadnall had died. He looked at the level of kerosene in the small glass lamp on the dressing table, opened drawers, peered into the wardrobe. A gaping Gladstone bag, still full of shirts and socks and underclothes, stood beside the room's one straight-backed chair. A little water in the china basin on the washstand, two empty glasses beside it. Without touching them he bent and sniffed inside each one. Spirits of some kind, he thought: whisky or brandy.

On the floor half under the bed was a cheap book with yellowed pages and a brightly-coloured picture of a cowboy on the cracked cardboard cover. He picked it up and tossed it on the chair.

Em watched him. 'Before I go, you'd better know Horry had a blazing row with his father last night. They were on their way to bed, and Horry waylaid Silas and started trying to persuade him over some kind of farm business — you know the farm still belongs to the old man, though the sons run it now. Anyway, Silas took exception to something, and the next thing you know they're shouting and yelling and waving fists at one another. Trotter heard more of it than I did.'

'All right, I'll check with Trotter and then find out what Horry has to say. What time was this?'

'Around eleven, thereabouts. The women had gone to bed earlier, but Silas and his sons sat up for a while with a bottle of port. Fran too — she was waiting for Leon. They weren't staying here; they spent the night round at Aubrey Venables's.'

'Right.' He turned for the door. 'Come on, I'd better lock this room until John Shapcott gets here.'

When Em had gone, Bowler went out through the side door where a few yards of path, sheltered by an iron roof, led to the outside dunny. He couldn't see any unusual signs in the muddy ground around the doorway; if the murderer had come in that way he hadn't left any traces to assist the poor hard-worked constabulary. Innumerable prints of men's boots, several of men's shoes, and half a print from the pimpled sole of what appeared to be a child-sized gumboot lay outside the door.

No child had twisted the cord that had choked the life out of Silas.

He'd better hear what Trotter had to say, then confront Horry Beadnall. Bowler didn't know Horry well — a hard-working farmer, and slightly pompous with it. No, not pompous, self-righteous. And a bit martyred. Not an attractive combination, though by all accounts anyone with Silas for a father had every right to feel martyred.

15

From the straight-backed chair beside the bed Horry, bristling with anger, bounced up to confront the policeman. 'Bowler! For God's sake, what's the matter with Trotter? He says I mustn't go out. What's going on?'

Brenda lay propped on pillows against the bedhead with the bedclothes pulled up to her nose. Remains of mascara smudged her eyes; for some reason she reminded Bowler of a sharp-nosed little animal peering from its lair.

She said, 'The man's run mad. He seems to think he has the right to order us about.'

This room smelt of Evening in Paris scent, a powerful sweet perfume that reminded Bowler of his brother's wife. He said, 'Not his orders, my orders. He was waiting for me.' He paused. 'Sit down, Horry. Bad news, I'm afraid.' He paused. Neither Beadnall showed more than mild curiosity. Anyway, he knew of no easy way to say this. 'Horry, your father is dead.'

Although he was watching closely, he could read neither of their faces. Perhaps they were surprised; yet there for a split second Brenda looked almost gleeful, while Horry's anger dissolved into a stagy sombre expression, the product of effort, not emotion.

'Poor old Dad.' Horry tried to sound sincere. Ponderously he added, 'It must have been his heart. He certainly indulged himself last night.'

'No. Your father's been murdered.'

'Murdered!' Horry shot to his feet, then slowly subsided to his chair. He looked horrified enough there, though was he still acting? 'Dad murdered! He can't be. What happened? I mean, how — what —?'

Deliberately provocative, Bowler said, 'If you don't already know how, I'm not going to tell you.' This man had to be the most likely suspect — he had motive, means, and opportunity by the bagful.

Red-faced and furious, once more Horry leapt from his chair. 'That's a bloody insult!' He waved his clenched fist under Bowler's nose. 'Don't you get funny with me.'

Unmoved, Bowler slapped his hand down. 'All right. If you didn't kill him, who do you think did? Have you seen anything, heard anything, that might point to someone?'

'Oh.' This time Bowler could see both of them eagerly searching their memories for a suitable candidate at whom to point the finger, and with obvious regret shaking their heads.

Horry started for the door.

Bowler barred his way. 'A couple of questions first.'

'Get out of my way. I must see him.'

'Later. Plenty of time. Horry, last night you had a row —'

'You have no right to stop me. He is my father.' Flat-handed, Horry shoved the policeman in the chest and tried to push past.

Bowler's reflexes acted too quickly. He had Horry bent over with his arm up his back before his more rational self realised this was no way to get cooperation from this pair. A cup and saucer on the corner of the dressing table, bumped in the scuffle, toppled to the linoleum floor and smashed. Against the pillow Brenda started so violently the iron bedstead shook.

'Behave yourself,' Bowler said, as calmly as he could manage, and released the arm. 'I have every right. This is murder, you fool, a crime. Of course I'm in charge.' To Brenda, watching wide-eyed, he said, 'Make him see sense. Otherwise I'll drag him over to the station until he damn well tells me what I want to know. Horry, sit down and answer my questions.'

Breathing hard, Horry kept on his feet with his back turned.

'All right. Late last night you had a row with your father in his room, as he was going to bed. What was that about?'

Horry did turn then, and glared. 'Who's been telling tales?' When Bowler didn't answer, he said, 'Bastards,' with deep feeling. In a loud angry voice, as though reciting a lesson against his will, he continued, 'It's no secret. Legal stuff, we were deciding this morning about the farm. Father was making last-minute difficulties.' He glanced at his wife and moderated his stridency. 'Just as well I did manage to talk him round or you'd be sure I did it.'

'So when you left him he was still alive and had agreed to whatever he was yelling about earlier. When he said, "I'm damn well not going to sign anything."'

'Oh yes,' Brenda said quickly before her husband could answer. 'Horry made him see our point in the end. They were going to talk more about it this morning. Fix the details.'

'I see.' Bowler was pretty sure they were lying. 'What had he agreed to sign?'

'Oh, just tidying up the status of the farm. He was still technically involved, you know.'

A bit more than technically if he still owned it, as Em had stated. 'Did your brother know you had talked Silas round? He left before the quarrel.'

'Leon?' Horry looked shocked as he realised where Bowler's thoughts were tending. 'Leon wouldn't.'

'Wouldn't what?'

Horry shook his head.

Bowler didn't push it. 'Did either of you hear anything in the night? Mrs Beadnall? A cry or a door shutting, voices — anything at all?'

'No.' She looked at her husband. 'We were pretty tired, the late night and the party you know, so once our heads hit the pillow we were asleep.'

For farmers, eleven would be one or two hours past their normal bedtime. And he wouldn't bother asking them if either had been out of bed in the night. These two were not going to admit to anything. Bowler squatted to collect the broken china and took it with him when he left the room.

16

As he pushed open Miss Margot Jennings's door, Bowler thought perhaps she should have been the first one to be told about the death. He'd gone burning off to interview Horry because he knew the man, and because he was keen to know what the quarrel had been about. This poor girl was perhaps more closely involved emotionally than any of them.

She was sitting, as Horry had been, on the chair beside the bed. She was swathed in a lot of greeny satin with matching high-heeled slippers, and the effect, he thought, should have been sexy, a pretty young woman in costly boudoir déshabillé; instead she was tense, her movements stiff and angular. Her carefully made-up face couldn't conceal from him the traces of recent tears.

So it didn't matter he'd seen Horry first. Gently he said, 'You know he's dead, don't you. I don't have to tell you.'

'Dead?' She clutched both hands to her well-developed chest. 'Who is dead? Tell me!'

A little less of the Mary Pickfords — the girl had been watching too many talkies — would have convinced him more. Damn her, why did she have to pretend? Did she imagine he would think she had murdered Silas? Or was she afraid of what the wowsers would think if she admitted to visiting the man's room in the night?

Probably the last.

He said, matter-of-fact, 'Silas Beadnall is dead,' and waited with interest to see her next reaction.

She gasped, 'No!' and twisted to fall face down across the bed while she burst into unconvincing sobbing. 'Oh Silas! My beloved Silas!'

Bowler waited, arms folded, leaning on the doorframe, until he thought she was running out of steam and might welcome an interruption.

'Come on, Miss Jennings,' he said. 'You're making yourself ill. Sit up and dry your eyes. I'm Mounted Constable Brown, I have to —'

'I have lost everything. Everything! He was the world to me!' She jerked herself upright into her chair, though only so that she could press to her lips the diamond ring she wore. 'Oh my beloved!' She shot a lightning glance at Bowler, as though to see how he was taking this.

'Save it for somebody else,' he advised. 'I'm a working man and a busy man, and I have other work to do. At the moment I don't suspect you of murder, but if you carry on like that I might begin to wonder what you're trying to hide.'

'I am hiding nothing,' she declared.

'Well then, stop it. Look, I'm a policeman, all I'm interested in is who killed Silas Beadnall. Nothing else.' He smiled, reassuringly he hoped. 'The other thing is, whatever you tell me goes no further.' Well, he could say that now, when he had no reason to suspect her of complicity. Later, the ground rules might change.

The smile worked. Margot dabbed at her eyes with a handkerchief and smiled back, a sad, brave smile. 'I'm sorry to be so emotional. It was the shock.'

'It was nothing of the kind. You are trying to pretend that you didn't already know that Silas Beadnall is dead. Lying to the police is a serious matter, so if you'll tell me the truth I'll forget the melodrama. Of course you're upset, but don't overdo it.'

For the first time Margot looked at him properly. She had intended her act to overawe a simple country bobby, but unfortunately this man was no backward rustic. He had an intelligent face, she thought, and the lean and wiry body relaxed against her door jamb had an air of contained energy about it, although he stood so casually. In fact he was a damned attractive man, in spite of his unshaven face and his uncombed hair.

Margot responded to attractive men. She found herself smiling at him, this time without artifice.

'That's better,' he said. 'What time did you find him dead?'

She considered briefly. Earlier, she had made up her mind that she would never admit she had visited Silas's room, partly because she didn't want to be an object of scandal, partly to ensure she wasn't suspected of the murder. She knew enough about men, however, to realise that this one wasn't going away until he got what he came for.

'Late,' she said, dropping her gaze as though in maidenly confusion.

'When everyone else was safely asleep,' he agreed, sounding amused. 'Do you wear a watch?'

'Yes,' she admitted.

'Then I have no doubt you looked at it before you left your room. What time was it?'

She hung her head and muttered, 'Just after two. Later than — I had dozed for a little while.'

He appeared to reflect for a moment. 'Did his skin feel cool when you touched him?'

Shocked, she exclaimed, 'I didn't touch him! I couldn't, he looked —' She shuddered.

'That's all right,' Bowler said at his most soothing. 'Never mind that now. His room is next to this. Did you hear anything before that? Anything at all? You must think very carefully.'

'I have been thinking carefully,' she said, with a slight return to her dramatic manner. 'For hours and hours. Can you possibly think I've been able to sleep?'

'No,' Bowler said softly, 'But then, neither can I think why you didn't rouse the place when you discovered he was dead.'

17

Margot herself hadn't been sure why she hadn't raised the roof when she found Silas dead. After one glance at the bed, shocked at what her candle had revealed, she had flown back to her own room with no other thought than to distance herself from the horror next door. There she had huddled, moaning softly, shuddering, until her chaotic thoughts had quieted enough for her to start sorting out her options. By then she realised she had nothing to gain and quite a bit to lose if she woke up the whole hotel in the middle of the night. No matter how many people came running, nothing anyone could do would help Silas now; and at the same time, by admitting her visit to his room she herself would be branded forever as a woman of easy virtue.

Then she had thought how delighted those damn Beadnall women would be if they found their suspicions of her justified. Give those bitches more reasons to despise and condemn her? Not if she could help it.

She had fought hard for the respectability of a formal engagement, the promise of marriage — she wasn't going to forfeit that advantage lightly. So she had decided to do nothing, say nothing, and wait until someone else brought her the news.

She couldn't, however, explain this to Mounted Constable Brown without also explaining what she had left behind to attain this respectability. She hid her face in her hands and said in a tremulous voice, 'I was too shocked to think straight.'

'You had hours and hours to get your thinking straight.' Bowler, unimpressed, was thinking of the hours wasted, of clues probably lost. She had given the killer plenty of time to get away — or to clean up after himself, if he was one of those still close at hand. 'You just said so yourself. I think you decided your reputation was more important than finding your beloved's killer.'

He didn't understand, Margot thought, what a good reputation meant to a woman like her. Or perhaps he did, and, sensing the chequered past behind her current standing, despised her accordingly. Was this what lay in her future, now her rosy dreams had vanished like a puff of magic smoke? Margot's face crumpled.

Bowler's sympathies were touched at last: he read real distress here. And he understood that, whatever her feelings for Silas had been, the man's death meant the end of all her hopes. He would have liked to comfort her, though that could be risky. He had registered her response to his smile.

'I do understand your grief,' he said sincerely. 'Look, just a couple of small things, and I'll go. You must have been still awake when Horry and his father were arguing — did you hear anything they said? Either of them?'

Margot's pretty features became pinched and venomous. 'They were in the passage, and they were shouting,' she said, making it clear she was not a girl who listened at keyholes. 'Silas was shouting that if they didn't like the present arrangements they could get off the place and he'd put a manager in, and then Horry shouted, "You can't do that! Over my dead body!"'

'What did Silas say to that?'

'He laughed.'

'And then?'

'Horry said, "You *wouldn't!*" and Silas said, sort of jeering, "You can't stop me," and went into his bedroom and shut the door.'

Miss Margot Jennings was happy to dob in Horry for the crime, he could see. After all, she didn't know any of the family except Silas; she had met them for the first time that evening. Now she was insinuating Horry had decided to substitute his father's dead body for his own. She could be right, too.

'Did you see Silas Beadnall again after that?'

'He came in and said goodnight to me. He didn't stay more than a minute. We were both tired, it had been a long day, driving from town, and then the accident, and then the party.'

'Accident? What accident?'

'Someone ran into us outside this hotel, just as we arrived. Of course Silas was angry about that, too. It put a dent in his mudguard.'

Bowler had seen Silas's old two-seater Delage parked behind the pub that morning, and didn't know which dent she meant. Several decorated the mudguards, and a few more were scattered over the bodywork. The car had the look of a veteran tomcat that had been in too many affrays, battered yet indomitable still.

'Do you know who ran into you?'

'No, but Silas did. I didn't hear his name, Silas didn't call him anything except swear words. And once they'd got the cars apart he drove away.'

'I see. Now, after Mr Beadnall said goodnight to you, did you hear anything else from that room?'

'No, I — Yes! I do remember!' She leaned forward eagerly. 'I heard voices, someone was in the room with him!' Of course there had been voices: that was why she'd been forced to wait before she went to Silas, and then while she was waiting she'd fallen into a doze. 'I didn't recognise the other voice,' she concluded sadly. 'Another man, I think. But I couldn't say who.'

'What time was this?'

'Somewhere around midnight, I think. Sorry, I wish I had listened harder.'

'Never mind, that's very helpful. One other thing, though — there are two glasses in Mr Beadnall's room, as though two people had a drink together. Know anything about them?'

'Yes, we had a drink, though that was hours ago, before we went to dinner. You'd think someone would have cleared them away before this.'

'They were pretty busy last night.' Bowler opened the door behind him. 'All right. If you think of anything else, let me know. That's all for now.'

He crossed the passage to rap on the door of Lilian Beadnall's room. Hearing no response from Miss Beadnall he opened the door six inches. 'May I come in?'

Nobody answered. He pushed the door fully open. The room was empty, the bedclothes stripped back on the bed, the wardrobe open and bare. Not only was Lilian Beadnall absent, no sign was left to suggest she had ever stayed in the room. Whatever she had brought with her — her suitcase, all her possessions — had been taken away.

Em was as surprised as he was. Nobody knew when she had left. Nobody knew where she had gone.

Until Johnson, overhearing, told them. While she'd been serving canapes she had heard Miss Beadnall's nephew arrange to take her out to his farm. Early.

18

Margot Jennings had dressed slowly — a soft woollen dress in smoky blue that Silas had liked, a chiffon scarf in a deeper blue to match her eyes, a marcasite brooch to pin it in place — and now sat at the dressing-table making up her face, taking as much care as she would have done to present herself to him.

But Silas was gone. What did she do now?

She had lain awake half the night sorting alternatives through her despairing brain and was no nearer a decision now morning had come.

If she left, she would be leaving the field to Silas's family and she'd have no further claim on them. She knew she wouldn't benefit under his existing will; he'd told her that, and explained why. Because he'd have to make a new will anyway, as soon as they were married, he wasn't going to make his lawyer rich in the meantime. Of course when he'd said it he hadn't believed there was the slightest possibility she could be disadvantaged by this delay.

With a slight narrowing of her eyes Margot wished her beloved, spendthrift in some ways, mean in others, had not chosen to pinch his pennies in this instance.

She sat back, her hands in her lap. Would she gain anything if she stuck around and tried to shame the brothers into making her some kind of settlement?

They weren't going to do that. Their wives would take damn good care they didn't do that. So she would be left with a wardrobe of expensive clothes and a diamond ring as her total gain from the affair.

Better than nothing? Peanuts, compared with what she had lost. Margot, not a believer that a few crumbs were better than no bread, didn't know which bastard had cheated her of a comfortable future, yet the mere thought of the sneaking murderous sod, whoever he was, made her furiously angry. If the law didn't hang him she'd like to string him up herself with her own two hands.

Or string her up. It could have been Lilian — she had motive enough — or one of the daughters-in-law.

And no matter what that cynical policeman thought, she had been fond of Silas. How could she not be? He had offered her unlimited admiration, paid constant attention to her every comfort, spared no effort to please and entertain her — he had cared about her. She had seen his abrasive manner towards others, though he'd never shown that side of himself to her. Tears filled her eyes; she compressed her lips.

A tap came on her door. 'Who is it?' she called.

'Johnson, miss. The housemaid.'

'Come in then. What do you want now?'

Undeterred by the impatient tone Johnson asked politely, 'I wondered if you would like a tray in your room, instead of coming to the dining-room for breakfast.' Poor Miss Jennings looked terrible. She said formally, 'You have my deepest sympathy. A terrible tragedy.'

A horrible one too, which she suspected Miss Jennings knew as well as she did; she hadn't forgotten those red-rimmed eyes when she went in with the early teas. Then she saw the girl had bent her head and covered her eyes with her fingers in an attempt to stop her tears getting away from her.

'Oh, you poor thing!' Johnson put an arm across the bowed shoulders. 'Poor girl, it's awful, don't cry.' Though why not cry? Miss Jennings had every reason to bawl her eyes out. Although not as cynical as Bowler, Johnson recognised that some of this girl's distress was caused by disappointment, not grief for a lover, yet her distress was real, her misery genuine.

Undone by sympathy, Margot twisted on her stool, flung her arms round the other girl's waist, and howled into her midriff in an unstoppable release of her grief and her fears. Johnson stroked her hair and murmured meaningless phrases of comfort.

After a moment she said, 'Look, I have to get back to the kitchen. When I've got a minute I'll bring you some tea and toast.'

Margot sniffed, and detached herself. 'Thanks. Sorry.' She mopped her eyes, and glanced at her bedraggled reflection in the mirror. 'I should front up to those Beadnalls in the dining-room. I don't want them to think I'm scared of them, or hiding from them. But I can't, not looking like this.'

'You'll feel better after some breakfast. Have something to eat, bathe your eyes, and then bounce out at them.'

19

Several years before, Aubrey Venables, fired by his newest vision of himself as gentleman farmer, had bought the disused Anglican rectory in Kularook at the same time that he had acquired an extensive acreage of local scrub. Bowler had never been inside the house, a large and rambling building. He rather wished he could afford something like that for his Joan, who had grown up in the spacious surroundings of an English Stately Home and naturally felt five small rooms behind the police station a little constrictive.

Not that she ever complained, or indicated in any way that she minded. She was far more likely to enumerate the disadvantages of life in a huge pile built several centuries before comfort had been valued above ostentation. The dissatisfaction was Bowler's, that he couldn't provide the kind of house she deserved.

He saw a Chevrolet tourer parked in the gateway and swore. That was Horry's car. He was hoping to get to Leon before his brother broke the news.

Somewhere a mole cricket, encouraged by the rain, trilled incessantly. Bowler left his car in the muddy street, stepped over a large puddle, and reached the gate into a garden allowed to run wild, where encroaching shrubbery lined the path to the front veranda and he had to duck and weave like a busy boxer. A whippy branch snagged his hair and unloaded water down his cheek.

Aubrey Venables opened the door. He was a slight man in his early forties, wearing a cream sweater over grey flannels and looking far too tidily dressed for a Sunday morning. He had even shaved. He raised his brows in mild surprise.

'Good morning, Bowler. A wet morning for visiting.'

Bowler was conscious of the fraying cuffs of his old grey jacket, his three-day beard, the mud on his trousers. Water trickled under his open collar; he took out his handkerchief and mopped the side of his neck.

'Not social, Aubrey. I need to see Leon Beadnall. Is Horry here?'

'No. Were you expecting him to be?'

'Isn't that his car?'

'Leon drove it over last night. He'd come in with Horry, so didn't have his own.' Aubrey looked as though he'd like to ask the reason for the call. After a glance at Bowler's set face he said, 'He's in here,' and led the way down the passage to the kitchen.

Although a couple of cupboard tops were filled with the usual clutter of a bachelor's establishment — books, a heap of opened letters and bills, pliers and a greasy wrench on a stack of newspapers — the room was clean. Bowler was damn sure Aubrey was incapable of doing his own housework. He must be employing some woman now that his mistress, the woman he had passed off as his sister, had left him.

A bright fire flickered behind the slots of the stove; the air was full of the smell of wood smoke and toasted bread. Bowler's stomach yearned for his postponed breakfast.

Leon Beadnall, wearing a navy blue woollen dressing gown over striped flannelette pyjamas, was sitting at the table in the centre of the room with a plateful of crumbs and a cup and saucer in front of him; he was frowning and heavy-eyed, and his hair stood up in a brush.

'Hello, Bowler. What brings you here so early? Would you like a cup of tea?'

'No thanks.'

Bowler didn't want anyone thinking this was a relaxed occasion. Leon appeared mournful enough to have already heard of the death yet was perhaps only wishing for his own. Normally an amiable, pleasant-looking man, this morning he had bags like a bloodhound's under his eyes and looked, to the policeman's experienced eye, to be severely hung over. He sat frowning, fiddling with his teaspoon in the saucer, barely able to keep his eyes open.

Bowler decided to wake him up. 'I have bad news, I'm afraid.' He paused, watching. 'Your father is dead.'

'Eh? What did you say?' Leon dragged his bloodshot eyes open.

Bowler repeated the statement. Leon stood half out of his chair then fell back on it again.

'Bloody hell. Dead? No.' After a moment he added, 'In his sleep? Do you know why?'

'He's been murdered.'

Behind him, Bowler heard Aubrey make a soft exclamation. Leon stared under heavy lids for several seconds.

'Well, I'll be —' Leon lowered his head carefully into his hands. 'Don't look at me like that, Bowler, I didn't kill him. Who did? How did it happen?'

Bowler still wasn't sure that the news was a total surprise to him. Hard to tell when he looked so haggard anyway. 'Possibly you didn't. All the same, I want to know what you did from the time you got up from the dinner table last night until now.'

So Leon explained how, after the three women staying at the pub had gone to their rooms and old Colly Gordon had left to drive the Misses Beadnall to their friend's house, he and his father and brother had sat for about half an hour over a bottle of port. About eleven-thirty he and Fran had left the pub and, because of the rain, Horry had lent them his car.

They found Aubrey had waited up for them, so Fran — he and Fran had sat up for a while with him, drinking whisky and talking over the evening's events. Leon wasn't sure what time they'd finally turned in, because in the end they'd made rather a night of it.

'A bit after one, I think,' Aubrey said. He looked in better shape than the other man; of course he hadn't indulged in cocktails, champagne and port before the whisky. And he had nothing at stake in these events.

Bowler thought he could believe Aubrey.

20

Aubrey said, 'Good morning, Fran.'

Bowler turned. Fran had come into the kitchen from the passage. She was dressed as her husband was, in matching striped pyjamas and navy dressing gown; her dark hair was tousled, her face scrubbed and rosy from sleep, her feet bare. Yet the effect, to Bowler's eye, was much more sexy than Margot Jennings's satins and carefully applied cosmetics. He noticed Aubrey was watching her too.

He twitched his thoughts into line. 'Good morning, Mrs Beadnall.'

'Morning all.' She stepped past Aubrey and raked her fingers through her hair. 'I slept like the dead. What time are we due at the pub, Leon?'

'Hell, we were going to make him sign — that's all off, Franny. Bowler says Dad's dead.'

'Dead!' She swung on Bowler, to read confirmation in his face. 'Silas!' She stood for a moment digesting this. 'How — too much Little Miss Muffet on top of too much good living, I suppose.' She shrugged. 'Sorry, I don't mean to be coarse, but really.'

None of the three men present had batted an eye, though the remark was not one they would themselves have made in mixed company. Horry had suggested much the same thing, Bowler remembered.

He said, 'No. Silas Beadnall was murdered.'

Fran's eyes widened. 'Somebody actually killed him?'

'Yes.'

She pulled out a chair and sat at the table beside Leon; she laid her hand over his where it rested beside his plate. 'Oh dear. I know we called him an old pest but that's as far as it went. And now you'll think one of us did it. How did he die?'

'He was strangled.'

'Ugh!' She screwed up her face in a grimace of disgust. 'How horrible.'

Leon raised his head to smile at his wife. He turned his hand palm up and gripped her fingers. 'Don't think about it, Franny. Think about —' He shot a lightning glance at Bowler and stopped himself, looking foolish.

'Think about what?' Bowler, watching attentively, realised Leon had nearly reminded his wife of the advantages attendant on his father's early demise. 'How you'll all be better off now?'

'Think about more pleasant things,' Fran finished for her husband, who nodded. 'Though of course we are going to be better off now, Mr Brown. We'd be stupid to pretend otherwise, however much we might dislike the way it's happened.'

Bowler approved of this plain speaking. He smiled at her. 'I hope none of you pretend anything and just stick to the truth until this business is cleared up. Who do you think did it, Leon?'

The man looked totally taken aback; and yet that was a reasonable question. All the same, Bowler hadn't expected serious suggestions from any of the Beadnalls. One of Silas Beadnall's offspring was the most likely suspect for his murder — they had the most to gain and at present the only obvious motives — yet he could hardly expect them to tell tales on one another.

Not yet. Given time and a bit of stirring and he might have them panting to tell tales on everyone within a radius of five miles, their nearest and dearest included, in order to exculpate themselves.

On the face of it, Horry was the most probable murderer. He was on the spot; he had quarrelled violently with his father; in a dangerous rage he could have gone back to the room and silenced him once and for all.

Only, where did he pick up that electric flex? Em disowned it, so it can't have been lying about for long.

Aubrey moved across to stand by the stove. 'You know, Bowler, if anyone started that car in the night I'd have been bound to hear it. My bedroom window overlooks the drive and I'm a light sleeper. And I'll swear on as many bibles as you like that it never moved all night.'

'Leon's a friend of yours.'

'And I am not a liar. If I volunteer information you can be sure of its truth.'

Bowler thought this was probably true too. He knew himself how intrusive a motorcar engine could sound in the deep night-time silence of the small settlement. Even distant engines had woken him on occasion. Leon, if he had gone back to the pub after everyone was in bed, wouldn't have risked waking the neighbours by starting the car. He would have gone on foot.

And a dirty night like last night might make anyone have second thoughts. He'd know he'd certainly get muddy and probably wet as well, evidence against him if his clothes were examined in the morning — as Bowler was going to do shortly — and he wouldn't have the faintest idea what to expect when he arrived at his destination. Would he plan to go in the front door and risk waking Trotter? Or risk running into one of the other guests in the passage, someone who had got out of bed to go to the dunny? A very chancy business. The same applied if he planned to use the side door.

Leon must have been at least partly drunk. Alcohol could have made him reckless, and it would also have made him clumsy. Could a drunken man have entered the pub unobserved and found his way to Silas's room without bumping into the furniture or being seen? And how did he know which room was his father's? A lot of chances to take. Bowler still fancied Horry in the starring role.

Probabilities weren't good enough in his job. 'Leon, can you show me what clothes you were wearing last night?'

'What?' Leon's head jerked up. 'You can't think I had anything to do with it!'

Bowler assumed his professional give-away-nothing expression. 'I don't know yet. Which is your bedroom?'

'None of your business, blast you.'

Fran had got the point immediately. 'Of course our clothes are damp. Even with the car, we got wet dashing from the hotel, and then to the door here. It's all right, dear old boy, I'll show him. We have nothing to hide.'

The shoulders of the dinner jacket were damp, the trouser-legs splashed with mud. Which proved nothing, as Fran pointed out. Although, if Leon had walked to the pub in the night, Bowler would have expected the jacket to be a lot wetter than that. And her coat, airing on a hanger on the outside of the wardrobe, was only damp too. When he asked about the clothes they had worn before they changed into evening dress she lifted a small suitcase to the bed and threw back the lid. Every garment he lifted out was bone dry.

He thanked her. Then he walked through the house from the front door to the back and established the place had only two doors; he looked out on the muddy path, intersected by a large puddle, that led to the dunny at the back fence; he saw that a gate in the side fence, opening into the church yard, was so overgrown by a rampant cotoneaster bush it could probably no longer be opened. So the only way out of the back yard was by the wicket gate between the house and the garage.

'A detective is coming from Adelaide,' he said. 'He'll want to see you too.' If the detective wanted to search further, he could apply for the damn warrant himself.

21

Joan Brown heard her husband go into the office and came up the passage with a cup of coffee for him. 'Did Em give you breakfast?'

'No, she was busy. Joan, I have to ring Adelaide before I do anything else.' He ran his finger down the list of telephone numbers stuck on the wall beside the telephone.

'I'll get Rosie to make you some toast. She can't play outside because of the mud, so she's in the kitchen trying to be helpful and she's driving me mad.'

'Leave the kitchen to her,' Bowler said, 'She couldn't do a worse job than you do.' He never knew whether he took a perverse kind of pride in his wife's lack of domestic skills, or whether her slap-dash housekeeping exasperated him.

Joan gave him a long-suffering look. Then she grabbed his ears and pulled down his head; she kissed him hard. She returned down the passage whistling the old wartime song 'Take me back to dear old Blighty.'

Her theme song these days. Bowler was resisting.

'I'm not going,' he yelled after her.

He had finished with his superior officer on the telephone and was sitting at his desk writing up his notes when his nine-year-old daughter Rose came in with a plateful of buttered toast. 'Dad, why don't you want to go to England? Mum says we might have to go without you.'

Through a mouthful he asked suspiciously, 'Is your mother trying to get you to soften me up?'

'No!' She sounded offended. 'I wouldn't do that. I wanted to know for myself.'

Probably she was old enough to deserve an honest answer. 'I don't want to go because I'd have to give up my job and so I wouldn't have any money. I don't want to live on your mother's money for two years. I'd feel useless.' And a parasite, and all those other unlovely names he knew for a kept man.

'Why not, Dad? She says she's got plenty.'

'I know she has.' More than plenty. Though give Joan her due, she had always been content to live on his (by her standards) meagre salary; she had understood his stiff-necked pride and had never thrown her wealth or her moneyed upbringing in his teeth. The only sums she spent which he hadn't provided were on her expensive hobby of photography, which meant so much to her he couldn't grudge her the extravagance.

'Mum says you've provided for her for thirteen years, why can't you let her do it for two?'

'It's not easy to explain. Though I don't want to stop you and Tom and your mother going. It's time you saw your English grandparents again.'

'I was too little last time to remember them much. You didn't come then either.'

'No I didn't.'

'But Mum says this time she wants to go because of you, Dad. She says you should have the chance to ride show-jumping horses in Europe, to learn things you can't all by yourself here.'

He scowled darkly at her. 'Your mother has hundreds of good reasons all designed to undermine my resistance, and you needn't recite them to me.'

With the air of one imparting useful knowledge Rose said, 'Undermine means dig under something to make it fall over. Mum isn't trying to make you fall over.'

'Oh yes she is. She'd like me to fall flat on my face so she could put her foot on my neck.'

'Don't be silly, Dad,' Rose said, grinning.

'You know nothing about it. Anyway, what's the point of show-jumping in England if I have to sell Imshy before we go? Just as he's going well.'

'Send him and Isma up to the farm, to Uncle John.'

'Your mother has been getting at you, hasn't she,' he growled. 'You've got all the damn answers. She's a devious woman and I don't trust her an inch. Now hop it, I've got work to do.'

Rose laughed, and skipped off back to the kitchen.

Bowler leaned back in his chair, his hands behind his head. Of course he would like to ride in England and learn from riders with a lifetime's experience, men who had grown up inheriting generations of European tradition who must know ten times as much about horses as a boy from the bush could ever teach himself. Some of them almost made a career of show-jumping.

Although he didn't aspire to such dizzy heights, a few years at the game would be enormous fun. And if he didn't do it now he'd be too old to start. His devious wife Joan had realised she had a powerful lever to move him after his successes at the recent Adelaide Show had whetted his appetite for more. And if he did go, he'd have to stop arguing about the money; he would have to let her buy him the right horses. She could afford to.

He'd taken his young bad-tempered horse Imshy to town more from curiosity than in hope of success. After the time and effort he'd spent schooling him over jumps for eighteen months he had wanted to know how he measured up against the best show-jumping horses in the state. To his own surprise the horse had performed well, placed first in the novice class and third in the open. Then Bowler had been offered several rides on other men's horses, and had done well on each.

Mounted Constable Bowler Brown, who was not nearly as arrogant as he pretended to his wife, had been made to see he was a bloody good horseman, at least in local company.

So of course then he wondered how he would measure up overseas, in the company of riders like Bruno Whatsisname, the Italian lieutenant he had met in London during the war — the men who rode the international show circuits. Damn Joan, who had wormed this admission from him. Now he didn't get a moment's peace.

Apart from pride, he had another, unadmitted, reason for refusing to accompany his wife to the land of her birth. He was afraid that, if once she got her whole family to England, she might not want to return at the end of the two years she was asking for. He could imagine nothing more daunting than spending the rest of his life in Europe, yet how could he refuse her if she wanted to stay? No matter how often she reassured him, he was always painfully aware of how little he and his country had to offer compared with what her wealthy aristocratic family and Europe could provide.

Of course he trusted Joan — when she said two years she meant two years and she would stick to her word — but he didn't trust himself. If he saw that she was happier there, would like to stay and bring up her children there, how could he refuse her? Yet how could he survive the rest of his life in that strange country?

If he remained behind he could harden his heart. At least he would be certain Joan would come back to Australia.

He muttered an oath, reached for a notepad, and unscrewed his fountain pen. Before he forgot he'd better write up all he'd learned that morning so that he could pass it on to the detective his bosses in Adelaide were sending him.

22

Through his office window Bowler saw Doctor John Shapcott's old two-seater Packard, mud to the windows, pull up at the side of the hotel; he laid down his pen and went to meet him, taking long strides over the waterlogged ruts in the road. A spider web the size of a dinner-plate, a spoked wheel outlined in tiny gems of water, trembled between the eaves of the pub and a veranda post.

'Hullo, Bowler. I don't know why I bothered.' The doctor, a large untidy man in his forties, pulled off his leather driving gauntlets, unwound the scarf from his neck, and threw them into his car. 'You could have done the paperwork just as well.'

Bowler shook his head. 'You couldn't keep away. You can't fool me, you enjoy all this gory stuff.'

With a slushy hiss of tyres a car drove past along the main street ahead of them.

Shapcott laughed, rubbing his hands together as though to restore the circulation. 'I suppose we'll see spring some time this side of Christmas.'

'The rain has stopped.' Bowler raised his face to the louring sky as though to test his statement. 'Perhaps the weather will clear.'

'And perhaps it won't. Come on, I haven't got all day, show me where you've parked the cadaver. Is it really Silas Beadnall? Couldn't happen to a better man — he's been asking for it for years.' He led the way in at the side door of the pub. Over his shoulder he said, 'And you'd better turn your back, because Sunday or no Sunday I'm going to ask Em for a stiff shot of whisky.'

'How do you know Silas Beadnall?'

'He was my patient of course, before he left the farm. You forget how long I have been ministering to this — hullo, Trotter. You can save my life.'

Behind the front desk the publican, another big man, tall and broad, looked up from leafing through the guest register. 'Not with him watching.'

'I'll go down to the bedroom,' said Bowler. 'Send him along when he's recovered.'

As he passed the lounge he saw the Beadnall brothers and their wives sitting together at one of the small tables. If they were now busy concocting fairy tales to beguile the coming detective he couldn't stop them.

A second glance showed him more accurately that, far from heads-together collaborating, the two couples were ill at ease with one another. Each married pair had drawn closer together at the round table, creating a slightly confrontational air by the way they sat on opposite sides. Horry stirred the ashtray with a match; Brenda stared down at her lap; Leon, with his hands in his pockets, gazed at the ceiling. Fran saw Bowler at the door and waved with a twiddle of her fingers.

He nodded and walked on. Did the brothers suspect each other? They would never admit it, of course, though they had to realise they were the most likely suspects. Perhaps if they tried to cover for one another with evasions and lies they might make his job easier. Sooner or later they'd trip themselves up.

John Shapcott arrived in the bedroom breathing fumes of whisky and looking smug. His expression changed when Bowler drew the sheet from Silas's face. 'Jesus! I've seen a few violent deaths but I've never seen one of them before.'

Bowler passed him the flex. 'This is what did it.'

'He wound it pretty tight, didn't he.' The doctor ran a finger down the corkscrew crimps, the spiral bends that persisted in the cord where the two ends had been twisted hard together. He fitted one end over the other in the original turns. 'What did he wind it up with?'

'I haven't found anything yet.'

'It's how farmers tighten fencing wire to a post sometimes. Use the handle of their pliers, or a stick or something.'

Bowler had already considered this angle. 'Are you trying to tell me something?'

'Hell, no. Don't quote me. Anyone might know how to wind up a tourniquet with a lever. Nurses, anyone who's studied first aid.' Shapcott bent over the body, moving limbs, looking into the eyes, prodding here and there. He said, 'He was a hard bugger, you know. Threw his teenage daughter out when he found she was pregnant.'

'I've heard something about that. What happened?'

'The bastard, she was only a kid. Thrashed her, dragged her into his car, drove to Kularook, pushed her out in the main street — dumped her like a bag of rubbish in the dirt by the road — and calmly drove home. Never saw her again. She told me about it when I delivered her baby, afraid he might have been damaged in the attack.' He peeled the bedclothes back to examine the rest of the body. 'Pissed himself, but that's normal. Probably sitting on the edge of the bed and his attacker rolled him into it after he was dead.'

'Was the baby — no, that would be Diggory Kenrick, I suppose.'

'That's right. Sound as a bell. Bears a charmed life, that boy. Born into a normal family in spite of Silas, because old James Kenrick immediately took the girl in, and young James was delighted to do the honourable thing and marry her.'

'Why charmed life?'

'He didn't die in the house fire that killed his parents.'

'I haven't heard about that,' Bowler said.

'He was only four, asleep in the next room, and at first everyone thought he'd died too. He must have woken, gone running off to get help, got lost in the dark. They found him a couple of miles away next morning, still crying, still trying to run for help.'

'Silas had left the farm before I arrived in Kularook.'

'Count yourself lucky, then.' Shapcott pulled up the bedclothes and straightened his back. 'Sorry, Bowler, I can't give you much idea of time of death. Eight hours, nine — less maybe.'

'One witness says he was dead by two am.'

'What do you need me for? There you are then.'

'Not sure the witness is reliable. You notice he's broken a couple of fingernails?'

The doctor lifted one heavy hand and then the other. The nails were clean and carefully tended. Three on his right hand were broken roughly across.

'Clawing at the tourniquet, no doubt,' said Shapcott. 'He'd be too busy trying to breathe to have time for much else.'

'Trying to break the grip,' agreed Bowler. 'But we can't be certain a man killed him, you know, a woman could have done it. Doesn't take a lot of muscle to wind up a tourniquet.' He thought for a moment. 'If Beadnall was sitting up in bed, unsuspecting, all you'd have to do is throw the cord round his neck and yank him sideways. He'd be off balance, sprawled on his back across the bed, and the murderer behind him would have both feet firmly planted on the floor and able to exert all his or her strength.'

Shapcott grunted. 'Probably.'

Carefully, by the rims, Bowler picked up the two glasses from the washstand, yanked a handtowel from the rail at the side, and started to roll them up. 'You don't want to test these for residues or anything fancy, do you?'

'Christ no. Cause of death is obvious enough without looking for poisons.'

'All the same, perhaps they should be tested,' Bowler had second thoughts. 'Sleeping pills, something like that, could have made our assassin's job a whole lot easier.'

'Nothing there; they're dry. Need a pretty sophisticated lab to get anything out of them. What did you want them for?'

'In case whichever damn detective they send to make my life difficult wants to check that there are no foreign prints on them. Miss Jennings says they're hers and Silas Beadnall's. I'm happy to believe her, but you don't know detectives.'

23

The doctor was taking his leave of Bowler in the front hall when Diggory Kenrick walked in from the street, ushering in a heavily built, well-corseted woman unknown to Bowler. They went past into the lounge.

'I'll send you the report, then,' Shapcott said, and went on his way.

Someone in the lounge exclaimed sharply; voices were raised. Bowler went to see what was going on.

The room smelled of cigarette smoke and the cold ashes of last night's fire; a fine bloom of ash lay like dust on the varnished tops of each of the half dozen small tables. The branches of cream-flowering melaleuca in a brass urn on the mantelpiece were shedding drifts of stamens.

Hands in pockets, young Kenrick stood just inside the door with his attention concentrated on the strange woman, who had collapsed into an arm chair. Her skin pale, wide-eyed, she was staring at Horry standing in front of her.

Horry said, 'There you are, Bowler. Let me introduce my sister, Lilian. This is Bowler Brown, Lil, our policeman.'

Joan wouldn't like that, Bowler thought; he should have introduced me to her first. Never mind, now I know who she is which is the main thing. 'How do you do, Miss Beadnall.'

The woman turned her head towards him yet he wasn't certain that she saw him. She seemed to be looking a long way off, at something he couldn't see.

'I have just told her that our father is dead,' Horry continued. 'And how he died. She didn't know. She left before breakfast with — with —'

The young man by the door smiled, apparently enjoying his relatives' difficulties. 'My name is Diggory Kenrick, as you very well know, Uncle Horace. It's about time you stopped pretending I'm invisible.' He turned to the women. 'You must be my Aunt Fran. And it's Aunt Brenda, isn't it. And my poor Uncle Leon, who has run into me once or twice and hasn't known in the least what to do about it. He's not nearly as good as Uncle Horace at pretending he can see straight through me.'

'How do you do,' Fran said, smiling at this interesting-looking young man. 'I've been hoping to meet you ever since I heard about the — heard you were back in Kularook. And I never knew you were invisible.'

'Only to the select few,' he said, making her a half bow. 'Now Silas is dead — is he really dead?'

'He is.' Horry snapped his mouth shut as though to prevent the escape of more words.

He still looked shaken by what he'd seen. Bowler had allowed him into the room to view the body as soon as Doctor John had finished, and either he was a pretty good actor or his father's contorted face had horrified him. Had he been acting? Bowler studied him more carefully while his attention was fixed on his sister. Was that ordinary, hard-working farmer Horry Beadnall a patricide? A terrible word. A modern Oedipus. At least Oedipus hadn't known the man he fought was his father.

Young Kenrick was saying, 'All right, if Silas is dead perhaps I can become more opaque in future. I'm perfectly willing. I have no quarrel with the rest of you.' When this remark was met by a faintly hostile silence he turned to Bowler. 'How did he die? Heart attack?'

'Murdered,' Bowler said, and watched for a reaction.

'The devil he was.' Diggory stared at him. After a moment he added, 'A fitting end for the bastard.'

Horry demanded, 'Is that all you can say? Aren't you at all concerned?'

'No. Why should I be?'

Leon muttered something to his wife at the same time that Horry declared, 'But he was your *grandfather*.'

Kenrick glanced at Leon, then brought his attention back to his other uncle. 'No. He swore I was no grandson of his, so he was no grandfather of mine. His choice.'

'All the same —'

'Why the devil should I give two hoots whether he lived or died? Or how he died? A man who treated my mother as he did? In my opinion he deserved all he got — he had it coming.'

Horry said, 'All right — where were you last night?'

Bowler wanted to know too; he watched Kenrick.

The young man seemed taken aback for a moment. Then he said, 'I went to the dance at the hall.'

'After that.'

'Well, I — well, after that I went home.'

'You were back very early this morning, then.'

'I'd arranged with Lilian I'd pick her up before breakfast.' Lilian Beadnall nodded. 'And why on earth would *I* bother to murder him? He won't have left me a dud penny.'

Horry shook his head irritably at this insinuation that others had been left considerably more. 'Of course not. But you said yourself he had it coming. You must have hated him all your life.'

'I never even thought about him. I had better things to do with my time.'

Bowler said, 'All right, you two, that's enough. Kenrick, did you know Silas Beadnall was staying at the pub?'

'No.'

Horry said, 'You did know. You saw him here last night when you came in to see Lil.'

'Saw him, yes, my very first sight of the bastard and one I could have done without. But that doesn't mean I had a clue where he'd be sleeping, dammit. He could have gone home with you.'

'I see.' Bowler looked at the young man reflectively for a few moments before turning his attention to the woman. 'Miss Beadnall, your room was across the passage from your father's — did you hear anything in the night?'

She took so long to answer he thought she must have heard something that would help him; she must be weighing up how to tell him some damaging detail. In the end she shook her head.

'No, Officer.'

'Didn't you hear your father and your brother quarrelling?'

She turned her head to look at Horry. 'Oh, that. Yes, I couldn't avoid hearing them. That was while I was getting ready for bed. I thought you meant later.'

'I meant at any time. Do you know what they were quarrelling about?'

'Of course.' She paused, her gaze on her brother; he was studying his fingernails. 'Hasn't Horry told you? We wanted to persuade Father to make a legal settlement of the farm's income. As it is, he helps himself and the rest of us share what's left.' She compressed her lips, apparently in disapproval of this unbusinesslike behaviour on the part of her sire. 'A trying situation for all of us, to say the least.'

'And for the rest of the night you heard nothing?'

'Nothing. I slept heavily, and didn't wake until after seven. Then when Diggory came he drove me out to the farm for breakfast.'

And when they went she had stripped her room and taken all her belongings with her. Had she meant to clear out, then something had changed her mind?

'Miss Beadnall, why did you take all your luggage with you, if you were coming back?'

'We weren't coming back until now, until ten-thirty, for the meeting with my father, and I imagined the housemaid might want to turn out the room before then, since I am catching the train to town this afternoon and not spending another night here. So I packed my case and took it with me.'

A perfectly logical explanation. Thoughtful of her. Did he believe it?

Did he believe any of them? Well, that wasn't his problem. Pretty soon headquarters would tell him when the detective would be inflicted on him. Was there anything else he should ask these people before he left?

Leon had been lounging in his chair; he sat up abruptly. 'I don't suppose anyone has told the Aunts?'

'Oh dear.' Lilian sounded distressed. 'I'd forgotten them, poor dears.'

'What aunts?' Diggory wanted to know.

'My father's two sisters — your great-aunts, I suppose. They came down for the party. They're staying with Mrs Borthwick, in Widows' Row.'

'I didn't know Silas had sisters,' Diggory said.

'There's a lot about this family you don't know,' Horry said, a sneer in his voice.

Bowler turned to go. He heard Brenda say in an authoritative voice, 'Well, you can't go back to town now, Lilian. There will be arrangements to make for the funeral, and business to discuss.'

24

Phemie Borthwick and her guests sat round her kitchen table discussing the dinner party. In the street outside a car door slammed.

Phemie said, 'That sounds like Sheba now. She said she'd call in to see you.' The big sulphur-crested cockatoo sidled along the top of the kitchen dresser muttering to itself about pretty boys and nuts.

From the back door a strong voice called, 'You there, Pheme? It's me.'

A large woman, big boned, untidy, walked into the kitchen. From the knot of fair hair on top of her head numerous tendrils escaped to float round her face; her grey cardigan, missing two buttons, hung half off the shoulder under which she had tucked a capacious brown handbag; the hem of her print dress had come unstitched at the back. She grinned cheerfully at her mother's friends.

'G'day, Aunts. Come to help merry old Silas celebrate? Was it his birthday, or his latest whore? I saw her yesterday, when the bloody man ran into our car. What a dust-up, Muir and Silas threatening each other like six-year-olds. Muir is still breathing fire.' She advanced on Ada and gave her a hearty hug. 'Have to feed you up, old girl. You're skin and bone.' The grey cardigan engulfed Joss. 'Now there's some meat on you, old-timer, you'd make some cannibal chief very happy. My word, it's good to see you both.' She dumped her worn leather handbag in the middle of the kitchen table, pulled out a chair, and regarded her company with satisfaction. 'Put the kettle on, Pheme, there's a darling. I'm parched.'

Delighted, Joss said, 'Sheba, you never change. I still expect any moment you'll hitch up your skirt and pull a shanghai and a half-eaten apple out of the leg of your bloomers.'

Sheba laughed. 'Poor mama. She's given up on me at last, haven't you, Pheme? She tried, Joss, you must admit she tried. But I'm not ladylike material, as she has finally realised.'

'We like you how you are,' Ada said.

'That's more than Pheme does.' Sheba was only half joking. 'Never mind. Tell me what she was like on closer acquaintance, this blonde bimbo of Silas's.'

'Trying hard to be genteel,' Ada said. 'Crooked her little finger no end. Pronounced her aitches carefully and in all the right places.'

Joss snorted. 'Your snobbery is showing, Sister. Although the real drama occurred when Silas announced they were engaged and war was declared. Brenda and Horry could see all their dreams of owning the farm fading every time she smiled on Silas. They'll find her a tough nut to crack, I think. Possibly Brenda will have to murder her before she can actually marry Silas, the old goat.'

'Goat as in silly ass, or goat as in lecherous?'

'Both,' Joss said.

Phemie put a teapot in a knitted green cosy on the table, set out four fine china cups and saucers, and added a plate piled high with three different kinds of homemade biscuits.

'Elevenses,' Sheba said with gusto. 'About the only good thing about being married to a farmer is that he expects five meals a day. Even now, when Muir's so angry middle age is catching up with him, at least he enjoys his meals.'

'You're getting fat,' her mother said.

'My frame can carry it. No need to worry for a while yet. How's

Lil, Joss? We tried her room at the pub last night before we went home but the party was under way by then.'

'More like her mother every day,' Joss said. 'All starched up. She's only your age, for goodness sake and she's beginning to look well-preserved already.'

Ada said, 'Diggory Kenrick called in to see her for a moment before the party. A pleasant-looking young man, we thought. It seems Lilian has kept in touch with him all these years in spite of Silas.'

Neither of the sisters took much trouble to act within their adopted characters with these old friends. Ada added, 'We'd never laid eyes on him before. Neither had Silas. He nearly blew a gasket.'

'Ah yes, young Diggory.' Sheba twisted her mouth sideways. 'Don't mention him to Muir. Grandfather Kenrick left him a perfectly good farm that he doesn't know in the least what to do with, and it frets Muir considerably. He'd love to get his hands on it.' She slurped her tea with unnecessary vigour, no doubt to annoy her mother. 'Not that he will — Diggory will take damn good care of that.'

'Why?'

'They don't get on, to put it mildly. All the same, I wish the blasted boy would sell up and go. I think my Stella spends too much time thinking about him, and if she imagines he's the stuff husband's are made of she's fooling herself. Last I heard he was carrying on with one of those girls from across the line.' She set down her cup. 'Poor old Stell, she was only married a year before Paul died and now she's been unmarried for just as long. Of course she gets lonely.'

Phemie said, 'She should still be grieving for Paul.'

Sheba stuffed a last biscuit whole into her mouth and got to her feet. She swallowed. 'Oh she is, she is. Problem is, she has always liked damned Diggory better.' Apparently satisfied that she had shocked her mother, she settled her handbag under her arm and bent to kiss her mother's cheek. 'I'd better get going. Come out for afternoon tea on Wednesday. I'll make sure Stell and the baby are home. You have to meet my grandson.'

'Wednesday is fine,' Ada said.

'See you on Wednesday, then.' Sheba hugged Ada and Joss in turn. 'Around two, if that's all right.'

25

When Joan gave him a message from Muir Kenrick that he had caught three boys shooting sheep, Bowler had suspected that his wife had misheard the words over a bad connection on the party line. Although he wouldn't put much past at least four young males he knew among his parishioners, those youths were all good shots, far too good to knock over a sheep accidentally. And if the shooting was deliberate — what would drive any of them to open war on woollies?

He had hoped that he was, by a reasonable and fair application of the laws of the land, helping those unruly youths grow into law-abiding citizens. Perhaps he was falling down somewhere.

The rain had stopped, the clouds had lifted a little, yet the unsealed road was still rutted with water and sloppy with mud. Bowler had to negotiate his Chrysler tourer through some dangerously slippery patches in the five miles to Muir Kenrick's farm.

Muir, a hardworking farmer, was young Diggory's uncle on his father's side. Bowler didn't know him well; he was not a returned soldier so their paths hadn't often crossed.

He turned over a grid, along a track across a paddock full of grazing sheep — Kenrick had more than a few spares, so why was he kicking up a fuss over one? — and pulled up behind the house. He got out and stretched. Cars always cramped him. When he had time he preferred to ride.

Bowler saw a small group huddled together on a bench on the homestead back veranda and his heart sank. These boys looked too young to be the hardened teenage villains he'd been expecting.

And then the boys scrambled to their feet and he recognised all three — two fourteen year old Wilson cousins, and a younger boy struggling to suppress unmanly tears.

His own son Tom. Aged twelve.

For too long they stared at each other before Tom closed his eyes and turned his head aside. Questions, words, jostled in Bowler's head and he couldn't utter one. He couldn't treat the boy differently from his mates. He was here as policeman, not father.

To give himself time he said, 'Stay there,' in as level a voice as he could manage, and headed for the back door to call the farmer.

From a shed fifty yards off a voice roared, 'Shut up!'

Bowler spun round to see Muir Kenrick charge from it and halt abruptly when he saw he had a visitor. His wife, a big fair-headed woman with fury in every tense line of her large frame, followed; she stamped past her husband and up the slope towards the house. Lips compressed, she twitched a minimal nod to Bowler and stalked on. The back door slammed.

'Mr Brown!' Muir waved recognition. In spite of the chill breeze his sleeves were rolled up and he was smeared with blood to the elbows. 'This is a bad business, Mr Brown,' he said, his voice raised enough to ensure the boys heard.

Bowler walked down to meet him. 'Yes.'

Kenrick was a tall man with a good opinion of himself and, usually, a genial manner, which at the moment was rather in eclipse. A .22 rifle dangled by the trigger guard from his left forefinger.

He offered his other hand to Bowler and then hastily withdrew it. 'Sorry, didn't realise I was so bloody. Just dressing the sheep, you understand, no need to waste the whole damn animal, bad enough as it is. One of my breeding ewes. Here, you'd better take this.'

As Bowler accepted the rifle he saw a girl, fair like her mother, pushing a big basket-work pram to the other end of the veranda. The widowed daughter of the house — he couldn't remember her name. He couldn't lift his hat to her either, because he wasn't wearing one. Muir's son Lyall, a young man of around twenty, as tall as the normal Kenrick pattern yet still carrying a bit of puppy fat, had followed her out from the back door. Bowler jerked his head and led Muir away towards his car, out of earshot.

Watching his hands while he checked the rifle was unloaded he asked, 'What's the story?' He felt as though Tom's gaze, fiercely concentrated like the sun's rays through a lens, was burning a hole between his shoulders. He locked his neck muscles, resisting his need to glance back.

'I heard the shots from the house. Thought probably someone was after rabbits, there's a couple of big warrens on the other side of that hill and no matter how often I rip them the buggers open them up again.' Kenrick waved towards a bare hill half a mile away behind the sheds. 'All the same, nobody had asked me if they could shoot there, so I drove down to see. And found those three, standing over one of my ewes dead on the ground. So I got their names and rang you.'

Bowler hoped Kenrick wasn't trying to turn the incident into a major row. Most other farmers he knew would have told the boys what he thought of them, and when they'd been reduced to pulp would have informed them that their fathers would be paying for the sheep in due course, and let them go. The row would have been contained within the families concerned.

But of course, he, Bowler, was part of one of the families concerned. 'What do the boys say?'

'Of course they say it was an accident — what would you expect? But they had to admit they had taken the gun without permission, Mr

Brown. They are totally irresponsible.'

'You're not pressing charges I hope.' At times like this Bowler liked to keep the incident quiet while he instilled a healthy fear of the law into the culprits to deter them from further transgressions and devised some fiendish punishment that made them sweat. Then he expected all hands to forget the matter.

'Good god no, nothing like that.' Muir shook his head. 'I just thought you might be able to scare the little devils into the straight and narrow better than I could. All the same, they should be punished somehow, I suppose. You won't go soft on them because they're Wilsons I trust.'

The two older boys were sons of highly respectable farmers who — like all the Wilsons — considered themselves a bit above their fellows; and those influential dads were not going to be pleased to see them in this kind of trouble. That consideration, however, carried no weight with Bowler. The boys themselves were his concern.

'Even less will I go soft on them because one of them is a Brown.' Bowler caught a slanted glance from Muir, a quick glance to assess how he was taking this revelation of his son's misdeeds, and realised Muir was deriving considerable pleasure from watching the biter bit. He always had been rather a stirrer. Bowler added, 'I'll see they're punished. Who does the rifle belong to?'

'Ralph Wilson.' Kenrick gestured at the tallest boy. 'Maurice's father. And he admits Ralph had expressly forbidden him to touch it. Apparently he shot the family cat last week.'

'Bloody kids.' Bowler leaned over his car door and stowed the rifle under the front seat. 'You'll get paid for the sheep, of course.'

Muir laughed. 'I know I will. It's not that, it's discouraging these lads from doing it again. So when you tell their fathers, I hope they give them a damn good belting.'

Not if Bowler had anything to do with it. 'Leave me to deal with the boys, Kenrick.'

'What do you mean?'

'Seeing you've brought me into this, leave it to me to decide what to do with them. Though I'll tell you now, they won't be beaten. I don't believe in violence.' And him an old soldier from the Great War, he thought ironically. But then, children were different. 'Anyway, not against kids.'

'I thought you'd want to see them punished.'

'They will be, believe me. In the meantime, I'd better get them back to their families and have a word with their parents.' He turned, and beckoned to the trio on the veranda. 'Come on, you lot. I'm going to take you home.'

Lyall smirked, and stood aside to let them pass. Bowler saw him mutter something under his breath; Ron Wilson, shoulders hunched apprehensively, stepped away from him.

As soon as they drove off the two older boys, side by side on the back seat, started simultaneously trying to explain how the accident had happened. Bowler flapped a hand at them over his shoulder. 'Save it,' he instructed them. 'I'll hear you all later. And one at a time.'

He had changed his mind. He would take the boys to the police station, and make their parents collect them from there. Both parents. Mums as well as dads.

Tom, sitting in the front of the car, saw with grave misgivings that his father was smiling to himself . Tom knew that smile. In the family it was known as 'Dad's spider smile', as in *Will you walk into my parlour, said the spider to the fly*.

26

'I didn't want to show you this with that Diggory boy looking on.' Brenda handed a small piece of paper to her sister-in-law and sat down heavily on the side of the unmade bed. 'Horry went to the post office this morning and cleared the box, and this was in it. We can't pay that.'

Fran pulled out a chair from the dressing-table. 'What is it? Oh, an account — crikey! Do you mean to say Silas paid a hundred pounds for that ring Miss Muffet is waving about? Damn it all, Brenda, we have to live on less than that for half a year.'

'I know. She'll have to give it back.'

Fran snorted. 'I can just see her.'

'Well, I told Horry he mustn't pay it. She can make her own arrangements.' Brenda's jaw jutted aggressively. 'I suppose someone has told her that Silas is dead?'

'She must know. I think I heard her crying when we passed her door just now.'

'Huh. Crocodile tears. You can't tell me she cared two hoots for Silas. All she cared about was his money.'

'Perhaps she's crying for the loss of all that lovely lucre, then.'

'And that's another thing. Who is going to pay for that room now? I'm damned if I think we should. We didn't ask her to come.'

'All the same,' said Fran, wrinkling her nose, 'she must have been expecting Silas to pay. She probably hasn't got much money. Probably we should honour that debt.'

'Nothing was honourable about any of his rotten debts, damn it.' Brenda jerked an edge of the counterpane between her hands as though she wanted to rip it in half. 'She's probably weaselled hundreds out of him already, as well as the ring. All those clothes. And that stupid expensive party last night, just for her. All that money he wasted on women and horses and — oh, I can't bear it. I'm glad he's dead, Fran. Don't tell anyone, I'm glad.'

'I won't tell. Though Bowler Brown's nobody's fool and I expect he knows that already.' She stretched her arms above her head and added reflectively, 'I wonder where he got that silly nickname.'

'Something in the war, Horry says. He'll never explain.'

'Not fit for our tender ears, then. I wonder when men will wake up to the fact that women can face nastiness just as well as they can.'

'Speak for yourself. Or would you like to kill the next ration sheep? Cut its throat, skin it and gut it and hack off the head?'

'You've made a point. If I was starving, perhaps, but not this week.'

Brenda smiled. She couldn't often make her sister-in-law concede she was right. 'Tell Leon about the ring.'

Fran said, 'Leon's gone to inform the Aunts about Silas. I'll tell him when I see him.'

Leon in fact had finished his mission. While Phemie was seeing him out the sisters looked at each other.

'Silas dead,' Joss said experimentally, as though the idea would take some getting used to. 'Murdered.'

'They must have known since breakfast.' Ada glanced at the clock on the kitchen mantelpiece. 'Why has it taken them all the morning to get round to telling us?'

'Probably forgot we exist. They usually do.'

'Leon seemed pretty rattled. Do you think he might be under suspicion? By the police? Who is the policeman here these days?'

'Mounted Constable Brown.' Phemie said from the doorway. 'I rather like him. He married an English girl in the war, sensible sort of woman even though her father's some fancy kind of a lord. Some people think she's stuck up, but it's only her accent.'

'I'll bet anything you like Leon's under suspicion,' Joss said. 'He and Horry must be front-runners. I do hope they didn't do anything stupid. This is awful.'

Ada made a sound as close to snorting as a well-brought-up woman could manage. 'Come on, Joss, we're not going to be hypocritical about this.'

'I only meant awful because of the boys, if they're mixed up in it somehow. All the same, not even Silas deserved to die like that. Though I suppose if you considered the number of people he rode roughshod over in the past it's surprising nobody did it before. There have been times when I almost could have done it myself.' Joss laughed. 'Don't look so shocked, Phemie. You know how he treated us.'

Phemie went to the stove. With an oven-cloth she opened the front, then took a log of wood from the box on the floor, threw it in, and yanked the door up to close it. 'You two are getting outrageous in your old age.'

'Dear Phemie, you know we only do it to shock you. We're models of discretion when we're home.'

'I get enough of that from Sheba.'

'If neither of the boys did it,' Ada said slowly, 'who did?'

27

As soon as Em had realised she was stuck with the Beadnall family for the day she had shoved a leg of lamb into the oven. Now the family had gathered in the dining-room for their midday Sunday dinner.

Their newly-reconciled nephew appeared strangely reluctant to leave them, hanging around until the housemaid called them in to their meal, so Horry had asked him to join them. In an undertone he apologised to his wife, saying that she needn't have anything to do with him afterwards if she didn't want to.

Brenda, however, had been pleased. In spite of his reputation they all needed to know more about this enigmatic nephew. She felt a vague unease that he might somehow prevent the brisk winding up she planned for Silas's affairs.

She glanced at Diggory, who sat at the foot of the table holding a triangular slice of bread in both hands, pinching off crumbs and posting them into his mouth while he studied his newly introduced relatives with a detached curiosity.

The blind was up on the window beside them, allowing in daylight which, although the rain had stopped, still had a dull underwater feel to it. After the party Em and Johnson had pushed the long table to its normal position across the back of the room, put away the silver dishes and candelabra, replaced the cloth — which had a wide yellow stain where Silas had slopped his wine — with a clean starched cloth, and put the small tables back into their places in the front half of the room.

The gala atmosphere of the previous evening had dissipated. The room now looked ordinary and dull.

Almost defiantly, Horry had taken the place which had been Silas's, at the head of the table. That would show them, Brenda thought with satisfaction, seating herself on his right hand. Her Horry was head of the family now and the sooner the others realised it the better. Nothing was going to be decided about Silas's money, or about the farm, without Horry's approval. And that meant her approval too.

At last she could control where the money went. Though there still wouldn't be nearly enough at least none would be wasted. In her view, the dining-room looked infinitely brighter this morning, as though bathed in golden sunlight. Everything looked brighter. Silas had been stopped at last.

'Of course I'm catching the train this afternoon.' Lilian turned towards Leon. 'Why not? It's a nuisance, because I'll have to come back for the funeral, only you don't need me now and my business does. I have to be there to open up tomorrow morning.' She saw Brenda's surprise at her decision. 'Horry will deal with the undertakers and write to the lawyers and I would be very much in the way — you would only become annoyed if I tried to put my views forward.' She stated this as a calm fact, which annoyed her sister-in-law instantly. Lilian added, 'I don't intend to stay only to give you the pleasure of overriding my wishes.'

Leon protested, 'But Lil old girl, we wouldn't do that.'

'Not you, Leon. Brenda.'

Brenda sucked in an outraged breath. 'What rubbish!'

'Is it?' Lilian shrugged and turned to Diggory beside her. 'I would be grateful if you could run me to the station in time for the Adelaide train, dear boy, before you go home. I think it leaves here shortly after two.'

'It will be a pleasure.'

'And where is home for you now?' Fran asked brightly from his other side. She wanted to know more about this unknown nephew-by-marriage. She had tried to cross-examine Leon about him more than once, and he'd put her off by saying that the young man was not a suitable associate for respectable women. Of course she had instantly wanted to know why. So far, at this meeting the young man had appeared as respectable as the rest of them.

And whatever his reputation he hadn't alienated Lilian, surely a stickler for convention. Why had Leon refused to discuss him?

Diggory raised an eyebrow. 'On the place my grandfather left me. That surely isn't invisible.'

'All I meant was, are you back for good now.'

'My two years hard slog hasn't convinced you?'

Two years? She hadn't realised he'd been back for so long. 'Though you were away a fair while, weren't you.'

'If you mean at school and then working for the papers, yes, for around thirteen years. Nevertheless, nowhere else has ever been home; I've always come back whenever I could wangle the time.'

'You weren't here often, though, before you moved to the farm.'

'I came whenever I had time,' he repeated with emphasis. Almost under his breath he added, 'Or whenever Grandfather needed me.' He raised his eyes and smiled straight into hers. 'Anyway, Aunt Fran, you can assure the rest of your family —' he turned a hand palm up to include the others at the table '— my present intention is to remain.'

Now, here was one to watch, Fran thought. A dangerously attractive young man; no wonder he had charmed starchy old Lilian. 'You don't call Lilian aunt,' she said. 'Why me?'

'She asked me not to.'

'And if I asked you not to?'

'I would of course call you Fran. I'm a most obliging fellow.'

She would bet he was. 'That's fixed then.'

The housemaid had wheeled in a loaded traymobile and was handing plates of roast dinner to each in turn. 'And about time.' Fran settled her plate in front of her. 'I'm starving.' Breakfast had been hours ago. What a muddled morning it had been.

'Don't blame my old mate Full Stop. She only carries the plates.'

'Full stop?' Fran saw an odd exchange between her new nephew and the housemaid: he met the girl's suspicious expression with a warm and friendly smile. Was he trying to get off with a *housemaid*? Her favourable opinion of him fell sharply. Young men who seduced the domestic staff had low tastes and weren't worth bothering about. Perhaps that's what Leon had meant. She turned towards her husband. 'Has anyone seen Miss Muffet this morning? Or is she too soggy with crocodile tears to appear?' And then, glancing back, she encountered a look of freezing disapproval from that same housemaid.

What was the matter with the girl?

Lilian laid down her knife and took a sip of water. 'I asked Miss Jennings but she is too upset to join us.' She raised her face towards the housemaid. 'Thank you, Johnson. This is very good, tell Mrs Musgrave.'

The girl nodded, and pushed her traymobile from the room.

From the other end of the table Horry harrumphed a couple of times as though uncertain how to start; then raised his voice. 'Diggory, do you intend to take up farming permanently now? It's a big change from what you have been doing.'

'Oh, I'm learning. Yes, I'll stick to it. Unless I feed a hand through the chaffcutter or remove a foot with the axe, that is. As Fran says, I've been a long time away.'

'You can always ask your uncle Muir for advice, I suppose,' Horry said. 'Been on the land all his life and he's only a mile or two from you.'

'Yes, I could do that. You're right, Muir has plenty of advice for me.'

His tone was bland enough, though Fran wondered what subtle nuance of intonation had made her so sure he would rather die than ask his uncle Muir for anything.

Diggory looked them over with that air of calm dispassion that was almost insulting in its detachment. He laid his knife and fork tidily together. 'Excuse me, aunts,' he said, and pushed back his chair. 'Uncles.' He nodded to the table generally and walked out.

Fran had no idea why he had left so abruptly, nor could she tell whether he meant to return.

28

Bowler allowed the boys to think they were in such disgrace they were unfit to mingle with his respectable family. He made them a plate of sandwiches and shut them in the police station office, the front room of the house, to get on with their lunch while he and Rose demolished another plateful in the kitchen. Joan had never adopted the local custom of a hot midday meal, particularly on Sundays; she wasn't much interested in cooking at the best of times and she had better things to do with her Sunday mornings than waste time at the stove. This morning, as soon as the rain had cleared, she had slung her camera bag and her binoculars on her back, saddled her horse, and ridden off somewhere in search of birds.

Bowler wished he knew where she'd gone. He wanted her help for the next part of his plan for dealing with his juvenile miscreants.

'Rose, do you know where your mother went? Or if she said she'd be back before dinnertime?'

'She said she was going out to Spog Wilson's place, to see if she could photograph the mopoke in that old palm tree in front of the house. You were there, Dad, she told you. When you came home for breakfast.'

Bowler scratched his neck. 'She did? Oh well, a lot has happened this morning, I expect I was thinking about something else. All the same, that's not so far away. With luck she'll be back soon.'

'I wouldn't count on it,' Rose said, licking her fingers. 'You know Mum.'

'Yes, and she'd skin you if she caught you doing that.'

'You won't tell,' Rose said with supreme confidence.

'Go and wash your hands, brat.' Her father gave her a push to send her on her way. 'And then you can make me some tea. I'd better get these boys sorted out.'

Rose sobered instantly. 'Dad, what's Tom done? Is it very awful? Please, Dad, don't be hard on him.'

'It's bad enough, but he'll survive. Don't worry about him, Rosie. Still, that's the reason I want your mother. She has to be part of this.'

Bowler had already rung Mott Wilson and his brother Ralph, the two other fathers involved. He'd explained the situation, and told them they could come to the police station to collect their erring sons at three o'clock that afternoon, provided they brought the boys' mothers with them. He would then listen to what the culprits had to say for themselves, and tell all parents what the boys had to do to reinstate themselves.

Luckily Joan's return coincided with the arrival of Ralph and Gwenny Wilson, looking to retrieve their eldest son Maurice. Bowler regarded him as the chief culprit, since he was the one who had taken his father's rifle without permission and who had, intentionally or not, drawn a bead on the unfortunate ewe. He couldn't assess, however, the extent to which he'd been aided and abetted by his cousin Ron, and Ron's best mate Tom Brown. Bowler intended to treat them as though the guilt was equally shared.

29

'Hello there, Full Stop. I was looking for you.'

Johnson, carrying an empty tray back from Margot's room, halted in the passage. 'What do you want?' She pushed her heavy horn-rimmed glasses up her nose with a forefinger as though to see him better.

'What have I done to deserve that suspicious tone?' Diggory looked pathetic as a scolded spaniel, which was overdoing it a bit. 'I thought we'd been getting on rather well.'

To herself she admitted that they had been. Too well to be comfortable. She didn't want to get close to anybody in Kularook, particularly not to anyone connected with the current crop of guests at the pub. The whole business of Silas's death was so horrifying she wanted nothing to do with those involved. Not even those on the fringes, she told herself firmly.

So far none of the relatives knew that she had been the one to find the body and she hoped they never would find out. They might want to ask questions. Even remembering that moment brought her out in a cold sweat.

'I'm working, Mr Kenrick. Will you let me pass?'

He stood aside. 'Come on, I'm Diggory. When you've been sharing supper with a fellow in the small hours you can't suddenly go all formal on him.' He followed her towards the kitchen. 'When do you stop working?'

'I don't, not on this job.' That wasn't being fair to Mrs Musgrave, who was a considerate boss. 'I mean, I never know ahead when my times off will come. The pub has to run twenty-four hours a day if people want it to.'

'You're hedging.'

In the kitchen doorway she half turned. 'When you take Miss Beadnall to the train, could you take Miss Jennings as well? She wanted to drive back to town but the Beadnalls won't let her take your grandfather's car. She drove down with him.'

'It will be a pleasure, you tell her. Particularly if it annoys my uncles. Though isn't there any knight errantry I can perform for you?'

'I manage my own affairs, thank you.'

'Ha! I've been snubbed. You really are being extraordinarily difficult, Full Stop. How am I going to get to know you better? What does a fellow do in a place like this when he wants to take a girl out? If I invited you to go walking with me it would be ludicrous in this weather. There's a concert party coming on Saturday — may I invite you to that?'

'Invite — what do you mean?'

'My dear girl, you must know what I mean. I would like to take you as my guest. I would then consider myself well rewarded if you consent to sit beside me so that I can enjoy your company. At the same time I do my best to make myself agreeable to you, so that you in turn, I hope, enjoy my company.'

Johnson said, 'I have no idea whether I would be free that night. I can't — what's the matter?'

He had cupped his hands together and was blowing on his fingers. 'I'm getting frostbite, that's what's the matter, you hard-hearted wench.' He glanced at his watch. 'But I can't stop now to continue this singularly unprofitable conversation, or Lilian will miss her train.

You wouldn't want that on your conscience, would you. But don't imagine I'm withdrawing from the lists. I'll be back.'

He went out the back door, to where his car was parked in the pub yard.

As he drove his ten-year-old Fiat sedately home after waving the women off on the train, Diggory considered these new relatives who had intruded into his life. He steered carefully through the puddle of muddy water lying in the front gateway of his farm. What was it his aunt Lilian had told him? For all her stiff manner Lilian was a good sport.

On his right cloud shadows raced across a paddock of growing wheat, green and rippling under the breeze; to his left a flock of white, newly shorn sheep grazed on the last of the winter grass.

The track followed a five-wire fence over a slight rise, down a hollow, then up to the homestead on a slightly higher rise beyond. He drew up under one of the tree-sized mallees that surrounded the shearers' cottage where he was currently living. He turned off the ignition, pulled on the handbrake, and growled, 'Lie down, Magnus' to the big black and white border collie barking and dancing at the end of its chain by the door.

Then he sat with both hands on the steering wheel while he considered the implications of his disowned grandfather's death, and his subsequent acknowledgement by his Beadnall uncles and their wives. Now they recognised his existence he would have to recognise theirs.

He didn't have to do more than that, though: he didn't have to become friends with them.

He had known all the Beadnalls by sight from boyhood, when he lived with his grandparents on the old farm. Although even in those days the two families didn't speak. Since he'd returned he had deliberately kept out of their way from a perverse kind of pride. If they chose to look straight through him he'd take damn good care it didn't happen often. He didn't like any of them much, anyway. Perhaps they would improve on better acquaintance.

Probably nothing would change. They were unlikely to start inviting him to visit them.

30

A kestrel fell out of the sky to the track ahead and broke Diggory's reverie. He watched it flap off again with something in its claws. A lizard, perhaps. Or a grasshopper.

Up the slope to the main house between the thickly growing gums and mallees an anomaly caught his eye: a square shape, the back of a car. Nobody was living in his house while he worked in every spare moment at making the place habitable. Frowning, he moved his head, trying to see more.

He debated whether he should restart the car. Quicker to walk. He got out.

His hopeful dog wagged its feathered tail, so he unclipped it in passing. It frisked around him as he jogged up the greasy track between the trees and stopped by the car, a Ford A sedan. His uncle Muir's car. What the devil was Muir doing here?

When his uncle came through the front door Diggory stepped out from behind the car. Muir's whole body stiffened with surprise.

Diggory, hands in pockets, strolled to the foot of the stone steps to the veranda. 'Hullo, Muir. What an unexpected honour. Just what do you think you're doing here?' He saw with pleasure that his uncle was highly embarrassed at being caught snooping. 'And why have you omitted to tell me you have a key to my house?'

Muir laughed. 'I haven't. The place was unlocked, and I was looking for you.'

'Not true. The place was securely locked because I have become a little bored with finding that someone has been prowling round in it when I've been out.' Diggory mounted the four steps to the veranda. 'And I doubt if you were looking for me. Lately I seem to have offended you in some way.' His eyes were level with Muir's; he held out his hand. 'I'll take the key.'

His uncle made no move. 'Wrong. I did want to see you. I'm starting shearing in a couple of days if the rain keeps off and I thought I should tell you I'll be using the woolshed.'

'Tell me? Not ask me? But it's my woolshed now.' The dog finished its investigation of the car's tyres and padded up the steps; it sat beside Diggory and leaned against his leg.

Muir shrugged. 'Your grandfather let me use it whenever I wanted it.'

'I suppose so; the place belonged to him then. Now it doesn't, though I expect I'll do the same if I'm not using it. But you could do me the courtesy of asking.'

'Sorry. Just forgot for the moment I'm not working both places.'

'Give me the key, and you can use the woolshed. As you know, I've finished shearing.' He held out his hand again.

Muir stood frowning for some moments before he took a Yale key on a twisted loop of fencing wire from his hip pocket and dropped it in Diggory's hand. 'Of course I had a key. I had to keep an eye on my father when he was living here alone, getting frail, his health failing. There's nothing sinister about that.'

Diggory tossed the key in his palm. 'No? I used to visit him too, don't forget. Why do you think this is the only farmhouse in the state with effective locks? I'm damn certain he didn't know anyone beside himself had a key.'

'Nonsense. Of course he knew. He gave it to me.'

'I'll be damned if he did. He liked knowing he held the only keys to the place because I think he was afraid of someone. Not of you, I suppose, probably of someone else. Perhaps even Silas. Though he could have imagined it. All the same, it's over two years since he died, and in all that time you might have remembered to give it to me. I didn't know *you* were coming here behind my back. I suspected the Pedler boys.'

'I did everything on this place when he couldn't manage it on his own any more. It wasn't easy, on top of what I had to do on the other place — I sweated my guts out. Then he leaves it to you.'

'You can't complain. He left you his original farm.'

'This one should have been Lyall's. He's been on the land all his life but you're no farmer. You run a farm! You're just a joke.'

Diggory put his hand on the dog's head as though to restrain it though the gesture was more to restrain himself. 'I'll manage. You're forgetting I grew up here. I'm as much of a country boy as your Lyall.'

'You go off to secondary school and we never see you again except for the odd holiday. You turned your back on Kularook and then you get this.'

'Muir, come on, get the facts straight. Old James had two sons, and when he died he left a farm to each.' Diggory sounded impatient; he'd been over this ground with Muir before. The problem was that Muir, when he'd been working both farms, had convinced himself that his father intended the second for Lyall; to find a barely-known nephew had benefited from those long hours of extra work had been a bitter pill. 'Your son will inherit your farm when you're dead. I inherited this one because my father, your older brother, is already dead. And however much you might resent it, you can't blame me.'

'I don't know about that.'

'Bloody hell,' Diggory said explosively. 'I'm not complaining because you, the younger son, got the better farm. Grandfather had a right to leave his damn farms where he chose. Now if you've finished snooping, I've got work to do.' He turned towards the door. Muir pushed past him and went down the steps to his car.

'Oh, Muir, one other thing. My other grandfather is dead too.'

'Your other — Silas is?'

'Yes, he was staying at the Kularook pub, and he was murdered last night. Isn't that a juicy detail.' Diggory had turned with the door knob in one hand. He gazed speculatively at his uncle. 'Now, why do I think you already knew that? Don't tell me you pushed the family feud to that extreme. That would be too much.'

'You bastard,' said Muir, meaning it. 'Bowler Brown was out this morning. He told me.'

'What a pity. I was hoping you'd taken to a life of crime.'

'Be your age, blast you. Silas's quarrel was with your father and grandfather, never with me. I was never part of it.'

'Neither you were.' Diggory tossed the key high and snatched it as it descended. 'But from now on just keep away from this house when I'm not in it, and that goes for Lyall too. Wait till you're invited.' Diggory went inside the house and closed the door gently behind him, leaving his uncle staring at the newly stripped and oiled panels.

The dog lay down, its nose on its paws, and watched the door.

31

On his way to bed, Bowler found he still had a wad of paper stuck in his back pants pocket, notes he'd made on sheets torn off his scribbling block in the course of the day, so he carried the lamp into the office to put them on his desk. He heard a car stop in the street. Thinking someone was visiting the pub he turned to go; then footsteps gritted on his cement veranda and someone banged on the wire door. The new fox-terrier pup in the house across the street burst into hysterical yapping.

As sure as he showed a light in the window after hours some bastard would think up a job for him, Bowler thought sourly. He growled, 'Who's that?'

A head came round the door. 'Strewth, Bowler, who are you trying to impress? Don't you ever knock off in the bush?'

'Bloody hell! Hugh!' Bowler jumped to his feet. 'I thought they were sending Macrea again.'

Detective Constable Hugh Morgan strolled in. 'You got lucky. He's busy.'

Bowler had never worked with Hugh before, didn't even know him particularly well, yet he had to agree. He hadn't got on with Macrea at all, whereas he'd always liked Hugh whenever their paths had happened to cross in the past. A hardworking man and nobody's fool. 'Good to see you, then.'

'And how are you going?' He shook Bowler's hand. 'Got the murderer locked up yet?'

'Give me a break, it only happened last night.'

'You're slowing down. Age, that's what it is.'

'Stuff you. Where are you staying? I'm sure we can squeeze you in somewhere.'

Hugh arched his spine and rolled his shoulders, then dragged a chair to the other side of the desk. The lamp's tall glass chimney was between them; he moved it to one side and half dozen fluttering moths, pale as animated flakes of ash, moved with it.

'Thanks all the same but I told them I'd stay at the pub.'

There had been a time five or six years back, Bowler remembered, when Morgan had looked to be going to the dogs a bit — morose and bad-tempered and (so the story ran) drinking too much. Once Bowler himself had run across him in a suburban pub, on his own and downing whiskies with an air of quiet desperation. Probably that had been about the time his wife had died. Now he looked better than he'd ever seen him — fit and tanned, exuding a relaxed self-sufficiency.

'I heard you'd married again,' Bowler said. 'Congratulations. Looks like it agrees with you.'

A slow smile spread over the detective's sunburnt features. 'You could say that,' he conceded.

'Anyone I know?' Like the rest of the force, Bowler knew that more than one of the office typists had been trying to catch the young widower's eye.

'No. From Eyre Peninsula — I met her on a case.' An enormous yawn took possession of Hugh's face; he tipped his head back and dragged a hand through his hair until his jaw returned to its moorings. 'I'm buggered. I reckon I'll hit the hay, Bowler. You can tell me all your brilliant deductions in the morning.'

'I'm leaving deductions to you. You're the one who's gone off and joined the ruddy Sherlocks.'

'I'll unpack my magnifying glass first thing. What time's reveille?'

All innocence Bowler said, 'I'm out by five. Want me to give you a call?'

'Bloody hell, no. You can keep that. I'll see you after breakfast.'

32

Em prodded at the bacon in her frying-pan. 'No, only the Beadnall lot and Mr Tillerman. We didn't have anyone else booked in on Saturday night. Why do you ask?'

Johnson had been trying to discover if she was the only one who knew Diggory Kenrick had slept in the lounge the night Silas Beadnall was murdered. She hoped she wasn't. She didn't like telling tales on anyone, not even on strangers, although she realised that her own illogical conviction of his innocence shouldn't stop her telling Bowler Brown he'd been there.

She said, 'No reason,' and lifted another stack of plates from the dresser and placed them on the traymobile.

'We had a late arrival last night, though. A detective from town.'

'A detective?'

'Yes, the city police have sent him, Detective Constable Morgan. I put him in one of the single rooms, though he seemed rather disappointed he wasn't sleeping on the scene of the crime. I don't know what he thought he could do there — crawl round in the night with a candle, looking for clues?'

'Isn't the — I mean, has someone taken —?'

'You're quite right, Silas's body is still there. Once this detective's had a look at him the undertakers will come today and take him away.

The funeral's on Wednesday, so Brenda tells me.'

A solidly built man in navy blue bib-and-brace overalls came in and put a galvanised steel bucket on the kitchen table; the room was filled with the cloying smell of new milk still warm from the cows.

Em turned. 'Morning, Durwin.'

The handyman nodded to her, ignored Johnson, and went up the passage to the bar where they could hear Trotter Musgrave coughing over his first cigarette of the day.

Johnson said, 'Mrs Musgrave, who do you think did it?'

'Murdered Silas? I don't know and you shouldn't ask. This is too serious to gossip about, Johnson. Don't you go round asking people who they think did it.' Em lifted the frying pan and slammed the stove-lid in place. 'Leave the whole damn mess to Bowler and this detective. Haven't you finished setting the tables yet?'

'Sorry, just going.' Mrs Musgrave needn't get snappish. Only three places had to be set in the dining-room anyway, for the detective and a couple staying overnight en route to Melbourne.

All the other guests had left the previous afternoon, the Beadnall brothers with their wives home to the farm, Miss Jennings and Miss Beadnall on the train to Adelaide. Johnson, setting out plates and cutlery on the tables, thought it would be interesting to know what they found to talk about on the long half-day journey. The murder? Their possible legacies from Silas's will?

No. Miss Beadnall was far too well-bred to discuss her personal affairs with a comparative stranger. She had a dignity and self-possession that Johnson admired in a single woman — not for her Miss Jennings's dependence on a man for security. The housemaid had her own reasons for believing that she too would go through life unmarried; she hoped she could be as self-sufficient as Miss Beadnall appeared to be.

She dropped the last knife in place and looked up to see a youngish man coming in through the door. Hastily she looked the other way.

Hell and damnation. This must be the detective. And she'd met him before.

Had he recognised her? Their previous encounter had been so brief perhaps he hadn't. Anyway, domestic staff were invisible to most people. Fervently she hoped he was one of the many who didn't even notice them.

Luckily the middle-aged couple came in just then, and allowed her to escape behind their bulky forms. What did she do now? She couldn't skulk in the kitchen; she'd have to wait on the table for breakfast and just hope she could contrive to keep behind the detective while she did it. This could upset all her careful plans.

33

Hugh Morgan spread Bowler's notes across the desk. 'That housemaid, the girl who found the body — is she local?'

'No.'

'What's her name?'

'Somebody Johnson.'

'Doesn't ring any bells. I don't think I've ever seen her before, and yet she's obviously keeping out of my way as though she's afraid I might recognise her. Perhaps she saw me at some station or other, if one of the boys brought her in — a shoplifter, something like that. She doesn't look like a street-walker.'

'She does not. She seems a decent kid.'

'How long has she been there?'

'A couple of months. You don't think she's the murderer, do you? For god's sake don't upset her. She might leave, and Em Musgrave would kill me. Em needs her.'

'Hell, no, I'm not going to make trouble for her,' Hugh protested. 'How can I? She might know me, but I don't know her from a bar of soap.'

Bowler leant back in his chair with his hands on his head. 'Where do you want to start?'

Studying the pages in front of him Hugh said, 'Nice goings on in a respectable family. Was the victim really such a bastard?'

'Most people are surprised nobody murdered him before this.'

'Your choice is the eldest son, I see.'

Bowler waved an airy hand. 'Take your pick. There's Horry, who had the well-publicised row with his father, and he was on the spot — it just seems easier for him than for anyone else. And he's lying, trying to pretend he'd talked his father round when Miss Jennings says, from what she overheard, he hadn't. The family was trying to persuade the old boy to make some kind of legal division of the farm's income because, reading between the lines, he always spent more than his fair share and left them scratching. But he had the whip hand, because he owned it. They only managed it.'

'What about the other son? I see he wasn't staying in the pub.'

'A possibility, though I see him as unlikely. He and his wife drove round to his mate's place when the rest of them headed for bed. Silas was alive then; he had his row with Horry shortly afterwards. Then Leon and his wife sat up drinking with their friend until after one o'clock, and according to Miss Jennings, Silas was dead by two. I don't altogether trust her account of time, though if true it doesn't leave a lot of time for Leon. He would have had to wait until his wife and friend were deeply asleep, and then walk round to the pub in the dark. No streetlights, the roads are slush, there aren't any footpaths, only weeds, and it was raining off and on. Yet none of his clothes are wet or muddy and, apart from his evening clothes, he brought only what he stood up in from the farm. Of course he could have provided himself in advance with a full set of wet-weather gear, but if he did he's hidden it where I couldn't see it without a search warrant.'

'Could he have borrowed gear from his mate?'

'I doubt it. He'd have to assume Venables would lie for him, and I don't think they're quite such good mates as that. Venables never went to the war; it's not as though they've been under fire together.'

Hugh grunted, and went back to the notes.

Bowler said, 'I should warn you, the whole bloody district knows exactly how the murder was committed. Em, your landlady at the pub, saw the body, and she could no more keep the juicy details to herself than she could fly. You won't surprise guilty knowledge out of anyone.'

'I don't suppose it will make much difference in the long run.'

'A terrible gossip, Em. She knows everything that goes on around here, often before we know it ourselves.'

'Has she any views on who killed Silas Beadnall?'

'Apparently not. She'd have told me if she knew anything.'

'Good.' Hugh nodded. 'Who else was at this famous dinner-party? I see, Beadnall's two sisters and an old mate, plus the fiancee and a daughter. Do you like any of them as possibilities?'

'I haven't got around to Colly Gordon or the sisters.' Bowler hadn't really considered them, and yet of course they must be interviewed. 'You'll have to make up your own mind on them. The fiancee is deeply disappointed at the disappearance of her meal-ticket, so it's highly unlikely she made away with him herself. The daughter is a strong-minded woman who obviously disliked her father, although I wouldn't have thought to the extent of patricide.'

'I'll have to get someone in town to interview that lot, then.'

'The Misses Beadnall are staying in Kularook for a few days, Colly lives a few miles out with his son, and the daughter and fiancee will both be back on Wednesday for the funeral.'

'Good. If I don't finish up before that I can grab them then. In the meantime I'd better interview the rest of them. How far out is this farm?'

'Fourteen miles of bloody awful track. Good luck.'

Hugh shuffled the pages together. 'Aren't you coming?'

'Do you want me? I thought you might get on better on your own. No preconceived ideas, all that.'

'You don't have anything else on, do you?'

34

Horry nodded to his brother to turn the handle of the grindstone, a wheel of yellowish stone more than two feet in diameter mounted vertically on iron legs. As it gathered speed he jammed the head of an axe head against it. Leon twisted his head away from the painful screech of dry metal on rough stone.

After a minute Horry lifted the axe off. He tested the edge with his thumb. His brother stopped turning to straightened his back.

Leon said, 'I can't imagine what he thinks he's doing, trying to run a farm.' Now he was allowed to acknowledge his nephew Diggory's existence he could admit he'd taken more than a superficial interest in the young man ever since he'd come back to the district. 'He'd know bugger-all about farming.'

'He knows less than that, according to Muir. He says the sooner Diggory sells up the better. If he goes on much longer it will take years to get the place back into production.'

'I doubt if he'd sell the place to Muir even if he did leave.'

Horry lowered the axe towards the stone. 'Why not?'

'They don't get on,' Leon said, and started the wheel with a yank on the handle.

The noise prevented a reply until Horry lifted the axe again. He ran his thumb across the blade again. 'That'll do. I'll finish it off by hand.' He turned towards the workshop in the nearest end of the machinery shed. 'That can't be true about the Kenricks. I heard Muir's trying to help Diggory, prevent him making mistakes, giving him advice. Only it seems he's too bloody independent to listen properly.'

'That's the gospel according to Muir. Not according to son Lyall.'

'I'd rather believe Muir than that spoilt pup.'

Leon shrugged. 'Lyall makes no bones about it. He swears both he and his father would like nothing better than to see Diggory make a proper stuff-up. They were expecting Topknot Hill to be left to Lyall. Now he reckons Diggory will stay on just to spite them.'

'Diggory's not been short of enemies, then.' Horry laid the axe on the bench. 'Lyall on his father's side of the family, Silas on his mother's.' He scratched his nose, his gaze on the floor. 'He's an arrogant young devil, from what I've heard.'

Leon had brought the conversation round to the point he wanted. He said, 'From what he was saying yesterday it's pretty obvious he hated Father. Pretending he couldn't care less, but he cared all right. I hope Bowler Brown could see it too.'

'You mean, perhaps he didn't go straight home after the dance? That's an interesting idea. After all, who's to say where he went at that time of night?'

Leon nodded. 'The side door of the pub is never locked, day or night.'

35

The farm kitchen was warm from the wood stove and full of scents of hot butter and vanilla and baked biscuits. Brenda put another length of wood into the stove, opened the oven, and slid the last tray of biscuits in. Then she turned to her sister-in-law, sitting sideways at the table. 'Leon's not still going, surely.'

'Why not? The funeral will be over by next week.' Fran stirred her teacup slowly, watching her hand. What plans Leon made was nothing to do with Brenda, yet how like her to make an issue of them.

'But Fran, surely it's not quite suitable. I mean, so soon after his father's death.'

'It's only a fishing trip for god's sake. He's not proposing a week of riotous living. Anyway, his mates are expecting him. It's been arranged for months.'

Brenda pursed her mouth. 'Nobody would think it odd if he cancelled. In the circumstances.'

'Perhaps not. The point is, he doesn't want to cancel. Honestly, Brenda, I can't see that it matters. They'll be camped miles from anywhere in the bush at Pondolowie; he can pretend he's in mourning there just as well as he can here.' The whole wide world must know none of us are really mourning Silas, she thought.

'Oh well, if you can't see the difference there's nothing more to be said.'

Only there would be more, Fran knew very well. Brenda was incapable of leaving a grievance alone once she'd discovered one. Why did it matter to Brenda if poor old Leon stuck to his plans for a few days' fishing? Who would be offended? Who the hell would know about it anyway, apart from the family? Let alone care about it.

Brenda was becoming far too managing, far too critical, now she saw herself as head of the family. Well, she told all and sundry that Horry was head of the family now — rubbed all their noses in the fact — yet Brenda believed she ruled Horry.

Fran knew differently.

Nobody ruled Horry: merely, he didn't bother arguing with his wife providing she didn't try to interfere in the management of the farm.

The farm was his obsession. In his single-minded pursuit of his ambitions for it he was very like his father, whose single-minded pursuit of more selfish ends had caused so much trouble. Because of this Horry's wife could do what she liked so long as she left him alone to run the farm; and that had given her an inflated estimate of her powers.

When they heard children's voices raised in argument coming from the next room Brenda went to quell whatever disagreement had arisen between the three of her young supposed to be working at their Correspondence School lessons.

Fran decided the time had come for her sister-in law to have something else to worry about instead of poor old Leon, so when she returned she said, 'What if Diggory Kenrick decides to take a case to law for his mother's share of Silas's estate?'

'What? He couldn't!'

That had jolted her, Fran thought with satisfaction. She had no idea if such a claim was possible in law, but it sounded good. 'I'm not sure how these things work.'

'Silas disinherited her!'

'Did Silas make a will?'

Brenda shook her head in irritation. 'We assume so, but we don't know where it is. Horry rang his lawyer, and it turns out Silas quarrelled with him last year and took his business elsewhere. Now we have to find the right lawyer.'

'Trust Silas to be difficult even when he's dead.'

'That disgusting man!' Brenda said. She grabbed an oven cloth, brown and tattered after many scorchings, from the hob and wrenched open the oven door to inspect her biscuits.

'I rather admired the old pest. He knew what he wanted, and didn't pretend he cared what any of us thought about it.' Fran considered. 'Mind you, that doesn't mean I liked him, because I didn't. I thought he was the utter end. If you want to know his lawyer, why not ask Miss Muffet? She might know.'

'We don't know where she lives.' Brenda slid the biscuits off the tray with the blade of a bone-handled table knife and turned them bottoms up on a wire rack.

'Lilian will know. They went up on the train together.' Fran stretched out a foot. Not bad ankles for a going-on-forty housewife.

She saw Brenda watching and smiled to herself. Brenda wore 'sensible' shoes round the house, and considered Fran's little heels — only little heels, nothing like the spikes she wore when she was in full war paint — a frivolous and expensive luxury that fed an unworthy vanity. And therefore, an affront.

A good many things were an affront to Brenda these days. She appeared to be living on her nerves, edgy and apprehensive; she was almost jumping at shadows.

Fran had walked across from the cottage this morning with the half-formed idea that she should show support. She'd meant the visit to demonstrate to her sister-in-law her belief that the family should present a united front towards the world and particularly towards the police.

And all damn Brenda could do was have a shot at poor old Leon. What price family solidarity now?

The eldest child, eleven-year-old Philip, ran into the room. 'I can hear a car, Mum. There's someone coming.'

'Have a look and see if it's a car you know,' his mother said. Brenda was pleased to have something to divert her frustrated anger. Damn Fran, she was altogether too casual — irresponsible really. She didn't care about the place at all.

Horry couldn't get away on fishing trips: he always had too much to do, too many things to see to. And, quite apart from the fact it didn't look right so soon after his father's death, Leon was ducking his responsibilities. He never pulled his weight on the place. She supposed it was Leon and Fran's own affair that they were wasting money on train fares and camping gear; still, she found it irritating when Horry didn't think he could afford that sort of thing.

People who had no children were selfish. There was no getting away from it, they were just plain selfish.

And, infuriating though she found the idea, Silas had probably left Leon a half share in the farm. Leon, the half-hearted worker with no dependents, could have as many rights in the place as Horry. If that happened, they would have to scratch up some money somewhere and buy Leon out.

36

'This is Detective Constable Morgan,' Horry said in the doorway. Leon walked past him and took a chair at the table beside his wife.

Brenda looked up from sliding the empty trays back into the oven. The detective was tall and much younger than she expected. He was younger than any of them, in his late thirties. Her apprehensions relaxed a little. They should be able to cope with a young inexperienced man. Then behind him she saw Bowler Brown who was just as tall and certainly no older, yet her dislike and fear mingled like acid on her tongue. Mr Brown suspected her husband of murdering Silas.

Horry turned from Bowler to Hugh Morgan and gestured introductions. 'My wife. My brother. My brother's wife. You all know Bowler. Sit down, we'll have smoko. Will you make the tea, Mum?'

'Do you mind if I ask a few questions while you do?' Hugh Morgan looked from one to the other as carefully as if committing their faces to memory. His smile, like the question, was perfunctory. 'You must realise why I am here.'

'Of course we don't mind,' Fran said, smiling her amusement. 'It's as good as a novel. Sleuth away, Detective Morgan.'

Brenda couldn't share her light-hearted attitude: Fran's husband wasn't the man the police suspected. She glanced at Bowler who, choosing to stand, had propped himself against a cupboard with his back to the window.

Although the detective, give him his due, treated them all alike she found his neutral manner unsettling. He was neither friendly nor aggressive, and she had nothing to respond to. Only questions. And if he'd intended his acceptance of their hospitality to put them at their ease he'd miscalculated.

No matter that he drank his tea and ate his share of her burnt-butter biscuits while he asked his questions and made his notes: nobody could imagine this was a social occasion. He was too watchful.

She could be watchful too.

He asked each one their movements on the night Silas died, their recollections of what had happened during the evening, what they felt about his engagement, what the row had been about, what they expected of Silas next morning. 'I should take you all one by one into a separate room and question you there,' he said, making a last note. 'But that would take too long, and anyway, by now you've discussed the evening so thoroughly between yourselves your memories must more or less coincide. Just tell me if there are any details one of you noticed, and not the others.'

'We left before midnight.' Fran sounded faintly regretful. 'We missed some of the fun.'

Brenda drew a breath. 'It wasn't fun.' Fran was dangerous, for all her flippant manner. She was pointing the finger pretty firmly at those who'd stayed in the pub overnight — at Lilian, Horry and herself.

Morgan said, 'So Mr and Mrs Leon had left the hotel before Silas Beadnall started shouting. You drove directly to your friend's house? You didn't stop on the way for any reason?'

'No.' Leon stirred his tea. 'It was raining. We wanted to get out of the wet as soon as we could.'

'And neither of you left again until next morning?'

Leon replaced his spoon carefully in his saucer. Without looking up he said, 'No. Neither of us. Fran — we sat up over a noggin or two with Aubrey until after one, and then we went to bed. After that, we were together all night, though I don't suppose you like alibis given by husbands and wives.'

'Not much.' Morgan made a note. 'Though Mr Venables seems to be in a position to vouch for both of you.'

'Of course Aubrey Venables is a very dear friend of ours, Mr Morgan.' Fran smiled mischievously. 'Perhaps you can't trust him either.'

The detective didn't smile back. 'You can leave it to us to decide whose statements are trustworthy, Mrs Beadnall.' He looked round the faces of the four seated with him at the kitchen table, and then he did smile, a well-worn and mildly cynical smile. 'Don't underestimate the police, will you. You might not like us but that doesn't mean we're idiots. After all, we have had a bit of practice — we've been lied to by experts and still come up with the right answers.'

Brenda felt a shiver like the tip of a cold knife run down her spine.

'Why would we lie to you?' Horry demanded angrily.

Morgan said, 'I can think of several good reasons though I don't know yet which is the right one. But I'll find out, you can count on that.'

'We're not damn well lying!'

The detective met his angry glare with a stony face. A small girl in navy bib and brace overalls, thumb in mouth, wandered in from the next room and stood staring at Morgan as though waiting for him to perform some interesting trick. His face relaxed into a smile; he held out his hand.

Without removing her thumb or changing her expression she backed away.

'You expecting Ross Lawson?' Bowler had turned to look out of the window behind him. 'He's just arrived.'

As though grateful for the interruption Horry immediately got up and left by the back door, letting the screen door bang behind him. Leon said, 'I didn't hear a car.'

'He's on horseback.' Bowler went out after Horry; after a couple of minutes put his head in the door. 'I've got to go, Hugh. Call in at Wisharts' on your way home and pick me up. Leon will tell you where.'

37

This was more his kind of job, Bowler reflected, as he sat beside Horry in his car listening to young Ross, in the back seat, explaining why he had come. This was nothing so dramatic as murder, just one of his jobs of keeping the peace in his 'parish', making his parishioners stay within the law, sorting out differences, making sensible judgements on who was telling the truth and who was lying — as Hugh had said, he'd had quite a bit of practice at that — and deciding what should and what should not be brought before a magistrate. He believed he was good at it.

Did he want to go on doing it for the rest of his life?

Ross Lawson, a slight, swarthy young man with an untidy thatch of dark hair recovering from a self-inflicted haircut, was saying, 'We couldn't start shearing at Wishart's shed this morning because the sheep were still damp, so with nothing to do — I'm shearing for Clive this year — I poked about a bit and couldn't find seven of your sheep, Horry, we'd left in the yards on Saturday. I reckon someone's been in the shed over the weekend after we knocked off so maybe the sheep got shorn after all. I thought you should know.'

'Unless damn Clive can provide a miracle and produce the sheep unshorn, those fleeces must be somewhere in the shed.' Horry wrenched at the steering wheel to dodge a large sheet of water across most of the track. 'He won't have sent any bales away yet.'

The tyres slurred through the edge of the water; Bowler ducked to avoid the drops coming over the door. 'You seem pretty sure he's shorn them.'

Horry snorted. 'He's been doing it for years. Always only a few, yet shear them and brand them and his clip is just a little bit bigger and so are his flocks. Silas always swore he had proof the sheep didn't stray by accident, that Clive came in and collected a few off our back paddocks every year, but he never pushed it. We put up a new fence last year so this time Clive hasn't any excuse about straying sheep, the bastard, and I want to push to the limit.'

'I'll need pretty solid evidence,' Bowler said.

Horry growled, 'Don't you go soft on me.'

'I'll do what I have to,' Bowler said. He wasn't going to invent evidence, not even to please another old digger like Horry.

He'd need to keep his prejudices under control on this one. He disliked Clive Wishart — one of those instinctive antipathies that had more to do with gut feeling than with logic. Although Horry might be a murderer he wasn't slimy.

They turned in at Wishart's gate and bumped along a weedy track to his sheds. The house was a small dun-coloured box standing alone on a slight rise to their left; no trees or shrubs or garden softened its hard rectangular shape, only a couple of clumps of spiky blue-grey agaves among the weeds. Bowler felt depressed just looking at it. What would life be like inside that box? How would you live in it with a wife and five children? Or was it six? He'd lost count.

Several hundred yards beyond the house, past the windmill and two sagging brush sheds that looked as though a few gigantic moths had been at them, they could see a straggle of stunted trees surrounding the woolshed, a low tin shed with an air of imminent collapse. The rusting sheets of corrugated iron were coming loose from the supporting timbers, none of which was on the square; the overhang of the roof had fretted to rust-bitten lace; one of the double loading doors at the end had fallen from its hinges and lay half hidden in weeds. In the paddock around it long ridges of limestone like the backs of whales broke through the thin soil.

In a corner of the fence nearest them a flock of about two hundred newly shorn sheep, white as cockatoos, huddled against the stiff breeze. All were branded in red branding fluid with a 'W' inside a triangle on their gleaming ribs. The men pushed down the top wire and stepped over the fence.

Bowler pulled up the collar of his jacket. That wind hadn't been tempered for these shorn lambs, poor brutes.

Horry hurled himself forward, reached into the scattering mob, and grabbed the hind leg of a sheep; he pulled it back and held it clamped between his knees while he examined the notches clipped from its ears. He threw out an angry hand. 'Look at that! This sheep is one of ours, I'll swear.'

'You can tell from the earmarks?'

'He hasn't had time to chop them about.' Stiff with anger Horry stalked after the flock. 'There's another. They're our bloody sheep.'

'Can you see how many?' Bowler stood with Ross in positions to hold the sheep penned in the corner while Horry walked through them looking at the ears.

'That one too I reckon,' Horry said. 'And that. I'd have to run them through a race to identify the lot.'

'No.' Ross pointed. 'Just look at the ones you picked. They've been tomahawked, all uneven wool and gashes. Neither Bub nor I shore those.'

'You're right. Of course, he's had to shear them himself.'

'I make it seven.' Bowler had been counting.

'That's it.' Horry squared his shoulders and set off for the shed. 'I want a look in his bloody bins. The beggar has been doing this for years and I'm fed up.'

38

A Rumly tractor with steel wheels, its engine pounding, was parked facing the shed; from its flywheel a wide belt turned endlessly into a gap in the shed wall.

Ross said, 'They've started without me.' Stripping off his coat he hurried in through a narrow doorway.

Inside, Bowler paused. The air seemed dense with noise: with the whine of machinery, the slap of the belt on the overhead shaft, the bleat of sheep from the pens. The whole ramshackle building seemed to be vibrating. He wondered how the shearers could endure it, day after day. Enough to send a man out of his mind. The place reeked of lanolin and sheep droppings.

Ross had stripped to singlet and pants and was dragging a sheep from the pen to join the shearer already head down over his sheep on the narrow board. In the middle of the shed Clive Wishart, a thin loose-jointed man, slouched over the classing table skirting the fleece spread across the slats. Snippets of raw wool clung to his greying hair; grease from the wool darkened the front of his blue collarless shirt.

Bowler didn't know him well, seeing that he hadn't fought in the war and so didn't attend RSL meetings and was usually too broke to drink at the pub. His inefficient farming practices coupled with his ever-expanding family kept him poor — 'Ignorant, bone lazy, and over-sexed', declared Trotter at the pub, who had known him for more years than Bowler and liked him even less.

He looked up with a frown when he saw them. His hands didn't stop moving round the edges of the fleece.

Bowler said, 'Good morning, Mr Wishart. We've come to collect those sheep of Beadnalls you had in the yards.'

Clive threw a fistful of wool into one of the bins behind him. 'Beadnalls? I haven't got any of your sheep, Horry.'

'Seven of them,' Horry said. 'We know they'd been drafted off on Saturday. Where are they now?'

Clive glanced towards the board, as though realising Ross must have told them. 'Oh, them. I let them go.'

'There aren't any unshorn sheep with the mob outside.'

'No, I put them in another paddock.'

'Which damn paddock?' Horry demanded at the same time that Bowler, who had strolled across to peer into the empty bins, turned round and said formally, 'Mr Wishart, I would like to look in the last bale you pressed. Which would that be?'

'That's insulting!' Clive blustered. 'You can't be suggesting I've shorn those sheep!'

'Suggesting? I'm damn well telling you.' Horry rammed his hands into his pockets as though to confine them in safety. 'What's more, you've been doing it for bloody years.'

'I'm damned if I'll open any bales. You're just trying to make trouble for me. You and your cosy mate the copper.'

'I hope you don't mean I'm playing favourites here,' Bowler said in a dangerous voice.

'Course you are.' Clive was shaking with rage. 'All you returned men hang together worse than the bloody Masons. Trying to make trouble. Picking on me. Why don't you look at some of your other neighbours, Beadnall? Why me?'

Horry said, 'You think I'm stupid or something?'

Almost as angry as Clive although hiding it better Bowler raised an open hand to shut them up. 'If you believe I'm acting unfairly, Mr Wishart, you go right ahead and complain to my bosses in town. In the meantime, certain allegations have been made and I have to find the truth. So you will open those bales or I'll impound the lot of them until I'm satisfied.'

Fists clenched, Clive walked away to the loading doors and stood silent, his back to them. He turned abruptly. 'Oh all right. That bale.' He pointed.

Ross had finished shearing his sheep and now stood watching. When Bowler raised his brows Ross moved his head slightly sideways, then rolled his eyes towards a different bale on the other end of the row. Clive's head swung round just too late to see this exchange.

Beckoning Ross over, Bowler went to the bale. 'Get Bub here too. I need witnesses for this.'

Clive was waving his arms. 'Not that one! Not that one! I said this one.'

'I know you did.' Bowler prised at the hooks holding the fat jute cube closed; as the fastenings gave way the compressed wool sprang up in a dramatic fountain. Clive plunged in his arm and started yanking out wool piecemeal.

Bowler's hand clamped like a vice on his forearm and pulled his hand out. 'Stand aside, Mr Wishart.'

Few men argued with Mounted Constable William Brown when he used that tone of voice. Clive twisted his hands together and made no further attempt to interfere as Bowler parted the fleeces in the top of the bale and carried an armful to the classing table. 'Don't you touch them either, Horry. Leave this to me.'

The fleeces were intact, the branded parts in place. Nobody could mistake a dark green B in a circle on the hind part of the fleece for a red W in a triangle on the ribs. Bowler was able to identify all seven fleeces while the two shearers watched. Although Bub, as was obvious from his nickname, was a large man with muscles like a draught horse and a mind that moved equally ponderously, it worked well enough to make him a competent witness.

Clive Wishart was astounded. He couldn't imagine how those fleeces had got into his bale. It must have been a mistake: the shearers in a hurry to knock off on Saturday, too busy to check the brands . . .

And it certainly wasn't him. He hadn't had the time. The shearers had been working on Saturday afternoon, and that evening his wife had dropped him off at the pub so that he could catch the Express to town on Sunday morning, three-thirty am yesterday morning. Then he'd spent all day yesterday driving his sister-in-law's car from town, to bring her and her children back with him. They hadn't got home until late.

'You had time on Saturday,' Horry said. 'Between knocking off time and going to the pub. They look as though they've been shorn in the dark. And don't think you're getting away with it this time. I'm going to press charges and make damn sure they'll stick.'

They all turned as Hugh Morgan's car pulled up under the loading doors.

'Another thing,' Horry added. 'Over a year now and we still haven't seen a penny towards that fence. We reckon pretty soon we'll start talking lawyers.'

Clive looked sick. 'Don't do that. You'll get your money. Any day now.'

Bowler watched Hugh climb in through the doors. He bared his teeth in a ferocious smile and crooked a finger at Clive. 'In the meantime, here's someone who'll want a word with you. He'll want to know everything you did and what you saw in the pub on Saturday evening.' When Clive looked mystified he added, 'Didn't we tell you? Someone killed Silas Beadnall at the pub during Saturday night.'

'Oh yes. Right,' Clive said, the comment of a man who had temporarily forgotten a fact, not one who was hearing it for the first time.

He hadn't reached home until late last night, his place wasn't on the phone — so who had told him? Was it possible that he had known before he caught the train? And if so, how and why had he known? Bowler would leave that for Hugh to sort out.

While he was waiting he'd better find a wheat bag or something so that he could take the fleeces away with him.

39

Diggory Kenrick met them at the door of the shearers' cottage. He was wearing paint-spattered khaki bib-and-brace overalls over a grey sweater unravelling at the cuffs and there were streaks of some yellowish paint in his dark hair. He smelt of turpentine. Under a tree a few yards away his big border collie bounced around at the end of its chain, barking madly.

'Hello, Bowler, what brings you my way?' He studied Hugh Morgan. 'And I know you — you're Detective Morgan. I covered the Port Mack case for the *Adelaide Times*.' He turned his head and rapped out, 'Lie down, Magnus.' The dog subsided.

'I wondered why your name rang a bell,' Hugh said. 'Don't you write for that paper any more?'

'I'm learning to be a farmer now. Come in.'

'We want a few answers from you,' Bowler said. The door opened directly into a narrow room with a table running the length of it towards a window in the opposite wall.

'Answers? Answers to what? Sit down, sit down.' The only places to sit were on a small couch with sagging springs just inside the door, or at benches on either side of the table. One of these was half covered in stacked books; the policemen chose the other bench. Diggory stayed on his feet, his back to the window.

Bowler said, 'You've been lying to us.'

'I have?' Diggory sounded mildly curious, and not at all abashed. The light was behind him, his expression hard to read.

'Don't try and play the bloody innocent.'

'All right,' Diggory said agreeably. 'Hang on, I'll put the kettle on.'

'This isn't a social occasion,' Bowler said.

'I know it isn't.' A wood stove, coals glowing through the slots in the firebox door, stood in a recess in the side wall; with the toe of his boot Diggory lifted the knob on the door and let it crash open; he threw in two split logs and hoisted the door shut again with his foot. 'But if you're about to give me the third degree I need to eat. Haven't had anything since six — forgot about lunch.' He glanced at his wrist-watch. 'It's damn nearly three o'clock.'

He adjusted the damper and topped up the kettle with water from a bucket on the floor. A few drops spilled on the stove-top boiled into dancing globules that spat as they dried. He delved into a bread crock in the corner, brought out a high-top loaf, dumped it on the end of the table, and started cutting thick slices.

Bowler said, 'You told me that you went home after the dance. Now Clive Wishart tells us he saw you asleep at the pub. When he got up to catch the train.'

'Bugger. I'd forgotten Clive.'

Keeping his temper on a tight rein Hugh said, 'Kenrick, this is serious. Why did you lie about your presence at the hotel?'

Diggory buttered his bread, took a plate holding a lump of cheese from a small flywire safe beside the window, put it on the table. He sat down beside the books and bit off a large lump of bread and cheese. With his mouth full he said, 'Thought if I told you it would only confuse you.'

'Lies confuse us a bloody sight more.' Bowler reached across and crumbled off a piece of cheese. 'Not only that, they arouse all our worst suspicions. What else have you lied about?'

'Nothing else.'

'So why were you there? Asleep in the lounge?'

'Couldn't get my car to start. Decided to be dry at least.'

'Did anyone know you were there? Did Trotter?'

Diggory hesitated. 'I came in after everyone was in bed. I've done it before. Trotter doesn't mind.'

'Did you see Silas Beadnall that night?'

'Once, early in the evening when I went to see Lilian. Not after that.'

The two policemen shared a glance. Bowler said, 'Voices were heard in your grandfather's room. Was that you?'

Diggory bit off another mouthful, chewed, swallowed. Finally he said, 'No. Why would I try to see him at that hour of the morning? I assumed everyone was asleep, my grandfather included.'

Hugh had waited with diminishing patience for this answer: it had been so long coming Kenrick could have been tossing up whether to admit or deny the voice was his.

Irritably he said, 'We don't think he was asleep. You could have seen a light under his door.'

Diggory raised his brows. 'Awake and waiting for the fair Miss Jennings, you think? I see. By all reports that would be his form. Was she the one who heard voices?'

'Never mind who heard, we want to know who they were,' Bowler said.

'Wasn't me. I didn't kill him, however much I detested him.'

'You admit you detested him.'

'Wouldn't you? You must have heard how he treated my mother. She didn't have many years of joy in her short life thanks to that bastard.'

Hugh said, 'Short life?'

'She died when I was four. Both my parents. In a fire.' He gestured to a small, cracked, black and white snapshot pinned with a drawing pin to the wall beside the stove. 'She's the reason I'm still here.'

Bowler got up to see more closely. The print showed a small boy in short pants with his arm over the neck of a border collie almost as tall as he was. The dog looked identical to the one that had barked at their arrival.

'You mean the dog?'

Diggory nodded. 'Magnus out there is her great-grandson. Her name was Maddie and she woke me when the fire started. So they tell me. I don't remember anything about it.' His expression said, *So don't ask.*

40

Hugh was not remotely interested in details of Kenrick's family. What did interest him were the details of the man's movements the night his grandfather died, and so far he hadn't heard them. He said, 'Saturday night. After the dance finished at midnight did you go straight to the hotel?'

Diggory's gaze had fallen on a pile of newspapers on the floor beside the stove. 'By the way, Bowler, congratulations. I'm weeks behind with the papers, I've only just caught up with how well you did at the Adelaide Show. You've done remarkably well with that horse. As a matter of fact I'm getting a horse, one —'

Hugh slapped the table with a flat hand, a loud smack that made Diggory jump. Or pretend to. 'Stick to the bloody point, Kenrick,' he growled.

Diggory gazed at him and scratched at the stubble on his cheek with a forefinger. 'Oh yes, after the dance. Yes. I went straight to the pub.'

'See anyone in the street? Anyone near the hotel?'

'Anyone near the hotel?' Diggory looked as though he thought this an odd question. 'In that rain?' Then he grinned and said, 'No. No, sinister strangers with knives up their sleeves.'

Hugh had taken out his notebook and was scribbling in it, so

Bowler took up the questions. 'Did you see anyone else in the hotel on Saturday night?'

'Sunday morning by that time. No I didn't.' Diggory cut a lump from the cheese and pushed it towards Bowler with the knife. Before cutting another for himself he raised his brows at Hugh, who shook his head.

'Then how did you know Wishart was there if you didn't see him? You said you'd forgotten him, so you did know about him.'

'How did I —? Oh. Oh, Em had left a lamp on the kitchen table, with some sandwiches for him. And — and a note. A note for him.'

Hugh took over. 'During the night did you hear anything? Did any noise wake you?'

'I have an immaculate conscience and I slept like a log.'

'Convenient for you. What made you give up journalism for farming?'

Diggory blinked at this abrupt switch to a different topic yet answered readily enough, 'My grandfather left me this place when he died so I have to give it a go. Anyway, I grew up here — well, on the place my uncle Muir has now — so I didn't feel strange coming back. Are you hoping to discover I'm fleeing some discreditable scandal in the city? Sorry to disappoint you.'

'It's rather an abrupt change.'

'I keep *telling* people, no it isn't. I'm just a country boy at heart, always have been.'

'I'll bet. What about your adventures in China?'

This was the first Bowler had heard of China in connection with Kenrick who, by the look of him, was not pleased to be reminded of it. He was scowling at Hugh.

'Wars are different,' Diggory said. 'The rules change.' He pointed at the RSL badges in their lapels. 'You two ought to know.' The sleeve of his old sweater slid back, revealing two shallow parallel scratches across the back of his right wrist.

He saw Hugh looking at them and pulled down his unravelling cuff. Hugh shot a hand across the table to grip his forearm.

The arm jerked minimally, then stilled. In rigid control, low and venomous, Diggory said, 'Get your hands off me.'

For several seconds they stared at each other. Then Hugh nodded, released the arm, and sat back.

Diggory took two slow breaths; his anger appeared to subside. 'You only had to ask.' He pushed his sleeve to the elbow. Previously he might have made his living tapping a typewriter yet the arm he held out was as muscular as any young farmer's. 'There are a couple of wire twitches on the chookyard gate. I scratched myself on them,' he told Bowler, apparently still unwilling to explain himself to the detective.

Bowler leaned to see. The scratches could have been made by blunt wires. Possibly.

Hugh said, 'When you were living in town were you in a boarding house? Or did you have your own digs?'

'I was renting a place at Glenelg, if it's any of your business. I gave it up when I moved here.' Diggory stood, stepped over the form, and went to the stove. With his back turned he asked, 'Why? Have you found a body under the floorboards? Nothing to do with me.'

'When you moved here did you bring furniture, things like that?'

'All my gear is in a heap in the house up the hill, waiting until I finish getting rid of the white ants and repainting the place. I should probably pull it down and start again but I have only one lifetime.' Diggory reached to the mantelpiece for a painted tin tea caddy, worn to shiny metal at the corners, and measured tea into an aluminium teapot on the hob beside the stove. Using a handkerchief from his pocket to protect his hand he lifted the heavy black kettle, filled the pot, slapped on the lid, and pulled a grubby woollen cosy over it. 'Why the hell do you want to know about my domestic arrangements?' He collected three large willow-pattern cups from a dresser beside the stove and returned to the table. 'You jokers have lost me.'

'Bring any kitchen things?'

'I brought everything I owned. I could give you better answers if you told me why you wanted to know.' From the safe he took a white china jug of milk and a handsome silver sugar bowl, worthy of any fine lady's drawing room, and set them beside the cups.

'Never mind.' Hugh stood up. 'We're not staying to tea. But before we go, we need your fingerprints.'

Diggory stiffened and turned his head alertly to study Hugh. After a moment he nodded once. 'All right.'

Wiping his fingers on a stained handkerchief , Diggory went with them to the door. 'Just so that you are perfectly clear on one thing — I didn't kill my grandfather.'

41

Bowler turned his car out of Diggory Kenrick's front paddock into the three-chain road heading back towards Kularook. He didn't bother with the graded strip of dirt in the middle, a slushy mess of potholes and ridges, and took the nearest sandy side track running closer to the belt of scrub along the fence. Wide paddocks, green with crops not yet maturing, stretched away on either hand.

Hugh said, 'I heard about your successes at the Show. One of the blokes in the police tent-pegging team is a mate of mine and he reckons they should have had you on the strength.'

Bowler glanced across at him. 'I'd be too rusty to be any use to them — haven't done that since I was demobbed.'

'Seems a long time ago now,' said Hugh, another old soldier.

'Sometimes I think it happened yesterday. What did you make of Kenrick?'

'Not an easy man to read.'

Bowler said, 'Fingerprints surprised him.'

'Yes. He gave them willingly enough in the end, though. I wonder what startled him originally.'

'I think he worked out he hadn't left them anywhere incriminating, so it didn't matter. But I'd like to know whereabouts he thought at first he might have left them.'

'He'll tell us eventually. I'll arrest him if I have to, for obstruction.'

'I hope he tells us before that,' Bowler said. 'What was that about China?'

'He was up there — Christ!' Hugh braced his arms against the dashboard as Bowler stamped on his brakes.

Only inches in front of the radiator a bunch of emus shot out at frantic speed from thickets of scrub along the left hand fence.

The engine stalled. Startled by the car the emus, half a dozen of them, swerved violently and raced off along the road away from them, feathered bustles bouncing.

Bowler let out his breath. 'Bloody hell.'

On the other side of the tangle of mallees, banksias, and yakkas growing along the fence appeared the tossing head of a chestnut horse, blowing hard. The youth on its back craned his neck to look out into the road at the departing emus, then back to the two in the car. Bowler got out and walked over, pushing through the scrub to the five wire fence.

He had to raise his voice over the sound of the mallees rattling in the stiff breeze. 'Hullo, Alan.'

'Chasing them out of the crop, Mr Brown.' Alan Pedler reined in his excited horse as it swung sideways. 'Did you nearly collect one? Sorry.' He didn't appear remorseful in the slightest; he was grinning as though at a good joke. 'Mum saw them from a window.' He gestured towards the farm house visible among pine trees further along the road.

Bowler realised young Alan couldn't be blamed for his near miss with the damn emus: nobody could be expected to allow for passing traffic on a road that at times would carry no vehicles whatsoever for several days straight.

'No harm done,' he said. 'Listen, I've been wanting a word with your Dad. Will you remind him his driving licence is due for renewal? Tell him to come in and I'll fix it up for him.'

'He'll come, Mr Brown. Spitting chips he was, when you got him fined last year.'

Bowler was pleased to hear it. Pedler senior was inclined to treat the law a bit too casually, an attitude that had rubbed off on his sons, particularly the eldest. Alan was the youngest.

The youth glanced back up the road, the way they had come. He took a breath. 'Been wanting to tell you, I saw Mr Kenrick on Saturday night going into the pub, I'd been out spotlighting with the Gordon boys and —'

'Yes, we know about him. We've just been to see him.'

'Right. That's all right then. Be seeing you.' Alan turned his horse and they heard hoofs drumming away along the fence towards the house.

Bowler went back to the car. 'Just sending a message reminding his ramshackle father about his ruddy driver's licence. They don't have the phone on.'

Hugh gestured with one hand. 'The boy can ride.'

'Yeah. Little bastard.' This youth and a couple of his larrikin mates were the culprits Bowler had been expecting to find waiting for him at Muir Kenrick's, when he'd been called out about sheep shooting. 'He's a wild kid. His eldest brother's worse, mind you, an unpleasant piece of work. There's not a lot of harm in this one. He'll grow up.'

42

After the boy had ridden off, Bowler trod on the self-starter. The engine fired immediately. The drive out must have topped up the car battery nicely. Pleased he didn't have to swing the starting handle he said, 'You were telling me what Kenrick was doing in China.'

'So I was.' Hugh turned half sideways in his seat. 'Didn't you hear about that? He was there two or three years ago, covering the civil war for his paper. When Peking was overrun apparently he did a bit of fighting on his own account, decided this time the sword was mightier than the pen and traded his typewriter for a gun.'

'You mean he took sides? In someone else's war?'

'Nothing so choosy. Seems he tackled anyone from either army who got in his way or tried to stop him. He'd taken charge of a group of European women fleeing the carnage, got them out of the city and eventually south to safety. One of the Pommy papers with a correspondent on the scene wrote him up. He did a good job, apparently.'

'He's no stranger to violence, then. I couldn't see for a minute where you were going, that stuff about his furniture, and I agree, he's the obvious one to have an electric jug in his effects. And if he took the cord with him from the farm the murder must have been premeditated.'

'More likely if it was kicking about the floor of his car, something like that, and he just happened to find it handy.'

Bowler said, 'He sounded genuinely puzzled about why you were asking, though.'

'Probably putting on an act. He doesn't give much away.'

'Does that make him your first choice?'

Hugh shrugged. 'Perhaps. And why did he go all vague and withdrawn when we asked if he'd seen anyone else? He's still not telling us everything. I still think it's possible he did go to see his grandfather.'

'You didn't push him on it.'

'What's the point? He wasn't going to tell me the truth. And he's not the only one — they're all lying. Mrs Horry tried far too hard to convince me they had talked Silas Beadnall round into making a fair distribution of the farm's profits, and I don't believe a word of it. There's no doubt he was treating them abominably, so I agree with you, they have the most motive. Mrs Leon, now — she sits back apparently hugely entertained by the whole business, the only one who didn't object to having her fingerprints taken, yet there's some tension in her too, no matter how hard she tries to hide it. Possibly she's afraid Leon did the deed. I don't know.'

'If he did he was pretty nippy. He and his mate sat up till late and then he'd have had to wait until Aubrey was asleep. Though if Miss Jennings is mistaking the time — she could be, she's pretty careless with facts — he could come into the picture.'

'What if he didn't wait for his mate to fall asleep?'

'Don't think so. Undoubtedly Fran and Leon would lie for each other, but I don't think Aubrey would. And I couldn't find any wet clothes anywhere and I think he'd have had to get muddy even if he didn't get rained on. All his stuff was present and correct.'

'The brass in Adelaide are going to get pretty toey if I don't arrest someone soon.' Hugh sounded gloomy. 'If only we could find something that pointed to one of them rather than to the whole lot of them.'

'We've been pretty casual so far,' Bowler reminded him. 'Probably we should get Horry to the station and grill him properly. Look, why don't you come over after dinner tonight and we'll go over what we've got?'

Bowler liked having things to do on Monday evening. Otherwise he might have to go and break up Trotter Musgrave's Monday night poker school, about which he was quite as well informed as anyone else in the township. He knew they didn't hold it at the pub and, seeing that he knew the identities of three others of the group, half an hour's prowl around the dark streets would find it. He tried to ensure he had no spare half hours on Monday evenings.

43

A scratch pad was lying on the blotter. Hugh twisted it towards him, uncapped his pen, and wrote 'Report' across the top of a page. Not that he would submit it to his superiors; this was a rough draft, just notes to get his thoughts in order before he went over the facts with Bowler Brown. When he got the case sorted out — he didn't even to himself admit the possibility of failure — these notes would also be a starting point for his official report.

The door into the rest of the house was shut. He could hear voices from the back of the house, probably Bowler and his wife in the kitchen.

Hugh didn't like how this case was going, how diffuse it had become. He hadn't expected it to be so difficult. These irruptions of murderous violence in small communities usually could be sorted out in a day. The suspects would be so thin on the ground that the perpetrator more or less named himself. In this case he had too many suspects.

He had to agree with Miss Jennings. With no trouble at all he could imagine any one of Silas Beadnall's immediate family deciding to do away with him. What had he overheard Fran Beadnall calling him? 'The old pest' — that was it. Someone had swatted an elderly man out of existence like a pestilent fly.

He hadn't yet spoken to Lilian Beadnall or Margot Jennings. If he was still tied down here on Wednesday, he'd interview them when they came for the funeral. And then Colly Gordon had been at the party too. He'd better be interviewed too, as soon as Hugh got a moment.

Not that he expected the man to be much help. Hugh really fancied only two of his suspects: Horry, because he had a bad temper, was on the spot, and had the most to lose; Kenrick, because he too was on the spot, had a long-term hatred of his grandfather, and was now hiding something. The young man had been apparently open and helpful with them, yet Hugh thought he had discerned a faint arrogance, as though Kenrick believed himself clever enough to fob off the police with any old lies he chose to tell.

He needn't think he was as clever as all that.

Hugh wrote:

Silas Beadnall was murdered after he arranged a party at the Kularook hotel to celebrate his sixty-sixth birthday and his engagement to a much younger woman. His grown-up children realised that this meant he would still take the greater part of the farm's income for himself. They had been hoping to get him to sign an agreement to share more equitably with them.

Horry manages the farm for the others; brother Leon works on it; sister Lilian draws an income from it. All three share only what's left after their father takes what he wants. All three believe they should have more.

According to Horry, Silas Beadnall's sisters do not derive their income from the farm so on the surface have no motive. Colly Gordon, according to the same source, is an old mate from Silas's youth, also with no obvious motive.

<u>*Horry Beadnall*</u>

From what Trotter heard of the quarrel, Horry in particular is desperate. Swore to his father that the farm isn't viable under the present arrangement and it must be made so, since he has no other skills to start a new life and support his own family elsewhere. So he stood to lose his livelihood and his life's work: must be the most likely suspect. Certainly he had the opportunity.

Problem is, he didn't have any way of covering up the crime. Unlikely that a man of his intelligence would believe he could stroll down the passage in the middle of the night, commit a murder, and get away with it. Unless he is counting on just that, that we won't believe any man could act so brazenly. Prompted by his wife, he's lying about the quarrel, and pretending he'd persuaded his father to agree to their profit-sharing scheme. A difficult man to read.

Mrs Horry

She certainly hated Silas Beadnall more bitterly than anyone else. She believes her husband does most of the work and all of the managing to provide income for the others who do nothing. She's lying about the quarrel, and is certainly tense and jumpy. She could have done it — she's a strong countrywoman and would have the strength to twist that cord, particularly if she took Silas unawares. But she, like her husband, had no way of creating an alibi to cover her movements. On the other hand, her nervousness could be because she suspects — or even knows — her husband did the deed.

Leon Beadnall

No doubt expected to be forced off the farm also if Horry decided he couldn't run it on his father's terms and left. Can't see him liking the idea of finding another job — when I was questioning them all at the farm he told me he isn't qualified for anything else.

If he killed his father he would have been forced to wait until Aubrey Venables went to bed before he returned to the hotel, and, if Miss Jennings estimation of the time when she found Silas Beadnall dead is accurate, I doubt if he had time after Venables was asleep. Though if she visited the room later than she at present estimates, he probably could have done it. All the same, it was a filthy night and so, seeing that Venables swears no cars moved overnight, Leon would have been soaked to the skin and mud to the knees by the time he walked round to the hotel, and there is no trace of water or mud on the floors of the passage or the deceased's bedroom. Bowler checked his clothes, and found no excessive mud or moisture. Gum boots? Check whether Venables has an easily accessible pair somewhere in his house.

Mrs Leon

The same objections for her. Here too I sense some tension behind her amusement at the bumbling constabulary. I'd like to know what she fears, or is hiding.

Miss Lilian Beadnall

Have to wait until I've spoken to her. Bowler says she'll be here tomorrow afternoon, for the funeral.

Miss Margot Jennings

The same for her. Though of them all, she seems to be the only one who stands to gain more from Beadnall alive than from Beadnall dead. Not really a suspect. When I finally get a word with her, I hope she can throw some light on what the others were up to.

Diggory Kenrick

This one also hard to read. Admits he hated his grandfather, lied about his movements on the night and is still keeping something back. Scratches on wrist — fingernails? His history proves he's no stranger to violence. We would have to search his house to find out if he has an electric jug minus a cord in his possession. I'd better do just that.

Em and Trotter Musgrave

No motive. If anything, a good reason not to kill Silas, to avoid scandal in their hotel. Bowler Brown trusts them, believes what they tell him, and he has known them for years. I've spoken to Trotter; I'd better find out if Em noticed anything he didn't.

Housemaid Johnson

This one too I must interview as soon as possible. She carries some mystery, something she's hiding. I doubt if it's to do with the murder, though she could be suppressing evidence against one or more of the others. Mrs Musgrave seems protective of her. Why?

Clive Wishart

Only in the hotel for a short time. Although he doesn't get on with Horry Beadnall, vide row over stolen sheep, I can't see he would gain anything by Silas Beadnall's death. Though he was pleased to dob in young Kenrick and prove he *hadn't gone home after the dance, which could have been to take my attention away from himself. His obvious prior knowledge of Beadnall's death, which Bowler had noticed, had an innocent explanation after all — his wife had told him. She had visited Fieldings on Sunday afternoon and heard it from Horry himself, when he had called in to collect his children whom Mrs Fielding had been minding overnight while the adults went to the dinner party.*

Hugh screwed the cap on his pen, clipped it into his top pocket, and sat back. He had the feeling he was overlooking something. Nothing jumped off the page at him.

The truth was he didn't yet have enough evidence to arrest anyone. A good lawyer could drive a team of horses through the evidence he'd got against the two chief suspects, Horry Beadnall and young Kenrick. His gut feeling was Kenrick. How could he improve the case there?

Ask him specific questions about electrical cords, that was how. He'd go back and do that next day. Would he need a search warrant? Probably not yet.

44

After breakfast on Tuesday morning, seeing that Bowler had gone off to get statements from the shearers about events at Wishart's woolshed the day before, Hugh Morgan pushed open the gate to Phemie Borthwick's cottage, the middle cottage in a terrace of three. They were small, old, and stood at the edge of the town just past the police station, at the point where the road petered out to the south in a muddy, little-used track.

The front garden was tiny. Hugh took three paces from the gate to the veranda, through a waist-high tangle of sword ferns and succulents, and lifted a brass knocker shaped like a horseshoe to bang on the front door. He could smell the musty geraniums in the next garden.

He was considering banging again when he heard a crash and piercing screams from inside the cottage. He flung open the door — it was unlocked — and raced down a short passage to the back of the house, into the kitchen.

'What —'

Three elderly women stood around a mess of shattered china in the middle of the floor. They were laughing uncontrollably, doubling over, rocking themselves, beating their knees, whooping with laughter. A large sulphur-crested cockatoo danced along the top of the dresser, teetering and flapping its wings and screaming, and a fat Pekinese like an animated fur rug backed away under the table yapping furiously.

Raising his voice above the din Hugh said, 'I'm sorry, I did knock. You didn't hear me.'

'Well, we wouldn't would we,' the tallest woman said, choking back her laughter. This almost set the other two off again as well.

The most portly of the three said, 'Do come in, Mr — the other room, this way.' She turned him round by his elbow and took him into the front room, small yet bright. 'Let it wait.'

He assumed she meant the disaster on the floor. 'Morgan,' he said. 'Detective Constable Morgan.' The furniture was old, and elegant enough to furnish a far more distinguished drawing room than this poky one. His wife would have been delighted with it. 'I thought someone was being murdered.'

'Augustus Caesar. Noisy bird when he's excited. Borthwick, Phemie Borthwick. My friends Ada Beadnall, Joss. The Misses. You're assisting our gallant Mr Brown.'

Not quite, Hugh thought. He didn't bother to correct her; he nodded. 'I want to ask the Misses Beadnall a few questions, if I may.' He smiled on the sisters as they seated themselves side by side on a chaise lounge upholstered in striped silk. Ada was the tall thin fidgety one, Joss the shorter sturdy one. 'I am investigating your brother's murder, you understand.'

'Pleased to tell you anything we can,' Joss said. 'Are we suspects?'

'Good heavens, no!' Hugh laughed.

Joss shook her head in reproof. 'We ought to be. We didn't like him.'

'Neither did a lot of other people, I've discovered. Did you murder him? Either singly or together?'

'No,' they said in unison.

'That's all right then. Now, you were at the dinner party on

Saturday evening. You know all the guests — did you notice anyone acting strangely? Or anything that suggested someone present was dangerously angry?'

Ada fluttered her hands. 'But officer, we didn't know Miss Jennings. And you can't expect us to notice things, we were talking to our nephews and nieces, chatting you know, and Colly Gordon tried to flirt with Joss, silly old thing, so as for noticing anything, you couldn't expect us to be watching *every*one. Really —'

'Colly was angry,' Joss said.

'Why was that?'

Phemie Borthwick said, 'Back a long way. When we were young.'

'If you want to know what I think,' Joss said slowly, 'I think Silas arranged this whole party to annoy as many people as possible. Oh, he pretended he was celebrating, but it was a celebration designed to rub salt into as many wounds as he could reach.'

Hugh wondered if she was right. Silas certainly had upset his sons, their wives, and his daughter. 'What was he doing to make Mr Gordon angry?' He knew from Bowler's notes that Colly Gordon, a widower, lived with his son's family on a farm north of Kularook.

'There was a girl,' Phemie said. 'Engaged to Colly. Silas took her away.'

'A long time ago,' Joss explained. 'A terrible scandal. Silas got her pregnant, abandoned her, then she committed suicide. This girl, Margot Jennings, is very like her.'

Ada said, 'If Colly had been able to find Silas at that time he would have murdered him there and then, I think. Just as well he didn't. That's why we think Colly was invited, to remind him of that other girl. He took a long time to get over her, before he married.'

'Silas pretended he was invited for old times' sake,' Joss said. 'One of his oldest mates, you know, lots of nudges and reminders of what devils they'd been when they were rip-roaring young bloods together. That sort of thing. They really were mates, too, until this business with Ann came between them.'

When he'd finished with his official questions Hugh said, 'I know it's none of my business, but I'm curious. What was so amusing about whatever you'd broken?'

The three looked at one another. Grinning, Joss said, 'Our wedding present to Phemie, a decorated china bowl. Father made us buy it and though Ada and I thought it pretty hideous we didn't have any choice and anyway Phemie always said she loved it. We'd just discovered Phemie loathed it too and only put it out on the bookcase when we were here. All these years! Over fifty years, all of us lying in our teeth and we never knew. So Phemie smashed it. Lifted it over her head and positively hurled it on the floor.'

'Relief,' Phemie said. 'A great relief.'

The other two nodded. Joss said, 'Good manners can be a trap, Detective Morgan.'

Hugh took his leave, and then wasted the rest of the morning driving out to Diggory Kenrick's farm and finding nobody home. The Fiat was standing by the shearers' cottage, but his other transport, the lorry, was gone from the machinery shed. Kenrick could be anywhere about the farm, anywhere about the district. Hugh drove back to Kularook in a sour mood, thinking dark thoughts about bloody clodhoppers who didn't have telephones installed.

Though Bowler had explained that to him. Telephone connections cost more than most farmers could afford when they had to pay for the miles of line running out to their houses.

45

Juliet Davidson put her elbows on her very good friend Joan Brown's kitchen table and raised her cup in both hands. Since she was never quite sure how much such lapses grated on her friend, who had been reared in the rigid formalities of an upper-crust Pommy family, she said, 'Sorry, Joan, smoko manners not tea-party manners. I'm not in the mood today.'

Joan replaced the teapot on the hob and returned to the table. 'Suits me.'

'So what's Bowler doing about these kids who shot Muir Kenrick's sheep?'

'How do you know about that? It is supposed to be confidential.'

'Well so it is, why else would I be asking? But you know it won't go any further.'

'It had better not. Bill would kill me.'

'Bill would do no such thing. And it can't be as confidential as all that because young Ron's mother told Archie — he's her brother — and she must have known he'd tell me. There aren't any secrets between husbands and wives. Come on, Joan, what happened?'

'I will never learn all the family connections in this community,' Joan said, shaking her head. 'That is another one new to me. One day you will have to draw me a diagram, arrows pointing and connecting, like a glorified family tree.'

Juliet took a sip of tea, swallowed. 'No good asking me; I don't know them all. I only moved here after I married Archie. For a properly detailed list of all the family ties you'd need someone like Mrs Harry Wilson, who was born here. Go on, tell me about the boys.'

'I suppose you heard our Tom was one of them?'

'Of course.' Juliet reached for the packet of coffee biscuits and shook one free. 'Joan, do you really like these things? They taste like tarted up cardboard to me.'

'No, I don't suppose I do. It's just everybody seems to buy them by the cartload, and they're easy. Bill hates them, so perhaps I ought to try a different sort.'

'You're impossible. Of course you ought to buy the poor man a different sort if you're not going to bake him home-made ones.'

'I'm a hopeless cook,' Joan said comfortably.

'You could always learn.' Juliet shook her head. 'No, not your style. Go on about the sheep.'

'Well, Bill arranged for the other parents to come and collect their young sprigs, and then stage-managed a dramatic production to satisfy everybody and drive his messages home. Really, Juliet, I had trouble not to laugh. He was solemn as a judge, the poor boys were quaking in their shoes, and the other parents were completely bemused about what he was up to, partly because he insisted the fathers bring their wives and they're accustomed to managing these affairs between men only. He turned it into a sort of court with himself as prosecutor and judge. When he questioned the boys he saw that young Maurice was the obvious ringleader and the one who actually shot the sheep, but he said they were all equally to blame since they'd known Maurice had taken the gun without permission. After he'd read them a lecture on firearms and safety he told them that seeing their fathers would have to pay for the sheep the boys would have to work off the debt. Then came the punch line — not by working for their fathers, because they did that anyway, but by working for their mothers.'

Juliet laughed outright. 'Trust Bowler.'

'We have the use of their spare time for two weeks,' Joan said. 'Washing up, sweeping and dusting — things like that — and we have to write down the hours they work, keep a record so Bill can check. You can imagine how that deflated the boys. Particularly young Maurice. He'd been a bit cocky at the start, and more ashamed of his appalling marksmanship than he was of killing the sheep — he claimed he'd actually aimed at a rabbit so he had all kinds of excuses. Naturally Bill didn't let him get away with that. They were all properly ashamed of themselves when he finished with them, because of course he was a Light Horseman in the war and knows what he's talking about when it comes to guns. Their fathers know about his gongs, too, even if the sons don't.'

'Archie told me.'

Joan smiled ironically. 'My war hero.'

'Don't pretend you're not proud of him.'

'Oh, sometimes.'

'I don't suppose you can tell me anything about old Silas Beadnall's murder, can you?'

'You *are* being diplomatic,' Joan said. 'You suppose right. And not because Bill has warned me not to say anything, only because I don't know anything to say. I'm as much in the dark as you are. And, I suspect, as he is.'

46

In the kitchen Em dragged the big wooden clothes horse closer to the stove and began draping it with towels from the cane basket at her feet. Her mind still seethed with the things she wanted to say to her husband Trotter; things she would have said that morning if he hadn't walked away. She wouldn't let him get away with it this time. They had to discuss the pub's finances.

A rattle and a rumble preceded Johnson, trundling in a traymobile loaded with dirty dishes from the midday meal in the dining-room.

Em slung the last towel over the rail. 'I'll be glad when the weather clears. It might have stopped raining, but everything is still damp as blazes.'

'Did the sheets get dry?' Johnson started packing the crockery in piles on the table.

'They're not so bad. I've draped them all round the laundry.' Em fiddled with the corner of a towel. 'Johnson, on Sunday I overheard young Kenrick trying to ask you out.'

Johnson continued unloading crockery.

'Don't be offended,' Em said. 'I know it's none of my business; still, I think I should warn you just the same. You were right to refuse him. You should be a bit careful about that one.' When the girl didn't answer she added, 'He's got a pretty bad reputation around here.'

'Reputation?'

'Where women are concerned.'

As if that wasn't enough, Em thought, he was part of her damn husband's Monday night poker school. What had got into Trotter lately? He wasn't going to lift the pub out of the red by playing sixpenny poker with that ill-assorted gang; and if, as she suspected, he was taking a free bottle of whisky with him every week he was only making matters very much worse.

Johnson set out the washing-up bowl and the draining tray on the table and went to the stove for the kettle. 'In what way, with women?' Steam swirled into her face as she emptied the kettle into the bowl.

The slightly amused tone of this question confirmed Em's suspicions: the girl was interested in young Kenrick and didn't want to believe the worst of him. Feeling satisfied she'd been right to issue the warning, she said, 'Well, there was the wild party he threw not long after he came back to live on the farm, when a carload of his friends arrived from town. They lit a huge bonfire and then apparently all got roaring drunk. There were women running all over the place with the men after them like dogs — one even had a hunting horn, I've been told. A couple of people driving past saw it all.'

'Probably stopped for a better look.' Johnson still didn't seem to be taking these disclosures seriously. She was watching her hand swishing the soap-saver, a small wire cage attached to a handle and containing laundry soap, to and fro in the bowl until the suds rose.

'Undoubtedly,' Em agreed. 'All the same, it's made people wary of him. I'd keep my daughters out of his way.' Em's daughters were safely in boarding school in the city, so this statement was hypothetical. She glanced at her housemaid, whose blank expression gave nothing away. Determined to get through to her, almost spitefully, Em added, 'And now I hear he's having an affair with one of the Gregory girls across the line.'

In Kularook this made her, quite literally, from the wrong side of the tracks. Johnson did look at Em then.

'I hear all sorts in the bar,' Em said. She patted the girl's shoulder. 'So you were right to say no. When you've finished the washing up you can take a few hours off. We won't start getting tea until around five.'

Johnson said, 'Thank you, Mrs Musgrave.'

Em couldn't tell whether she meant for the advice, or for the time off.

47

Johnson wandered aimlessly round the six streets of Kularook —
three down, three across — wondering what she could do to
entertain herself before she had to start work again at five. She saw
Diggory's Fiat tourer pulled up on the weedy verge on the other side
of the street, in front of the corrugated iron shed that was Niels
Petersen's workshop.

Around the turn of the century old Petersen, then in his thirties
and the carpenter on one of the big Scandinavian windjammers, had
jumped ship in Port Adelaide and walked south, following the railway
line, until he'd believed himself far enough from anybody connected
to the sea to be safe from discovery. In Kularook he'd married a local
girl and raised a family. Now his wife was dead and his son and both
daughters had left home; he lived alone, and continued to make his
living as a carpenter.

Propped on the Fiat's front mudguard Petersen was watching
Diggory, on his knees in the weeds peering into a baby's carry basket
on the ground before him. A thin, pale girl stood over him, fingering
a twist of golden hair that lay on her neck below her beret.

They were both smiling, he with delight at the hidden baby, she
with unguarded affection at the back of his head.

Johnson crossed the unsealed road towards them.

When he heard her footsteps he jumped up. 'Full Stop! Well met, young Johnson. Do you know my cousin? Stella White. And baby Andrew, who is to be christened tomorrow. Come and pay homage to Andrew. He expects it.'

The two girls smiled rather warily at each other.

'Hullo.' Hands on her knees, Johnson leaned over the basket. She hadn't much experience of babies. 'How old is he?'

'Seven months.'

Petersen lifted a steel toolbox from the ground and lowered it to the running board of the car. He bent to secure it with a length of thin rope.

Stooping, Diggory gave the baby a finger to grip. 'Aren't babies astonishing? So tiny, and yet perfect working models. Young Andrew here's a credit to his mama.'

'There's someone over by the post office waving at you,' Johnson said.

He glanced up. 'Hey, Stell, it's Muir. Seems he wants you. Make him wait. Do him good.'

'Not a good idea to keep Dad waiting,' Stella muttered. 'I'll have to go.'

Diggory lifted the basket by the handles. As she took it from him Stella said, 'Come over for morning tea some day, why don't you.'

'I'll do that.' He pecked her cheek and she walked off to where her father waited.

Diggory seized Johnson's arm. 'You're an elusive wench. I'm just collecting Niels and taking him out to the farm to do a couple of jobs for me. Why don't you come too?'

She looked into the car. The back seat was piled with lengths of timber that protruded above the doors, leaving no room for passengers. 'There's not enough room for three.'

'Of course there's room. It will be a squash, but I'll make Niels sit on the bonnet if I have to. Come on.'

Johnson, who had resented Em's lecture quite as much as that well-intentioned woman had feared, said briskly, 'All right.' She glanced at Niels; he was nodding complacently. She walked round and got in.

When Petersen also climbed in beside her they were indeed squashed, wedged so tightly Johnson half expected one or other of the doors to fly open under the strain. Diggory barely had room to move his gears.

Petersen looked past her. 'Trotter has spoken to you, Kenrick? He says not next Monday. Not if this detective still hangs himself around.'

'All right,' Diggory said.

Johnson knew very well they were discussing the Monday poker school, so she pretended she wasn't listening: not difficult when she had so much to see.

This was the first time she had been out in the country around the small township and everything was new, the pleasures sharp with discovery. She had learned to appreciate misty mornings, magpies singing, the scent of wet earth, the trees; now she took pleasure in the views she glimpsed in gaps in the scrub along the roadside fences: long views of dark green paddocks, undulating paler grazing land speckled with grey sheep, belts of gums, an occasional farmhouse surrounded by sheds and more trees. The sky was in the background everywhere she looked; it came a long way down to meet the plains.

At his farm Diggory drove past the woolshed and the barking dog at the shearers' cottage and up the rise to the homestead beyond, where he stopped the car under one of the small eucalypts that surrounded it and they all got out. Johnson stood looking about her, at the old house with its wide verandas, at what had once been a garden behind a collapsed wire netting fence, at a small flowering gum full of excited parrots, while Diggory crossed the veranda to unlock the back door. He helped Petersen lug in his tools, then he turned to her.

'Welcome to my humble abode.' Hand on heart, he bowed deeply. 'Sorry, Full Stop, I should have a hat with a big feather in it, to sweep off before you.'

'You're doing all right without it,' she assured him. She studied the house for a further moment. 'And that house is far from humble where I come from. You should have seen — no, never mind.'

'Are you being difficult again? Going all mysterious on me?'

She laughed. 'Probably.'

'What do I have to do to prove you can trust me?'

He sounded serious. Lightly she said, 'Of course I trust you.'

'I hope you mean that. Come on, I'll show you the inside of the place.'

They went in through the back door to the kitchen where the old man, setting up a couple of sawhorses in a sea of curly russet wood shavings, smiled warmly at her. The room smelt of timber and new paint.

The house wasn't large, though because every room had a window or door to the veranda it seemed bigger. Their footsteps echoed on bare floors. Furniture was stacked in the centre of the rooms away from the newly painted walls. 'Whenever we get a good strong breeze I open every window and door in sight.' Diggory sniffed experimentally. 'I think the paint smell is fading.'

On the front veranda he pointed between the trees. 'That's my uncle Muir's place, about a mile away. I grew up there, when my grandparents were alive. Now I might plant a couple more trees to block it out.'

'Don't you like your uncle?'

'Not a lot.' He wagged his head and gazed at the distant house. 'It's a family thing. I think he's always resented me since my grandparents took me in when I was four. He was a teenager, still living at home, and I suppose from his point of view I was definitely

175

a cuckoo in his nest. He's probably all right to other people.' Grinning, he added, 'And now I have mortally offended him by inheriting this farm. James — that's my grandfather, his father — left it to me. So Muir's fuming, because he thought his son Lyall would get it, though I can't imagine what gave him that idea. So mostly we keep out of each other's way.' He offered his arm. 'Come down to the cottage. That's where I'm living at present — I'll make you tea or something. And I want to let Magnus off his chain.'

She tucked her hand inside his elbow and they strolled together through the trees down the slope. The sun was shining, drawing up scents of damp earth and rank grass. Three magpies flew up from the track and regarded them balefully from a low limb on the nearest gum.

'I don't want tea,' she said. 'Show me around.'

Chaperoned by a frisking Magnus, they first inspected the woolshed, dark and dusty and smelling strongly of raw wool. Then he took her behind it, past the sheep-yards, to where two fences meeting at an awkward angle had left half an acre of unusable ground, a triangle where the original scrub still flourished. The highest bushes were only shoulder height.

He walked in through the bulloaks and banksias, planting his boots between the smaller plants in the understory, and pointed to the leaf litter in a little clearing. 'Spider orchids.'

Entranced, Johnson knelt on the damp earth. 'Really truly orchids?'

'Really truly orchids. Wild ones. Those blue spikes are orchids too, and those greenhoods. Pick them if you like.'

'They'd only die. Leave them here.' She looked at him in some awe. 'You have orchids growing on your land. It sounds like a fairy story.'

'They don't survive when we clear the land,' he said. He sounded brusque, as though he too regretted the destruction of such beauty.

'Come on, I'll show you the rest of the sheds.'

So they walked past the open front of the machinery shed, which housed the big steel-shod tractor, the harvester, and a heap of bagged superphosphate; stuck their noses into the farm workshop, where Diggory said he was still, after nearly two years, discovering tools he didn't know he owned in the heaps of metal, furred with dust, that lay jumbled in dark corners; and came to the cowshed. This was smaller than the others and built of brush, instead of corrugated iron.

'No cows at present, because I detest milking,' Diggory explained to Johnson, as she stood on the bottom of the cow-yard rails and leaned over to look into the shed. It had a dirt floor worn into hollows and two sets of cow bails close to the back wall. 'I always went missing at milking time when I was a kid, if I could manage it. Not only does it set your wrists on fire until you get used to it, you're then, like it or not, tied to the place twice a day for the term of your natural. Still, I don't have much option.' He leaned beside her. 'I'm getting a couple from Archie Davidson next month. The end of my carefree life. Still, James wanted me to grow up years ago, I should have —' He gave his head a quick twitch as though to dislodge an uncomfortable thought. 'Oh, well, probably only fair he's forcing me into it posthumously.'

'Why get cows, though, if they are so much trouble?'

'So I can start sending cream-cans to the butter factory in Edgerton. I need more paint and plaster.'

'The house looks almost finished.'

'There's a bit to do yet. James was pretty frail in his last few years; it wasn't his fault he let the place go.' He turned and leant his back against the rails while he looked over his property. 'Last month I had to borrow a nag off Pedlers to muster the sheep for shearing, so I need a horse too. Still, I'm getting one on the never never from a mate at Gumeracha — it's coming by train on Wednesday.'

She climbed up the rails and perched on the top one beside him, her gaze following his. 'How does it feel to be monarch of all you survey?'

He dragged his hand over his face and didn't answer. Then he cleared his throat and growled, 'Not good. Worried stiff, if you must know.'

Johnson got her feet under her and stood up, balancing precariously. The rails were just rounded poles cut from the scrub and gave insecure footing; she teetered, flailing her arms, and Diggory reached up a hand for her to grab. She walked along the rail as though on a tightrope and he paced beside her, his hand stretched high.

Without raising his head to look at her he said, 'What do you do when you're not housemaiding in country hotels?'

She nearly lost her footing. Gripping his hand like a lifeline, she recovered. 'I'm a good housemaid. What makes you so damn certain I'm something else?'

'That, I couldn't tell you. However, I know I'm right so don't start inventing lies for me.'

Johnson considered this for several moments. Then she said, 'I can't tell you. I will, I promise, just not yet.'

'You can also tell me what I can call you besides Full Stop.'

'All right.' She compressed her mouth. 'But there's something I have to do first.'

'You sound as though it could be difficult. If you need any help, let me know.'

They had come to the corner of the yard. He reached up both hands, took her waist, and lifted her down before she could protest.

For a few seconds he held her, his hands on her ribs. 'I mean that. If there's anything I can do, let me know.' Then, before she had a chance to become embarrassed, he grabbed her hand and towed her off to the chook yard, where he raided the nests and presented her with a warm brown egg.

'I know it should be a golden one,' he apologised. 'Maybe next time.'

'Time!' Johnson grabbed his arm. 'Diggory! What's the time?' He showed her his wrist watch. 'Hell! Ten to five! I'm supposed to be back at work at five.'

'It's all right, I'll take you in now. You'll be there by half past, about. Hang on, I'll tell Niels.'

'I wasn't thinking,' she said, angry with herself. 'I shouldn't have come. Now you'll have to make two trips.'

'A small price for the pleasure of your company. Of course you should have come.'

48

Hugh was pleased to discover that the Gordon farm did have the telephone installed. He made sure Colly Gordon was at home and waiting for him, then drove five miles north along the railway line. Seeing that this was the main road to Adelaide, capital of the State, it left a considerable amount to be desired, since a few hundred yards out of Kularook it degenerated into two worn ruts in the earth with a ridge of weeds between. Hugh, however, was unsurprised. He'd travelled that road when he'd driven from Adelaide on Sunday.

He recognised the farm, the trees, the sheds, from Bowler's description. He turned east, bumped across the railway line without obeying the painted sign to LOOK OUT FOR TRAINS (in that vast silence he would have heard a train long before he could have seen one), and drove to the homestead half a mile away. The track leading to the front of the house appeared virtually unused. He pulled up near the back door.

When he knocked a woman opened the door. She was middle size, going grey, and wore a worried expression. He introduced himself.

She said, 'Gramps is in the kitchen. He's expecting you, come in.' She led the way across a closed-in veranda littered with cardboard boxes, collapsing gumboots, and unidentifiable pieces of metal from larger machines. 'He's not too clever, one of his asthma attacks coming on I think.'

'This won't take long,' Hugh said. 'I'll keep it short.'

A thin, white-headed man in his sixties, Colly Gordon was seated in a kitchen chair close to the wood stove. He didn't get up. His daughter-in-law introduced them and then went out through the door into the rest of the house.

Hugh said, 'A couple of questions about Saturday night, that's all.'

'Like to help if I can,' Colly said. His breath squeaked and rasped in his chest.

Hugh pulled over a second chair and sat down. 'You were an old friend of Silas Beadnall's?'

'Known him a long time, if that's what you mean.'

'You weren't friendly, then?'

'Were once.' Colly paused for several difficult breaths. 'Fell out, expect they've told you.'

'They?'

'That bloody gossip at the pub.' He paused again. 'That Em woman. Or Horry.'

'I have heard something,' Hugh admitted.

'Not sure why I was invited.'

'Miss Jocelyn Beadnall believes her brother wanted to score off his guests.'

Colly grinned, a death's-head grimace. 'Good old Joss.' A breath. 'Reckon she got it in one.' Two breaths. 'Shouldn't have gone.' A breath, three. Hugh waited. 'Only wanted to see the girls.' A breath. 'Joss and Ada.'

'Did you drive yourself in to the party?'

Colly nodded. 'Son's car.'

'When did you leave?'

'When the girls left.'

'Did you drive straight home?'

'Got me there.' Colly grimaced again, wheezing. 'Drank champagne.' He heaved in several hard breaths. 'Got me bloody money's worth.' He wheezed and breathed. Obviously his attack was getting worse. 'Off bloody Silas.'

'You didn't come straight home, is that what you're trying to say?'

'Trying, nothing,' Colly said angrily. A couple of breaths later he said, 'Am saying. Fell asleep.' The grey pullover covering his bony chest rose on every wheezy breath.

Hugh wasn't certain whether all the old boy's attacks ran this course, or whether agitation at answering police questions was making him worse. Still, they were pretty innocuous questions unless Colly had something to hide, and so far he appeared to be answering openly without fear.

Colly said, 'Got home around —' he flapped a hand, wheezing '— three.'

It appeared increasingly uncertain to Hugh whether Colly could draw in enough air with his next breath to sustain life; certainly he now had none to spare for more questions. Hugh got up, went to the door into the passage, and called, 'Mrs Gordon!' She hurried towards him. 'I think Mr Gordon is getting worse. I won't stay. He's told me what I wanted to know anyway.' Well, he hadn't actually wanted to know that yet another of the dinner guests had no alibi to cover the time of the murder; he'd hoped he'd be able to eliminate Colly from the investigations. He might have known he wouldn't be so lucky.

Mrs Gordon went directly to her father-in-law; she lifted one of his hands.

'Medicine,' Colly gasped.

Hugh left.

Five hundred yards the other side of the railway crossing he felt the signs and realised one of his rear tyres was flat. Almost immediately afterwards he remembered he never had topped up the air in the spare tyre as he'd intended doing before he left Adelaide on this trip. Swearing, he got out of the car, leaned over the back door, and groped beneath the back seat for the hand pump as well as for the jack.

Muttering profanities he pumped up the spare, changed the wheel and examined the flat tyre. He found the shining head of a fine nail, driven in as neatly as if someone had done it with a hammer.

49

When he got back Hugh remembered he hadn't yet heard what Em Musgrave had to say about events on the night of the murder. By that time she was busy in the kitchen getting dinners and she brushed him off comprehensively. It would take more than a mere detective-constable ten years her junior to overawe Em when she was in *that* mood.

Hugh went to his room and consoled himself by writing a short letter to his wife and an even shorter one to his two children. He spent a few minutes more speculating on the sex of his third child, due to arrive in this world shortly after the new year; although, seeing that he already had one of each, he really had no preference for which sort of baby his new wife brought forth. She had professed herself equally indifferent and he wondered if she meant it. This after all would be her first child.

He looked for Em after the evening meal and couldn't find her. He finally tracked her down the next morning.

Em said, 'What is it you want to know, Mr Morgan?' She was in the middle of pegging out washing on the line in the paddock beside the pub and was still not pleased to be interrupted.

The line of sheets billowed and cracked in a stiff breeze. Fast cloud shadows slid over the town, momentarily dimming the light before they fled away to the north. They could hear the intermittent thud of a horse's hooves from over by the police station, where Bowler was exercising Imshy over jumps, and short bursts of huffing from the engine of a goods train as it shunted trucks in the railway yards.

Although convinced she'd been avoiding him Hugh chose to be conciliating; he said, 'Sorry to be a nuisance, but you're always so busy I can never find you at a convenient time. I haven't asked you what you know about people's movements on Saturday evening.'

Em rammed down a peg. 'Not much. Johnson and I were flat out in the kitchen with the food for most of the time, and when we finished cleaning up I just fell into bed.' Em glanced towards the other end of the line where Johnson, from a separate basket, was pegging up white towels banded with red lettering down the middle.

'Did you hear any of the row Silas Beadnall had with his son Horry?'

'No, that was Trotter. He was doing his rounds before he turned in and he heard them. Couldn't help hearing them, they were yelling at each other.' She bent for the next sheet, threw the end over the line.

A small dog yapping hysterically shot towards them from the back door of the pub. A short woman followed, remonstrating. 'Dandy! Come back! Bad boy, Dandy, come back!' The Skye terrier took no notice and continued to yap and snap, dancing round Hugh's ankles. Its hairy grey coat flopped up and down like a skirt.

'No, don't.' Em smiled, seeing him take his weight off one foot.

'No,' he agreed. 'Better not. Though I'd like to lift the little mutt into the middle of next week.'

'They'd never stay at this pub again and we need their custom.'

The woman hurried over, out of breath. She was dark and plump, holding a wide straw hat to her head and wearing a shapeless grey dustcoat over her coat and skirt. She scooped up the dog with her free hand, let go her hat, and tapped its nose gently with a forefinger. 'Is Dandy-Pandy a bad doggie then? Naughty Dandy.'

Em said, 'Good morning, Mrs Crocker. Are you leaving now?'

'My husband is just putting the cases in the car. I'm giving this naughty little doggie a teensy weensy run before we go.' She tucked the dog under one arm and turned to go, turned back. 'We've been very comfortable, thank you, Mrs Musgrave. A pleasant stay.'

'Thank you,' Em said. 'That's good to know.'

The woman walked away past the old stone stable towards the side street. Hugh said, 'Look, Mrs Musgrave, I won't take up much more of your time. Did you see anyone besides Silas Beadnall and his dinner guests in the hotel that evening? Any strangers?'

Em frowned, bringing her thoughts back. 'No. Apart from the Beadnall contingent we only had one of our regular travellers, Mr Tillerman, staying overnight, and Clive Wishart for half the night. We gave Mr Tillerman his dinner early, and then he went up to the hall, to the dance, so he was out all the evening. Clive arrived about nine o'clock, and I showed him to his room because Trotter was looking after Silas's dinner party. Oh, and earlier I ran into Diggory Kenrick looking for his aunt, Miss Beadnall, so I showed him which was her room. She can't have been in it, though, because Trotter says he finally caught up with her in the lounge, before they all went to dinner.'

'Kenrick apparently made himself at home in the lounge later, after the others had gone, settled down to sleep. Does he often do that, without asking?'

'Often? Well, now and then. Trotter doesn't mind. They're mates, play — they play cards together. Sometimes.'

'Bridge I suppose,' Hugh said, expressionless.

'That's right.'

'And do you mind Kenrick coming in uninvited? You are joint licensee with your husband, I notice. I saw it on your sign.'

Em looked at him as though he was mad. 'Mind? Why the hell should I mind? He doesn't get in my way.'

Johnson, with her empty basket under her arm, walked past on her way to the pub back door.

'I need a word with her,' Hugh said, and turned to follow.

Em caught his arm. 'She's only a kid, she knows nothing about it. Leave her alone.' Although she was annoyed with the girl Em still felt protective towards her. The little fool had so wilfully disregarded her words of warning the previous afternoon that she had apparently gone straight out and spent all her time off with young Kenrick; he'd driven her home — and late at that — at the end of the afternoon. Em wished now she hadn't meddled.

Hugh shook off her hand. 'I'm not going to give her the third degree, dammit. But you know I can't leave anyone alone. She's over twenty-one, Bowler says. She might have seen or heard something important.'

50

Bowler had shut the other two horses, his wife's and his son's, in the second paddock and was exercising Imshy over the varied jumps he had constructed in the police paddock beside his house. They had made several circuits; a couple more to clear and they would stop. The horse was going well, and he felt both satisfied and elated. Such exercise was exhilarating on a fine morning.

They were poised to take off at the triple-rail obstacle on the far side of the paddock when a yellow straw hat came cartwheeling towards them, closely followed by bundle of greyish fur, shrieking shrilly.

The horse was already committed to the jump. In mid take-off it shied violently away from this horror, was wrong-footed yet couldn't stop, carried by its momentum halfway up the rails and too close to clear them cleanly. It caught its leg and somersaulted over in a tangle of legs and wooden rails. Bowler rolled clear.

The dog was still yapping. Sore and shaken Bowler lurched to his feet. He didn't seem to have suffered any major damage. He grabbed for the reins, still on Imshy's neck, as the horse heaved its haunches under it in efforts to stand.

It staggered, nearly fell again, and then managed to get to its feet. To three feet. The right foreleg hung useless.

Bowler put his hand on the horse's shoulder, bent to run his other hand down the leg and froze.

No. This wasn't true.

He could see blood, and splintered bone protruding through the fine black coat.

He felt a heavyweight's punch in his guts. He was sick and breathless with shock. Sick with disbelief. This wasn't happening.

The dog was barking even more frantically. A woman was hurrying across the paddock towards them. 'Oh, dear,' she puffed. 'Dandy has been a naughty boy. Come to mother, naughty doggie. Is the poor geegee hurt? Naughty Dandy.'

Bowler opened his mouth. At his second attempt he got his voice working. 'Madam,' he croaked. He tried again. 'Madam. Take that dog away. I am going for my rifle. If that dog is still here when I get back I'll shoot it too.'

He mustn't give himself time to think. He didn't want to consider anything. He didn't want to think. He threw the reins over the post at the side of the jump and he ran.

He walked back, fitting a round into the breech of his 303. He wouldn't trust his handgun with its smaller charge.

The horse hadn't moved. He laid the rifle carefully on the ground while he unbuckled the girths and took off the saddle. Then he removed the bridle, rubbing round the bases of Imshy's ears as he always did, saying, 'There you are, that's better.' Wanting the right words to say and finding none, so what, what was the point of words to an animal? The horse stood shivering, ears flicking at his voice. Bowler picked up the rifle.

With his hand wrapped round the breech and the barrel pointing to earth he laid his forehead to the warm, silk-covered bone of Imshy's forehead. In the distance some female was screaming.

He stepped back, cocked the rifle, and raised the barrel. Imshy's head came up and ears swung forward as the horse watched him.

Bowler closed his eyes and the barrel slanted down.

He rolled his lips between his teeth to stop the tremors. He dragged his eyes open, sighted blurrily along the steel, pulled the trigger. The horse collapsed untidily into a heap, a bright, shining bay heap.

Bowler's hands were shaking so much he couldn't work the bolt to eject the spent shell. He sank to the ground. That was where Joan found him.

She had been watching him through the kitchen window, filled with love and admiration for her man and his horse and the picture they made as they raced effortlessly over the different kinds of jumps.

Then she had seen them fall, and had watched in dread until he was on his feet again, controlling her impulse to dash to his side. She had been trained to keep out of male accidents in case she embarrassed anyone by unstiffening an upper lip.

She'd known exactly what was wrong when she saw Bill sprint towards the house, heard him dash in the front door, saw him run out with his rifle.

This was disaster. Joan ran. She dropped to her knees beside her husband and cradled his head against her breast.

51

Hugh had caught up with Johnson in the washhouse at the back of the pub. She was using a piece of broken broom handle to lift clumps of steaming fabric from a boiling copper. She dumped them, streaming scalding water, on a tin scrubbing board which slanted over the gap between concrete laundry troughs and the copper. Water drained back. Steam wreathed round her head.

She looked across at Hugh in the doorway though didn't stop what she was doing. She had no way of hiding her face here.

He said, 'Miss Johnson, I've noticed you've been avoiding me. I think I must have seen you somewhere before.'

She slapped another loaded stickful of washing on top of the last. 'I knew you'd recognised me.' As bravely as she could she added, 'I don't have to explain.'

'You do, though,' he said, keeping his tone light, trying not to sound like a bully. 'Seeing that I'm investigating a murder. I have to know why you have been involved with the law before. Where did I see you? A police station somewhere? In court?'

'You think I'm a criminal! Really, I —'

Somewhere a woman was screaming, high-pitched, terrified.

Hugh turned his head. 'What's going on?'

They heard a loud report.

Old soldier Hugh exclaimed, 'That's a rifle!' and ran out.

Through the wide back gates of the pub yard he could see a woman standing rooted in the middle of the side street, a dog under her arm. She had stopped screaming, and as he passed her he saw her eyes stretched wide with fear. She turned and hurried into the pub back yard.

Then he saw Bowler and Joan kneeling together beside the body of the horse, and he started towards them. Over her husband's head Joan saw him, and waved him away with a vigorous, almost angry, gesture of her arm.

52

In the stockyards at the railway station the brown mare rocketed sideways away from the saddle, felt the check of the bridle tying her to the post and reared violently. The leather reins snapped. With her head free she staggered back towards the other side of the yard and stood quivering, head up, watching the man with a saddle over his arm. Sweat darkened her muzzle and brown flanks. The broken reins dangled in the dirt.

The mare had recently been released from hours confined in a small box while all kinds of alarming loud noises assailed her nerves, while periodic jolts and jerks had her hoofs scrabbling for balance, while the landscape tore extraordinarily past. She was thoroughly rattled, and in no mood to be nice about it and overlook such indignities.

Diggory dumped the saddle on the top rail and walked slowly towards her, his hand out. He should have brought some oats, something with which to bribe the animal. She hadn't been so intransigent the day he had tried her paces at his friend's farm — the day he had bought her.

At the last minute the mare jumped away, keeping the trailing reins out of reach, then found herself more or less cornered. She charged past Diggory, knocking him off his feet with her shoulder.

Swearing, spitting out earth, he scrambled up and found another player had entered the arena. Bowler Brown had materialised like a ghost and caught the reins.

He looked grim as any ghost, yet his voice was conversational and soothing as he addressed the mare. Legs braced, he had a strong grip on the reins, yet was making no move to approach her as she pulled back on the other end of them.

Still in the same even tone Bowler said, 'You all right, Kenrick? A bit toey, isn't she. Understandable. Come on, old girl, nobody's going to hurt you. We're on your side.'

After a few more minutes of this sort of nonsense, delivered in Bowler's calm and somehow authoritative voice, the mare gradually lowered her head and let Bowler walk up to her. He stroked her sweating neck, still talking, and rubbed round her ears and under her jaw. Tired and unhappy, she relaxed and stood docile under his gentle hands.

Killer's hands, Bowler thought. Hands that knew a Lee-Enfield so well that it had become an extension of themselves. In the desert, here — how many horses had those hands killed? How many men? Would he ever get away from the killing?

Diggory said, 'Thanks, Bowler. I don't know what I did to scare her.'

'She's a bit tucked up. Better get her a drink.'

'The trough here's rusted out. I'll take her to the pub when she calms down.'

'Good-looking youngster — where did you find her?'

'A mate of mine at Gumeracha breeds horses. Let's see if she'll let me saddle up now.'

The mare had made her point and submitted quietly to the saddle. Bowler asked, 'What's her name?'

Diggory swung into the saddle. He leaned to scratch between her ears. 'Turtle. As in dove, I think it's supposed to be. Thanks for your help.'

'You'll be all right now?'

'Yeah. She's not vicious, you know.'

Bowler nodded. He walked over and slid the bolts on the tall gate; he held it open until horse and rider had passed through; he shut and bolted it again. Then he turned and strode away, round the horsebox standing on the spur line, across the little hump of stony ballast carrying the sleepers and rails of the main line, towards the mallees beyond.

Surprised, Diggory wondered what business took him over there, and on foot. He was riding away when he heard, muted by distance, a terrible roar of rage and anguish.

The mare swung an ear back, listening.

53

That afternoon Gerard Talbot, the rector from Edgerton, drove forty miles to Kularook. In front of Saint Chad's, a small stone church in a back street, he parked his mud-splashed Austin sedan and picked his way along a path through wet and rampant weeds to the steps at the western door. At the top, in the act of unlocking the door, he paused, shaking his head sadly at signs of decay in the large rectory beside the church. He'd lived there very comfortably once; now the house belonged to Aubrey Venables, who was letting the maintenance slide.

Inside he flicked a duster here and there and opened a couple of windows a crack to let the raw cold air dispel the musty smell before he unlocked the vestry and put on his surplice. He heard the toot of a train leaving the station. The Beadnall family would be there shortly. He walked the length of the church, tucked his hands in his sleeves, and waited beside the door.

The figure that slipped in, furtive as a thief, didn't see him in the shadows as it crept into a pew, fell to its knees, and buried its face in its hands.

Gerard didn't disturb it. Anyone had a right to the comfort of prayer in his church. All the same, he wondered why Fran Beadnall wanted to pray so intently before the service for her late father-in-law had even begun. Previously she had exhibited a casual, take-it-or-leave-it attitude towards her religion; an attitude that, regrettably, the majority of his parishioners shared.

Meanwhile Horry and Brenda collected Lilian from the railway station and, to Brenda's fury, were obliged to collect Margot Jennings also. As Horry pointed out, they could hardly leave the woman standing while they drove off.

Brenda hadn't realised the brazen hussy would come back for the funeral; she had thought they'd got rid of her for good. And yet here she was pretending she cared enough for that dreadful man Silas to want to attend his last rites. What a hypocrite, thought Brenda, feeling self-righteous, as though the rest of them had come because of affection for the dead man and not solely because of concern for convention, for the look of the thing.

'We'll go straight to the church,' Horry told Lilian. 'I've fixed it with Talbot and the undertaker that we would start as soon as you arrived. Leon and Fran should be there by now.'

He braked to let a dray piled high with brown jute wool bales cross the track into the railway yards. Perched on the front Vince, the second of the three Pedler sons, bunched the reins from his six-horse team into one hand and lifted the other in acknowledgement of this courtesy.

Only five mourners other than the family entered the church. Aleck Fielding, Billy Miller, Archie Davidson, and Bob Norman arrived together, four old diggers who were there not to show respect for Silas, whom they had to a man disliked and avoided in life, but to show solidarity with their digger mate Horry. Aubrey Venables came with Leon and Fran. The minister kept the service short.

Then the men went with the coffin to the cemetery in the scrub two miles out of town while the women drove to the pub, where they had arranged for afternoon tea.

Brenda would have liked to omit this ceremony — more expense for no benefit, in her opinion — but Horry had insisted they observe the proper forms. Stripping off their gloves, the four women trooped into the pub lounge where Ada and Joss, who had declined to attend the service, were already waiting.

Joss professed to despise formulaic religious observances. Ada didn't care one way or another, and so chose to keep her sister company.

In the lounge Em had lit a fire in the basket grate, more to give a cheerful atmosphere on this overcast afternoon than for warmth. Cakes and sandwiches, covered with clean tea towels, lay waiting on a couple of tables. Fran sneaked her hand in under a corner and helped herself to a curried egg sandwich.

Brenda said, 'I think we should wait for the men before we start.'

'Oh so do I,' Fran said with her mouth full. One sandwich wasn't a start. Only she would bet that Brenda would make an issue of it; if not of that, of something else. To her eye Brenda was obviously spoiling for a fight.

Margot, again wearing her good grey suit, again better dressed than any of them, walked to the fireplace and spread her hands above the fire. Her diamond ring winked red and blue in the firelight.

And that was provocation, Fran thought. Little Miss Muffet was flaunting her colours. She must have a hide like a rhinoceros if she didn't know how much Silas's family resented her.

In this, she misjudged Margot Jennings, who knew exactly how the family felt about her, and who would gladly have forgone the expense of the train ticket and a night at the pub now that she had no prospect of future advantages from her connection with Silas. The trip in fact represented a considerable sacrifice to her, seeing that she had given up her job at his insistence and would need to watch her pennies carefully before she found work again.

Margot couldn't miss Silas's funeral. There had to be at least one person at his funeral who had been fond of him. One person who hadn't hated him.

54

Brenda had come armed this afternoon, determined to stop Lilian making her intolerable insinuations. She saw her sister-in-law standing in front of the mirror over the fireplace while she re-pinned her hat — pulled out two long hatpins, adjusted the black straw, pushed them through again — and thought now was her chance. Stepping to Lilian's elbow Brenda hissed, 'If you repeat that lying slander about Horry, that you think he's been keeping the farm's profits to himself, I will tell everybody the truth about that man Connery.'

Without haste, brows raised in some hauteur, Lilian turned to face her. 'Good heavens! That ancient history. What is there to tell?'

'I'll tell them —'

'That when I was too young to know better I fell for a man who was both a liar and a cheat? Who could possibly care now?'

'A bit more to the affair than that, I've heard,' Brenda said, her voice loaded with innuendo.

'And if there was? I'm not saying there was, Brenda, I would not gratify your salacious imagination so much — even so, I am merely wondering who the deuce it could matter to after all these years.'

'It might make some of your la-di-da friends look a bit sideways at you.'

'Nonsense. How small-minded you are. My la-di-da friends, as you call them, probably know a great deal more about what happened than you do. They were my friends at the time, and they are my friends still. Tell whomsoever in the world you please, you won't do me any harm.' With a disdainful look down her nose at the shorter woman Lilian walked away and seated herself, back rigidly upright, on a hard chair at one of the small tables.

All the same, Brenda thought with satisfaction, Lilian was angry. She might pretend she didn't care what anyone could say of her yet she did care. That would teach her to make slanderous accusations against Horry. She wouldn't do it again in a hurry.

Then Brenda saw Hugh Morgan in the doorway and bustled over. Better to take the initiative, she believed, than wait for the police to start issuing directives. Besides, she was the senior woman here and she didn't want any of the others fancying themselves as hostess. 'Good afternoon, Mr Morgan. Are you looking for someone?'

'Afternoon. I'd like to speak to Miss Beadnall or Miss Jennings if they're here.' Hugh had hoped to have Bowler with him, to remind him of what had transpired at the earlier interviews, but he couldn't expect much help there for a while. He knew how these Light Horsemen felt about their horses.

'Oh yes, indeed they are. This way.' Brenda went ahead of him. Margot had joined Lilian at the table by the wall though they hadn't apparently been finding much to say to each other. Brenda introduced the detective. 'I expect he wants to grill you both,' she said brightly. 'If that's the word.'

'No,' Hugh said. 'That's not the word. Miss Beadnall, could I see you for a minute? Not here, in the dining-room. I won't keep you long.'

'Certainly.' Lilian rose, her composure as rigid as her whale-boned corset in spite of the angry flush on her cheeks.

As he turned to usher her from the room Hugh heard Brenda say under her breath, 'And don't believe everything *she* tells you.'

Although the words were said softly, as though not meant to be overheard, he believed he had been meant to hear; although, seeing that the two women radiated such blatant hostility towards each other, it could perhaps have been a gibe to unsettle Lilian Beadnall.

However the words were meant, Miss Beadnall proved an exemplary witness. She answered his questions readily and concisely and, as far as he could judge, told him no lies. She described the dinner party, explained why she had left the pub early the following morning, and stated that she hadn't heard of her father's death until she returned around half past ten. Yes, she had heard the angry exchanges between her father and her brother at bedtime the evening before, though hadn't paid much attention — her father was always having rows with someone and she knew what this one was about. She had been at one with her brothers in their attempts to get Silas to sign an agreement on the farm's income.

Much later she heard voices from his room; she hadn't recognised the second voice, a man's voice.

'Have you any idea where a length of electrical flex could have come from?' Hugh would have liked to show it to some of the suspects, but its gruesome associations ruled that out. 'One with a round plug for a power point on one end, and a flat rectangular socket on the other.'

Lilian said dismissively, 'A cord like that could come from anywhere — that sort fits any electric jug or toaster. Every kitchen has one or two.'

'Not in Kularook,' Hugh said. 'There's no power supply here, so no electric jugs or toasters.'

'Oh yes, of course. I'd forgotten for the moment.' She considered briefly, her eyes cast down. 'No. In that case, no, I can't think where it came from.'

When pressed she refused to speculate on the identity of the murderer, and would not enter into any discussion about the members of her family. Apart from the judgement that Miss Margot Jennings was a reasonably intelligent girl though probably no better than she should be, the detective got no opinions from Miss Beadnall.

She reminded him of his great-aunt, his grandmother's starchy sister, although she couldn't have been much past forty, not more than half a dozen years older than he was. Wearing an expression of fastidious distaste she allowed him to take her fingerprints before he escorted her back to the others.

55

Without being asked Miss Margot Jennings jumped up to accompany the detective to the dining-room as though eager to give him her version of events. Her practised, slightly coquettish smile made Hugh wary. Recently married, still full of wonder and delight at his young wife, he felt slightly repelled by this assault, however mild, on his sexual responses. Still, if she wanted to flirt he supposed that professionally he should exploit such behaviour to the limit.

The dining-room smelled of stewed mutton from midday dinner and had been rearranged since the dinner party. The long table now stood across the back of the room and three smaller ones had been added closer to the door into the passage. Hugh pulled out chairs at one of the latter, seated himself opposite his witness, and tossed his notebook to the table.

He said, 'Miss Jennings, who do you believe murdered Silas Beadnall?'

'It could have been any one of them!' she declared in throbbing tones. 'They all hated him. Hated him! And he their father!'

'That's not much help,' Hugh said flatly, to keep a lid on the drama. 'Don't you suspect one more than the others?'

'There's not a penny to choose between them. Horry wants the farm and was trying to take it away from Silas. Brenda wants more money. The other two were in it too, after what they could get out of him.' Margot paused. 'Probably Lilian did it — Silas was threatening to disinherit her she made him that angry. Because of Diggory, you know.'

He didn't know; so he made her tell him about the confrontation between Silas and his grandson before dinner, Lilian's subsequent intransigence, Silas's threats. Hugh realised he would have to talk to Lilian again, and ask a few more personal questions.

'Did you have a drink with Silas in his room at any time?' When she started to shake her head he added, 'There were two glasses on the washstand.'

Margot became flustered. 'I'm sorry, I'm sorry, I was forgetting, I've already told Mr Brown about them. That was in the afternoon, Mr Morgan, before we went to the lounge, before dinner.'

He wondered why she was overreacting, as though he might suspect her. If she was a reasonably intelligent girl, as Lilian Beadnall believed, then she must know he didn't.

Back in the lounge Fran plonked herself down beside Lilian and said, 'Did he give you the third degree? I hope you were discreet.'

'Don't be absurd. What information could I give him that could possibly harm any of us?'

'I think Brenda is afraid he is looking at Horry.'

'Naturally enough. That doesn't mean he believes Horry is the criminal.' Lilian shrugged. 'I wish I knew.'

'Do you think we ever will? I'm hoping this detective never finds out who killed Silas. If you look at it in a practical light, he's a public benefactor, whoever he is. It seems a pity to punish such a praiseworthy act.'

Lilian permitted herself a smile. 'What nonsense you talk, my dear Fran.'

'Not me. By the way, I saw your photo on the society pages in the *Adelaide Times* a couple of months ago, at some charity do at the theatre. However did you get a ticket for that?' She sounded slightly envious. 'You are consorting with the nobs these days.'

'That was Diggory's doing. He had the tickets through some connection with his old newspaper, so he took me; a most enjoyable evening. The picture was only because he knew the photographer — they'd been in China together.'

'China? What was Diggory Kenrick doing in China?'

'I didn't think you knew about that,' Lilian said with satisfaction. 'Your despised nephew was a highly regarded war correspondent for two years.' She watched while Fran digested that.

'No, we didn't know.' Fran arched her brows. 'And none of us knew you'd been keeping in touch with him, either.'

Irritated, Lilian said, 'I have not been "keeping in touch" with him. He is my nephew. I am very fond of him, as I was of his mother, and I hope he is of me.'

'What if Diggory was the one who murdered Silas?'

'Don't be ridiculous.'

'The night of the murder he spent sleeping in one of those chairs.' Fran pointed. 'And then lied to Bowler Brown about it.' She smiled innocently at her sister-in-law. 'I didn't think you knew about that.' She smiled sweetly and crossed the room to speak to Brenda.

'Rather a self-centred woman,' Ada commented, coming up behind Lilian.

56

Just inside the door to the passage Aubrey Venables, standing beside his friend Leon Beadnall, said, 'I expect you're glad that's over.'

Leon grunted. 'Won't be glad anything is over until this damn detective goes back to wherever he came from. Nosy beggar, wants to know details about private matters that are none of his business.' Across the room Johnson set a large teapot on a table beside the stacked cups and started lifting the tea towels from the food.

Aubrey said, 'Who is that girl?'

'Em's latest housemaid. She's not local.'

'I didn't think I'd seen her before.'

Leon wasn't listening. 'Franny says we have nothing to worry about.' He lowered his voice. 'Aubrey, what if it was Horry? What's going to happen to us then?'

'Do you really suspect your brother did it?' Aubrey thought, none of them were saying anything as crude as 'killed Silas'. And was Leon pretending to pass on these worries only to make sure nobody suspected him? Though it might be to protect Fran; she was much more capable of straightforward action than he was.

Like the night before. She'd really surprised him the night before, when she and Leon had come in after the dinner party. They had put Leon, staggering drunk after unaccustomed amounts of alcohol, straight to bed, and then Fran had stayed up to have a nightcap with him. One thing had, surprisingly, led to another.

He'd been very careful not to catch her eye this afternoon, even though he thought she was trying to catch his. For goodness sake, Leon was his friend, he wasn't going to get involved there, pleasant though the unexpected episode had been. Surely she didn't think . . .

He wiped his thoughts clear of Fran and listened to Fran's husband.

'For God's sake, Aubrey, don't say I said so, it's just hard to think of anyone else it could be.' Leon shook his head as though bothered by an insect. 'He's got a rotten temper, just like Silas.' He started, as Johnson appeared at his elbow with a plate of sandwiches in either hand.

Smiling, she held them out. 'If you want tea, it's help yourself from the table over there. Or Mr Musgrave is getting a couple of jugs of beer, if you'd like to wait.'

'Thank you, my dear.' Aubrey took two sandwiches and smiled on this fresh youthful face. An attractive girl. Not exactly a beauty yet pretty enough in spite of her heavy horn-rimmed glasses, clear-eyed and friendly, with a good figure. 'Could you be a kind girl and get me a cup of tea? Not much milk, and no sugar. Thank you.'

Obviously surprised at this request when she had just told him to help himself, she recovered swiftly. 'Of course.' She corrected herself. 'Of course, sir.'

'Black and two sugars,' Leon said.

Aubrey watched her walk away. She was an attractive little thing, quite an air about her, not at all like the usual housemaid. Well spoken, too. He saw so few new faces in a small community like Kularook. Perhaps he would talk to her later.

Perhaps . . .

All sorts of possibilities opened before him, setting his spirits dancing. When she returned with his tea he contrived to squeeze her fingers as he took the cup. She didn't appear to notice, and turned away to carry plates of food to Lilian, seated at one of the small tables.

Horry needed a beer. He poured Gerard Talbot, another old digger, a glass from the jug he carried before he filled one for himself. He gulped half, wiped his mouth with his wrist. He said, 'Thanks, Gerard. The service was just what we wanted. Brief and dignified.'

'I wouldn't perjure my immortal soul by inventing eulogies about your father,' Gerard said. 'Yet he was a man, he was hustled out of this life prematurely, and he was part of my flock once. We don't have to judge him, Horry. I think he needed our prayers, but it's out of our hands now.' He wondered whether he should tell Horry about Fran's appearance in the church before the service and decided against it. After all, her actions were nothing to do with him.

Horry said, 'This damn detective is still hanging around, I see. I wish he'd find the culprit and go back where he belongs.'

'You don't think the criminal was one of your family, then.' Gerard made it a statement, not a question.

'Of course not. Ridiculous idea. It must have been somebody who sneaked in at the side door. A swaggie, looking to pick up a few bob from someone's pocket, and Silas woke up at the wrong moment.'

'I hope you're right. I must go and have a word with Miss Jennings.'

'I wouldn't bother. All she's grieving for is the loss of a meal ticket.'

'You're pretty hard on her, Horry.'

'It's no good being mealy mouthed about it, she's a gold-digger, and would have chiselled every penny out of Father she could get. She'll find somebody else soon enough. And although of course I regret Father's death sincerely I have to admit it happened in the nick of time. Otherwise the whole family would have been on the streets.'

Gerard Talbot looked grave. 'I must respect honesty, Horry,

though I think you should remember to whom you are speaking. I would be dishonest in my profession if I didn't advise you to examine your heart and your conscience.'

Startled, Horry said, 'You're not accusing me —? No, of course not. And for your information my conscience is in fine shape.'

57

Aubrey Venables moved towards the tea tables. He wanted to intercept the housemaid, who was tidying up the plates of sandwiches and cake, collecting scattered remnants on to one or two plates and stacking the empty ones. He handed her his cup and asked with suitable diffidence if she could possibly give him a refill.

'So kind. Thank you, my dear. May I be permitted to know your name? I am Venables, Aubrey Venables.'

She kept her head turned, pouring tea. 'Johnson, sir.'

'And your first name?'

'Just Johnson.'

She spoke with such finality he let it go for the moment. He asked, 'And how do you like working here at the hotel?'

'It's all right.'

'You're a taking little thing, my dear. Really, I think you're too good for this kind of work.'

'Too good —?'

'How would you like to come and keep house for me, instead? Don't you think you'd like that? I think we'd get along very well together.'

'Keep house for you? Why ever would I?' She handed him his teacup.

'I'd be good to you, dear.'

'Good to me? What do you mean? Mrs Musgrave treats me well enough. I don't want another job.'

'With me you wouldn't have to work all day, a smaller house, only me to look after, you understand. It would be a little bit different — I mean, with me you'd be more like my friend, my little friend, if you understand me.' His confidence grew. 'I can say without boasting I'm a generous man, my dear, I'd give you more than you could possibly earn in a place like this. You have quite taken my fancy with your pretty ways.' He set down his cup and smiled fondly, gazing into her eyes with a quizzical expression while he reached for her free hand and held it closely within both of his. 'I do so want you to be my little companion. I am very taken with you.'

She wrenched her hand free, her face clearly showing her astonished distaste as she understood the implications of his offer. 'Are you propositioning me?' She didn't bother to lower her voice. 'The answer is no.'

She turned away and saw Margot, in the doorway after her interview with the detective, watching with an expression of complete understanding. Scowling, Johnson gritted her teeth and pushed past her on her way to the kitchen. She nearly ran into Leon and Fran, standing heads together in the passage.

Fran looked after her. 'Do you think that girl has a guilty secret? She jumps every time anyone speaks to her unexpectedly.'

Leon ran a finger around inside his starched funeral-going collar. 'I don't suppose she could be one of Silas's cast-offs?'

'Never in a million years. Silas liked them meaty and preferably blond. Perhaps she's some barmaid's little mistake who thought she could palm herself off on the old pest. Whatever she's up to, he can't tell us now, and I am certainly not going to ask her.'

Muir Kenrick appeared in the lounge doorway. His lofty gaze travelled over assorted Beadnalls without connecting with any.

Horry glanced up and muttered, 'What's bloody Muir want? He wouldn't have the nerve to come because of Silas, surely.'

Gerard Talbot set his empty teacup on the table. 'No. He's looking for me.' He took his watch from his pocket and clicked it open. 'Is that the time? I had no idea. I'm supposed to be christening Stella Kenrick's baby — Stella White she is now. Very sad about her husband.'

'Yes.' Although Horry wasn't much in sympathy with any of the Kenricks he supposed a girl widowed as young as Muir's daughter deserved some compassion. 'Thanks again, Gerard, for the service.'

The departure of the minister saw the rest of the tea party beginning to break up. The four old diggers took their leave of Horry; Aubrey went down the passage to the kitchen to try for another word with the housemaid; Fran and Brenda went the other way, towards the loos.

Margot followed Lilian, and carried her empty cup across to the table to add it to the stack of dirty crockery. She asked, 'Who was that man? The one who came for the Reverend?'

This grated on Lilian's ear though she answered civilly enough, 'He is Muir Kenrick. Diggory's uncle. Do you know him?'

'Not to speak to, no. Silas ran into his car.'

'Silas is — was a shocking driver, a minor failing when you consider his numerous more serious sins.' Lilian added, 'Have you decided to stop wearing your ring, Miss Jennings?'

'No.' Margot looked down. 'Oh. No, I took it off just now to wash my hands. I must have left it on the washstand.' She hurried from the room.

Brenda had returned and was gathering up the empty glasses. 'I suppose we could find a bed for you tonight if you want one, Lilian, although it's a long way out, you know, and we've already driven in once today. Horry would have to bring you all the way back tomorrow for the train.'

Lilian smiled. 'How welcoming you sound. Horry wouldn't mind, you know.'

'What wouldn't I mind?' Horry had come up behind them.

'Taking me home for the night.'

'Of course I wouldn't. You're not planning to stay in the pub again, are you? Of course you're coming home with us.'

'I don't think Brenda feels there is any of course about it.'

Horry gave his wife a puzzled, slightly suspicious look. 'No, that's nonsense. You want Lilian to stay, don't you, Bren?'

'Oh, naturally, naturally, she must come, there's nothing more to be said.' Brenda turned away as though to hide her anger.

Lilian said, 'All the same, Horry — Miss Jennings! Whatever is the matter?'

Margot, wide-eyed, almost staggering in her haste, had run in at the door. 'It's gone!' she cried. 'Gone! My ring! I can't find it.'

'Where have you looked?' Brenda asked, in a tone that suggested Margot must be jumping to premature conclusions. 'It must have fallen down.'

'Don't be a fool, I've looked everywhere — what do you think?' Margot said scornfully. 'It's gone, I tell you. Someone must have taken it!'

'Where did you leave it?' Horry put his hand on his wife's arm to prevent her exploding at this affront. 'We'd better find out who's been down that way.'

'I put it on the shelf above the washbasin, in the bathroom.'

'It wasn't there when I washed my hands,' Brenda said. 'Fran?'

'No,' Fran said. 'I didn't see it.'

As though reminded of them, Brenda twisted her own rings on her finger. 'I did see that housemaid Johnson in the passage a few minutes ago.' She closed her eyes and brushed her hand across her lips.

Lilian, who had left the room when the alarm was first raised, now returned with Hugh Morgan. He looked a long way from pleased at being asked to look for a ring. 'One at a time. Miss Jennings, you first.'

Margot explained where she had left the ring, where she had searched. Brenda and Fran each denied seeing it.

'Show me,' Hugh said.

58

Already frustrated enough in his investigations, Hugh was annoyed at having to divert his attention from his murder investigation to a piddling lost ring.

Though if what Miss Jennings told him was true the ring wasn't so piddling, and worth a good bit. Worth pinching? Who would know how to turn a ring into cash? He supposed most people would expect to make only what a pawnbroker would offer them. No ordinary person, moved by impulse to pocket a valuable ring, would know where to find a proper fence.

And which of the upright citizens at present milling about the hotel's public rooms had been unable to resist the lure of such an expensive bauble?

He searched where Margot had searched before, tried to think of an explanation for the disappearance of the ring that didn't involve theft, couldn't — and then remembered that Mrs Horry said she had seen the housemaid in the passage. And he remembered more, that the girl had been avoiding him when first she saw him and he hadn't yet discovered why. Perhaps she had a police record. He'd better interview her next.

He found her in the kitchen with a tea towel in her hands standing beside Em at the table. They had the washing up bowl and tray before them, the cups and glasses stacked to one side, and were conferring together in low voices.

Hugh stood in the doorway and beckoned. 'Miss Johnson, I want a word with you. Come into the dining-room.'

With a glance at Em she laid down the towel and followed.

He seated himself at one of the small tables. 'Sit down, sit down.' When she remained rigidly standing he gestured impatiently. Was she scared? He opened his notebook and wrote her name. 'Miss Johnson, we were interrupted when I was asking you some questions this morning. Why are you hiding from the police?'

'I'm not!' she protested. 'I'm —'

'You were trying to keep out of my way.'

'Yes, that was because I know you, not because I'm a criminal. You should remember me too.'

'Then tell me where I've seen you.'

She half smiled. 'At Unley Park primary school. I was teaching your daughter Sophie.'

Frowning, annoyed with himself for his faulty memory, Hugh studied her face. 'Yes. I would have remembered eventually. Why have you left teaching?' He made a note. When she didn't answer he looked up and saw that she had flushed scarlet. 'Well?'

'I —'

'Resigned?'

After a pause she whispered, 'No.' She pulled out the chair and sat opposite him.

'Sacked, then.'

She didn't answer. Hugh asked, 'Why?'

'It wasn't true!' she said passionately. 'None of it was true.'

'Miss Johnson, I can soon enough find out the truth. I have only to telephone CID in town.'

She took a breath as though to steady herself. 'The headmaster — it was the headmaster. He wanted — he was horrible, he tried — I wouldn't do what he wanted and so he made up a story and got me dismissed. Nobody listened to me. And he was lying; nothing he said was true.'

'What wasn't true?'

She folder her hands in her lap and stared back at him, stony faced.

That face showed determination, disillusion, strength. Hugh remembered his daughter Sophie had adored Miss — not Miss Johnson, she'd been Miss Johns then. He found it sad to see her brought to this. He said, 'Your name is Johns. Why are you using a different one? Did you forge some references?'

'No!'

'And I suspect you were sacked for dishonesty. What did you take?'

'Nothing. It was all lies.'

'I can find out, and I will.'

Now she was as white as she had previously been red. 'You must believe me.' She closed her eyes. 'What can I do, what can I do,' she whispered. She was talking to herself.

Hugh hardened his heart against her distress. A naturally chivalrous man, in normal circumstances he'd have turned her over to a woman officer at this point. He didn't have that option now. He said, 'Where have you put Miss Jennings ring?'

'*What!*' She jumped to her feet; the chair crashed over. 'I don't have to listen to this.'

He caught her halfway to the door, grabbed her arm, and swung her to face him. 'You do, you know.'

'I haven't taken it! What do you think I am?'

Hugh thought he had made it admirably plain what he thought she was. 'I am going to search your room. Come with me.' He asked Em Musgrave to accompany them, and opened the door to her bedroom.

Em went as far as the doorway. Johnson turned out her pockets as requested then sat on the bed with her eyes closed, pretty obviously in an agony of embarrassment, while he went through her wardrobe, looked in and behind her drawers, opened her empty cases stacked in a corner, searched the windowsill, and peered under all the furniture. He asked her to move so that he could search the bed and she jumped up as though stung. He thought she would burst into tears. She didn't; dry-eyed she stood waiting until he had finished.

He found nothing.

Feeling a twinge of remorse and not liking it Hugh said, 'You brought this on yourself. You must be straight with me. Now tell me what you are doing here under an assumed name.'

'No!' she yelled. 'Bloody hell! No!'

She pushed past Em, who didn't try to stop her, and before Hugh could follow they heard her feet flying down the passage. The back door banged.

By the time he got there she was nowhere in sight.

Em said, 'She can't go far. Let her go for now.' When he came back she added, 'I think you're making a mistake, anyway. I wouldn't put it past that Jennings woman to steal her own ring.'

'There's something off about this one, though. I wish I knew what.'

'What was that about an assumed name?'

'Her real name is Johns. She was a teacher, and she's been sacked for some reason. She more or less admitted it was for dishonesty.'

'Really?' Em raised her brows. 'That does surprise me.'

59

Diggory Kenrick parked his car by the post office, vaulted the veranda rail, and bent to unlock his mail box. He had to count the rows by touch to find it. Kularook, with no power supply, had no streetlights. Clouds blacked out stars and moon.

He was tired, cold, and damp. He had ridden his new horse home and turned her into a paddock. Then, because none of his neighbours had been available to do him a favour, he had set out late in the afternoon to walk the whole six miles to Kularook to collect his car from where he had left it at the stockyards. A change had come through while he was on the way so he had been rained on twice during the last two miles.

The car could have stayed there for a week without much inconveniencing him but, now he had run out of meat and bread at the farm, he needed the stores he had loaded into it before he drove to the railway stockyards to collect the mare. He might as well collect his mail as well before he drove home.

'Who's that?' He thought he heard something move against the side wall of the post office, in the sheltered angle where it joined the garden wall of the postmaster's house. He leaned over the rail. 'Is anybody there?'

It sounded like whimpering, a puppy perhaps. He ducked under the rail and immediately tripped over a body. A shivering body crouched huddling in the corner. He was trying to regain his balance; his hand touched a bare arm, cold under his fingers.

'Hey! Who are you?'

A wobbly voice asked, 'Diggory?'

'Full Stop! What on earth are you doing here?'

Even as he spoke he was gathering her up, holding her against him, wrapping his arms around her as though to ward off the cold.

That brought him to his senses. He let her go, stripped off his jacket, and wrapped jacket and arms around her together. She let her head fall against his shoulder. She was shaking violently.

'What's happened?'

She mumbled something through her chattering teeth.

'Never mind. We'd better get you back to the pub — somewhere warm, somewhere dry.'

'No! I'm not going back.' Not only her head, her whole body shook with the force of her denial.

'Mrs Brown then. She's a sensible woman.' Diggory, like many in the district, had come to have considerable respect for Bowler's aristocratic Pommy wife.

'*No!* Not there! Not anywhere.' She shuddered.

'I've got to take you somewhere,' he said reasonably. 'You can't spend the night here.' He tried to think of the married women he knew round the town and rejected them all for one reason or another. 'Would you come out to the farm with me?'

This time she nodded.

Although intensely curious about what had happened to her, Diggory didn't ask questions during the drive and she offered no explanations. She stayed silent, her head back, her eyes closed. At the cottage he went in first; he lit the big metal kerosene lamp on the mantelpiece and stirred up the fire in the stove before he went out and helped her from the car.

For his bedroom he'd been using the only room that opened off the kitchen — what would have been the cook's bedroom in the old shearing seasons. He lit the candle on the small chest of drawers, took out his best sweater and a pair of thick socks, gave her a towel, and left her alone while he got a bowl of scraps from the safe and went outside to feed Magnus.

The dog gulped its meal and followed him inside. The alarm clock beside the lamp read half past eight and he'd had no dinner. He lifted the frying pan from its hook beside the stove.

When Johnson padded out, wearing the multicoloured afghan from his bed wrapped round her as a skirt to cover her bare thighs, he said, 'Feeling better?'

She walked over to stand beside him at the stove. 'Yes thank you. Dry, and I'm getting warmer.' She leaned a little to peer into his frying pan. The dog pushed its head under her hand.

'I assume you haven't eaten either. I'm starving. Chops will be ready in a moment.'

'Look, I must explain, I have to —'

'Whenever you're ready.'

'No,' she said. 'Now. You have to know. That detective thinks I'm a thief.'

'Well, don't get excited. I know you're not.'

Curiously she asked. 'How can you tell?'

Diggory smiled. 'I can tell the difference between honest indignation and a put-on job.'

'That's reassuring. I wish damn Detective Morgan could tell too.'

To make room for her to sit at the table he lifted a pile of books from one of the benches and stacked them on the floor against the wall, beside several other haphazard piles. 'To the despair of my dear Gran, who brought me up, I've always treated the floor as an extra shelf.' He gestured at the books. 'Lots of useful space on floors.'

When she smiled he said, 'That's better. Nothing is so terrible, after all.' Then he saw her looking at the .22 rifle propped in the corner behind the books. 'Rabbits,' he said. 'Mostly Magnus gets them, though now and then I keep one myself. A change from mutton.' He reached for the rifle with one hand and picked up a canvas case, lying across the books like a discarded snake skin, with the other. He slid the rifle into it and stood it in the corner again.

60

Over the meal of fried chops, shapeless pieces of cooked tomato, and as many slices of bread and butter as they needed, Johnson told Diggory, in exact detail, what had occurred between herself and Detective Constable Morgan.

The fire cracked, a breeze sang in the mallees outside. The window glass reflected them gesturing against the night. A fawn-coloured moth bumped repeatedly against the milky glass shade of the lamp now standing on the end of the table.

He didn't interrupt until her voice started rising as she described the unbearable violation she had felt when the policeman had searched her room. Even her pockets, her bed.

He said, 'And why were you sacked? From teaching?'

His matter-of-fact tone brought her back to the present, to the warm room and the yellow lamplight. She coloured, yet said steadily, 'For dishonesty. Just as that damn detective thought. But it wasn't true.'

'Tell me.'

The dog had been lying asleep by the stove. Now it lurched to its feet, fur rising along its neck, a growl in its throat, and took two stiff paces towards the door. Diggory considered a moment and then got up to open it; the dog shot off into the darkness. They heard barking diminishing into the distance.

'Fox, probably,' Diggory said, reseating himself. 'The damn things have been after my chooks. All right, if that wasn't the reason tell me what was.'

She licked her lips, then said in a rush, 'The headmaster, a horrible man, he wanted me to let him make love to me and when I tried to complain to the Department he'd got there first and invented a nasty story that got me sacked. And of course it makes me look bad now, with this damn ring lost.'

Equally unmoved by this recital, Diggory said, 'Next question. Why are you using a different name?'

She shook her head. 'Sorry. Don't think I can tell you yet. Soon.'

'All right. Next. What am I to call you instead of Full Stop?'

She started to shake her head again, then relented. 'That's an easy one. Martine.'

'And why the devil,' said Diggory, getting to his feet to collect up the debris of the meal, 'have you been hiding that? Martine is a perfectly unobjectionable name. I thought it must be something you disliked.'

'I just didn't want people using it.'

He thought about that, and then he nodded. 'Unfortunately I have to say I see your point. It would let people be too familiar, when you couldn't use their first names in reply.'

'That's it exactly, though I never put it in words so clearly to myself.'

Head tilted a little sideways, he was gazing steadily at her across the table. He said, 'How old are you?'

Surprised at the sudden question she said, 'Don't you go all senior and superior on me.'

'I wouldn't do that. You're no baby. You've known tough times and it shows.'

She frowned doubtfully. 'I didn't know that. I don't think I like it.'

'Not to everyone. But I've had a bit of experience in reading people.' He added reflectively, 'Some of them didn't want to be read and were pretty angry with me when they saw what I'd written. Look, we'll leave the dishes, I'll do them in the morning. In this light I can never see if they're properly clean.'

He climbed out from behind the bench, threw his arms wide, and arched his back. 'At this point of the evening I usually adjourn to the sitting room. Come on.' He took three steps and folded into a corner of the old leather-covered couch. He patted the seat beside him.

61

Martine rose slowly into consciousness. She had drifted, warm and well fed, into drowsiness and then into sleep in her corner of the couch. Now she found she had slipped sideways. Her head was on Diggory's shoulder, his arm around her.

They were almost lying, their legs stretched out in front of them. The lamp had been turned low. She was very comfortable. This was …

She jerked upright, fully awake. The dog, lying in front of the stove, lifted its head.

'What's up?' Diggory asked sleepily.

'I must have been asleep.' She didn't remember him turning the lamp down, or letting in the dog.

'You were.' He tightened his grip on her shoulder, pulled her back, and kissed the end of her eyebrow, the only part of her face he could reach without sitting up. 'You're very beautiful when you're asleep.'

Martine felt herself blushing. 'Nonsense.' She turned to see whether he was joking; he slid his hand behind her head and pulled her down to kiss her lips.

She enjoyed that more than she believed she should and let it go on longer than her conscience told her was proper. When she tried to pull away he kissed her again and this time she didn't resist.

Some minutes later she hardened her resolve and pushed him off. Her heart was thumping. 'Are you trying to seduce me?'

He smiled. 'I wouldn't mind. But no, not this time. I was merely taking the chance to enjoy myself. If you weren't enjoying it too then I apologise.'

On a breath, almost to herself, she admitted, 'But I was.' When the headmaster had grabbed her and kissed her she had felt physically sick and, even before that, when young men had taken her out she had refused to permit them more than a chaste kiss on her cheek, believing she didn't like a man 'slobbering' over her. Now it seemed that she did. Sometimes.

'That's all right then.' He pulled her close. 'Where were we?'

'No, don't start again. You might forget where enjoying yourself left off and seducing me began.'

He shook his head. 'Believe me, I wouldn't leave off enjoying myself if I was seducing you. On the contrary.'

'That's the problem, then. Some other time.'

'Tomorrow?' he asked hopefully.

Laughing, Martine stood up. 'You don't give up, do you? No, not tomorrow.'

He pulled his feet back, sat up, and yawned widely. 'Anyway, I expect it's time I took you home.'

'What is the time?'

He consulted his wrist-watch. 'Hell, it's ten to one. We've been asleep for hours. Will anyone at the pub be waiting up for you?'

'I don't want to go back there!' In the exciting diversions of the present she had forgotten the distresses of the past, and the chain of events which had led to her presence here, in Diggory Kenrick's cottage, in the middle of the night. She flopped on a bench, her back to the table, and put her head in her hands. 'But there's nowhere — I don't know —'

'You're going to give up your job, then?'

After a moment Martine lifted her head. 'No, you're right, I can't. I'll just have to convince Mrs Musgrave somehow that I didn't take that damn ring. I don't have anything else to live on or anywhere else to go. Not until next year.'

'What happens next year?'

'School starts. I've got a job lined up when school starts.'

He got up and leaned across the table to turn up the wick on the lamp. 'Can you get in without waking Em? I should have taken you back hours ago.'

62

In spite of her late night, Johnson had the stove alight, the kettle heating, and the cups set out on the traymobile ready for the early teas when Em came into the kitchen next morning.

'Good morning, Johnson.' Frowning, lips pursed, Em studied her. 'Are you all right? I didn't hear you come in last night.'

Pleased that her stealthy entry in the night had been undetected and that apparently Diggory's complicity was unsuspected, Johnson said, 'No, I — I walked about, I don't know what the time was.' She took a breath and faced her employer squarely. 'Mrs Musgrave, I didn't take that ring.'

'Detective Morgan thinks you've parked it somewhere, to retrieve it later.'

Angrily Johnson yanked her apron over her head. 'All right, sack me. I'll go and pack.'

'Hold your horses.' Em caught her arm. 'Come on, settle down. I don't agree with him and I'm not going to sack you. I don't know what's happened to that damn ring but I don't think you had anything to do with it. Satisfied?'

Johnson closed her eyes, weak with relief. 'Thank you.'

'Probably one of the riff-raff who sneak in to use our dunny put his head in the door and saw it.' Em released the girl's arm. 'But

Detective Morgan also told me you're using a false name. Your name is Johns, not Johnson.'

'It's not for any sinister reason, truly. Please, Mrs Musgrave, let me go on being Johnson.'

'I might.' Em nodded. 'I'm beginning to get ideas about you. Can you —'

'I'll tell you about it. Soon. There's something I have to do first.'

'I imagine there might be.'

Johnson was uneasy at the idea that Mrs Musgrave might know more about her than she'd been told. She said, 'You won't tell anyone —'

'Not a word. All right, get on with the teas for now. Four of them: Miss Jennings in six, a couple who arrived late in number three, and Mr Gafoops, you know, the commercial traveller, in ten. Don't let him hold you up. He'd talk the hind leg off a donkey.'

When she tapped on Miss Jennings door Johnson was reminded of the morning — was it only five mornings ago? — when she had finished her round of teas in Silas Beadnall's room.

And the detective still hadn't found who had killed him. In the difficulties of her current position she tended to forget that the crime had not yet been solved. She wished she had been brave enough to ask Diggory if he had done it.

A stupid idea — he wouldn't admit that to anyone. Though he had something on his mind and, although of course he was delightful company, she couldn't rule out the possibility he had lost his temper with a man he hated. She didn't really know him. Just because he'd been kind to her didn't mean he was a saint.

She found she was hoping he hadn't done it just as fervently as she hoped the other one — even in her mind she had difficulty naming him — was in the clear.

Miss Jennings was calling 'Come in!' impatiently for the second time. Recalled to the present, Johnson opened the door and pushed in the traymobile.

Wearing ice blue satin this time, Miss Jennings was curled up into a small space on her pillow, staring fixedly at the wall. She looked annoyed. And nervous. 'You took your time. Get rid of that spider.' She pulled a hand from her armpit to point then hurriedly tucked it out of sight, as though she feared the spider might leap on any such outlying parts of her person.

Johnson looked where she had pointed. Above the dressing table, high on the pink kalsomined wall and just below the paper frieze of roses, a brown huntsman spider, legs reaching further than could be covered by a teacup, sat immobile.

She shook her head. 'They're harmless. He won't bite.' She set a cup on a saucer, lifted the teapot. 'I can't remember, do you take milk?'

'No. And I can't drink tea with that thing watching me. Hit it with something.'

Johnson looked around. Blue satin mules — how many sets of matching night things did the woman have? — lay on the floor though they didn't look suitable for swatting spiders. She untied the laces and pulled a sturdy shoe from her own foot, then dragged a chair close to the dressing table. She climbed on.

She would have to lean at full stretch to reach the spider and now she could see it at closer quarters she didn't want to flatten it. The thing was too big. It would almost be like trying to squash a mouse, a disgusting thought. She leaned and banged her shoe against the wall, and the spider obligingly danced instantly out of sight behind the mirror on the dressing table. With luck it would be too frightened to show itself before Miss Jennings left the room.

'I think I got it.' Johnson sounded confident. As she stepped down she glanced across to the wardrobe further along the same wall. The top was finished with a wooden parapet of symmetrical carved scrolls and in the space behind it, among a number of dead blowflies, a live silverfish, a couple of twists of screwed up paper, and a man's sock white with dust, she glimpsed an iron. An electric iron.

The iron shone, free of dust. She couldn't see a cord.

She brought her other foot to the floor and stood on one leg to replace her shoe. Miss Jennings didn't appear to have noticed her momentary hesitation. When she had finished serving the tea she pushed her traymobile back to the kitchen. Em wasn't there.

As she passed the dining-room she'd seen Hugh Morgan waiting for his breakfast and she left him waiting. She wasn't going to do the detective any favours after the way he'd treated her. She ran across the road to the police station, where she banged on the front door and, in another repetition of Sunday morning, Bowler jerked it open. He looked tired, grim, and no better pleased at being disturbed than he had been last time — yet she wasn't afraid of this policeman.

'I've found an iron.' When he just stared at her looking totally confused she explained, 'An electric iron, in one of the bedrooms. Without its cord.'

That brought him awake. 'Have you now. Where is it?'

'I didn't touch it. I'll show you.'

As they walked back to the hotel Bowler asked, 'Which bedroom? Who was in it on Saturday night?'

'The same one who's in it now,' Johnson answered. 'Miss Jennings.'

63

Bowler had been hoping Hugh wouldn't need his help this morning, although he didn't know what else he wanted to do. Get on with the digging, probably.

He had woken in the night shouting and sweating, in the grip of one of his nightmares, the first for many months. The dream had left him dry mouthed and shaken; its recurrence had left him depressed. He'd thought he was getting over the damn things.

Usually, when he had to cope with bad temper or bad news, he would saddle up Imshy and head out of town, anywhere to be alone with his thoughts, until the rhythms of the horse's motion, the steady beat of hoofs, soothed him into a better frame of mind. He couldn't do that this morning.

He knew Joan would have lent him her Isma, if he'd asked. Since he also knew that she had planned one of her photographic excursions that morning he had brought the horse from the paddock, buckled on her saddle, and tossed her into it.

'Don't worry about me,' he had said, reading the love and concern in her face as he handed up her camera bag. 'A good time to catch up in the office. Bloody paper work should keep me out of mischief.'

'Paperwork? Huh! I'll believe that when I see it.' She had leant down from the horse, kissed him hard, and ridden away with her camera slung across her back.

So he'd been thinking of his Joan and her staunchness and how utterly he depended on her and trusted her when young Johnson interrupted him. Now he must collect his wits and find Hugh, to tell him what this girl had discovered.

When they entered her bedroom Margot was still in bed, sitting up reading a paperback book with brightly coloured covers, which she tucked under the blankets as the two policemen followed the housemaid through the door.

'What do you want now?' she demanded.

Johnson pointed to the wardrobe, and withdrew.

'Just come to check on something,' Bowler said, walking over and reaching a long arm to the top of the wardrobe. Miss Jennings, he was interested to see, had turned nearly as pale as her sheets: she had instantly realised what he was groping for. 'Is this yours?' He held out the iron.

Wide-eyed, both hands clutching the blankets to her breast, she exclaimed, 'No! No! Not mine!'

'Come on,' Bowler said. 'Why not tell us the truth? This was your room last weekend.' He knew damn well her little-girl act was assumed.

'What happened to the cord?' Hugh stepped for a closer look — not that he gained any insights from that.

Bowler put the iron in his hands. 'Didn't you know Kularook was without power when you packed to come here, Miss Jennings?' When she didn't answer he added, 'All the others know.'

'I didn't kill Silas! It wasn't me!'

'Nobody says it was.' Bowler wished she'd stop overacting. And stop pretending she thought they might suspect her. She knew damn well they didn't. 'We just have to know where you last saw the cord from your iron. You must tell us the truth. It's important.'

Margot looked from one to the other of the two policemen. 'I took the iron to Silas's room,' she admitted, her head turned aside as though embarrassed. 'I wanted to ask him where I could find a power point, seeing I couldn't see one in this room, so of course he explained there weren't any, no power points anywhere. And then we had a drink together, and when we left the room I forgot it, and left it on a corner of the dressing-table.'

'So you took the iron with its cord to Mr Beadnall's room?' She nodded. 'How did the iron get back here?' Though Bowler thought he could guess.

In a small voice she said, 'In the night, when I found him — found him, and the cord — anyway, I brought the iron back here. I was frightened, and so I hid it.'

'That was concealing evidence,' Hugh said. 'You should have known better.'

'I was too shocked to know what I was doing.'

Hugh grunted in disbelief.

'Let's get this clear,' Bowler said. 'You took the iron and the cord to Silas Beadnall's room before you went to dinner on Saturday evening. You left it there, and then took the iron away in the night when you found Beadnall dead with the cord round his neck.'

She nodded, still wide-eyed, still pretending to be frightened of them.

'When you have dressed you must come across the road to the station and make a formal statement for us,' Hugh said. 'And sign it.'

'Oh, I'll sign it,' Margot said meekly. 'Then can I catch the train to town today?'

'Certainly. We have your address if we need any more information from you.'

'And that's no bloody use to us,' Hugh complained as they shut the door behind them. 'Any bastard could have waltzed into Beadnall's room, picked up the cord, and wrapped it round his damn neck.'

Bowler agreed. 'And seems to me if the cord was just lying there, the murder is much more likely to have been a spur of the moment thing. Someone in a rage, the means to hand — too easy.'

'And every last one of them was in a rage with him for one reason or another,' Hugh said morosely. 'Every last one of them had a motive. I was hoping when we found where the cord came from it would point to one or other of them, dammit.'

'What now?'

'I've got to catch Lilian Beadnall when she comes in, before she catches her train. According to Miss Jennings, Silas was threatening to disinherit her.'

64

Hugh decided to wait at the railway station to interview Lilian. He hoped she wouldn't cut it too fine before her train arrived: he wanted a few words with her first. Then, in the front hall of the pub he nearly ran into her, standing beside her brother Leon and talking to Bowler.

'Yes, I was going to catch the train,' Lilian explained. 'Then we found this letter had arrived from Father's lawyers. It's addressed to Horry, and as he didn't come in with us today we can't open it. We expect it contains a copy of the will, so I have sent a couple of telegrams and will stay for another night on the farm.'

'We all want to know what's in the damn thing,' Leon said.

'I'm sure,' Hugh agreed. 'Miss Beadnall, we need to ask you a couple more questions. Will you come into the dining-room?'

Leon started to follow. 'What's this about?'

Hugh waved him back. 'Just a word with your sister. Shouldn't take long.'

'All right. I'll go and see if I can find that thing of Fran's.' He disappeared into the lounge.

In the dining-room Hugh held a chair for Miss Beadnall at a small table and seated himself opposite. Bowler followed, and propped his shoulders against the door frame.

Hugh said, 'Miss Beadnall, we have been told your father was threatening to disinherit you.'

With an air of freezing disapproval she said, 'And I hope whoever told you that — was it Brenda? No, never mind, I know you can't say — I hope she also informed you that I told my father he couldn't control me by that means or any other.'

'Telling your father is one thing. If he had actually cut you out of his will you —'

'He was a bully, and I would *not* allow him to bully me.' A flush of anger stained her cheek though she didn't raise her voice. 'I make a comfortable living from my business.'

Hugh nodded. That could be easily proved if he needed to check further on her. 'I see.' He had a feeling he should believe her, though he tended to mistrust anyone as self-controlled as this woman. Even when she was angry she didn't lose her careful, slightly pedantic manner of speech. He wished he could rattle her somehow.

'You didn't tell us about your father's threats to you.'

'Why on earth should I? He was always ranting and raving at someone. It just happened to be my turn.'

'So you didn't believe he'd really do it? Cut you from his will?'

'I thought he might. That would have been disagreeable. Not disagreeable enough, however, to drive me to murder.'

'So you say.'

She remained unruffled. 'Have you found Miss Jennings's ring yet?'

'No.' Now the damn woman was putting him on the defensive. 'I have had other things to do.'

'I'm sure you have, Officer.' In her most measured tones Lilian said, 'I am not holding anything back. I didn't kill my father, and I hope you find who did. May I go now?'

Hugh gazed at her reflectively for a moment. 'Oh, yes, you can go. We have your Adelaide address, and so if we need more answers I'll see you in town.'

'I am not returning until tomorrow's train. Good afternoon.' She stood up, arranged her handbag over her arm, and walked in unruffled dignity from the room. Bowler stood aside to let her pass.

Hugh asked him, 'Did you believe her?'

'She might be as indifferent as she pretends.' Bowler compressed his lips. 'Then again, she's got such rigid self-control she could be lying like billy-o.'

65

Leon Beadnall, on his hands and knees half under a table in the hotel lounge, saw that a pair of sturdy brown shoes had come to rest, tidily side by side, close to his right hand. He looked up, saw the housemaid, and hoisted himself to his feet.

His face red, partly from the effort, partly from embarrassment, he said, 'My wife left a cigarette holder here on Saturday evening, a long black ebony one. She has only just missed it. She thinks she must have dropped it here.'

Johnson said, 'Not on that floor. I have swept that carpet four times since then.' She sounded on her dignity, as though he had suggested she skimped her work. Relenting, she added, 'I found it on the mantelpiece. Your wife must have put it down and then forgotten it. Mrs Musgrave has it in the office.'

'Thank you,' he said. Then, because the housemaid was regarding him with an abnormally intent gaze, he asked, 'Is something the matter?'

Johnson had spent hours imagining the right moment, planning what she would say, how she would lead up to her revelation. Instead now, the first time she was alone with him, she blurted, 'I'm Celeste Johns's daughter.'

For a second she regretted her impulsiveness. Then she thought, why not. If she was going to tell him, she would never easily find the right time.

Leon was obviously surprised. 'Celeste! After all these — Christ!' His eyes widened and his mouth fell open as he realised what else she was telling him.

His gaze never left her face. He groped behind him for a chair and collapsed onto it.

'Silas,' he croaked. 'Silas made me —'

Johnson said, 'My mother died six months ago. She left me a letter.'

Leon closed his eyes and slowly turned his head from side to side in negation. 'You must give me a minute or two. A shock, to put it mildly. I thought she was going to — I mean, I believed —'

'You chose to think she would have an abortion,' Johnson said harshly. 'You and Silas.'

'I had no idea —'

'You didn't make much of an effort to find out, my mother said.'

Leon covered his mouth with one hand and sat staring at her.

Johnson gazed steadily back. She saw the back of his sunburnt, scarred, farmer's hand, his dark eyes above, and thought, this man was her father. She could tell he knew it, too. She said, 'I can show you my birth certificate, with the date, if you want to see it.'

'Celeste is dead,' he said, as though he needed to say the words to believe in the fact.

'Yes.' Now wasn't the time to tell him of her mother's long struggle with cancer, of their desperate poverty after the headmaster's machinations got her sacked. She intended to make sure he knew eventually. She believed that, in fairness to her mother, he should know these details eventually. If he retained any vestiges of a conscience she intended giving it a hefty jolt pretty soon.

'Look — what do I call you? What's your name?'

'Martine.'

'Look, Martine, what do you want me to do? To say? You'll have to give me time to get used to this.'

'I'm not sure I want you to do anything,' she said. 'I just thought I should let you know I exist. I don't want anything from you. It's a bit late now.' She saw him wince. 'I've done all right without you so far, I can go on very well the same way.'

'Who else have you told?'

'Nobody. Is that all that's worrying you, the scandal? It makes no difference to me, so I thought you should decide that one.' She turned away. 'Though I think Mrs Musgrave guesses. Excuse me, now I have work to do.'

'You can't throw a bombshell like that at me and then calmly walk away,' he expostulated. 'We have to talk, there are —'

'What is there to say?' She went away up the passage.

Leon stayed sitting in the chair in the lounge, his eyes closed. Martine went into her bedroom, shut the door, sat on the side of the bed, and put her head in her hands.

She was shaking. She couldn't stop shaking. She had done it.

She had done it, yet nothing was changed. She hadn't expected this feeling of emptiness. Her father had just looked at her, acknowledging her existence, believing what she told him, yet not seeing her, Martine, as a person, only as a problem he had to resolve. But then she had to admit she had no idea what she did want from him; her speculations had never got her past the first moment of her revelations.

So she was being unreasonable to feel so let down. And she would have been repelled if he had tried to embrace her, or made any dramatic gesture like that.

She went to the dressing-table and combed her hair. Her familiar face looked back from the mirror, her ordinary face, the one she lived with every day. She wondered how it had looked to Leon Beadnall — how her father had seen her.

She scowled at the image and slammed down the comb. After all these years without him she was stupid to care what he thought now. She straightened her shoulders and went out to see what needed doing in the kitchen.

66

In the lounge Lilian found her brother sitting at one of the tables. She said, 'There you are. Did you find it? Fran's holder?'

Leon looked up. 'No. I mean, it's in the office, I have —' He shook his head as though to clear it.

'Are you all right? Leon, what is it?'

'Do you remember Celeste Johns? She was teaching at the school here for a while, a good many years ago now.'

'Perhaps that was after I left home.'

Leon shook his head again, more wildly. 'It could have been, I can't work it out now. All I remember is I was eighteen when she left.'

Lilian sat in the chair beside him and took his hand. 'Dear boy, whatever is the matter?'

He turned and gripped both her hands. 'I was in love with her. With Celeste. Father found out and there was hell to pay, said she was no good. I wasn't twenty-one, I couldn't fight him. So he broke it up, she left. Now this girl says she's Celeste's daughter.'

'Which girl?'

'Don't tell Horry, will you.'

'Leon, which girl?'

He released her hands and sat back; he screwed his eyes shut and tilted his face towards the ceiling. 'The girl working here, in the pub, Johnson or whatever she calls herself. Her name's Martine, she told me.'

Slowly Lilian said, 'She told you?' Frowning, she made connections. 'Do you mean this girl thinks she's your child?'

'Dear sister, not only thinks, she is.'

'Leon!'

He sprang to his feet and walked to the window. 'She has to be, if she's Celeste's daughter.' He turned, stopped in front of her. 'She offered to show me her birth certificate.'

'What would that prove? Your name can't be on it.'

'No. But I knew — we both knew, Father and I — that Celeste was pregnant. That's why he was so furious. The date would prove it. At least to me, if to no one else.'

'Why haven't you mentioned this before? I didn't think we kept secrets from each other.'

'Celeste was supposed to have an abortion. I thought Father gave her money for an abortion. Perhaps he didn't. Anyway, Celeste died recently and left this girl a letter. So she has come to see me.'

'What does she want? Money?'

'No. Nothing.'

'Leon, that can't be possible. Why would she bother to find you if she wants nothing?'

'Lilian, you are not thinking straight. She is curious to see what sort of a bastard abandoned her mother. That's all. I can understand it perfectly.'

'You're very trusting. If you admit this — this relationship, you don't know what she might decide to ask for.'

Leon smiled. 'You don't know her — well, neither do I, but I can't let you think badly of her.' He stopped, as though listening to what he'd said. 'Quite mad. Already I feel I have to defend her. And before you ask, she hasn't told anyone else; she says that's up to me.

Though she thinks Em Musgrave guesses.'

'I am absolutely dumbfounded,' Lilian said.

'What the hell do you think I am?'

'You'll have to tell Fran. And Horry.'

'I suppose so. But not yet. Don't say anything to them yet, Lil. I have to get used to the idea myself before I can let the others know. I don't even want to talk about it until we've got this business of the will out of the way.'

'Yes, all right.'

'You have a grown-up niece, Lilian. I hope you like her.'

A servant, Lilian thought. Liking might be a problem. She hoped she wasn't a snob, yet she didn't think she could welcome a servant girl into the family on the same footing as the rest of them. She remembered that she had in fact liked the girl when she had been staying in the pub; that, though, had been liking for a clean, willing and polite housemaid. Not for a niece.

Driving home rather squashed together in Leon's Austin 7, Lilian said, 'What will you do about this girl, Leon? I suppose you'll want to get to know her.'

'Of course I want to. It's going to be difficult, though. I'll wait and see what Fran says. She might have some ideas.'

Lilian was pretty sure she knew the kind of ideas Fran would have, and Leon wasn't going to like them. He was fooling himself if he believed Fran would acknowledge this girl as readily as he seemed to be doing. His wife might appear easy-going, but that was only as long as she was getting her own way: she wasn't going to put up with anyone for five minutes if the interloper threatened to take any part of Leon's attention away from her. Or any part of their admittedly meagre income.

Lilian said, 'Has it occurred to you that if what this girl tells you is true, she also is related to Silas? His granddaughter?'

'Hell, no.' After a moment he added, 'I hope you aren't hinting she had a motive for murder.'

'No more than the rest of us.'

'Come on, Lil, the only ones who benefit are the three of us. Well, that's what Bowler Brown seems to think. And that detective.'

'Brenda benefits.' Lilian seized the chance to share her suspicions.

'Brenda!' He jerked his head round to look at her; the wheel twisted under his hands.

'Look out, for god's sake! You'll have us into the fence.'

'Brenda!' he repeated, hastily correcting the steering.

'Yes, Brenda. Why not? I'm sure she hated Silas more than any of us.' Although Lilian could tell this was a new idea for Leon, she was hoping that the police were more perceptive. She didn't want to be the one to point this possibility out to them: she didn't want to demean herself by dobbing. Reasonably she added, 'Who else could it be? I don't believe you did it, or Horry.'

Leon took one hand from the wheel to rub the back of his head. 'Crikey, Lil! Brenda! I'll have to think about that.'

Satisfied she had sown the seed, Lilian sat back.

Although Lilian would spend the night in the cottage on the ridge with him and Fran, Leon stopped the car at the main house to deliver the letter to his brother. When he took it from inside his jacket and started to pass it to Horry, Brenda pounced on it and nipped it from his fingers. 'The will!' she exclaimed.

Angrily, he snatched it back. 'That's addressed to Horry.'

'Don't be stupid, Horry has no secrets from me.' She held out her hand.

Lilian, from the doorway, said, 'It's nothing to do with secrets. If that letter contains my father's will it concerns Horry and Leon and me. Neither Leon nor I thought we had the right to open it. You keep out of it.'

'Well! You've come back, have you?'

Lilian looked her over coolly. 'As you see.'

They were in the farm kitchen. Horry glanced from his wife to his sister and said nothing. He took the letter, seated himself in his usual place at the head of the kitchen table, and put his thumb under the flap of the long envelope.

Brenda would have sat beside him except that Lilian got there first. The three Beadnalls were edging her out, and she was furious.

'Horry!' she said.

'All in good time, old girl. This concerns us all.'

Horry pulled several sheets of paper, held together with a paperclip, from the envelope; he unfolded them and smoothed them flat on the table. Leon and Lilian bent to read beside him.

67

Em said, 'Johnson, will you dash up to the post office and clear the box while I dish up the teas? There should be letters from the girls today, and I forgot to go this afternoon. Here's the key.'

In the west the sun had sunk behind a belt of leaden clouds solid as a mountain range, though the vault of the sky still showed blue. The air was clear, unshadowed, deepening into dusk. Pleased to be out of doors, Johnson ran lightly up the centre of the road, along the strip of rutted dirt that the occasional cars kept free of weeds, and arrived at the post office slightly out of breath. Four letters were in the pub's box, two of them probably bills, the other two the ones Em was waiting for, from her daughters in boarding school. More sedately Johnson walked back.

On the left of the road she passed a stone building with a pretentiously grand facade and an entrance raised by several broad steps from ground level, the town's only bank.

The accommodation for the bank manager opened from a less ornate porch beside it; it too was on high foundations — to allow for a vault beneath, apparently — so that the side window was a little above her head. Martine saw Diggory standing close to the glass and looking back into the room as though he had just turned from gazing into the street. He was barely ten feet away.

The lift of his head, the line of his bare throat, caught at her senses. She was surprised by her physical response to what was, after all, only an unexpected view of him. The sight had taken her unawares.

What was he doing in the bank manager's quarters? Probably the family were his friends. She had to acknowledge she knew nothing about him. She didn't know his friends, or what he did with his time when he wasn't working on the farm.

He hadn't seen her; she could study him without embarrassment. A light was growing behind him. Whoever had entered the room and caused him to turn was carrying a lamp. The light illuminated the line of his cheek, and outlined his hair in fire.

She didn't know anything about the bank manager's family, either. The other shadowy figure, now further into the room, was a woman. She couldn't see who carried the lamp.

If he turned his head again he would see her watching. She jumped into movement as though galvanised, running across the road as silently as she could lest her footsteps alerted him to her presence; running across the road and in the front door of the pub; running into hiding.

She didn't understand why she wanted to get away before he saw her. Why would that have mattered?

The surge of her emotions had been too intense, that was why. She needed to re-establish control before she met him again.

He came to the pub after dinner. Johnson, coming back from throwing the washing-up water under the stunted almond tree by the shed, met Diggory in the passage by the kitchen door.

She thought, handsome young men couldn't help looking as though they'd disarranged their hair artistically on purpose, even though the result was merely from the attentions of a stiff breeze. Diggory looked tired, even haggard, yet dramatically romantic all the same.

He reached as though to take her hands, and then dropped his own. 'I should have told you, but it didn't seem to matter.'

Johnson paused in her admiration. 'What are you talking about?'

He closed his eyes as though awaiting a blow. Then he met hers squarely. 'I had no right to — I'm pretty much of a louse, but not so low that I'd let you find out from someone else. I have to tell you myself. My wife arrived in Kularook this afternoon.'

When she just stared at him he closed his eyes again. 'I never expected to see her again. I was going to explain — I thought I had time, I thought —' He shook his head helplessly. 'The marriage was over, she'd left me, I was waiting — oh, what the hell. Now she's back and I don't know what the devil to do. I should have told you and then things moved too fast for me.'

She kept silent. What could she say? That of course he should have told her? As soon as he had realised how strongly they were attracted to each other he should have told her. He must have known she'd been beginning to fall in love with him. He had intended that she should, which was why he was so disgusted with himself now. A bit late for that. She wished she could pretend that she didn't care.

She wrapped her arms over the tightness in her heart. He should have been too honest to permit her to start, let alone encouraged her. Too honest, too kind.

Yet she had believed him both those things, both honest and kind. She started to move away.

'Full Stop, please!' He put his hand on her arm and removed it immediately when she halted. 'I'll sort something out, I must, I can't — I was waiting until I could divorce her, desertion, now I'll have to see what else I can do. It will take time, though, and in the meantime you'll understand why I have to keep away from you.'

'Yes. You will have to.' If he hoped she would contradict him, she couldn't. Confused and angry, she turned and walked with what dignity she could manage down the passage and into her own room.

She closed the door gently, turned, rested her knuckles on the dressing-table, and stood with her head hanging. She wasn't sure whether she felt more anger, or more loss.

He had been growing into a delightful friend, and one whom she had trusted. Then with astonishment she remembered she had known him less than a week. So quickly had he taken a hold on her affections!

She thought with disgust, perhaps she had been like a homeless pup, ready to attach herself to the first person who showed her kindness.

No, that wasn't true. Diggory had made the first moves.

Anyway, after so short a time, perhaps all she had lost was the expectation of greater friendship, of good times to come.

This was the second time she'd taken refuge in her bedroom that day. Hidden herself, run away from confrontations with men she cared about. Perhaps she was a coward. Perhaps she should have stayed, faced them, demanded answers from them.

The problem was, she hadn't begun to formulate her questions, even to herself. She didn't know what she wanted from Leon, and didn't believe there were any questions she could reasonably ask Diggory that would give her the answers she wanted.

He'd said he'd been waiting to divorce his wife. Did that make his sins less?

He must have believed himself free to love again in every other way than under the law. If he could 'sort something out', would she be pleased?

She wouldn't allow herself to consider this. Less than a week of burgeoning hopes shouldn't be difficult to erase. She would get on with her life as she had planned before, and forget Diggory as though she had never met him.

She'd give up on men. She hadn't had much luck with them so far.

68

Diggory was standing looking after Johnson when Em came from the kitchen and almost ran into him.

'What are you doing cluttering up my passage?' she demanded. 'Out of my way.'

He stood aside. In a voice he tried to keep light he said, 'You can be the second to know. My wife has arrived. I am taking her out to the farm now.'

She stopped. Her gaze followed his, to Johnson's closed door. 'You bastard!' When she could get her breath she added, 'Get out of my pub. Now.'

He pushed past her and went up the passage towards the front door. He stopped, turned. 'For what it's worth, I thought she was in Hong Kong. Permanently.'

'That doesn't let you out,' Em muttered, though she didn't think he heard. She went to Johnson's door and knocked softly.

To Em's relief the door opened instantly: she'd been afraid the girl would shut herself away to nurse her humiliation in isolation, like a wounded animal. Unkind to remind her, to say I told you so, I did warn you about him: the kid needed help now. She looked awful.

'Diggory told me, the mongrel. Are you all right?'

Johnson nodded, and cracked her stiff face into a smile. 'I'm fine,

Mrs Musgrave.' She came out and shut the door behind her. 'I'll finish clearing up in the kitchen and then I'll set the tables for breakfast. Will there be anything else tonight?'

'That's all.'

Outside in the street, daylight lingered in the west; a cool breeze rustled the ranks of elms lining the white metalled street. Ada and Joss, on their way back from a brisk after-dinner constitutional in the twilight, paused outside the pub. They could hear bottles clinking inside as Trotter cleaned up ready for next day. The yeasty smell of beer seeped out from a partly opened window.

A man had emerged from the pub's front door and stood still. His arms were by his side, fists clenched; his face was tilted to the sky though he saw none of it, for his eyes were screwed shut. They thought he could be drunk.

Then a patch of light fell through the frosted bar window and they recognised their great-nephew Diggory Kenrick. Believing that probably he didn't even know of their existence they had been hoping to see him again; they hadn't had time to speak to him on Saturday evening when he'd interrupted Silas's party so briefly to talk with Lilian.

For years the sisters had followed his journalistic career with intense interest, searching the paper for anything he had written, any reference to his activities. They had felt a personal pride in him, pleased that they knew of the connection though he might not, and had occasionally indulged themselves with a little mild boasting to the other residents of their boarding house. And here and now, drunk though he might be, they couldn't possibly miss the opportunity to introduce themselves.

Joss stepped forward. 'Mr Kenrick? Diggory!' He lowered his head to stare at her. 'I'm Jocelyn. Your aunt Jocelyn.'

'Aunt?' He jerked his head, a short abrupt movement as though to shake his thoughts into order. 'What the devil are you talking about? I know all my damn aunts.'

'Great aunts really,' she said. 'Silas's sisters.'

'Oh yes, Lilian said something about you. You must forgive me, this was the first I'd heard of you.'

'We thought you might not know.' Diggory turned as though to walk away and Joss, greatly daring — she was not sure how far drunken men could be trusted — laid her hand on his sleeve. 'We were at the party on Saturday and saw you come and speak to Lilian.'

'Silas's merry little party,' he said. 'So Silas was your brother. Congratulations.'

'Don't be cross.' Ada joined them. 'And don't blame us. We didn't choose him.'

He smiled. 'Neither did I. So we're all better off without him. I don't suppose you have any views on to which benefactor we owe this happy state of affairs?'

'We think — no, of course we don't know.' Joss was annoyed with herself for being so unguarded.

Ada said quickly, 'We were fond of our niece — Helen, your mother — and we are very pleased to make your acquaintance at last.'

Diggory switched his speculative gaze from Joss. 'Then I am pleased to make yours.'

'Would you come back with us now? We're going to make a pot of tea as soon as we get in.'

'No. Not now. I can't stay now. Damnation, I —' He swung round until his back was towards them. Over his shoulder he asked, 'How long are you staying in Kularook? And where?' When they told him he said without turning, 'Yes, I know Mrs Borthwick. I'll try and see you later. Now isn't a good time.' He repeated, more to himself than to the women, 'Not a good time.' He walked quickly away towards his car, waiting further along the street in the darkening night.

Ada said, 'He seemed upset about something, poor boy. Not

about us, something else. And I don't think he was drunk at all, do you?'

'No.' Joss, in her role of a more worldly woman, gave her considered opinion, although in truth she had encountered as few inebriated men as her sister. 'And you're right. I'm sure he has something on his mind.'

'No wonder Stella likes him. He's a good-looking boy, and that slight air of raffishness would make him irresistible to any girl his own age.'

Joss laughed. 'Ada, Ada, even to old girls like us.'

69

Johnson was lying on her bed reading — trying to read — by the light of a candlestick on a chair beside her pillow. She wasn't making much progress with *Robbery Under Arms*, which she had borrowed from the bookshelves of Em's absent daughters. Unwanted images kept getting in the way of the story.

She had taken up the book to switch off an unproductive round of speculations about Leon. Now she found she couldn't stop thinking about Diggory. She was angry that he so possessed her thoughts, yet no matter how she tried she couldn't get free of him. Whenever it seemed she'd succeeded she found that after a paragraph or two Diggory had easily ousted Captain Starlight and the Marston brothers and was back in occupation of her mind.

She wondered what his wife was like. Wondered why she hadn't joined him in Kularook before. Wondered what Diggory was doing now, and whether he was thinking of her — though she quickly shut a mental door on those speculations. Whether Diggory thought of her or not made no difference now. Anyway, most probably the presence of his wife had driven all memory of her, Johnson from his head, and that was as it should be.

The idea that he should now forget her brought her no comfort at all.

The candle burnt low. She slapped the book shut and twisted to put it beside the candlestick on the chair. It must have been nearly midnight. Time she got undressed and into bed.

Yawning, she rolled from the bed to her feet. Then she heard a scuffling sound under her window. She picked up her candle and went over.

The light reflected off the glass put a barrier between her and anything that might be there. A dog, she thought, even a fox: something sniffing at the veranda posts for scent of previous canine visitors.

A voice said, 'Psst! Full Stop!'

She hadn't yet started to undress. She took her candle and went to the back door.

When she stepped outside the wind instantly stripped the flame from her candle. The light of a hazy quarter moon showed her Diggory, a tall shadowy figure, waiting for her. He took her arm.

She pulled herself free. 'What do you want?' The wind was cold on her bare arms.

'I have to talk to you. Please.' When she said nothing he added, 'This might not be important to you but it is to me. Five minutes, that's all.'

She took a few moments to think about that; then she said, 'All right.' This time she didn't shake off his hand, and she allowed him to lead her into the shelter of the old open-fronted stone stables on the other side of the yard. He took the candlestick from her, put it on the bonnet of Trotter Musgrave's T-model Ford beside them, and struck a match. The candle flame streamed sideways, yet held.

His face downturned, watching the flame he said, 'Look, Katya's arrival surprised me as much as it did you.'

'Hardly. You must have noticed when you got yourself married.'

'Yes of course, I didn't mean that. It's just that she swore blind she would never leave Hong Kong, ranted and raved about it, and I believed her. Now there's something odd going on and I have to find out what.' He lifted his head and reached for her hands. His expression looked very serious in the flickering light. 'When it's fixed, I'll come back to you. Tell me I can come back when I've cleared up this mess.'

What did she say to that? She knew exactly what Em Musgrave would advise her to answer. But she was Martine Johns, not Em Musgrave, and she was beginning to realise that now she was free of the crippling responsibilities of her mother's last illness she had a freedom to act for herself she'd never known before. She could throw off the burden of grief and guilt; she could make her own choices and be answerable to no one. This was her life. She would make her own decisions.

She took a deep breath.

He said quickly, 'I know what you're going to say, you hardly know me. All I'm asking is permission to try to change that. When I've sorted everything out.'

She said, 'All right.'

He lifted her hands and lowered his face into her palms. 'Thank Christ for that,' he muttered. And for what seemed to her a long time they stood like that, unmoving.

She looked at his bent head. Was she making a terrible mistake? Plenty of time to discover that later. She freed one of her hands and laid it on his hair.

He lifted it off, kissed the tips of her fingers, straightened. 'Now I can survive, even though I have to keep clear of you until I find out what she's up to. In the meantime, you can do something for me. Please.'

A stronger eddy of wind snuffed out the candle. The smell of hot candle grease rose from the smoking wick and was snatched away like the flame. 'What?'

'Mind this for me.' He had taken something propped against the wall beside him and was pushing it into her hands, some kind of rod, something long and unyielding inside a canvas cover. With a shock she realised she held his rifle.

'I was going to shoot her,' he said conversationally. 'It seemed like a good idea, solve everything. All those acres to bury her in, nobody would ever find her and I could pretend she'd caught the next train out. So I'd rather you took charge of the damn rifle.'

'Diggory!'

'Are you horrified? Don't be. Goes on all the time in a war and nobody turns a hair.' He gave a half laugh. 'Sorry, of course you're horrified. Anyway, I didn't do it and I won't. Mind you, I was thinking why not. It's all too damn easy after the first time.' He was gazing over her head at the moonlit yard, the back wall of the pub, and seemed to be talking more to himself than to her. 'I'd like to think I'm not such an arrogant bastard. Murder's just arrogance, you know, bloody-minded selfishness and arrogance.' He brought his attention back to her. 'So I got in the car and brought it to you. I had to see you, anyway.' He took her by the shoulders and bent as if to kiss her, then pushed her away. 'Not yet, damn it. You mustn't be mixed up in my disasters. Just keep that bloody thing away from me.'

Johnson found her voice. 'Diggory, I —' His fingers fell gently against her mouth.

'Hush. I promise I'll find another way.' Seeing that she was holding the rifle gingerly in both hands he picked up the candlestick. 'Come on, I'm keeping you out here like a brute and you're shivering. Time you were inside.'

She wasn't sure whether she was cold or shivering from tension. She couldn't help herself: she was involved in the fate of this man she hardly knew. At the door of the pub he hung the sling of the rifle on her shoulder and handed her the candlestick. 'I will be back,' he promised. She watched him walk away and heard his footsteps going up the street towards the front of the pub and the main street.

The insignificant weight of the twenty-two rifle on her shoulder felt huge and threatening as a cannon. In her bedroom she lit the misshapen stub that was all that was left of her candle and looked around for a hiding place. Though why did she have to hide it? It had been used in no crime.

For whatever reason, she wanted it out of her sight. So she wouldn't prop it inside her wardrobe. Carefully she laid it on the floor and with the toe of her shoe pushed it under the bed as far as it would go. She was the only one who ever swept that floor. The unsettling weapon was safe for the moment.

She hurried into her pyjamas. Her hand was cupped round her candle flame, ready to blow it out, when she heard a crash and a yell from the bedroom next to hers. She hadn't known anyone was staying there: Em used the poky little room only if every other room was occupied or the guest was someone she didn't like. Johnson slung her dressing gown round her shoulders, grabbed her candlestick, and ran to investigate.

When she opened the door of the room a puddle of flames was leaping and flickering on the floor by the bed, and in the uncertain surges of light she could see the occupant standing as though mesmerised, shaking his head at the fire and trying to drag his heavy eyes open. A stringy middle-aged man, in socks, shirt, and pants with braces dangling, he was making no attempt to control the flames.

The fool had knocked his lamp to the floor.

She had to move fast or the whole room would be ablaze; already the fire had licked up to take hold on a corner of the bedspread. Johnson slammed her candle on the dressing-table and shouldered the man aside.

For a split second she considered throwing the bedclothes over the flames then she would only have to find more bedding and spend half the night making up the bed again. She snatched off her dressing-gown, dropped it over the mess of broken glass and burning kerosene — she didn't think the sight of her pink flannelette pyjamas the stuff to incite lust in strange men — and pulled the burning bedspread to the floor so she could stamp on it.

The man peered at her as though trying to see through fog. 'Thang you,' he said. 'Akshiden, yunnerstan.'

She lifted her candle and saw he was Clive Wishart, a man she had encountered briefly on the night of the murder. He'd been waiting to catch the train to the city then. What was he doing now?

'I didn't imagine you did it on purpose.' Just as well the fire was now extinguished or he could have been at risk of igniting his breath; he was very drunk. She almost gagged on the stench of burning wool as she bundled up the charred remains of her dressing-gown. 'You'd better open the window. I'll get a dustpan.'

She also brought a second candlestick. When she had swept up the remains a black hole eighteen inches across was revealed in the linoleum, where scorched wooden floorboards showed through. It could have been worse.

'Try not to knock over your candle,' she said as she left.

The incident had changed her mood. She felt light-hearted, almost light-headed, as she crawled into bed. That would show the capricious fates she could still control the course of events when she wanted to.

70

On Friday morning Hugh sat in the dining-room, a plate smeared with the remains of his bacon and eggs before him, picking his teeth with a match and watching Johnson pour his third cup of tea. An unpleasant smell of burning hung in the air this morning and tea washed it temporarily from his palate.

'Thank you,' he said. She made no answer; back straight, she carried the teapot from the room. Whenever she was forced to wait on him she radiated a cold hostility: to mask a guilty conscience, he supposed, seeing that he still believed she had the ring hidden somewhere and his suspicions undoubtedly showed.

Bowler came to the doorway and beckoned impatiently with his arm.

Hugh stood. 'What is it?' He gulped his tea, set down the cup, and joined Bowler.

'Horry Beadnall is here. He's all steamed up about something he thinks we should know, though he won't tell me, he wants us both there. I'll bet he thinks he's solved the case for us.'

'Be nice if he has. I for one won't grudge him the kudos.'

In the police station, in the cramped space between the door and the counter, and under the slightly disdainful gaze of King George V in full naval fig framed on the back wall, Horry Beadnall paced to and fro, as though the news he carried was too unsettling for him to keep still.

The two policemen nodded to him and went behind the counter; Bowler sat at his desk and started pulling out drawers looking for the right form, while Hugh put his hands on the counter and faced Horry.

'You have something to tell us?'

'We got a copy of my father's will in the post yesterday,' Horry said. He thrust his hands into his pockets, took them out again, rubbed a hand over his face. He glanced at Bowler. 'You're writing this down?'

'Of course. You tell us, we write it down, you read it to be certain we aren't making anything up, and then you sign it.'

'You want to tell us something about the provisions of the will?' Hugh prompted. 'Something surprising?'

'Not about how the farm was left. We already knew that, Father always said he'd leave it jointly to me and Leon.' Horry compressed his lips, as though he wasn't completely satisfied with this disposition. He shook his head and continued, 'And we knew about Lilian's legacy. We expected all that. What we didn't know was that Father's first wife had money of her own, and when she died she left it to him in trust for her daughter Helen. Or Helen's children, her 'issue' or whatever they call it, you know how these things go.' Horry paused, apparently waiting for some reaction from the policemen. He prompted, 'That means now it goes to Diggory Kenrick.'

Horry didn't add how furious they all had been — still were — not only to discover the existence of this sum they couldn't touch, but also to realise how that *bloody* old pest Silas had been spending the interest off it all these years without telling them of his added income.

Bowler could sense some of the anger in Horry. He said, 'So Kenrick inherits under his grandfather's will. You were there when he told me he was sure he wouldn't get a bean.'

'How much?' demanded Hugh.

'Nearly ten thousand bloody pounds,' Horry said savagely. 'Christ! It's a bloody fortune! Though Kenrick was right as far as the will goes — Father left him nothing. It came from his grandmother, Father's first wife, so Father only held the money in trust. Knowing the old pest it's a wonder he didn't embezzle the lot.' Horry paused, possibly, Bowler thought, to grind his teeth. 'What I'd like to know is if that bastard Kenrick had any idea this money was coming to him on Father's death.'

'Naturally we would too,' Hugh said. 'And now we will find out. Look, thanks for telling us this. Now we need the name of your father's lawyer.'

When Horry had gone over the story twice more to make sure they had missed none of the implications, and sworn a few fearsome oaths against his nephew Diggory Kenrick, at least some of them fuelled by a bitter envy, Bowler handed him a statement to sign. After that, he departed.

Hugh waved the paper to dry the ink. 'That's a tidy little sum. I'd almost commit murder for that myself.'

'And we know Kenrick is having difficulties making ends meet at present,' Bowler said.

'We do?'

'No, perhaps I haven't got round to telling you. That's the word from a farmer mate of mine, Archie Davidson. He told me some time back. Kenrick's buying a couple of cows from him, going to send away cream cans to the buttere factory in Edgerton to supplement his income.'

'Interesting,' Hugh said. 'Now if we can prove he knew about this . . .'

'If there are lawyers involved, they can probably tell us how much he knew. What do you want to do now? Ring the lawyers? Or tackle him?'

'First the lawyers. Then we'll know our next move.'

71

Bowler walked down the passage to where he could hear his wife thumping saucepans about in the kitchen. Brought up in a household where meals involved no effort on the family's part yet always appeared on the table as though by magic whenever needed, Joan still resented the time she spent in preparing and cooking food.

When she had chosen to marry her soldier, however, she had known the life she would lead, and in her code one did not complain of one's obligations or fail in them — only now and then the saucepans suffered.

As he entered she turned from the sink and smiled on her husband. He crossed to her, moved the saucepan from her grip to the sink, and took her in a tight embrace.

She pressed her face into the side of his neck. 'Darling.'

Over her head he looked through the window at the paddock, where his circuit of jumps still stood gleaming white in the sun. Thankfully he could no longer see the horse's carcase lying by one of them.

After the accident — after the death of Imshy, even in his mind he mustn't try to gloss over the hard facts — he had taken the other two horses across the road and shut them in one of the pub's paddocks before he set about digging a grave. He had chosen a corner of the second police paddock, as far from the house as possible and hidden from it by a clump of mallees. All his waking hours he had been conscious of the body of the dead horse waiting by the hurdle.

He had dug for most of Wednesday afternoon and in every spare moment on Thursday. There had been stones in the hard earth as he got deeper; he'd been sweating with a pick and a crowbar as well with his spade, and he had plied all his tools with a ferocity driven by rage. The exercise had helped him gain control of his fury at the horse's unnecessary death. He could scarcely believe such trivial events could lead to such a major catastrophe blowing up out of nowhere.

Rage had seemed more bearable than dwelling on what he had lost yet that had got him nowhere. He had to get over it.

Early that morning he had finished digging. In a windless dawn, as the eastern sky was layered in saffron and rose, he had roped the stiff carcase to the back bumper of his car and dragged it to the grave site. He had heaved it in. He had shovelled in the earth. He had tramped it down.

Tramped it down over that once-bright bay coat. Trodden his anger and grief into the earth, the cold earth, the clay.

Then he had lifted stones one by one from the heap he'd dug from the earth and had stacked them carefully into a small cairn in the middle of the mound.

He returned to the present, aware Joan was looking up at him and obviously wondering where his thoughts had taken him. He'd show her the cairn, later.

Now he said, 'The perfect wife. You've stopped nagging me about bloody England.'

'It isn't the right time. I haven't given up.'

'I didn't think for one second that you had. But I'm still not going. For one thing, I'd have to be polite to your damn brothers.'

Joan snuffled a laugh. 'And that exercise would do you a great deal of good.'

'No it wouldn't. I'd murder them first.' He wondered why the women in Joan's family were so normal when the men were such arrogant twits. He released her and went to explore the bread-crock and the safe, to find something for his lunch. 'We've got to drive out and see young Kenrick again as soon as Hugh's had lunch,' he told her.

'Has something new come up?'

'Yes. Apparently he gets some money now Silas Beadnall is dead, money his grandmother left him, and he knew he was getting it. So that puts him in the picture again and we have to talk to him.'

'Do you think he did it? That now the case is solved?'

'I wish I did,' Bowler said. 'But no. I don't think it's going to be so easy.'

72

Hugh and Bowler were going over their notes in the police station office, getting ready to drive out to Kenrick's, when an old sedan car stopped at the gate. Its original blue colour had turned chalky with age and was almost hidden beneath tan layers of dust and mud-spatters. The driver, a dark wiry man in his forties, bounced out and walked briskly up the path to the veranda. His tie flapped over his shoulder with the speed of his advance.

Bowler opened the door before he could knock. 'How can we help you?'

'It is rather,' the man replied, bustling in and obviously delighted to be given such an appropriate opening, 'a matter of how I can help you.' He looked around, nodded familiarly to his sovereign's photograph on the wall, and beamed in happy anticipation on the two policemen. 'My name is Tillerman.'

'Ah!' they said in unison.

'Call me Tip, everyone calls me Tip. Tip Tillerman. I was here —'

'We were hoping for a word with you, Mr Tillerman,' Bowler said. 'Come through and take a chair.' He waved the newcomer round the end of the counter. 'You were staying in the hotel on the night of the murder.'

Tillerman nodded eagerly. 'I've only just heard about it, knew I must talk to you people immediately. Immediately, you know. I've driven up from Aston this morning, flat out, wonder I didn't bust a spring or two, rotten road, but I knew you'd want to know what I can tell you.' He paused for effect, his eyes round with excitement, and took a breath. 'Probably I saw who did it. Saw who murdered that man.' He sat back, looking from one to other of the policemen and enjoying their expressions of surprise.

For a moment neither of the policemen said anything. Bowler's instinct was to mistrust anyone as cheerfully informative as Tip Tillerman.

Hugh said, 'When did you see this?'

'In the night, late,' Tillerman said. 'I'd been to sleep, and then voices in the next room woke me up. I looked at my watch, a luminous dial, it was after one, ten past I think it was, and I was going to bang on the wall, but then they stopped, and they were quiet so long I assumed the second man had gone away, and I tried to get to sleep again. But I was wakeful, a bit of tossing and turning, you know, and then I heard someone call out in the room next door, the sort of cry people make in their sleep. Not quite sure why, but that did get me up to open my door, and I saw Diggory Kenrick closing the door next to mine.'

This wasn't Bowler's investigation, so he was taking notes and leaving the questions to Hugh; who now repeated, 'You saw Diggory Kenrick.'

'I thought at the time it was probably his room so I asked the girl next morning while I was having breakfast — I had an early breakfast, wanted to be on my way, you know — and she told me that was the room Mr Beadnall was staying in.'

'You know Diggory Kenrick by sight?'

'Oh yes. I got talking to him at the dance, I was up at the Institute that night, I'm very fond of dancing, tripping the light fantastic, never miss a chance when I can manage it. We got chatting on about this and that, you know how it is, standing around between dances. I always get chatting to someone. Not a common name, Diggory, sort of stuck in my mind.'

'This man at the door — how could you recognise anyone? Did he have a light?'

'No, no, just the moonlight, shining in through the side door, must have been a bit of a gap in the clouds between the showers. Nearly full moon that night when it wasn't raining.'

'The side door was open? Didn't you think that strange?'

'Thought someone had nipped out to the lavvy, actually.'

'And you're sure it wasn't Beadnall you saw at the door?'

'Oh yes. Quite sure. Mr Beadnall was shorter than the man I saw, bit of a stoop, more thickset. I'd seen him the evening before in the passage, before I went up to the dance.'

'After the dance, did Kenrick walk back to the pub with you?'

'We didn't walk. It was raining that night, you know, heavy showers, a dirty night, I took my car. When I dashed across the road to get into it I saw Kenrick helping a girl into his car, a girl he'd been dancing with. Drove up to the railway crossing, didn't see where they went after that.'

Bowler looked at Hugh. Kenrick had stated he went straight to the pub when the dance finished. That was after they'd made him admit he didn't go straight home to the farm as he had originally claimed. He seemed to have lied about his movements from the start.

Hugh said, 'First you heard voices, at ten past one, then you heard a cry in the night. How much later was that?'

'Twenty minutes? Could have been half an hour. Actually I did look at my watch after he's gone and it was twenty to two, I think.'

'Could one of the voices you heard have been Kenrick's?'

'Oh yes, definitely a man's voice. They sounded angry, the two of them.'

'When you looked out, and saw Kenrick coming out of the room next door, did he see you?'

'I'm sure he didn't. He looked round very carefully, sort of sneaky, and I'm sure he'd have reacted somehow if he knew I was there.'

'And you're sure Kenrick was the man you saw?'

'Oh yes. Absolutely positive. I'd been talking to him only a couple of hours before.'

Bowler said, 'Two other men were staying at the hotel that night. How would you describe Kenrick?'

Tillerman thought about that for a moment. 'Tall,' he said. He pointed at Bowler. 'Bit taller than you, probably, and more your build than his.' He pointed at the more heavily-built Hugh. 'Not skinny but not hefty. Dark hair, needs a haircut, thin face. How'm I doing?'

'Pretty well,' Hugh said.

'What was he wearing?' Bowler made a note on his pad. If Tillerman was right it couldn't have been Horry or Clive: neither was as tall as he was.

'An overcoat, darkish. I saw him put it on when he left the Institute. Dark pants.'

'You could see him clearly enough to see he wore an overcoat, and not just a jacket?'

'Overcoats stop at the lower leg.' Tillerman sketched a shape in the air. 'Could only see a short part of his legs.'

Bowler nodded. 'Did you see which way he went, when he left Beadnall's door?'

'Which way? He turned towards the side door, so I had to shut my door or he'd have seen me.'

'Why did you do that?' Bowler asked. 'You didn't know then about the murder.'

'Not many people like being spied on. I didn't want a punch on the nose. Anyway, I heard his footsteps even though he was walking pretty quietly, and I risked another peep in time to see him going out the side door. He'd left it open, but he shut it again after himself.

Very very carefully, you know, so that he didn't make a noise.'

They went over and over his story with him while Bowler wrote it down, getting the details filled in, until they had a statement for him to sign.

'We've got your city address,' Bowler told him. 'I got it from Mrs Musgrave, when we weren't sure you were coming back this way. If we need more from you we'll be in touch.'

Tillerman handed back the pen. 'Glad to have been of help. If I have helped at all.' He sounded slightly miffed, as though he had been hoping for some greater effusion of praise and gratitude from the police than that which had so far been forthcoming.

'You've been a great help,' Hugh assured him, and went with him to the door. 'You haven't heard the last from us. And we wish everybody was as public-spirited as you are.' He patted Tillerman on the back and closed the door behind him.

Bowler screwed the cap on his ink bottle, dropped the steel-nibbed pen in the tray — he didn't let others use his fountain pen — and passed the statement to Hugh. 'Seems pretty straightforward.'

'I knew that bastard Kenrick was lying,' Hugh said. 'We've got him nailed now. He's only been admitting as much as he couldn't get out of, facts we've confirmed from other sources. I'd like to see him talk his way out of this lot.'

'He's got nerves of steel if he can murder his grandfather and then curl up in a chair under the same roof and go to sleep.'

'I think he proved in China there's nothing the matter with his nerves,' Hugh said. 'All the same, he could have been only pretending to sleep when Wishart saw him — he wouldn't want anyone thinking he was prowling about the premises in the night.'

'Clive saw him around three, when he got up to catch the train, over an hour later than Tillerman did. What possible reason could he have for sticking around after committing murder? You'd expect him to clear out fast, while the going was good. He didn't know he'd been seen.'

'Most likely he really did want to sleep, then.'

'And why would he go out through the side door if he intended to sleep in the lounge?'

'Because that was the quickest way to get clear of Beadnall's door, probably. Once outside, if he was seen he had no connection with any room. If he'd stayed inside he must have thought someone in one of the other bedrooms might have chanced see him and drawn conclusions.'

'It's only circumstantial,' Bowler said. 'A good lawyer could make it bloody hard to get a conviction.'

'He's been identified in the right place at the right time and he's got a whopping great motive. I don't think we'll get anything better than that.' Hugh snapped his fingers. 'Those scratches! Don't forget those scratches on his wrist. All right, let's get out there and grab him. Let's see what the bastard has to say this time.'

73

They took Hugh's car. Bowler said, 'Once I've lined up a couple of JPs and got him remanded to town, will you take him with you when you drive back?'

'No, not on my own. It's a fair way, and he'd have to go in handcuffs. I'd prefer he went by train. Can you do that?'

'If I have to,' Bowler said without enthusiasm. Hugh grunted.

At the cottage they couldn't see the dog, so they didn't expect to find the owner at home. They only knocked as a matter of form.

They heard footsteps behind the door. As it opened they were watching a spot level with their own heads, expecting Diggory Kenrick, then were taken aback when they had to lower their gaze to meet the dark eyes of a woman, a much shorter woman.

She had a pale skin and a mass of crinkled black hair down her back; her feet were bare and, although it was the middle of the afternoon, she wore a faded pink silk dressing-gown, flounced and trimmed with lace. She wasn't wearing much else except some strange Oriental scent, if Bowler was any judge.

Hugh said, 'Good afternoon, Miss. We are looking for —'

'Mrs. I am not Miss, I am Mrs. I am Mrs Kenrick.' She turned her suspicious gaze on Bowler. 'What do you want?'

Young Kenrick was married? This was the first Bowler had heard of it. He relied on Em at the pub with her infallible nose for gossip to keep him informed of such goings-on among his parishioners; surely she hadn't missed anything quite so juicy as this.

The woman had a marked accent, was obviously foreign, and, in her present déshabillé, was equally obviously considerably older than Kenrick. Bowler wondered where on earth Kenrick had acquired her. And when. Not recently, and not locally. Where had she been during the last couple of years, when he had been living a bachelor's life in Kularook? And the life of a pretty fancy-free bachelor at that, if half what Bowler had heard was true.

Hugh said, 'Police. We are looking for Diggory Kenrick.'

'Police?' On the second syllable the woman's voice rose dramatically. 'What you want with my husband?'

'Where is he?'

'My husband is at the house. Not this serf's hut, the house.' She clutched Hugh's sleeve and leaned to peer up into his face, opening her eyes wide for maximum effect. 'Why you want him?' she demanded, her deep voice rising in alarm. 'Tell me!'

'All in good time. We'll see him first.' Hugh shook off her hand. They turned away.

The dog began barking as they walked up the slope towards the house, though it stood aside and merely waved its plumed tail at them when they banged on the back door.

Kenrick shouted, 'Come in.' He was in the kitchen, reaching over the stone sink to paint the wall behind it a pale cream. The room held a kitchen table, on which chairs had been stacked, and two cupboards pulled away from the walls. In one corner worn linoleum, green darkened almost to black, had been peeled back from the floor so roughly that pieces had broken off. Obviously Kenrick intended replacing it, not re-laying it. Piled in another corner was a tangled nest of grey blankets topped with a stained pillow without a case, as though he had slept there.

Perhaps he hadn't slept much; he looked tired and rather forbidding when he swung to face them. 'Not you lot again. What the devil do you want this time?' He wiped his brush on a rag and laid it across the paint tin. 'Haven't you got anything better to do?'

Hugh said, 'We want you to come with us, answer some questions.'

'Ask away, then.'

'Not here. Back at the station.'

'I'm busy.'

'If you don't come, I will arrest you and take you in whether you like it or not.'

'What?' Kenrick stepped back. 'You can't be serious.'

'Perfectly serious.' Hugh reached to put a hand on his arm. Kenrick batted it aside and jumped out of range; he stood braced, scowling.

Bowler said, 'Don't be a fool, Kenrick. There are two of us.'

After a moment the young man gave a small abrupt nod and relaxed. Shouldering aside Hugh's attempts to take his arm he walked back to the sink, where he put the brush into a jam tin of thinners, replaced the lid on the paint tin, and hammered it in place with the handle of a screwdriver lying beside it. His movements were deliberate and controlled and they made no move to stop him.

This time when Hugh took his arm he didn't resist, though once outside he pulled free and turned to shut the back door. The Yale lock clicked. 'Nosy neighbours,' he explained. He stood facing them. 'Look, I've told you before, I did not kill my grandfather. This is stupid.'

'We'll talk about that when we get to the station,' Hugh said. 'Now we have some new evidence.'

'What new evidence?' When they didn't answer he shrugged, resigned, and walked down the hill towards the car with a policeman on either side of him. 'You'll have to let Katya — let my wife know what's going on.'

Bowler said, 'We will. She was a bit of a surprise. You've kept pretty quiet about her.'

'I thought she'd left me. Permanently.' He grimaced. 'But bless her grasping little heart, she finally got wind of this farm I've inherited, and where she comes from land means wealth. Well, before the revolution it did, and she knows we haven't had any revolutions here lately. She had visions of big houses and serfs to do the dirty work, so to find I was only a poor bastard of an Aussie battler was not what she expected.'

'Does she know about this money you're inheriting from your grandmother?' Bowler asked.

Diggory swung to face him. 'How the hell do you know about that? I only got the letter yesterday.'

'But you knew before that.'

'No I didn't.'

'The lawyers say otherwise.'

'The devil they do. Anyway, for god's sake don't tell Katya.' He added glumly, 'Though I suppose I'll have to increase her allowance if I find I can afford it.'

Now dressed in a form-fitting black jacket and skirt, her hair piled on top of her head, she was waiting for them at the door of the cottage. She flew to her husband, gripped both his arms, turned her face up to his. 'Where are you going? What is happening? When will you be back?'

Kenrick stood straight, hands by his side, and nodded towards Hugh. 'You'll have to ask him.'

Hugh said, 'He won't be back.'

This was news to Kenrick as well as to his wife, Bowler could see. She started screaming, hammering his chest with her fists, screaming and shouting in some foreign language and on the edge of full-blown hysteria, and all the policemen could do was step aside and let

Kenrick deal with her.

At first he answered with short words in her own language, then longer sentences. It took him some time to calm her. Then he said, 'I've just told her that Jack Pitts at the bank will look after her. I'll get him to come out tomorrow and help her sort out whatever she wants to do.' To his wife he added, 'Don't worry, he'll arrange whatever you decide. Take your time, think about it. In the meantime, don't forget to feed the dog and shut up the chooks tonight.' He turned to Hugh. 'I'll be allowed to do that? Fix this with Jack? He's the bank manager here, he knows all about her — I had to arrange with him to send her allowance every month.'

'Of course,' Hugh said.

'See? You don't have to worry. I'll make sure Jack looks after you. And you'll have the car if you want anything from Kularook.' When the dog tried to follow him he said, 'Stay.'

Bowler would have liked to know what was going through Kenrick's head, how he felt about Hugh's blunt announcement that he wasn't coming back. His set face gave nothing away.

74

Bowler glanced at the big round clock on the wall when they brought Kenrick into the police station. Four-thirty. The children should be home from school by now though he couldn't hear them in the house or in the yard. They must have gone off to play with their mates somewhere. He hoped Tom had checked with his mother that she had no need of his services until teatime.

They sat Kenrick in a chair at the desk behind the counter. During the drive in Hugh had refused to tell him their reasons for arresting him. That could wait until they could interrogate him formally at the station, with everything written down, everything by the book.

As soon as they'd told him his rights Hugh said, 'Now tell us why you murdered your grandfather.'

'Get stuffed.'

'You were seen,' Hugh said. 'We have a witness. Someone saw you leaving Silas Beadnall's room in the night.'

Kenrick gazed at him reflectively while he considered this. Twittering sparrows were foraging in horse droppings along the street outside. The clock ticked.

Hugh insisted, 'You were *seen.*'

'Every bastard in Kularook must have been watching me that night,' Kenrick said bitterly. 'A whole team of them, taking turns.' He heaved an exasperated breath. 'So what? He was alive when I left him.'

Bowler was surprised by this admission, and a little disappointed. He hadn't believed Kenrick a murderer. And of course he would say his grandfather was alive — what other answer could he possibly make? He took his pen from his breast pocket, uncapped it, made a note on his pad.

Hugh said, 'Why did you kill your grandfather?'

'I didn't. I just told you.'

'If you didn't kill him, why did you lie to us? Say you hadn't been near him?'

'Because I thought you'd jump to the wrong bloody conclusions, that's why. Turns out I was right, doesn't it.'

Hugh said, 'You let us decide which conclusions are right and which are wrong. Now all you've done is make sure we won't believe a word you say.'

'Not something I foresaw at the time. I thought you'd fasten the murder on Leon or Horry and it wouldn't matter.'

'Fasten it on one of them? Not that one of them had committed the murder, but that we might think so and you would get away with it?'

'A bad choice of words. I thought one of my uncles was probably the culprit, and hoped the keen minds of the constabulary would discover which.' Kenrick had pushed himself back from the desk and folded his arms across his chest in an attempt, Bowler suspected, to appear at ease; yet he was pretty sure the hands tucked out of sight were clenched into fists.

'You've been lying from the start,' Bowler said. 'You told me you went straight home after the dance. Then, when we told you Wishart had seen you at the pub, suddenly you remembered that's where you were after all. Then you stated categorically you hadn't seen Silas Beadnall that night and now we have a witness, you admit you did.'

'You lot are so pigheaded you can't be trusted with the truth.'

Neither Hugh nor Bowler thought that worthy of an answer. Hugh said, 'You went to his room. Why? If you didn't go to kill him, why did you go?'

'Forget.'

'Don't get funny,' Bowler said. 'Tell us why you went to see your grandfather. You've been pretending you hated him too much to want anything to do with him.'

After a moment Kenrick shrugged. 'Wanted to annoy him, I suppose. He nearly had a stroke when he first laid eyes on me so there was always a sporting chance he'd really burst a blood-vessel this time.'

Hugh took a breath to control his temper. 'Try again,' he said. 'The real reason you went was to kill him.' Kenrick appeared to have withdrawn into thoughts of his own. Hugh barked, 'Kenrick!'

His head jerked up. 'Oh yes, my grandfather.' He appeared to collect himself with an effort. 'I prefer not to think about him. As it happens, I really did want to annoy him. Seriously.' He looked from one to the other of them, all innocence — far too innocent, Bowler thought. 'I'd just laid eyes on the bastard for the first time in my life, the bogey-man who had haunted my childhood as the personification of pure evil, and when I saw the light under his door I thought I couldn't let this chance go by without saying something to him. I wanted to look at him properly to see that he was just an elderly man and didn't have horns and a tail. And perhaps to remind him there were still people around who hadn't forgiven him. Look, I just went.'

Hugh appeared to accept that. 'So what did you say to him?'

'That I wanted him to know that throwing my mother out was the best thing he ever did for her, because she spent the rest of her short life with people who loved and respected her.' That answer came briskly enough to be true.

'What did your grandfather say to that?'

'He gobbled a bit, and then he ordered me out of his sight. I'd had enough too, so I went. He disgusted me.'

'Disgusted you so much that you killed him.'

'No.'

'Saw the flex lying there and killed him.' No point in being coy about the means of death, seeing that Em Musgrave, with her enthusiasm for gossip, had ensured that every man woman and child in Kularook knew how Silas Beadnall had died. 'Picked up the cord and wrapped it round his neck.'

Kenrick shut his mouth and closed his eyes. A car pulled up outside the hotel opposite; the door slammed, and brisk footsteps crunched away and dwindled to silence.

Bowler said, 'What time was this?'

Without opening his eyes Kenrick said, 'No idea. After one, anyway.'

'You said you went straight to the hotel after the dance. We know in fact you didn't. So what were you doing between midnight and one a.m.?'

'Bloody hell, hasn't anyone around here got better things to do than to watch my every effing move?' They waited. 'If you must know, I drove a girl home, raining cats and dogs, she lives across the line. Then the car wouldn't start so after buggerising about for hours I walked back across the railway yards to the pub.'

This at least tallied with what Tillerman had told them. Bowler asked, 'Which girl? You must know we'll have to ask her about it.'

Kenrick thought about his answer. Finally he said, 'Flo Gregory. But keep her out of this — it's only her bad luck I chose to do the chivalrous thing and drive her home.'

'We'll be discreet,' Hugh said.

Which was more than Flo was, Bowler reflected. Most of the local boys who drove Flo home were hoping for a good bit more than a few words of gratitude from her as reward for their chivalry. Had Kenrick been rewarded? A side issue, of no importance. Bowler said,

'What did you use to wind up the cord?'

'Wind it up? What do you mean?'

'Like a tourniquet.'

'Is that how it was done. I didn't do it, I wasn't there.'

Hugh said, 'You needn't pretend you don't know. You were seen.' Kenrick said nothing. 'You needed the inheritance from your grandmother. Plenty of other suspects were around to take our attention from you. You took your chance and killed him.'

Kenrick turned his head to look directly at Bowler. 'I did not kill my grandfather.' Then he shut his mouth, fixed his gaze on the desktop, and refused to utter another word in answer to their questions.

In the end they gave up. They let him make a telephone call to Jack Pitts, and then Hugh formally charged him with the murder of Silas Beadnall. Bowler said, 'This way,' and stood holding the door open.

Keeping the same stony silence Kenrick got up and went out where he was directed, off the veranda and down the side of the house to the back yard, where the single-cell lockup, in size and shape like an overgrown dunny, stood against the back fence. The sun was low in the west; their long shadows slid and rippled over the uneven ground before them. Bowler again opened a door and stood aside.

At the sight of that constricted space, nearly dark in spite of the small high window, Kenrick hesitated. Only for a second. He walked steadily in, turned around, and was facing the door when Bowler shut it on him, and locked it.

When Bowler came back, Hugh said, 'Even if he went to see his grandfather with no thought of murder in his head, the cord was just too handy. Once we established the cord was already in the room, the murder never looked premeditated, did it.'

'No. Now I'd better see if I can get hold of a couple of Justices, get him remanded to town.'

75

Tip Tillerman, staying overnight at the Kularook hotel again, wanted a bath before dinner — 'covered in dust off the road, you know' — so Johnson carried a bucket of kindling to the bathroom to replenish the wood-box under the chip heater. As she passed the front hall an imperious voice accosted her.

'You! Girl! A room. I must have a room.' A dark woman in a black coat and skirt stood by the front desk looking disdainfully around her. 'Now, it is now I want it. And my cases carried. And dinner. I must have dinner.'

Her accent was strange and she looked foreign in some undefinable way. Who was she and where had she come from, this abrupt woman? 'I'll tell Mrs Musgrave,' Johnson said. Resisting a strong urge to stand and stare she put down her bucket and went to get Em.

Johnson was in the pub kitchen loading the traymobile with crockery for the dining-room when Em, shaking her head in disbelief, came back from registering the new guest. 'Know who that is? No? Diggory Kenrick's wife, that's who. Throwing her weight around like a damn duchess.'

Johnson made no attempt to hide her surprise. 'What's she doing here?'

'Diggory's been arrested. So she couldn't possibly — sorry, I should have broken it more gently.'

Gripping the edge of the table in both hands, Johnson held herself upright. 'Arrested,' she said, wondering how her voice could sound so calm. Words jumped into her memory, words she had only half understood at the time. It's easy after the first one, Diggory had said. Had he meant Silas Beadnall was the first one?

Em was saying, 'Yes. She says they went out and got him this afternoon — two policemen, it must have been Bowler and this detective. So now she has come bolting in, because she couldn't possibly stay on the farm alone, she's far too fragile and sensitive.'

'Where is Diggory now?'

'In the lockup at the police station I suppose. Ask Detective Morgan, he's having a beer in the lounge.'

'No,' Johnson said. She wasn't going anywhere near that disbelieving man, not voluntarily.

Em said, 'I forgot to tell you, Miss Beadnall was looking for you around lunchtime today. Lilian Beadnall. Did she find you?'

'No, I didn't see her.'

'She had to catch her train. Why would she want to speak to you?'

Johnson didn't want to explain. The matter was private, between her and Leon. Yet if he had already told his sister she had better brace herself for the relationship being known more widely. And Mrs Musgrave deserved the truth.

'I've told Leon about my mother,' she said. 'But please, don't spread it around.'

'I thought that might be it. No, of course I won't tell anyone.'

'Thanks,' Johnson said, not realising she had just confirmed the suspicions of the second most dedicated gossip in the district.

She looked up as Bowler, who always used the back door of the pub, headed up the passage to the lounge.

He found Hugh sitting in the lounge with a beer in front of him

'No, I won't have a beer. The bad news is I can't arrange anything until Monday morning. I've got the Justices lined up for Monday, and I've fixed the time for ten o'clock. Ten o'clock in the cloak-room at the institute. It shouldn't take long.'

'Monday? You beaut!' Hugh jumped up from the small table. 'That's not bad news — I can go home for the weekend. If I start now I'll get halfway tonight. Then I can catch the Express back on Sunday night, take Kenrick to town on the afternoon train on Monday.' Beaming, he did a little jig of pleasure. 'I'll see my family tomorrow.' He lifted the glass and drained it at one draught.

'See you on Monday, then,' Bowler said.

76

Bowler walked back across the street to Joan, deeply thankful he didn't have to wait until tomorrow to see his family. Now he had time on his hands, all those hours he would have spent schooling Imshy, Joan was his strength and his comfort.

Not that she had mentioned the accident or said a word about the horse after they had knelt together by its cooling carcase. Then, as she had held his shuddering body against her own, she had made her only comment on the catastrophe. 'Bill, my darling Bill, what a *bloody* thing.'

Yet, although she invested the occasional kisses and hugs she bestowed on him with no more meaning than usual, he knew she expected him to understand that she grieved with him and for him. She was there, in his house, in his life, calm and accepting. He knew too that if ever he felt the need to unload his rage at his loss on her she would be ready to take that too, and help him manage it.

Without Joan's steadfastness over the last two days he wouldn't have been able to carry on working normally with Hugh while his mind kept distracting him with an itch about unfinished business, about something else he should be doing.

A false itch. Joan kept him anchored in the present.

She was in the kitchen when he walked in; she smiled at him, and nodded towards Tom, beside her, who was carefully — and very slowly — peeling a potato. 'We've been writing down his hours, Bill,' she said. 'I think you'll be satisfied.'

Tom poked the tip of his tongue from a corner of his mouth, as though in intensified concentration. His father, ignoring this provocation, picked up the penny notebook from the table.

'I'll check on the other two tomorrow. Your mate Ron and that devious little wretch Maurice.' He glanced at his son. 'You were going to say something?' Tom shook his head decidedly. 'Never mind, I can find out for myself.'

After dinner, while Tom was busy at the sink washing up, Bowler took a clean plate to the stove to dish up a meal for Kenrick. Then the thought of anyone having to eat in the lockup, in that dark and horrible little hole between those four steel walls, rather turned his stomach, and so he changed his mind. He went down to the lockup, opened the door, jerked his head, and brought Kenrick to his feet and outside.

'Dinnertime,' he said. 'Come up to the kitchen. And behave yourself.'

'Thanks.' Kenrick walked out stretching his arms and arching his back. 'I thought you might expect me to eat in that stinking little hutch and I've been in more salubrious places.'

'It's been scrubbed out with phenol since the last fool was in there.'

'That's what I mean — carbolic stinks.'

'Bad luck,' Bowler said. 'But I'm buggered if I'll prop up the door while you eat so that I can take the lantern when you've finished.'

Kenrick smiled, as though he saw through this attempt to disguise an act of kindness. 'Thanks anyway.'

Bowler sat his prisoner at the kitchen table and put a plate of boiled potatoes and Joan's watery Irish stew in front of him. 'Are you going to stay put? I'd better find you a blanket or two.'

Kenrick appeared to give the matter serious thought. Eventually he nodded. 'I'll stay.' Then he grinned at Tom. 'You can watch me for your dad.'

77

Johnson wheeled the traymobile into the dining-room. Diggory's wife was at a table by herself. Mr Tillerman had seated himself with the only other guests, a young married couple staying overnight to break the long drive to Mount Grenfell. They didn't seem to mind his non-stop chatter.

'Just luck, really, that I knew who he was,' Tillerman said, leaning back to allow his dinner to be put before him. 'I'd been talking to him at a dance at the institute earlier, saw him put on his overcoat at the end, so I recognised him instantly. Coming out of the room where the murder was committed.' He lowered his voice confidentially. 'I overheard the two policemen in the lounge just now and apparently he's admitted it. Once he knew he'd been seen, you know.'

A plate in either hand, Johnson froze. Diggory — It couldn't be true.

'Admitted to murder!' the young wife said, suitably agog. She was small, with blue saucer eyes and a lot of almost frizzy blond curls. 'Thank you,' she added, as a steady hand lowered a plate in front of her.

'Well, he admits he went to see his grandfather, which amounts to the same thing. Yes, the murdered man was his grandfather, didn't I say?'

'How shocking,' said the husband comfortably. A solid young man, also fair, he had the air of one not easily shocked. He nodded his thanks to the waitress.

'Really!' breathed his wife, leaning across the table as though avid for more details.

'He's locked up now, they're going to take him to town on Monday.'

'Tea?' Johnson interrupted. She hoped she didn't sound as disconnected with reality as she felt.

'Girl! Where is my dinner? Why have I not yet my dinner?' Diggory's wife beckoned vigorously.

'Coming.' Johnson set out three cups, poured the tea, then took her trolley to the other table.

'What is this?' Diggory's wife — Mrs Kenrick, that's who she was, Mrs Kenrick — peered short-sightedly at her plate.

'Lamb chops and mashed potato, Mrs Kenrick.' Johnson kept her voice low. She didn't want that man Tillerman bouncing over, all excited to meet a murderer's wife. Luckily the wife herself spoke in a strange deep growl, not easily understood.

'You know me?'

'No. I know who you are, though.'

'You know perhaps my husband.'

Johnson said carelessly, 'I have met him. Do you want tea? I can make you lemon tea if you like.'

Russians were supposed to like lemon tea. Em had assured her this middle-aged female was Russian. She looked years older than Diggory. Did late thirties count as middle aged?

Why had he gone to his grandfather's room in the night when he told her he was going to sleep in a chair in the lounge? Had he murdered Silas Beadnall?

She wanted to speak to him, ask him straight questions face to face. He wasn't far away, just across the road behind the police station in that strange corrugated-iron box, yet he was so far from her reach he might as well have been in another country. She didn't like thinking of him caged like that.

'No tea.' The woman had begun eating; with her mouth full she gestured with her fork to stop Johnson leaving. 'That man is talking about my husband?'

'Yes.'

'He saw my husband? When he went to kill the man?'

'So he says. Mrs Kenrick, are you going back to the farm tomorrow?'

'Never. Never will I go back. I am treated badly, my husband has left me all alone.'

'He didn't choose to be arrested.' Perhaps she had sounded more partisan than she had intended because Diggory's wife gave her a hard, suspicious look.

'So that man who talks so much saw him. He is angry too quick, my husband.' As though Johnson had protested she added, 'You do not know him in the war. Those years in China.' Her manner was faintly superior: she owned Diggory; she had shared his past.

Johnson said, 'Did you bring the dog with you?'

'Dogs I do not like. Dirty.' Smiling a little, she turned her head to stare up at Johnson.

Her expression was brightly malicious. Somehow she must be seeing that Johnson's interest in the dog — or her husband — was more than casual. 'I will not be followed. I tie it to the table. I see a belt of my husband, I buckle it. The dog is tied up short, it is stopped.' Knife and fork suspended, she continued to stare for several moments.

Johnson kept her expression blank. 'Is someone going to untie it?'

'I see my husband's bank in the morning. The man there, he can arrange it.' She lowered her gaze. 'He will arrange other things as well,' she said with satisfaction. 'I will go when the money is arranged. You will be pleased?'

'Nothing to do with me,' Johnson said. The woman saw too much. And why the devil couldn't she use Diggory's name? 'My husband' this, 'my husband' that: she was making sure nobody was in any doubt who he belonged to. Johnson turned away.

'One moment.' Mrs Kenrick grabbed a handful of her skirt and tugged her backwards. 'I have telegrams must be sent.' She began rummaging in a large handbag on her lap.

Johnson loomed over the table, so outraged she couldn't utter the furious protests burning in her brain. This arrogant woman had laid hands on her, pulled at her as though she were a dog on a leash. After a moment she unclenched her teeth enough to say reasonably calmly, 'The post office is shut. They will have to go in the morning.'

'The morning? Well if they must.' Mrs Kenrick thrust a sheet of paper into Johnson's hands. 'In the morning. Early.'

The writing was in block letters. 'And the money to pay for them?'

'The hotel sends them. A courtesy, surely.'

'I don't think so.' Johnson dropped the paper on the table. 'Send them yourself.' She grabbed the handle of her traymobile and stalked out.

As her fury subsided she remembered the dog Magnus, held by a man's belt looped through its collar and around a table leg. She didn't like the thought: the poor brute would hardly be able to move. And left like that all night —

In the kitchen she explained her concern to Em.

'She's a piece of work all right,' Em said.

'His car's outside, and she's not going to use it. After they've finished dinner and I've cleaned up here, I could go out and untie the dog.'

'Thus earning Diggory's undying gratitude.' Em poured custard over the last plate of tinned apricots. 'I suppose now you've seen

Lady Muck in there, you think he was justified in leaving her. Don't forget he married her first. His choice.'

'I know, I know. But what about the dog? It could choke itself.'

'Check with Bowler, whether you can help yourself to the car. If he says yes, you might as well go.'

78

Bowler came out onto his back veranda and closed the wire door behind him. 'I don't think you can. Why do you want to see him, Miss Johnson?'

Johnson explained again about Diggory's wife, and the dog.

'I'll talk to him,' Bowler said. Three large hurricane lanterns stood in a row on a cupboard against the brick wall of the house. He lifted the glass on one, rattled the matchbox beside it to check it still contained matches, and lit the wick. 'Wait here.'

She watched the light bob across the yard towards the lockup. A door creaked; the light disappeared. Why wouldn't he let her go with him? She only wanted to see Diggory, not mastermind a gaol break.

A goods train was huffing quietly to itself in the railway yards and the breeze brought the smell of steam, and the sulphurous tang of coal smoke. Somewhere in the distance a cat squalled.

Bowler returned. 'Yes, Miss Johnson, Kenrick will be grateful if you would drive out and release his dog tonight. And he says the car is at your disposal for as long as you like. If his wife objects, refer her to me.' He didn't think it necessary to pass on that Kenrick was unsurprised 'that twisted little madam' had been unkind to his dog, or that he would be delighted if Full Stop removed the car before the same madam could flog it, along with everything else he owned.

He said, 'Why does Kenrick call you Full Stop?'

'Oh. That was a joke, the night he came to the hotel to sleep in the lounge. I wouldn't —'

'You didn't tell me that you saw Kenrick that night.' Bowler, very much on the alert, kept his voice level. 'I should have been told of this before.'

'I thought you knew,' she said. 'Of course I thought Diggory had told you.'

'He said he didn't see anyone.'

'Did he?' She frowned, somehow displeased by this information.

'He lied about a lot of other things, so I suppose it's no surprise he lied about that.' Bowler considered. He'd have to get some sort of a statement from her, what she'd seen, and at what time. 'Look, you'd better come up to the office, so I can make a few notes.' Holding the lantern high to light her way he opened the back door. 'It won't take long.' He saw her reluctance, and added with deliberate guile, 'You must understand we need to know everything that happened on Saturday night. Then we can be sure we have the right man. This way.'

As he intended, she followed him willingly after that.

He ushered her behind the counter, settled her in a chair, lit the big table lamp on his desk, and blew out the lantern. As he uncapped his fountain pen his gaze fell on the towel-wrapped bundle he'd stowed on top of the cupboard against the wall.

He said, 'By the way, I've been meaning to ask you — there were two empty glasses in Silas Beadnall's room on Sunday morning. When did you take them there?'

'I didn't. They're just the tumblers we put in the rooms with the water carafes. I don't know why there were two. I did take a couple of drinks to that room earlier, but I collected up those glasses during dinner.'

'I see.' The tumblers had been used: two people had shared a drink in Silas's room some time after the dinner party. He'd better look for recognisable fingerprints on both. Hugh should have done that. Had he shown the glasses to Hugh? Bowler couldn't be sure. The towel looked rolled up in pretty much the same way as it had been when he had put it there on Sunday. Damn. He'd better stop churning personal problems round in his head and concentrate on his job.

The girl was looking at him as though wondering where his thoughts had gone. He said, 'What time was it when you saw Kenrick?'

'I looked at the clock, it was a bit after half past twelve. About twenty to, something like that.'

'What were you doing out of bed at that hour?'

'Doing? Nothing. I woke up when Diggory came in, it must have been the back door shutting woke me. I didn't know who he was at first, and then I recognised him, he'd called in to see his aunt earlier, I'd seen him then. So I followed to see what he was up to.'

'I see. You followed Kenrick along the passage. What did you do then?'

'Well, I asked him what he was doing, and he said he'd come to sleep in the lounge because he couldn't start his car. He said Mr Musgrave wouldn't mind. Then we sat in the kitchen and talked for a while, and then he said he was going to the lounge to sleep and I went back to bed.'

'How long did you stay talking?'

'Not long. Twenty minutes at the outside. We pinched a couple of sandwiches that had been put out for Mr Wishart; he was catching the train. Plenty were still left for him, though.'

'Did you think Kenrick was angry?' When she shook her head he added, 'Did he have something on his mind? A bit absent minded, as though he was thinking of something else?'

'Not remotely. He was teasing me. Having a bit of a joke.'

Without a doubt Kenrick would know how to make himself agreeable to young women, Bowler thought. No wonder she didn't want to believe in his guilt. He said, 'Did he mention his grandfather?'

'Only that he'd met him for the first time that night, and was going to take care to keep out of his way so it never happened again.'

'And why did he decide to call you Full Stop?'

'He wanted to know my first name and I wouldn't tell him. I said I was Johnson full stop.'

Bowler didn't look up from his notes. Casually he said, 'And what is your first name?'

'Martine. I'm Martine Johns.' She caught his glance and smiled. 'It's no secret now I've told Leon. I'm Leon Beadnall's daughter. Illegitimate of course, a bastard. My mother wanted him to know about me.'

'You're very forthcoming all of a sudden,' Bowler said, more startled than he cared to show by these revelations. He was also impressed by the straightforward way she delivered the information: self-possessed, unembarrassed. 'Your mother —?'

'She's dead. She left me a letter. And Leon knows it's true, you can ask him. Though probably he doesn't want the news spread around so you'd better not tell anyone. Except Mrs Musgrave, she's guessed.' She gathered herself, ready to stand up. 'Is that all? Because I want to get to that poor dog.'

'Hang on, I just have to get this straight.' He read through his notes. 'He came in after half past twelve, you talked for twenty minutes or so, and he was in a cheerful frame of mind.'

'That's right. Only you're forgetting to add Silas Beadnall was my grandfather too. I thought you ought to know, that's why I told you about Leon.'

Bowler smiled. 'Do you want me to add you to our list of suspects?'

'Of course not. I just didn't want you finding out from someone else and then wondering what sinister motive I had for trying to hide it, and my motives weren't sinister. Just that I couldn't tell anyone until Leon knew.' She paused. 'Anyway, I think Detective Morgan has torn up his list. He believes Diggory murdered Silas.'

'And you don't?'

'Of course not,' she said again. She wondered why suddenly she was so sure. Because she had just realised that Mounted Constable William Brown also was by no means certain of Diggory's guilt, that was why: that gave her reassurance. The policeman was a dispassionate observer, not a rabid partisan as she was.

'That's all then. Off you go.'

After Johnson had gone Bowler sat at his desk, his notes before him.

He compared the times Johnson had given him with the times Tillerman had provided. Kenrick's could have been the angry voice the traveller had first heard in Silas Beadnall's room. A bit after one — that would be when he left Johnson. Then the loud voices had stopped for a while until a cry had disturbed Tillerman.

Had Diggory Kenrick spent the time talking more softly with his grandfather? If so, what about? Or had he left when he said he did, while his grandfather was alive, and then a second man had gone in and killed him? Tillerman perhaps had confused the time he saw Kenrick emerging from the room — perhaps that had been before the cry, not afterwards.

Bowler considered himself better than most in judging whether a man was lying. When Kenrick had turned from Hugh Morgan — making the point that what he said was for Bowler, not the detective — and looked him in the eye while he declared that he had not killed his grandfather, that had sounded like truth to him.

He'd better grab another interview with Tillerman before he left the pub in the morning. Probably now would be as good a time as any. He'd check the glasses for prints later. If Kenrick's were on either, it just proved he'd been telling more lies about his visit to his grandfather. If they weren't, perhaps someone else had visited the room later.

79

When Johnson opened the door of the shearers' cottage her torch revealed the dog Magnus lying panting, its head close to the table leg and one of the heavy benches overturned beside it; it looked past her at the door, as though expecting Diggory. Then its tail started thumping enthusiastically as she bent to remove the strap holding it. She sat on the floor, the torch beside her, and hugged it fiercely while it tried to climb all over her in a frenzy of welcome.

When they were calm enough she got to her feet and lit the lamp on the end of the table. Diggory's books had begun spreading again since she was there before. As well as on the floor they were stacked on one bench, on the table, on the wrecked couch in the corner. From the safe she took the tin, full of various scraps, she'd seen Diggory empty for the dog's meal. The dog frisked around her as she carried it outside and tipped the mess onto a leprous white enamel plate. She topped up the water tin.

It wouldn't eat while she watched. Inside, she opened a book titled *Working Bullocks*. A novel, it looked interesting: she might borrow it.

She carried the lamp into the bedroom. The bed was unmade, the air heavy with Mrs Kenrick's oriental scent. Johnson shut the door, pushed a few books aside, and settled on the couch in the kitchen.

After a while the dog scratched on the wire door, so she let it in. It sat down on her feet — actually on her feet, its full weight across her insteps — and watched the door. It seemed expectant, as though waiting for Diggory to walk in now his car was outside.

'Poor old Magnus,' she said. 'You're a good dog. Come on, you're coming home with me.' Then she remembered the chooks. She might as well shut the gate of the yard, if foxes hadn't already cleaned up the lot of them. She left the car beside the cottage and together she and the dog walked up the hill towards the house at the top of the rise. The chook-yard lay beyond it.

A misshapen moon was not long risen. She switched off the torch, easily able to follow the well-used track. From somewhere near the woolshed a mopoke was calling. The breeze rustled the stiff mallee leaves overhead.

She couldn't tell if all the hens were present and correct, or whether a fox had already begun its depredations. No feathers were lying about, anyway. She pulled the gate across the uneven ground and dropped the hook in the staple. She turned back towards the house and saw the figure of a man on the veranda, at the back door, working his arms as though trying to lever it open.

'Hey!' she shouted, at the same time that Magnus, barking furiously, leapt from her side.

The man bolted, with the dog gaining on every step.

After she'd called the dog a few times with no result she went to inspect the door. Splinters of wood had been levered off beside the lock; a heavy pinch-bar lay on the cement veranda. Diggory had shown her where he kept the key so she let herself in, though she wasn't certain why she wanted to check inside the house when she had so obviously interrupted the burglar, if that's what he'd been. All the same, she walked into the kitchen and shone her torch around.

Diggory must have been working in here. She saw a tin of paint in the sink, strips of linoleum pulled from the floor, a tumble of grey blankets heaped in a corner.

She lifted a chair off the table in the centre of the room and sat down to wait for Magnus to come back.

She couldn't relax in the hard straight-backed chair. After a while she lay down in the blankets. They smelt of Diggory, a rather sweaty Diggory. She dozed, half listening for Magnus scratching at the door.

80

'What happened to you?' Em Musgrave, arms akimbo, stood in the kitchen doorway watching her housemaid set a match to the fire laid in the kitchen stove.

'I'm not late, am I?'

'No,' Em conceded. 'But you've only just got home. I heard the car.'

'The dog ran off,' Johnson said. 'I fell asleep waiting. And when it got back it didn't seem worth uprooting.'

'So was the dog all right?'

'Pretty uncomfortable, nearly throttled but surviving. Pleased to see me, anyway. Then it ran off — after rabbits I think. I brought it in with me.' Johnson wasn't going to tell anyone about the man trying to break into the house. Not yet, anyway.

'We've got this concert party booked in for tonight. With Lady Muck still in residence and a couple of travellers booked we'll need all the rooms made up, even that one next to yours with a hole in the linoleum. You can take the hearthrug from the lounge to cover it up.'

'All right,' Johnson said.

'I hope insurance will take care of it,' Em brooded. 'Damn Clive won't, that's for sure. And Trotter was only trying to do him a good turn — when the bar closed he was so incapable Trotter carted him there and dumped him on the bed to sleep it off. So he repays us by trying to burn the place down.' Em shook her head. 'He hardly ever comes into the bar yet that day he was swigging whisky like lolly-water. As if we don't have enough problems.' She heaved a rather theatrical sigh. 'By the way, I've ordered you a new dressing-gown from Meyers. Should come any day now.'

'Thank you.'

'Though you'd better watch yourself. I've had complaints, you were insolent to one of our guests.' When Johnson didn't answer Em said, 'I realise you can't like the woman; at least you could be polite. Another time, refer her to me about who pays for what. I'll just stick her ruddy telegrams on her bill.' She smiled sourly. 'So as soon as the post office opens this morning you will trot up there like a good girl and send the damn things.'

'Do you expect her to pay her bills? She'll take damn good care Diggory pays.'

'Why the devil shouldn't he? She's his wife, for heaven's sake.'

With a comfortably long length of rope Johnson had tied Magnus to the front bumper of Diggory's Fiat, which was parked in the pub yard outside the old stone stables. At nine o'clock, with Mrs Kenrick's messages and a handful of coins from the pub's petty cash in her pocket, she went out and untied the rope from the collar, intending to take the dog with her to the post office for a bit of a run. Immediately it shot off like a racing greyhound, across the road, down the side of the police station, to the lockup by the back fence.

Johnson, following more slowly, stopped at Bowler's front gate when she saw the dog drop to its belly, its nose pressed to the crack of the door.

Could Diggory hear it? Probably he didn't know it was there. Still, the dog wasn't going to run off now it had found where he was. She turned and walked up the street towards the post office.

The first telegram she printed carefully on the form given her by the postmaster was to a hotel in Adelaide promising to send the money next week. On the second form she copied: HUSBAND IN GAOL STAYING HOTEL COME SOON into the spaces and added the sender's name KATYA. The address was to someone called Pollock at a North Adelaide address.

81

'How can you believe the little bitch?' Fran cried. In exasperation she leant over her husband where he sat at the kitchen table and shook her two fists in his face. She would have liked to shake him. 'Leon, Leon, she's no more your daughter than I am. She's got no proof, nothing, she's just trying it on, hoping you're soft enough to believe her pathetic story. Pathetic is right — it's got whiskers on it. Honestly, Leon, you can't be taken in by such tripe.'

Leon didn't look up; he went on adding up figures on the rain-gauge chart and transferring them to a ledger. He wasn't answering back; but then neither was he agreeing with her.

'Some trollop feeds her daughter a pack of lies and you go along with it. You're as weak as water, you fool. Stand up to her, send her packing. If you won't I will. She needn't think she's taken me in with her damn insinuations.'

'I knew her mother.' Leon put down his pen. 'When she lived in Kularook.'

'So what does that prove? Even if you slept with her, that doesn't mean this girl is your daughter. I'll bet she was playing around with half the men in town.'

Leon shook his head. 'No. That's just it. She wasn't. We had to go to extraordinary lengths to get time together. Anyway, she was in love with me.'

'How can you possibly know that?'

'I knew Celeste. You didn't.'

'No man could ever understand how devious her sort can be. You're all too gullible, too easily taken in.'

'Fran, listen. Celeste told me she was pregnant before she left, and wanted money for an abortion. Of course I had none — working on the farm for Silas, he never gave us a penny for ourselves. I always assumed he'd given her some money, and she'd had an abortion somehow. If this girl is really Celeste's daughter and she's the age she says, I don't think you can go on putting your head into the sand. She has to be mine too.'

'Dear old boy, I'm only trying to protect you. From your own good nature among other things.'

'You're not protecting me from anything,' Leon said. 'I'll be pleased to have a daughter.'

Fran felt a chill along her arms. Years ago she had told him she didn't want children, and had persuaded him — successfully, she thought — they were better off without a family. Now some unknown trollop had given him a daughter and he was pleased about it, for god's sake.

'What does Horry say?'

Leon picked up his pen. 'I haven't told him yet. Only Lilian.'

'All right, when you've finished that we'll walk over to the big house and see what Horry and Brenda have to say.'

'I can tell you now,' Leon said. 'Brenda will carry on exactly as you have, if not more so, and Horry will listen to me.' He paused, considering. 'Anyway, she won't be a complete surprise to him. He knew about the row I had with Silas over Celeste's pregnancy.'

'But —'

'I don't know why you're kicking up such a fuss, Fran. Martine hasn't asked me for anything.'

'Hmph. She's just softening you up. She soon will.'

'In that case, time enough to stack on a turn when it happens.' He flipped the chart to the next month's figures. 'I'm nearly through here.'

'I suppose you realise she has a motive for murdering Silas. If she really is his granddaughter she must have hated him — he would have murdered her before she was born if her mother hadn't had other ideas.'

'Fran, you're getting muddled. She came to Kularook to find me, and couldn't possibly have known Silas would be here too.'

'She could have seized the opportunity.'

'Dammit, she's not a monster. Look, all I want is for us to get to know her better before we make any judgements.'

As his brother had foretold, Horry took the news calmly and agreed the family had no need yet to get defensive, leaving Brenda and Fran to explain to each other why the girl's claims were outrageous.

82

Gwenny Wilson rumpled her short dark curls. 'No, Mr Brown, when you put it like that, I can't.' Her round face showed an almost childish anxiety. 'Maurice hasn't. It's — well Ralph thinks women's work is demeaning for a boy, so he won't make Maurice do what he promised. I can't make him. He never listens to me.'

The three of them were standing in Wilsons' kitchen. Coldly angry, Bowler turned to the boy. 'Did you think I wouldn't check? You have broken your word to me.'

Maurice Wilson turned his head away and looked down at the mottled blue linoleum floor. He was trying to appear contrite and not managing very well. The little sod had traded on his mother's inability to demand his help when his father backed him up. Obviously he thought he had got away scot-free.

Well, Bowler had a little surprise for them. For both father and son.

'Maurice,' he said. 'Look at me. That's better. You have two options, so listen carefully.' This would wipe the smirk off the devious little bastard's face. 'You haven't done the work for your mother you said you would. Your mother is not a liar, and if she says you haven't lifted a finger to help her, I believe her. So, you can come in with me now and spend this afternoon helping Mrs Borthwick, and then go there every afternoon after school for a fortnight and do whatever she asks you to. She's old, and a widow, she could do with some help, and you'll be in Kularook where I can see you.' He had Maurice's full attention now. 'On the other hand, if you don't want to do that, I'll take you to town next week to face a juvenile court and let them deal with you.' Judging from the boy's dropped jaw, Bowler thought he was shocking some sense into him at last. 'You don't make undertakings to the law and then not fulfil them. I was trying to let you off lightly. I doubt if a court would. Here, sit down.'

He dragged a chair from under the kitchen table and pushed Maurice into it. The boy looked sick; Bowler hoped he hadn't overdone it. His mother looked almost as horrified. He would have reassured her if he could have done it without reassuring damn Maurice.

'Mr Brown, I will, I —'

'Let's get your dad in to hear what you've decided.' Bowler had, with difficulty, excluded the boy's father from the initial interview. He opened the door and said, 'Ralph? Here a minute.'

Ralph Wilson, still affronted at being shut out, stalked in and stood behind his son's chair, a protective position. 'What's going on?'

'I will tell you what I have just told Maurice — if he disobeys me this time he'll front a juvenile court in Adelaide.' Bowler was, if anything, more angry with father than with son. 'He's coming —'

'Hey, there's no need to get nasty about it!' Ralph interjected, laying a comforting hand on his son's shoulder. 'There's no need for that! When all's said and done there's —'

'It's his choice,' Bowler said. 'Either that, or he works for Mrs Borthwick for a fortnight. Because he's proved I can't trust him, this time it will be in Kularook where I can see him.' He wished he could add, *And you've proved I can't trust you either, Mr Ralph bloody Wilson.*

'All right, all right, of course he'll work, of course he'll do it — we had no idea you'd take it like this.'

'Take it like what, for god's sake? You both promised. Doesn't that mean anything to either of you? And you had better get this clear — I do not consider I am asking him to do anything beneath his damn dignity. I do not believe that women's work demeans women, so why the hell should it demean men?'

In his head he could hear Joan's voice saying fondly, *Good boy.* He said, 'Maurice, go out and get in the car.' To Ralph he said, 'You can collect him any time after one.'

Ralph followed to the car. 'I hear you've arrested young Kenrick.'

'Detective Morgan has. That's right.'

'Clive Wishart was in town that night.'

'We know that. Are you suggesting we've got the wrong man?'

'You know your own business best.' A faint flavour, the merest whiff, of a sneer inflected Ralph's voice. 'Did you know Clive blamed Silas for the fire that destroyed his tractor and all his bagged wheat one year? Just waiting to be carted to the railway stacks, his year's income. Clive reckons Silas chose the wrong day on purpose to burn off a bit of stubble, though Silas always said Clive started the fire himself, with a cigarette.'

'Before my time. How long ago?'

'Seven, eight years.'

'A goodish while to wait.'

'Clive carries grudges forever,' Ralph said. 'Never bloody gives up. He's a woeful farmer, yet it's never his fault, it's every other bugger keeps cheating him. It's nearly as many years since I sold him a ram, and he's still whingeing I robbed him.'

Bowler said, 'And did you?'

'Course I didn't. You don't diddle locals.'

Oh yes you do, Bowler thought. If you think you can get away with it, you do. 'Apart from that incident, do you know any other reason why Wishart would murder Silas Beadnall?'

'Well, they were arguing over paying for a new boundary fence.

313

Horry and Leon put it up, and Clive hasn't yet paid his share.'

This scratching around for motives was beginning to sound like spite to Bowler. 'I know about that.' He'd heard Horry mention it that morning at the woolshed. He trod on the self-starter. 'Any time after one,' he said, and let in the clutch.

He wished he could ask the youth sitting beside him if he knew why that pillar of society Ralph Wilson was sooling the law on to Clive Wishart, but Bowler had a strongly-developed sense of fair play. One did not ask kids questions about their parents.

He had better ask Em. She could fill him in on any long-standing antagonisms between his parishioners.

Once Bowler had introduced young Maurice to Phemie Borthwick's wood-heap and shown him where she kept her axe he went in search of Em Musgrave, and found her as usual in the pub kitchen. She turned from whatever she was stirring at the stove to listen to his question; then she laughed.

'I always thought Clive was the aggrieved one. Mind you, whenever he catches sight of Ralph he starts ranting and raving as though it happened yesterday so I suppose Ralph has got sick of him. Oh yes, some years ago now, but most people can remember that little dust-up. Not funny for Clive, though most of the blokes thought it a huge joke. Ralph sold him a ram for a fat sum, supposed to have some fancy breeding, next best thing to a ram from a named stud. Well, perhaps its breeding was all right, only Clive reckoned the damn thing turned out to be a poofter and as much use to him as a wether. He swore Ralph knew, that's why he was selling it. Knowing Ralph, I'd say he was probably right.'

'I see. Thanks, Em.' The incident if anything gave Wishart a motive to dob Ralph Wilson, not the other way about.

83

The concert party, four women and three men, arrived soon after lunch, straggling across from the railway station with the smaller pieces of their luggage in hand. The leader, a middling-sized man with a humorous rubbery face and a banjo case over his shoulder, embraced Em like an old friend. His name on the posters was Penrith Parry.

'Good to be back, dear lady, lovely to see you again and looking so well, younger every day I do declare, quite our favourite digs this pub of yours, always look after us so well, spoil us my good lady says, Gladys, you remember Gladys.' The stout woman standing at his side responded with a practised smile; she patted the improbable golden waves adorning her head and said nothing. Probably she had given up trying to interrupt her husband years ago. He rattled on, 'Seems like yesterday, must be all of twelve months. Can Trotter collect our luggage? I'll go too, tell him what to bring here and what goes straight to the hall. Who has the keys to the hall these days? The storekeeper still? Right, I'd better see him straight away. We'll need to set up this afternoon.' He turned to Johnson, waiting patiently to show the group to their rooms. 'Show my good lady the room if you would, I'll be back when I've got the baggage organised.' He winked. 'Treat her nicely and she'll give you a free ticket.'

Johnson took this offer calmly: Em had already told her that the hotel staff received free tickets as a matter of course from Pen Parry's group. She hadn't yet decided whether she would use it. One of the younger men brushed his body closely against hers as he headed back towards the bar.

It had been deliberate. She glared after him. She saw that Parry had seen it too; he was looking after the man with a thoughtful expression although it hadn't interrupted the flow of his speech. 'It's a good clean family show, you know. And new numbers, we have a lot of new numbers as well as the old favourites, well the public expects them, they'd be disappointed if we didn't leave them in the program. New talent, too, dear lady, tell your friends we have new numbers and new talent. One of our young ladies hasn't toured with us before.' He patted Johnson on the shoulder in a fatherly way, almost as though he meant to reassure her, nothing in the gesture at which she could possibly take offence, though he spoke still to Em. 'Time presses, dear lady, now I must find your good man.'

Johnson picked up one of the cases and went to show the group to their rooms.

84

'Do you want to go to the concert tonight?' Phemie Borthwick asked her guests. 'I usually go. They put on quite an entertaining show. And their musical numbers are surprisingly good. The pianist in particular.'

'A concert would be pleasant,' Ada said. 'We don't get out much in town. Yes, a concert will be most acceptable.'

'You must come as our guest, old girl,' Joss said. 'Do we have to book our seats?' She exchanged a look with her sister.

The sisters had long perfected a system of silent communication between themselves. This time the looks conveyed their shared belief that an evening out would be a happy diversion for their hostess, who had been withdrawn and patently very worried indeed since the disastrous afternoon-tea party at the farm.

When they'd arrived at the farm house on Thursday afternoon Phemie had used a mother's privilege to walk in without knocking, and then they had been too embarrassed to let anyone know they were there. Because, as they stood in the front hall, they could hear Sheba and Muir in the kitchen at the back of the house in the middle of a loud and furious quarrel. They'd been shouting abuse at one another, dredging up past grievances, raking over old differences, reopening old wounds in a nasty, brutal, vindictive exchange. There had even been occasional crashes and bangs, as though small articles had been hurled about.

It had been some time before Stella, escaping from the war zone with her baby in her arms, had discovered the three women. She had taken them to the sitting room, and gone to warn her mother.

Conversation over the tea-cups had been stilted after that, although Sheba, smiling and chatting airily, had done her best. Baby Andrew in the end had salvaged all that was possible from the occasion: they could each admire him, respond to his gurgles and smiles, and pass him from lap to lap.

Now Phemie said, 'It's a good idea to book if we want to sit near the front. The institute doesn't have raked seats like a theatre. There'll be someone at the hotel this afternoon who can arrange it. Shall we take a little stroll?'

So it was that Johnson, coming back from taking a tea tray to Gladys Parry's room, found the three elderly women looking about themselves in the front hall. 'Can I help you?' When Ada explained their mission she said, 'Mrs Parry left a plan on the counter here. Mark off the seats you want, take the tickets that correspond, and put the money in that tin. Reserved seats are a shilling extra, she told me.'

She watched them while, heads together at the counter, they made their decision. Those two were her aunts, she thought. Great-aunts she had never known she possessed. In finding her father she had found a great many more relations than she had bargained for, though she shouldn't have been surprised. Just because she had never been surrounded by an extended family she shouldn't have expected Leon to be the same. As well as these two great-aunts she now had an aunt Lilian, an uncle Horace, and several little cousins she'd never met. And another grown-up cousin; though he was only half a cousin. She switched her mind from thoughts of half a cousin.

Had Leon told any of them about her?

She was surprised to find that she wanted them to know about her. She wanted them to recognise her as something more than a willing housemaid. Wanted them to see her as an individual, not some amorphous member of the servant class. She would rather be an embarrassment to them than invisible to them.

She had more or less told Leon she would let him decide how widely their relationship was known. And yet — after all, she didn't owe him any favours. How would these women react if she turned round and announced, 'Miss Beadnall, I'm Leon's daughter'. Would they regard her with curiosity? With disdain? With blank stares that looked straight through her?

The three women were taking a long time deciding about their seats. They seemed to be arguing over who would pay. Johnson walked to the front door, catching the scent of lavender water and talcum powder as she passed them.

A few piled meringue clouds drifted across the blue overhead. Sunlight laid a yellow patina like old varnish over the white metalled road. Accompanied by a pack of at least a dozen dogs, sheep dogs and roo dogs mixed, a horse and jinker was trotting past; staccato hoof-beats echoed off the pub's front wall. The driver, small, bald, and brown, raised his hand to her.

She was becoming irked by her servant role. She had needed a job while she found Leon; now that was done she could give notice any time. With care, she could make her savings last until the end of January, when at the start of the school year she would begin teaching in the post she'd secured at a privately run school in the Dandenongs, outside Melbourne. She must remember to reserve enough money for her rail fare.

She must give Mrs Musgrave enough time to find another housemaid, though. Em had been good to her, had believed in her. She owed the woman a debt of gratitude. Even her unfortunate advice had been kindly meant.

Even so, Johnson thought, she didn't have to give notice. The job wasn't onerous, the pay was at least as good as she could get in any non-professional job considering she got her keep thrown in. The only reason to leave would be this niggling feeling she was not meeting any of the Beadnalls on even ground. Not only would they despise her for a bastard, they would despise her for her lowly job.

Though it was hard to understand why, seeing that the work was no different really from that of any housewife — cooking and cleaning, washing and ironing, emptying the slops and making the beds. Why was she socially inferior because she was paid to do it?

'Excuse me,' a voice said behind her. She was blocking the doorway and Miss Jocelin Beadnall was waiting to get past.

'Sorry.' She stepped aside.

Joss gave her a friendly smile. 'Do you get time off for the concert? We are looking forward to it.'

Johnson nodded.

85

Bowler opened the door of the lockup. The black and white sheepdog — Kenrick's dog, he remembered — which had been lying outside, bolted past his legs into the cell. He heard Kenrick exclaim, and then start murmuring to the animal. He pushed the door wider.

'Hey, Kenrick, a word with you. This way.' Without looking round to see if his prisoner was coming he set out up the side of the house to the front, to his office at the end of the half-veranda. He opened the door and stood aside as Kenrick, closely followed by the dog, stepped past him.

Kenrick walked through the flap in the counter and took the chair Bowler pointed at. Although black-eyed from lack of sleep, unshaven, he appeared perfectly self-possessed. The dog sat and settled its weight against his leg.

'I thought prisoners were only allowed tame rats as pets. How come I get to have a dog?'

'The dog's decision, not mine. Your friend Full Stop at the pub brought it in this morning.'

'Thank her for me, if you see her.'

'Make the most of it, she'll have to take charge of it again in a minute. In the meantime, I've got a few questions for you.'

'Fire away. I've nothing better to do so take all the time you like.'

Kenrick smiled down at his dog and laid a hand on its head.

Bowler grunted. 'Kind of you.' He picked up the pages of notes he had made so far to check a couple of points. 'And this time, if it isn't too much to ask, try to stick a little more closely to the truth than you've bothered to do so far. Straight answers.'

'I don't know why you keep insisting I haven't been straight with you. Thanks to the self-appointed vigilante squad I've had to own up to every damn lie I ever told you.'

'Not all of them. Now I know another.'

Kenrick groaned. 'What now?'

'You said you saw nobody at the pub the night you went to sleep in the lounge. Miss Johnson says you chatted with her for some time.'

'For Christ's sake, does it matter? She can have nothing to do with this sanguinary business.'

'As she pointed out to me, she's another of Silas Beadnall's grandchildren.'

'She's what?' Kenrick was on his feet, leaning across the desk into Bowler's face. 'You're not serious!'

'She's Leon Beadnall's daughter. She told me.' Bowler didn't think he was breaking any confidences passing on the information to this young man, who seemed to be the nearest thing she had to a friend in Kularook. 'Her name is Martine Johns. Now Leon knows about her she didn't mind telling me, though for his sake she isn't broadcasting the fact too widely.'

Kenrick subsided into his chair. 'Bloody hell. Martine I knew, not the rest. She said she'd tell me later.'

'That makes you cousins.'

'Half-cousins. That's an idea will take some getting used to. Is she all right? How does she get on with Leon?'

Pretty obviously Kenrick's thoughts were all over the place as he assessed these new facts.

Bowler said, 'She seemed fine when I saw her, and I have no idea how Leon took the news. Enough of this. I have questions that need answers from you.' Kenrick was still shaking his head as though in disbelief. Bowler said, 'I want to know why you went to see your grandfather. The real reason, not whatever vague piffle you told Hugh.'

Kenrick idly rubbed round the dog's ears while he thought about that. 'All right. I don't suppose it matters if you know, and no doubt someone has already filled you in on the quarrel between my grandfather James and Silas. It was over my mother — James never forgave Silas for throwing her out, and Silas never forgave James for taking her part. Well, when I was young they used to have slanging matches every time they ran across one another, until one day James bailed Silas up and they had an almighty bout of yelling and shouting and swearing that lifted roofs all over town and left James shaken and Silas crowing. They never spoke again. After that James seemed almost frightened of Silas, and would never let me abuse him or go anywhere near him. Before he died I asked James why he was nervous of Silas, and he wouldn't tell me. I thought Silas might. That's why I went.'

'Did Silas tell you?'

'He thought it was deliciously funny that James had been afraid of him, but no, he wouldn't answer. He just said James knew if he didn't keep his mouth shut Silas would turn his family inside out. Sounded like some kind of blackmail to me. And before you start getting excited, I didn't murder him to shut him up.'

'"Turn his family inside out",' Bowler repeated.

'Probably thought he could lay some legal claim to me when I was young, after my parents died, something like that. I don't know, it must have meant he could get at James through me somehow. Or else that James had some disreputable secret he knew about, though I'd say that was highly unlikely. I've racked my brains and I still can't come up with an answer.'

'What about your grandmother's family, your mother's family?'

'Nothing disreputable there, far from it. A stuck up starchy lot, Sydneysiders, far too good to be true and far too important to take any notice of me.'

'All right, leave that for the moment. What time was this, when you went to his room?'

'Must have been a bit after one.'

'What did you see? Tell me everything, where he was, how he looked, what else was there, on the bed or on the dressing table. Start with the light — a lamp, or a candle?'

Kenrick closed his eyes, as though to see the room better. 'I had a candle I'd taken from the kitchen. Silas had a lamp, a small glass one, on a chair beside the bed. He was in bed, sitting up with the eiderdown round his shoulders; he had his glasses on his nose and he was reading, some Western with a lurid red and yellow cover.' He squeezed his eyelids together with effort. 'An electric iron on the dressing table — well, you know about that, Em says.'

'The electric cord for the iron?'

'Wound round the handle. Wasn't me unwound it.'

'What else?'

'Nothing else. A basin and ewer on the washstand, a water bottle and a couple of tumblers.'

'Sure about that? There were two?'

'Yeah. I had to shove them out of the way to put down my candle.'

'You didn't use them? Sit down and have a drink with your grandfather?'

'Are you out of your mind? I wouldn't share the time of day with that bastard, let alone a drink. I don't drink or break bread with my enemies.'

'So the glasses were there when you went in. Good. That's a great help.' Bowler wouldn't have to chase up those damn drinking glasses if they were already in the room before the murder was committed — before Kenrick or some other man strangled Silas with the cord from the iron lying so conveniently handy. He would still like to know who had used them, though they wouldn't offer any clue to the murderer no matter how many fingerprints dotted their surfaces. 'What else did you say to Silas?'

'I've already told you that. I told him I was glad he threw my mother out because it meant she and I didn't have to put up with him in my childhood. We had the two Jameses instead, my father and grandfather, a much better bargain. He was furious and told me to get out. I got. Back to the lounge where I spent the rest of the night in blameless slumber and didn't go near him again.'

'How long were you in his room?'

'Five minutes? Seven at the outside.'

There had been no candlestick in the bedroom on Sunday morning so Kenrick must have taken it when he left. 'You took your candle — was it alight or blown out?'

'Alight. I'm not a bloody cat can see in the dark.'

'A witness saw you leaving the room a bit after half past one.' When Bowler had checked with Tillerman the evening before the man wouldn't admit to any possibility of error in his original statement. He knew what he'd seen, and when. He repeated that it had been nearly one forty-five when he had seen the man in the overcoat, and even in just a patch of moonlight he couldn't possibly have mistaken Kenrick's tall, loose-limbed build for any other man. All the same, he had made no mention of a candle.

'Wasn't me. I told you.' Kenrick shook his head. 'And here I was thinking you were beginning to believe me.'

'Never you mind what I believe,' Bowler said. 'It's what a jury will believe that counts.'

'Shit.' Kenrick heaved an audible breath. 'Not a good thought.'

Bowler looked through the notes he'd made. What more could he ask? Nothing there proved that Kenrick was lying. Neither, of course, did it prove he was answering truthfully. He leaned back in his chair, his hands behind his head, while he regarded his prisoner thoughtfully. The prisoner stared back with a steady gaze.

Bowler sighed and got to his feet. 'Come on. You have to get back in your box now.'

Once the lockup door shut on Kenrick he went in search of his wife, and found her sitting at the dining-room table with a selection of her photographs spread before her. She had a trimming knife and board at one elbow, a cup of cold scummy tea at the other, and was studying a flashlit picture of a frogmouth through a powerful magnifying glass. Bowler paused, to admire the detail and beauty of the photographs. Some were like portraits of birds, some captured the grace of birds on the wing, some explored more a mood: the bird in its habitat. One, of three emu-wrens on a strand of barbed wire, he turned round with his forefinger, to see better.

She looked up. 'Finished giving him the third degree?'

'Joan, this isn't a joke. I think we've got the wrong man. What am I going to do?'

'Find the right one, stupid,' Joan said, and pulled his head down to kiss him.

Bowler, holding his cheek against hers, had to laugh. Such sublime confidence in his powers was as engaging as it was ludicrous.

86

A cold breeze was rattling the leaves on the street elms and whipping Johnson's hair into her eyes as she pushed through a cluster of men having their last cigarettes on the footpath outside the institute. Parked cars lined the street on both sides.

She became conscious of a looming presence, a tall man in her way. She tried to step round him.

'Just a minute.' She looked up. He was Bowler Brown. He said, 'Miss Johns, are you going out to Diggory Kenrick's place tomorrow? If you do, could you collect up a few respectable clothes for him? Hugh can hardly take him to town in paint-stained overalls and elastic-sided boots.'

'To town?' Adelaide was a long way off. While Diggory remained in Kularook his situation seemed contained, a bit of a misunderstanding where she could imagine a few easy words of explanation to Mounted Constable Brown could set him free.

Not in Adelaide. Adelaide meant officialdom, more policemen, a bigger gaol filled with criminals, an impersonal system of law and law-courts. That could also mean an indifferent system, full of more rules and regulations than one country policeman chose to impose. She had no confidence that the larger machinery of administration would recognise the individual in Diggory, and believe his denials.

She felt sick. 'What's going to happen to him?'

To Bowler she sounded frightened. 'He'll be able to brief a lawyer before his trial.' He wished he could tell her he shared her worries.

'He'll still be in gaol?'

'Unless his lawyer can get him bail. I must tell you, though, that's almost impossible in a case like this.'

'Oh.' She swallowed. 'Can you tell him — I mean, that I —'

'I'll tell him you were asking about him.'

'Thank you. And of course I can collect his things, as long as I can use his car. What should I get?'

'He's given me a list, and instructions where to find everything. And he asked if you would check the trough for water and throw a couple of sheaves of hay to the mare.' Bowler handed her a used envelope with notes pencilled on the back in Diggory's handwriting, the same she'd seen on the flyleaf in his books. Bowler looked around. 'Are you by yourself this evening?'

'I was going to come with Diggory.' She remembered that she had in fact refused Diggory's invitation, when she'd still been feeling defensive and disobliging. That attitude hadn't lasted long. Now she could imagine how pleasant it would be if he was beside her, making her laugh as he so easily did, making her heart light just by his exciting presence.

Diggory was locked in that corrugated iron cell against the police station back fence, and it seemed almost like disloyalty to be here without him. What was he doing, all alone there? Not much he could do: he would be sitting or lying on whatever bunk was provided with nothing to do except let his thoughts run wild.

Bowler said, 'I'm sorry about that.' He paused, his gaze on her face, as though considering adding something more. Abruptly he said, 'Excuse me,' and walked over to beckon Clive Wishart aside.

Inside, while Johnson waited in line to show her ticket to Mrs Parry, who sat at a small table in the foyer, she saw ahead of her

Diggory's cousin Stella, her baby against her shoulder, standing beside her father and a woman presumably her mother. The girl turned and smiled at her.

Johnson would have liked to speak to Stella, to explain that she too was Diggory's cousin. Stella would be able to share her renewed fears for him: fears so intense they ached in her viscera like a badly digested meal. By the time she entered the hall Muir Kenrick and his family had gone to find seats.

The hall was half full already; a loud hum of voices, punctuated by children's shrill cries, rose from the rows of seats set out on the polished hardwood dance floor. A voice called, 'Martine!'

She started; she hadn't heard that name in a long time, on only a handful of occasions since her mother died. Who in Kularook knew it? She'd told Diggory, yet he'd continued to call her Full Stop.

It was Leon.

He left the small group where he'd been standing, in the space behind the ranks of seats, and came over to take her arm, smiling down into her face with genuine pleasure.

'I've been hoping you'd be here,' he said. 'You must come and meet my brother. And my wife.'

This was going too fast for Johnson. She hadn't expected this encounter; she'd had no time to get her thoughts in order, no time to brace herself, before she met them in her new guise. Of course she had met them before, though they wouldn't count that: one wasn't introduced to domestic staff, one ran into them and ordered them about, and very often one didn't even know their names. She ran her tongue over dry lips.

She was surprised by her father's eagerness to recognise her, to introduce her to his family which was now also her family. Surprised and extraordinarily warmed. Her father wanted others to recognise her as well as himself.

Perhaps she would be able to learn affection for this unknown man.

As he made the introductions Leon had his arm round her shoulders, a possessive and also a protective gesture. She could smell Lifebuoy soap on his skin, wood-smoke on his jacket. Although previously she had shrunk from the idea of his embrace, the arm didn't bother her. In her present state of dread his presence was almost comforting.

She was so preoccupied with analysing her feelings at being so close to him she hardly heard the introductions he made.

'Unnecessary,' Fran said, stony faced. 'We have met Miss Johns before.' She turned and walked away.

Brenda said, 'How do you do,' very formally. She didn't offer to shake hands. 'I must find places for the children before the seats fill up. They need to be able to see the stage.' She lifted the toddler to her hip, beckoned to the other three children behind her, and followed Fran down the centre aisle between the rows of seats.

Smiling, Horry stepped forward. 'Don't look so alarmed — we won't eat you,' he said, and took Johnson's hand. 'Welcome to the family.' Left to himself, he might not have been so complaisant about recognising this unknown girl but he, being fond of his brother, had perception enough to see how important she was to Leon. 'And here are two more who want to meet you. Aunt Ada and Aunt Joss.'

The two elderly woman were looking rather bemused. 'We have only just heard,' Ada said, looking at Leon. Slowly she shook her head in a whatever-next kind of way, then inclined it in a small bow. 'He has threatened us in the most unprincipled way.'

Joss said, 'Not nearly brave enough to withstand him.' Her smile made plain to Johnson they were teasing her. 'Welcome, my dear. New niece and nephew, all in one week — exciting.' She did better than her sister, and kissed Johnson's cheek. 'Silas would be furious,' she added with great satisfaction. 'What a pity he didn't know.'

Ada smiled slightly. 'You are fortunate.' She didn't elaborate.

Even while she realised they were doing this for Leon, motivated by affection for him and not for her, Johnson was moved by their ready acceptance of her place in the family. She felt her eyes pricking. Before she realised what she was doing she had turned to hide her face in her father's jacket.

'Sorry,' he said, stroking her hair. 'I'm afraid I was a bit sudden, springing the family on you like this. My fault. I just couldn't wait for them to get to know you.'

'Leon.' Fran, her whole body stiff with anger, came up behind them. 'It is time we took our seats.' Looking up and meeting her gaze, Johnson felt as though two daggers and a tomahawk had flashed past her ears.

Phemie had been standing a little aside. Now she came forward and held out her hand. 'Phemie Borthwick,' she said. 'Your father's honorary aunt. Knew your mother when she taught here. Interesting young woman — you're very like her.'

Leon said, 'Come along and sit with us.'

'Another time.' Johnson wasn't going to sit anywhere near Fran. 'I'm with someone.' A rank lie. She wanted to spare him the necessity of choosing between her and his wife.

All the same, some gesture was needed to conclude the encounter without awkwardness. She stood on tiptoe and kissed his cheek.

She hadn't expected to be able to do that, and mean it, until some very long time in the future.

Since she had first been old enough to understand why her mother pretended to be a widow she had resented and despised the unknown man who had abandoned them. Then once she had identified him, making herself known to him had been meant as some kind of retribution.

She was astonished to find she was beginning to like her father.

87

The concert ran late. There had been long delays between the items, as though matters were not running smoothly backstage, and for the last sketch they were obviously a man short, as Pen Parry had acted one of the parts with the playscript in his hand. When the lights came up and the audience scrambled to its feet to sing a petition to the deity to save their noble sovereign, the time was nearly midnight. Johnson avoided all Beadnalls, and walked back to the hotel alone.

While she lay awake some time later, her chest constricted by fears for Diggory and her head a muddle of speculations about Leon and her other relatives, Johnson thought she heard someone trip over the big brass ash-tray full of sand that stood beside the desk in the front hall. If whoever-it-was hadn't been able to see it, that meant the hall was dark, and that meant Trotter Musgrave had counted in his guests like a good farmer counting sheep, and had then removed the lamp.

She had heard a car go past in the main street a short while before. This must be some benighted traveller looking for a bed. She waited a moment, listening to hear if Trotter emerged to deal with him, then picked up her small torch and padded up the passage on bare feet, reflecting that this time she was unlikely to find anyone as interesting as Diggory Kenrick waiting for her.

When she got to the cross passage she could see a man at the front desk holding a lighted match to read the registry book. If he was hoping for an empty room he was out of luck. She was about to step forward and tell him so when the match went out.

She was reluctant to confront this stranger. The man's face, what she had seen of it above the match, had not been reassuring, though she couldn't have explained why: only a slight youngish man, with a round face and dark slicked-back hair. In the pitch dark she heard his footsteps come further into the hotel.

He struck another match and turned along the passage to her left, holding his hand close to the doors to read the numbers. She was debating whether she should wake the Musgraves when a door opened, throwing a patch of weak candlelight across the carpet strip. It silhouetted the woman in the doorway as he slipped quietly past her into her room.

Silhouetted Mrs Diggory Kenrick.

88

One of the reasons why the Kularook Hotel was so popular with Pen Parry and his group was Em Musgrave's generosity in allowing them to sleep until late on the mornings after their concerts. She didn't expect them in the dining-room for breakfast, she didn't ask them to vacate their rooms for the convenience of the staff; instead, she made up breakfast trays and carried them down the passage whenever any member of the troupe chose to surface.

Because of this change in the pub routine Em told Johnson she could make her trip to the farm early as long as she was back in time to serve lunch. They would make up the rooms after that.

Johnson collected what she needed and went out to the car.

'What the devil are you doing with that rifle?'

She started, and looked up to see Bowler Brown frowning at her from the back of his wife's horse. She had been handling the canvas case gingerly as she crossed the pub yard.

The sun's rays, slanting from the east though the trees in the railway yards, turned the horse's bay coat to fire. The earth smelled fresh and damp with dew.

He slid off the horse's bare back, looped the reins through his arm, and reached to take the rifle from her. 'You don't know how to fire that thing, do you.'

It was a statement, not a question. She shook her head.

'Nobody should lay a finger on a damn firearm if they don't know how it works. Who does it belong to?'

'It's Diggory's. He left it here.' She wasn't going to tell this policeman why Diggory had left it there. 'I was going to take it back to the farm.'

'If there's nobody living at the farm you shouldn't leave it there either. I wish to god a few people around here took firearms seriously.' He pulled the rifle from the case, inspected the breech to make sure it wasn't loaded, shoved it back. 'You'd better leave it with me.'

'Would you show me how to use it?'

Still frowning, Bowler regarded her steadily. 'Why? What do you want to shoot with it?'

She couldn't explain that she intended to stay at the farm that night, and would feel a little safer with the gun for protection if the intruder came back. That would suggest she wanted to shoot a person, something Bowler most certainly would discourage. And she couldn't tell him about the intruder in case he became protective and wouldn't let her go.

She said, 'I am going to stay at the farm. That's why I am moving all my things, including the rifle.'

After a moment he said, 'Come along, then. There's a tree with a good fat trunk across the line. You can aim at that.' He led the horse towards the gate to the street. 'But you'll have to wait while I saddle up Isma first. My wife's going out after birds.'

Surprised, Johnson said, 'Does she shoot birds?'

'Only with a camera. She says she had more than her share of watching birds shot with guns when she was growing up in England.'

The dog Magnus, which had been sitting up in the front passenger seat of the Fiat, hopped over the door and followed them.

So Johnson, after a short delay learning how to load and fire a twenty-two rifle while listening to a forceful lecture on the safe use of firearms, drove out on the pot-holed road to Diggory's farm that fine spring morning in a mood of savage resentment. If she hadn't carried this burden of anxiety over Diggory she would have been enjoying herself.

She liked driving and didn't often get the chance. The sky was a cloudless soft blue, the sun was shining, and the paddocks were green and high with growing grain. Scents of earth and the mallees along the road blew through the car.

On a morning like this Diggory's disastrous predicament was an obscene affront against nature.

The dog lay down across the seat and rested its head on her thigh.

89

Bowler sat at the desk in the police station making a list of those people who, he believed, could conceivably have had a reason for murdering Silas Beadnall.

The night before he'd been on the point of telling that loyal girl Johnson not to worry over Diggory Kenrick, that he was sure now the young man was innocent. Though that would have been cruel, because Bowler knew that, whatever his own beliefs, Kenrick would have to convince a judge and jury before he was a free man again.

Unless he, Bowler, could find the real criminal in the meantime. He felt a desperate urgency. Time was running out. But where to start? Not many names were on the pages of his notebook. Although a lot of people disliked Silas Beadnall it seemed to Bowler that few had enough reason for murder. Outside the family, that is.

Old James Kenrick, if he were alive, would have been a prime favourite. Young James also, though he had died young. Now that Diggory Kenrick had convinced him of his innocence, that took care of the Kenricks.

Apart from Muir, of course. He, however, was on such bad terms with his nephew he'd never risk his neck to avenge a wrong done to that young man. Muir, in fact, appeared to have adopted the view that whatever lay between Silas and Old James was none of his quarrel, and to have kept on good terms with Silas.

Of the Beadnalls, it looked as though Leon was in the clear. Aubrey Venables had come round to the police station on Friday morning and signed a statement that Leon had arrived at his house after midnight on that wet and windy Sunday morning too drunk to walk straight, let alone saunter back to the pub on foot and wind a cord round his father's neck. He'd have had difficulty finding the pub, let alone his father's room. Fran had driven them both to his place, then had come inside to get his help. Together, he and she had dragged Leon from the car, supported him inside, rolled him onto a bed, and left him snoring.

So that left Horry and Lilian; and don't forget the wives, he reminded himself. Brenda hated Silas quite as fervently as any of his offspring. Did Fran? He wasn't sure about Fran. Her air of amused detachment didn't fool him: she was worried about something and after Aubrey's statement it couldn't be about her husband. She had been sober enough that night to walk back to the pub if she'd wanted to, though the weather would have discouraged most people. And he had found no wet clothes at Aubrey's the morning after.

When he'd told Clive Wishart the night before to come and be fingerprinted this morning, a very flustered Clive had admitted his prints would be on the two tumblers found in Silas's room. He explained he'd seen Silas's light on, late, a bit before midnight, and he'd taken a bottle of whisky and gone to ask Silas to give him more time to pay for the boundary fence because Horry was being bloody-minded and demanding instant settlement. Silas, however, had refused to intervene, so Clive had taken his whisky and his worries away and tried to sleep before train time, leaving Silas very much alive. He repeated several times that when he left the room Silas had been alive.

That time, yes, Bowler thought. But he could have gone back later. He didn't appear to have the guts to be a murderer, though you never could tell with someone as devious as Clive Wishart.

He'd better go over his notes of the interviews, to check if he had missed something. He was reaching for them when the wire door opened and Pen Parry hurried in.

'Are you the policeman?'

'Mounted Constable Brown.' Bowler got out of his chair and walked to the high counter. 'Can I help you?'

'We've been robbed.' Parry seemed to be short of breath, as though he'd been running.

'We? Who's been robbed?'

'All the members of my company. All our money, all our valuables.'

'Come through and sit down. Take your time, and tell me all about it.'

Parry almost threw himself into the chair. He clutched his head in a melodramatic way. 'I have nothing to pay them with. Not a farthing. That bloody McBain.'

'You think you know who did this?'

'I'm damned sure who did it. Look, I'll explain. We've been having a bit of trouble with one of our young men, and last night it came to a head and I sacked him. In the middle of the performance. We just couldn't put up with him any longer.'

'Why? What had he done?'

Parry fussed in his chair, pursed his mouth, open and shut it a few times. With finicking distaste he said. 'Lately he's been making himself disagreeable to the girls. I don't like to say — and getting worse no matter what we did, and last night he'd been drinking and it was, well,' Parry bit his lips, 'ah, well, most unpleasant, to put it plainly you'd have to say it was assault. An, ah, personal assault.'

Bowler pulled a pencil towards him, opened his notebook, and made a note. 'On one of the girls in your company?'

'Yes. So I told him to go. While we were all onstage, though, he

339

must have gone through our things in the wings, where we'd been using it as a dressing-room, handbags and pockets, anything he could find. We were tired last night, we always are after a show, and we didn't realise then. Now we know he must have come back to the hotel to collect his bag and went through our rooms there as well. All our money is gone, and all the women's rings and bracelets and trinkets and my wife's good wristlet watch.'

'Does he have a car, this man?'

'No. We all came by train.'

'So unless he left by train he's still around. Does he have any friends here? No? All right, I'll see if I can locate him.'

After he'd taken a description of the missing man and established that Parry and his troupe, hopeful that the thief would be found, were going to stay at the pub for another night, Bowler went out to his car. At the gate he met his wife just dismounting from Isma, and informed her he had to go out for a while. He didn't add how frustrated he felt at being forced to postpone his researches into Silas's murder; Joan saw it, yet knew him too well to think she could placate him.

90

Attended by Magnus, Johnson fed the chooks, topped up their water tin, and let them out for the day. Then she walked down past the cowshed to the haystack, sending a flock of sparrows exploding out of the grass before her feet, and threw a sheaf over the fence to the pretty brown mare waiting, ears pricked, on the other side.

When she saw the horse tossing the sheaf about in its teeth she realised she should have taken the twine off. She ducked between the wires of the fence.

Close to, the horse looked very large and powerful. Apart from stroking the noses of the big dray horses when she came across them waiting in the streets of Adelaide, Johnson had no experience with horses. This one, although constrained by no harness, seemed as docile as the Clydesdales. She bent for the sheaf, wishing she'd had the forethought to bring a knife, and worried the loop of twine from the packed stems of hay.

A magpie started warbling in the gums by the sheds. While the horse chomped, Johnson boldly stroked its shining shoulder, smooth and warm: a novel and pleasant experience. She had never had much to do with animals of any kind, yet here she was on good terms with Diggory's dog and his horse. She liked the idea of herself as comfortable with animals; how pleasant it would be to take such familiarity for granted.

Perhaps she could cope with life in the country — possibly even enjoy it.

She reminded herself that coping or enjoying couldn't possibly matter once she started work at her new school next February. What was she dreaming of? She had known Diggory Kenrick exactly a week.

Someone shouted. She turned to see Diggory Kenrick's superfluous wife waving her arms by the back door of the farm house at the top of the rise. Beside her stood the man who had entered her room in the night.

In an angry voice the woman called, 'What are you doing?'

'Dancing on my hands. What does it look like?' muttered Johnson as she climbed back through the fence and trudged up the slope towards them. 'Feeding the horse,' she said, as soon as she was close enough to make herself heard without yelling.

'Who asked you feed that horse?'

'Diggory.' When Mrs Kenrick opened her mouth Johnson added, 'You said you weren't coming back here.'

'George Pollock,' the man said, looking her over in a scrutinising way she found uncomfortable. 'How d'ye do.' His accent was as unmistakably English as Mrs Bowler Brown's. He held out his hand.

Mrs Kenrick pushed it down. 'A servant girl only. And insolent. Girl, you know place of the key? For the house?'

This was awkward. The key was in her pocket and she didn't want to give it up.

When she arrived at the farm she had carried Diggory's rifle and all her own possessions into the house, stowed them in one of the cupboards in the kitchen, and then let the Yale lock click behind her when she left. Now she didn't want to admit to this woman she not only had the key in her pocket, she planned to return later, when she'd finished work, and spend the night there.

She spread her hands palms up, a gesture and so not exactly a lie.

Mrs Kenrick shrugged, as though she expected nothing but ignorance from the lower classes. She stepped up on the veranda and leaned, her hands beside her face, to peer in the kitchen window. 'He's got a bit of furniture. Perhaps we could sell it?'

'Not if it's all like that lot,' Pollock said, peering beside her. 'And there's nothing in the cottage worth a brass razoo. I thought you said he had things worth taking.'

'He has some jade,' Mrs Kenrick whispered. 'Three pieces that German gave him for thank you, for taking care of his wife.'

Pollock lowered his voice. 'Too easily identified, that sort of stuff.'

'It matters not, you fool. I am his wife, I am not stealing this.'

'Look, the bank manager said you'll still get your allowance even though Dig's in prison. We can live on that.'

'I can live on that,' Mrs Kenrick corrected him. 'I have told you. I can live on that. Not you too.'

'We'll be fine. I can always threaten to go home, make m'brother up the ante on my remittance. Time I touched him up a bit.'

They seemed to have forgotten Johnson. Obviously, she was beneath their notice. She walked away down the slope to collect the eggs.

Pollock was coming after her.

She turned to face him. For some reason his expression, the way he walked, held a distinct menace.

He halted at arms' length. 'How much did you hear?'

'Nothing. None of my business.'

He was silent, staring her down. Then he said, 'Keep it that way. Or I might make it my business. Understand?'

They must have realised that if Diggory heard of their plans he would have reason to stop his wife's allowance.

Pollock looked quite capable of violence. Johnson nodded, abruptly conscious of her isolation, of the wide open paddocks all around with never another soul in sight.

Then, in the most unexpected and reassuring way, Magnus stalked, throat rumbling, hackles raised, to her side; he fixed his gaze on Pollock's face and lifted his upper lip in the merest hint of a snarl.

Pollock backed off. 'Just remember.' His words, no longer frightening, sounded merely like bluster.

Johnson felt her taut muscles go slack. She smoothed Magnus's hackles and rubbed his ears while she watched Pollock retreat towards the house,

'Good dog,' she breathed. 'Oh, what a good dog you are.'

91

In a dangerously bad temper Bowler came home to find Joan and the children eating their midday meal.

'When I finally ran the stationmaster to earth, out visiting neighbours, he told me the idiot did catch the train, the express, but only bought a ticket as far as Edgerton. Why the hell couldn't he have gone far enough to be out of my way?'

'Come and have lunch.' Alone of all the women in the district, Joan didn't provide a midday roast dinner on Sundays.

'First I'll have to ring Edgerton, tell Clarrie Palamountain to keep an eye out for this joker. He won't be happy having his Sunday interrupted.'

'What about your Sunday?'

'What gives you the idea I'm any happier than damn Clarrie? Anyway, keep your fingers crossed. He's a lazy bastard, and with luck he won't find the man.'

Crossed fingers averted no evil that day. After lunch Bowler had barely had time to settle to his lists again before Mounted Constable Palamountain rang back to say he had Robert McBain safely locked up and would Bowler please come and take charge of him.

'Full house here,' Bowler said. 'You can keep him.'

'Well, you'll have to bring someone to identify him, lay charges. And to identify his swag. He was carrying quite a bit of money and jewellery in his suitcase, pushed in amongst his dirty clothes.'

Swearing, Bowler hung the telephone ear piece in its bracket. 'Expect me when you see me,' he growled to Joan in passing, as he went to get out his car.

He returned almost immediately. 'Don't forget to feed young Kenrick if I'm back late. Explain what's happened, and he won't give you any trouble.'

'Give me trouble? Me, who has sorted out dukes in my day?'

Bowler laughed, and kissed her. 'It's a brave duke would take you on,' he agreed. 'But Kenrick's all right.'

Edgerton lay at the end of forty miles of bloody awful road. Well, not even a road, nearly thirty miles of it was just a two-wheel track through the scrub. It would take damn nearly all the afternoon to get there, never mind getting back. Bowler swore again. His whole day would be gone and he'd be no closer to finding Silas Beadnall's murderer.

Once Kenrick was taken to the city and fed into the system there would be yards and yards of red tape to cut before he could be released. For his sake, for the sake of a clean ending to the affair, Bowler had hoped to find the real criminal before Hugh took him away.

Probably he'd been fooling himself that the search was possible in the time left. All the same, he was in no mood for Parry's cheerful prattle. Once settled in the car the man was positively effusive. He praised Bowler's skills in tracking down the thief; he expressed his gratitude. Then he said it again in different words. And not only him, Pen Parry, he explained — the whole troupe was delighted, grateful, and impressed; they had asked him to pass on their thanks, and if any one of them could do anything for him . . .

Bowler had become irritated by the praise, to say nothing of Parry's good spirits, before they had gone two miles. Though he supposed he should be grateful someone was pleased by his efforts.

92

Brenda said, 'Horry, can't we find a way to buy Leon's share of the farm?'

'Why would I want to do that? He's my brother.' Horry, sitting in a comfortable armchair in the middle of the afternoon, reading his way through a week's supply of daily newspapers, smoking his favourite pipe, was only half attending to his wife. Sunday's luxurious leisure lasted for almost eight hours, from milking to milking, and he liked to make the most of it.

Brenda, sitting opposite, had no such privileges on Sunday or any other day. She had just finished washing up after the midday roast dinner; now she had her workbasket on a table at her elbow and a pillow-case full of mending in her lap. 'It isn't right that you do all the work and he reaps the benefit. We should be working for ourselves, not to keep Leon in fishing rods and Fran in fancy shoes.'

'Look, old girl, I think Leon does more work than you give him credit for. Anyway, even if we could afford it, I don't think he'd want to go.'

'Fran hates it here. She'd persuade him.'

'I think you've got that wrong. I think Fran has more friends here than in town.'

'Isn't there any way we could buy them out? I do hate to see you put upon like this.'

Horry lowered his paper. 'Put upon? Me?' He studied his wife for some moments. 'You leave me to deal with Leon, old girl. I see that he pulls his weight. And I couldn't run the place without him, so put this notion out of your head.'

'I was only thinking of you.' She pulled a woollen sock from the bag and threaded it over her left fist. 'And now he's got mixed up with this grasping little nobody at the hotel, Leon will want even more than his share, I bet.'

'Brenda, he has convinced me the girl is his daughter, and what he chooses to do about her is his business. What's the matter with you? And he can't take any more from the farm's income than he already does. You know very well he and I do the books together, and divide what money is left after expenses. And of course until now we had only what was left after bloody Silas took his whack. Thank heaven we've got rid of Silas.'

Brenda nodded. 'That Kenrick boy did us a good turn, really.'

'He's claiming he's innocent. If so, he could still prove it.'

'I wish you wouldn't talk like that. Of course he did it.'

'If you're worried they'll arrest me if he is cleared, forget it.' Horry shook out his paper. 'They can't pin anything on me.' After a pause he added, 'Or on Leon.'

Fran had ensured that her husband could not be suspected of the murder when she had asked Aubrey Venables to fulfil a promise, and tell Bowler how drunk and incapable Leon had been after the dinner party. She hadn't made use of his evidence to begin with because of what had happened later. At that point she had been nervous of the truth coming to light.

Aubrey seemed if anything to be regretting the incident. He wasn't going to tell. So if he and his fortune were out of her reach — and she must have been mad to consider him as a possibility for even a second — she would stick to their arranged story: they'd had a drink, a bit of conversation, and then gone their separate ways to bed. Nobody else could contradict her.

She had thought of it as an adventure, a breaking out of the housewifely mould in a deliciously sinful and dashing way (she didn't like to acknowledge that Aubrey's comfortable fortune had somehow been one of the incentives). Aubrey had seen it differently. Not only had he been a pretty dull lover, he had taken her so much for granted she had felt insulted.

So she had been left confused, disappointed, and even guilty. Because her religion, which she had conveniently disregarded for so long, had come creeping back in the watches of the night like the sea repossessing tidal flats. Her beliefs had not gone permanently. Only receded.

As if that wasn't enough, now this purported daughter of Leon's had pushed into their lives. Seeing that she couldn't persuaded him to repudiate the girl altogether, Fran would have to put a good face on it and pretend to welcome her.

Still, it might not be so bad if the daughter didn't want any money or attention from him, made no demands, lived her own life as she had before. Fran would have to wait and see. She wanted Leon's involvement kept to a minimum, though it wasn't going to be easy: the blasted little nobody seemed to have bewitched him.

She would have to smooth Leon down a little. She *was* fond of him. And she could manage him, too, if she was careful. Someone had to look after him; he was far too trusting.

Particularly now that damn Brenda was trying to persuade Horry to buy his brother out. She could wring Brenda's neck, the grasping bitch. She was trying to sideline Leon when she knew very well that he, like her precious Horry, wouldn't have any sort of a satisfactory life anywhere else. Farming was all he knew. Here at least he was Leon Beadnall of Hawksnest Flat.

93

Bowler didn't get back from Edgerton until after midnight.

He walked into the bedroom, struck a match, and lit the candle on the dressing table. 'On top of everything we had to get a puncture,' he said, sitting on the side of the bed to kiss his wife. 'And it's a miracle I didn't kill that bloody Parry. He's the biggest bore this side of the black stump.'

Her arm round his neck, Joan asked, 'Did they get their possessions back?'

'Every last trumpery brooch, every last ha'penny. I don't think the bloke who nicked the stuff can be the full quid.'

He sat up, kicked off his shoes, drew a long and weary breath and heaved himself to his feet to pull off his jacket, moving awkwardly, wincing, because of a bandage on his right upper arm under a torn and bloodstained shirt sleeve.

Joan leapt out of bed. 'Bill! What have you done to yourself?'

'Not me, a bloody horse. Bit me, the mongrel. No, I can't show you, John Shapcott stitched it up. No lasting damage.'

'How on earth did it happen?' Joan slid her arms under his shirt, around his waist.

Carefully, he embraced her. 'Bloody animal was tied to a veranda post in the street where Clarrie and I were standing talking, just swung its head and grabbed my arm. Clarrie knows the owner, he'll be getting a warning. Joan, do you know if Hugh is back?'

'Yes. He saw the light I'd left for you in the kitchen and came over when he got off the train.'

'Did you tell him I'm having second thoughts about Kenrick?'

'I know my place. I left that for you.'

'You know your place!' he scoffed. 'Kenrick is still here, I trust?'

'He behaved with all the decorum of an honoured guest and took himself back to his hutch without argument. He's an interesting man.' She started unbuttoning his shirt. 'Now come to bed. You can talk to Hugh in the morning.'

Whether because of the pain in his arm or the speculations about Silas Beadnall's murder circling endlessly through his head, Bowler couldn't sleep. He must have been keeping Joan awake too; she rolled over, snuggled up to him, and kissed his chin.

'What's on your mind? Diggory Kenrick, or a trip to see my mother?'

'Mainly Kenrick,' he admitted. 'I've given up the idea of England. You and the children must go, but I've lost interest in jumping horses.'

'You cannot give up just because of Imshy, Bill. You're good, and you could be better.'

'Perhaps.'

'No perhaps about it. And apart from that, my mother would love to see you again, you know that. She hasn't seen you since the wedding.'

Joan's mother had supported him when the rest of her family wanted to set the dogs on him, metaphorically speaking. He owed her a lot. From out of the darkness a certainty came to him.

'She's ill, isn't she.' He felt her nod against his shoulder. 'Why didn't you say?'

'She wouldn't let me tell you. She said that's not fair, if you didn't want to come she wasn't going to blackmail you.'

'That's not blackmail. Is she dying, my only love?'

'Probably,' Joan said. 'Oh, Bill, it's hard.'

'We'd better get you on a boat immediately. The children needn't wait for the end of school. Why didn't you tell me? All this on your mind, you could have told me.' Joan was crying. He held her close. 'We'll get you on the next boat, I'll put in my resignation and come as soon as I can. Of course I'll come with you.' Gently he raised her face and kissed her wet cheek. 'You bloody Poms, with your stiff upper lips. What am I to do with you?'

'Come with me.' Snuffling back her sobs Joan pushed herself against him and twisted her head to kiss his mouth. She murmured. 'Oh, Bill, hold me tight.'

94

'Detective Morgan is over at the pub.' Bowler, at the stove with his back to the kitchen, prodded at a black iron frying pan. He winced at the strain on the stitches in his arm. 'He'll come and take you in front of the Justices at ten.'

Kenrick leaned back in his chair, hands clasped on the back of his head. He was unshaven, and his bloodshot, sunken eyes looked as though he hadn't closed them for the four nights he'd spent in the lockup. 'What happens there?'

'He'll tell them as many of his reasons for arresting you as he sees fit, they will then remand you in custody to Adelaide, where he will take you on this afternoon's train. In the guard's van.' He slid a plate of bacon and eggs in front of his prisoner.

Kenrick said, 'What's this? The condemned man's hearty breakfast?'

Bowler sat in the chair opposite with his hand on his sweater sleeve, over his wound. It was throbbing a bit; he hoped it wasn't infected, though who knew what wogs infested a horse's mouth.

He said, 'You can take it that way if you like.'

'So what's the drill once we get to town?'

'You'll go to Adelaide Gaol to await trial. That's when you'll be able to get hold of a lawyer.'

'Looks like I'm going to need one.' Kenrick reached for another slice of toast. 'What are my chances?' He sounded cynical, as though he didn't believe he had many.

'Ask your lawyer.'

'Believe me, I will. Something I take more than a casual interest in.'

Bowler said, 'I haven't had time to see your mate Miss Johns yet — she should have your clothes for you.'

'When I'm gone can you keep an eye on her? She doesn't know anyone here.'

'She's got Leon Beadnall now, pleased as punch to find he has a daughter.' Bowler had seen Johnson and Leon together before the concert. 'He'll take care of her if she'll let him. She'll be all right.'

'I don't trust any damn Beadnalls.' Kenrick paused, his fork halfway to his mouth. 'What's the matter? Have I grown another head?'

'Just trying to make up my mind about you.'

'Your damn mate Morgan has already made up his mind.'

'With good reason.'

'But you haven't? You're beginning to have doubts?'

'Doubts aren't the same as certainty,' Bowler said.

Kenrick shook his head. 'Better have doubts than the wrong certainty.'

'Got all the answers, haven't you.' He pushed back his chair to answer a knock on the front door.

Johnson handed Bowler a small suitcase. 'I couldn't bring Diggory's overcoat from the farm. It isn't there. It's been hanging up at the pub ever since Saturday night.'

'Hanging up?'

'On the hooks by the back door. It was very wet that night, and he took it off and hung it on a chair by the stove when he came in, before we got talking. It was in my way next morning when I went to light the fire, so I put it in the passage. I suppose he forgot about it. It's been there ever since.'

Bowler didn't appear to be drawing any conclusions from this.

Johnson said, 'I overheard Mr Tillerman in the dining-room one night. I thought he meant he'd seen a man wearing an overcoat.'

'Did he?' Bowler sounded non-committal.

'Diggory's coat was in the kitchen sopping wet when he went up to sleep in the lounge. It was still there next morning. He wouldn't have come back and put it on just to visit his grandfather.'

'I don't suppose he would,' Bowler said.

Johnson would have liked to shake him. 'So if Mr Tillerman saw a man in an overcoat it wasn't Diggory.'

Bowler smiled. 'It's all right, I understand what you're telling me. Is the coat still there? You had better show me. And then you must come to my office and sign a statement of what you know about it.'

'Oh yes!' she breathed. 'Oh, yes.'

No sooner had they reached the back door of the pub than Em, in the kitchen and sounding cross, called to Johnson to help her. Now. Immediately. So the girl identified the coat for him and said she'd be over to make her statement as soon as she had a spare minute. Bowler walked back with the overcoat over his left arm, reflecting that now he had some definite statements to offer Hugh that would, he hoped, convince him they had the wrong man.

Hugh was not convinced. He sat in the chair opposite the desk in the police station reading Bowler's notes. 'Dammit, Bowler, the light can't have been too good. Tillerman could have been mistaken about what the man was wearing.'

'If the light was as bad as that he could have been mistaken about which man he saw, too. You can't have it both ways.'

'What are you trying to say? We should kick Kenrick loose? I can't do that. There's too much against him.'

'I suppose there is. I wish you didn't have to go on with it, all the

355

same.'

'Where's that length of flex? I'll have to take that with me, present it in court, cause of death and all that.'

'It's in this shoe box.' Bowler lifted it out, careful to preserve the kinks where it had been twisted. 'There's a cut in the cotton sheathing there, see? It's frayed a bit more with handling, I didn't notice it before. Inside the place where the lever was used, as though it had a sharp edge.'

'We still haven't found what he used to wind it up. Does Kenrick wear a sheath knife round the farm? Plenty of country blokes do.'

'Don't think so. I've never seen him with one.' Bowler's gaze fell on the small suitcase just inside the door. 'Bloody hell, I've been forgetting the bastard.' He ran down the passage to the kitchen. His prisoner was not there.

He hadn't gone far. Bowler found him sitting on the edge of the back veranda, feet in the dirt, elbows on knees, chin on his clasped hands, looking at the sky over the trees in the railway yards.

He got up when he heard Bowler. 'I was beginning to think I should abscond.'

'Not this time. I've got your clothes, you can use the bathroom to change.' Bowler took him inside and pointed the way. 'You'd better shave too. You can use my razor. Hugh's here. Come up to the office when you're ready.'

Hugh was on the telephone. He stood aside and handed the earpiece to Bowler without a word.

'Jack Pitts here,' the voice said. 'That you, Bowler? Tell Diggory his wife and some slimy piece of work she seems to be hooked up with came into my office just now, as soon as I opened the doors, and asked me to sell the farm for them.'

'Bloody hell. Can you do that?'

'No, not on, title's in Diggory's name alone. They got very abusive when I told them they couldn't, too. I think you should get out to the farm and see what else they've nicked.'

'I'll speak to Kenrick. He'll be going to town on today's train.'

'Poor bugger,' Pitts said with feeling. 'When he gets hold of a lawyer he'd better tell the bloke to get in touch with me, if he needs funds or anything.'

Curious, Bowler asked, 'Don't you think he's guilty?'

'Can't see it,' Pitts said. 'I suppose I could be wrong.'

95

Her heart lighter than it had been since Diggory's arrest, Johnson ran across the road to the police station. This statement she was going to make was a positive step she could take to help him. And Mr Brown believed her, believed the overcoat proved Mr Tillerman had identified the wrong man, so perhaps they could let Diggory go now.

She opened the door, and found herself surrounded by three tall men, a thicket of male bodies, just inside. Then she saw that Diggory was holding out his right arm so that Detective Morgan could clip a handcuff on his wrist. Her heart lurched.

Diggory saw her shocked face. 'Hey, it's all right, I'm all right.' He reached out with his free hand to touch her cheek. 'Don't worry, I'll get this lot sorted out eventually.'

Bowler was frowning at the detective. Then he said, 'This way, Miss Johns,' and opened the flap in the counter to usher her through.

Hugh pulled Diggory's arm towards him so that he could snap the free end of the cuff round his own left wrist.

Johnson said, 'I wanted to see you but they wouldn't let me.'

'I wanted to see you, too, to tell you I didn't touch damn Silas. A bit of luck really, your barging in like this.'

'Can I go on using your car?'

'All my possessions are yours to command,' he said grandly. He made a slight bow, his right arm held behind him so that he didn't drag on Hugh's arm.

Hugh said, 'Time to go.'

'All right, I'm as ready as I'll ever be. Goodbye, Full Stop. Don't worry, I'll be back. And think how silly these two will look then.'

She forced a smile. 'Of course you'll be back.' She couldn't say goodbye: it sounded too final. 'See you then,' she said, and went through the counter after Bowler.

'Don't get too carried away, you two,' Bowler said. 'He'll be back in about half an hour, to wait for train time.' To Johnson he said, 'Here, write what you told me, leave it on the desk. I have to drive them to the institute.'

Hugh and Diggory, joined wrist to wrist by steel links, followed him out.

When she had finished writing her statement Johnson went back to help Em make up the rooms after the concert party had finally departed.

Em flapped a clean sheet across the mattress and tried to forget her worries for a minute while she studied her housemaid, reaching for the sheet on the other side of the double bed. The girl looked ghastly. 'Didn't Bowler let you make your statement?'

'Oh yes. Only it hasn't made any difference. They've taken Diggory anyway.'

'They couldn't turn him loose at a moment's notice, you know. It will help him in the long run, of course it will.'

'I hope so.'

'Don't worry about him. You've convinced me, if that's any comfort. And if he's innocent he'll be fine.'

'It is a comfort,' Johnson said. 'Mrs Musgrave, would you mind if I moved out to the farm? I can start and finish at the same times as usual, but it would make looking after the chooks and the horse a lot easier.'

'Now you've found your father I don't suppose you want to go on working here anyway.'

'I can stay as long as you need me. Until school starts next year, that is — I've got a new job arranged then.'

'The point is,' Em said, 'we can't afford you, Johnson.' She had finally made Trotter sit down and go through the books with her, had made him look at several alarming sets of figures, had hammered at him until she was convinced he understood what she was telling him. The pub was going to be forced into cutting a number of corners. 'Not full time, that is. I'm sorry, you must know it's not because we are dissatisfied with your work, you've been very good. Only Trotter and I have decided we'll have to manage without help, except for an hour or two in the mornings to do the beds and clean the rooms.'

'I would be happy to do that for you,' Johnson said.

'You would have to see if it's worth it, if you have to buy petrol. I assume Diggory is lending you his car.'

'Yes,' Johnson said. She wished she'd had longer with Diggory: she should have asked him several questions before she took up squatters' rights on his farm.

'Lady Muck is leaving, did I tell you?' Em had switched sides in the matter of the Kenrick marriage when, taking Katya early tea on Sunday morning, she had found George Pollock sharing her bed. If that was how his wife carried on it was no wonder Diggory believed she had left him. He certainly had grounds for divorce, and she could provide evidence of them.

Johnson said, 'Leaving the hotel? Perhaps she's going back to the farm.'

'I think they're leaving Kularook. Johnson, you will be careful how far you commit yourself to Diggory Kenrick, won't you. You can't really know anyone after only a few days.'

'It seems longer.'

Em shook a pillow into a fresh case and thumped it down on the bed. 'I've no doubt it does,' she said drily. 'I'm just not sure how far you should trust him. I wouldn't like him to break your heart.'

'But he's my cousin, Mrs Musgrave. I'm allowed to be concerned about a cousin.'

'I hadn't even considered that,' Em said. 'You're going to take a bit of getting used to.' Then she smiled. 'I should keep my mouth shut. Whatever you decide, I hope it works out for you.' She had enough worries of her own without involving herself in the affairs of this capable and independent girl. She'd become rather fond of her, that was the trouble.

96

When Bowler came back from escorting Diggory and Hugh to the train, he found Horry Beadnall leaning against the counter in the office waiting for him.

'I have to show you this,' Horry said. 'Came in today's post.' The down train from the city arrived an hour earlier than the up train; the postmaster always sorted immediately whatever mail had arrived.

Bowler took the envelope Horry gave him. 'What are you doing in Kularook on a Monday? Not your usual day for stores, is it?'

'Leon wanted to see Martine. I had business with the stock agent.'

The letter was typewritten under the letterhead of an Adelaide jeweller, who wrote to acknowledge the return of the diamond ring purchased by Silas Beadnall, deceased, and to assure H M Beadnall that all accounts issued in connection with the ring were now cancelled.

'How the devil did the ring get back to the jeweller?' Bowler demanded. 'Do you mean to say that whoever stole it from Miss Jennings returned it to the jeweller?'

Horry looked embarrassed. 'Looks like it.'

'Do you know who took it?'

'No.'

Bowler realised he could guess and, by the look of him, Horry could too. 'Did your wife come in with you today?'

'No. Bowler, what are you going to do about this?'

'Don't know. Haven't had time to think about it.'

'It wasn't really stealing. The ring was just returned.'

'It was stealing all right. Ask Miss Jennings. Or Miss Johns — it was cruel to let her be blamed.' He folded the letter and pushed it into the envelope. 'I'll have to keep this for the present. Oh, stop looking like a funeral, Horry, I'm not going to arrest your wife. Just the same, you'll have to come to some arrangement with Miss Jennings, I think. Give her the money, or buy the ring.'

'Do you really think that's necessary?'

'Of course it's bloody necessary. I'm going to tell her what happened to the thing, so unless you want to get mixed up in an unpleasant legal wrangle of course you have to put it right.'

Horry heaved a breath and levered himself away from the counter. 'So we're no better off after all that.'

Annoyed, Bowler said, 'You're worse off, you bloody fool. Your wife has committed a criminal act, and I could charge her if I chose.'

'Now look, Bowler —'

'I said, I'm not going to. Let me know when you've fixed the matter up with Miss Jennings, and I'll give you this letter back. That'll be the end of it.' He lifted the flap and went behind the counter, bent for a black steel cashbox, unlocked it, and locked the letter inside. 'Now, unless there's anything else you want, I'm going over to tell Miss Johns the ring has been found and she hasn't the slightest stain on her character.' He smiled sardonically at Horry. 'You should be pleased about that, now she's one of your family.'

Let Horry chew on that, Bowler thought. His niece was innocent, and his wife was guilty.

Over at the pub the interview between Johnson and her father was not going as smoothly as the last. They sat opposite each other at one of the little tables in the lounge, both frowning.

Leon said, 'But I'd like you to come out and stay with us for a while. It'd give us a chance to get to know each other better.'

'It's too soon.' Johnson polished the table top with a duster she happened to be carrying. 'We will have to take it slowly. I will, anyway.' He hadn't mentioned his wife. Unless Fran's hostility had abated, Johnson wasn't going to intrude into the woman's household, eating her meals, sleeping in her beds.

'I have a lot of lost time to make up.'

Certainly he did, and that was part of the trouble. He meant it differently from how she understood it. Leon felt he had been deprived for years of the pleasure of a daughter, an addition to an otherwise reasonably full life; Johnson knew she had been deprived of a great deal more than that. She wanted — not exactly an apology from him, more a recognition of the difficulties she and her mother had struggled to overcome without a male breadwinner to help them. Women teachers were paid a lot less than their male workmates.

She said, 'I will come, you know, but later.'

'Well, what about just for a couple of days, then? I have so much to ask you. About your mother especially.' He reached across the table and laid his hand on hers, over the duster. 'I wouldn't want you to think — you must know I was in love with her.'

'No, it's all right, her letter made that plain.'

'Can I read — no, of course not, but can't you tell me what she wrote about me?'

'One day. Not yet. And even if I thought it was a good idea to come and stay with you, which I don't, I can't come today because I have promised to look after Diggory's place while he's away.'

Astonished, Leon reared back in his chair. 'Diggory Kenrick? What's he to you?'

Calmly she said, 'A cousin. Had you forgotten? He's your nephew too.'

'He's a murderer, a criminal. He's not coming back.'

'He's not a murderer, and he will be coming back. Ask Mr Brown.'

'Ask me what?' Bowler said behind her.

Embarrassed to be caught using his name for her own ends, Johnson said, 'I just meant you don't believe Diggory is a murderer, either.'

'Don't I? Don't you go putting opinions into my mouth, Miss Johns.' Bowler pulled out a chair and seated himself between them.

'I'm sorry, I didn't mean —'

Bowler flicked a hand. 'Never mind. I came to tell you that Miss Jennings' ring has been found, and that you are completely cleared.'

Johnson could have kissed him. She heaved a deep breath. 'That's wonderful. Who took it?'

'That I can't tell you. Police business.'

'Never mind, as long as Detective Morgan knows now it wasn't me.'

'He'll be told,' Bowler said.

Excited, laughing, she jumped up. 'I must tell Mrs Musgrave. Though she has always believed me she'll be pleased it's official.' She danced out.

Leon said, 'Where was the ring?'

'Back at the jeweller's, where it came from. Horry will explain.'

97

Bowler went back to his desk, back to his notes, back to his frustrating search for some discrepancy in the various statements he had taken, looking for something, any tiny detail, to lead him to a murderer. After an hour he was getting nowhere, had in fact put himself almost to sleep, so he went out to his wife's dark room, a cell he had built into the back of the garage, to shout through the door and ask if he could take Isma out for a while. All this desk work was driving him bats.

This was the first time he had been in the saddle since Imshy was killed. He turned the horse out of the pub yard and up the street, heading for the oval and one of the roads leading out of town — leading to Kenrick's place, among others.

He'd have a look round. After what Jack Pitts had said, perhaps Kenrick's wife and her partner were helping themselves to anything that wasn't nailed down. His wife might once have been entitled to a share of his belongings, though not, in Bowler's view, now she had brought her fancy-man with her. According to Em, the Musgraves could provide enough evidence for Kenrick to divorce her.

He relaxed, soothed by the rhythm of the horse's movements. He'd have to get himself another horse. Though now he was committed to this trip to England with his family, that would have to wait until they got back.

In the meantime, there would be show-jumping in Europe. He felt a faint stirring of excitement and then disgust. Any thought of other horses felt like disloyalty to his hapless Imshy. Bowler put his hand on the warm neck of the animal under him.

Anyway, he wasn't going to England or anywhere else until he had found who killed Silas Beadnall. Kularook was only a small place — it was ridiculous that he couldn't find the truth between such a handful of suspects.

Ahead in the distance he saw the red roof of Pedlers' farmhouse. Young Alan belonged to that self-appointed squad of Diggory watchers, the various people who had seen that young man in the night and had, much to his annoyance, dismantled his lies one by one.

Bowler had taken statements from the others. Could Alan add anything to his original remarks? Perhaps he should ask more questions, in case the youth had seen anything else in the night.

He turned into the short track leading to the farmhouse and continued on to the sheds behind it. A voice yelled, 'Don't! Leave me alone!' and Isma shied violently as Alan raced out from behind a big wooden waggon immediately in front of him. Close behind pounded his father, Jack Pedler, slashing the air and trying to hit him with his heavy leather belt.

Both skidded to a stop when they saw Bowler. Skinny adolescent Alan, more angry than frightened, stepped aside a few paces to keep beyond reach of the belt.

Isma was trembling, ready to spin and bolt if more nasty surprises erupted. Bowler kept a strong hand on the reins, murmuring, soothing the horse with his voice. As the tensions wound down in animal and Pedlers alike he said, 'I want a word with you, Alan.'

'What's he done now?' demanded Jack, a black-browed, surly-looking man.

Bowler swung out of his saddle. 'Nothing at all. I'm after information, that's all.'

Jack wound his belt round his hand, spat on the ground equidistant between his son and the policeman's horse, and stumped off towards the house.

Alan stroked Isma's nose. Cautiously he asked, 'What is it, Mr Brown?' He emanated a slight air of injured innocence, as though ready to deny whatever he was accused of.

'I just want you to tell me again what you saw after midnight night on Sunday morning. You said you saw Diggory Kenrick going into the pub, late. Can you make a guess at —'

'No I didn't.' Alan looked puzzled. 'I didn't say that.'

'You did. The day you were chasing the emus, and I nearly ran into the buggers.'

'No, you've got it wrong. I didn't see Diggory, I saw Muir. I told you.'

So many thoughts started whirling through Bowler's mind he could hardly take this in. 'You said —' What exactly *had* the youth said?

Alan said, 'Anyway, you said that you'd just been to see him, you knew all about it.'

'We'd been to interview Diggory. You saw *Muir*?'

'Yes.'

'Any idea what time it would have been?' Muir Kenrick! Had Muir murdered Silas? What business would Muir have at the hotel in the small hours?

Alan pondered, scratching patterns in the dirt with the toe of his boot. 'I'd been spotlighting with the Gordon boys, and it had gone twelve fifteen by their kitchen clock before I left the house. I wasn't hurrying, and I sheltered under a tree a couple of times, when the rain was heavy. So over an hour, I'd say. Hard to tell.'

'You were on horseback,' Bowler said.

'Dad doesn't let me take the car,' said Alan. 'If I go anywhere it's on horseback or on foot.'

They had moved together, and were leaning side by side against the tray of the waggon. Isma snatched at a patch of grass by the wheel, crunching, jingling the bit.

Bowler's arm was hurting like buggery. 'And you saw Muir Kenrick going into the pub. You couldn't be mistaken, and it was Diggory you saw? It was a pretty dark night.'

'Yeah, but every now and then the moon came out. And of course they're alike, but hell, I know them both.'

Bowler thought, they're neighbours, this youth would know both well. This was a more reliable identification than that of a man who had met Diggory for the first time the same night. Anyway, if Alan left Gordons', five miles out, around twelve fifteen he couldn't possibly have seen Diggory entering the pub; that had been at twelve forty-five, according to Miss Johns.

'Did he see you?'

'Don't think so. I was at the corner by the bakery — I was heading out to Davidsons', help muster their back scrub for a couple of days — and by the time I was level with the side door of the pub Muir had gone inside.'

Muir Kenrick. Bowler couldn't take it in.

Alan said, 'Anyway, I saw his horse. He'd ridden in, too. He'd left it tied up by the common, in a patch of mallee. I wouldn't have seen it only it whickered to my horse, and you can't miss that ugly damn brute, a white face and one blue eye.'

Bowler knew the horse too. Muir Kenrick's horse.

Muir Kenrick had gone into the Kularook hotel at — twelve fifteen plus an hour or more — say between one fifteen and one thirty in the morning. Tillerman had seen a man he thought was Diggory around one thirty. Uncle and nephew were both Kenricks, with a strong family resemblance in build and features. A stranger could easily mistake one for the other.

If Muir Kenrick had been in Silas's room in the night, Bowler needed to know why. Though what possible reason would Muir have for murder?

He had stayed on good terms with Silas for all the years his father was feuding with him. What had changed? The accident, of course — Muir had been furious when Silas ran into his car that afternoon — though that surely was not enough reason for killing a man.

Bowler rubbed his arm. He had been silent too long. Alan was looking at him curiously.

'You mustn't tell anyone what you've just told me. Not yet. This is serious, Alan. Can you keep your mouth shut? Not anyone, not your father, brothers — nobody.'

Alan said, 'Then it was Muir? Not Diggory?'

The boy wasn't stupid: he couldn't be fobbed off with lies. 'Could be. That's what I have to find out. And that's why it's important nobody knows until I've had a chance to ask him a few questions. I'm trusting you.'

'Righto, Mr Brown.'

Bowler would have to go home and get his car before he approached Muir Kenrick.

But why? Why? What did he say to the man? 'I know you murdered Silas Beadnall, but I haven't the foggiest why you did it?'

Muir could laugh at him, brazen it out, unless confronted with more evidence than that.

98

Back in his office Bowler hastily wrote down Alan's evidence. It would have to be put into a formal statement and signed eventually; in the meantime he had to make sure the information was recorded while it was fresh in his mind.

The collision between the cars — something must have happened then to set Muir off. Before that Bowler doubted that the two men had met in years. Even when Silas had made one of his occasional visits from the city he'd have been staying at Beadnalls' farm, miles out the other side of Kularook, and unlikely to run into Muir.

How could he discover if the exchange had been more than a slanging match when Silas's car ran into Muir's? Two women had been present; perhaps they had heard some details of the quarrel and could tell him about it. He couldn't ask the man's wife, though. His source would have to be Miss Jennings.

Was she on the telephone? He would use the excuse he was letting her know about the ring.

He went down to the kitchen and asked Joan for a couple of aspirin. While she was rummaging for a packet through a drawer full of old bills, pencil stubs, bits of saved string, rubber rings and rusting clips off Fowlers jars, he related what he'd learned from Alan Pedler.

'I told you to find the right man,' Joan said smugly. 'Clever boy.

Here you are. I'll get you a glass of water.'

Fired up now, he hunted through his notes for Margot Jennings' address. It was of a boarding house in Kent Town and yes, he'd written a telephone number there too. He went to the telephone on the wall, wound the handle, and told the postmaster he wanted to make a trunk call to Adelaide.

Then he had to wait while some adenoidal female searched for Miss Jennings. He wished he had time to go to town and interview her face to face. Hugh could do that, if she had any worthwhile information to offer.

He drummed his fingers impatiently. Heaven knew what the call was costing. He hoped the damn Department would reimburse him. It was inclined to look on telephone calls as unnecessary frivolities: serious research was always done in person.

Finally she was on the line. Before he could get a word in she was asking eagerly if they had found her ring. So he explained that yes, the ring had been found, they had no idea who had taken it, and Horry Beadnall would be in touch with her about it.

He said, 'Miss Jennings, you were with Silas Beadnall when he ran into another car. Do you remember what either of them said?'

'The other man was very angry. Well, Silas was too. The other man got out of his car and came to Silas's door and he was swearing and calling him dreadful names.'

'That was Muir Kenrick. Did Silas call him by name?'

'I don't remember that. The man said Silas would have to pay for the damage to his car and Silas said he'd see him hanged first.'

The sort of thing anyone might say in anger. 'Then what?'

'The other man said he'd make sure Silas paid and Silas said he didn't think he would. Because he knew about the fire.'

'Fire? What fire?'

'I don't know,' Margot said pettishly. 'I'm just telling you what they said. And I can't remember it all, they were so angry with each other.'

'All right, all right.' Bowler tried to sound conciliatory. 'What did Muir say to that?'

'I can't remember. Silas said something about trains, he'd seen him on one, and the other man said he didn't believe it. And Silas said, "When I told your father, he believed it all right." Then he said he wasn't going to pay a penny, and the other man went back to his car. I don't think he saw I was there.'

Fire? What had he heard recently about a fire? Someone —

Diggory Kenrick's parents had died in a fire. He felt his hair rising on his nape. Suppose Silas had been hinting he knew Muir had lit that fire?

Jackpot, Bowler thought.

Margot's voice went on, 'When I asked Silas what it had been about he said not to worry, it was just something that happened a long time ago.'

Now he couldn't get away quickly enough. He had to ask someone about the fire. Em would know; Em knew every last detail of local history since Adam was a pup. 'Thank you very much, Miss Jennings. You'll be hearing from Horry soon.'

He hung up and went to his desk.

Bowler felt he was making a good many assumptions in his efforts to find Muir's reasons for murder. All the same, he was in no doubt that Muir had committed it: he'd been seen in the most compromising circumstances for which there could be no innocent explanation. He wasn't going to be able to talk his way out of that in a hurry.

Bowler would have to go on making assumptions until he could get admissions from the man himself. If, as now seemed likely, Silas had threatened to reveal him as a murderer, that gave Muir a motive in spades.

To find out the details of the fire that killed Young James Kenrick and his wife, Bowler would have to get hold of the coroner's report and the findings of whatever investigation preceded it. In the meantime, he would consult Em Musgrave. He found her in the pub kitchen cutting up vegetables for soup, for the guests' evening meal.

To begin with she thought his interest had been sparked because of Diggory's arrest, that he was merely following up the story of an ill-fated family. Her ears pricked up when he asked if she knew where the rest of the family were at the time of the fire.

'What are you after, Bowler? That's ancient history, it can't have anything to do with Diggory now.'

'Put it down to curiosity. Tell me anyway.'

'The whole family was in town, Old James and his wife, Muir and Sheba. They'd gone up for the Royal Show. Helen and Young James had stayed behind to milk the cows and feed the dogs. They were supposed to be away about a week, but of course came home in a hurry when they were told of the tragedy. What's it matter now?'

'Just curious,' he repeated.

'Rubbish.' She put her head on one side, considering. 'Good heavens, don't say you've heard the rumour that Silas knew something about it. Is that it? I thought that died out years ago. We've always believed he was just throwing hints to make himself interesting.' She paused, thinking. 'You could always check with Colly Gordon. If Silas told anyone, he would have told Colly.'

'Thanks. I will.' He looked around. 'Where's Miss Johns?'

'She's gone out to the farm. She's living there now, seems to think she has to look after it in some way now that Diggory's not there.'

'I see. Okay, thanks Em.'

On his way home he pulled his watch from his pocket, clicked it open. Five thirty. He'd let Muir eat his evening meal at home, and then go out and bring him in.

99

Bowler could hear the clink of china from the kitchen, where Sheba and her daughter washed the dinner dishes. From further in the house he could hear the mutter of voices on a wireless.

Bowler knocked on the back door.

Sheba, wet hands dripping, opened it, jerked her head. 'Go through.' She didn't appear at all curious what his business might be with her husband.

Muir was relaxed in an easy chair in the sitting room. 'G'dday, Bowler.' He switched off a broadcast about Scotland on the wireless set beside him yet didn't get up. 'Take a pew. What's on your mind?'

Standing in the doorway, probably looking as grim as he felt, Bowler said, 'I'd like you to come with me. Answer some questions.'

Muir surged to his feet. For a second Bowler read wild fury in his face, before it was replaced by controlled hostility.

'I don't have to stand any nonsense from you.'

'Not nonsense. Will you come?'

'I'm damned if I do.'

'All right. Muir Kenrick, I am arresting you for the murder of Silas Beadnall and —'

'What!' Muir lunged for him.

Muir was a tall strong farmer. Bowler was younger, just as strong, and far more experienced in this sort of scuffle. If he hadn't had stitches in his arm the contest would have been over before it began. As it was, they knocked over two chairs and smashed a crystal vase before Muir, panting and swearing, was in handcuffs.

The noise had brought Sheba and Stella, white-faced, to watch.

'I'm taking him in,' Bowler told them. He could feel his arm bleeding. Far from exulting in a case he now believed solved, he found the sight of the women's shocked faces deeply depressing. They would inevitably be affected by all the unpleasantness that now would follow.

'You can't get away with this,' Muir snarled. 'You've got nothing on me. My god, I'll make you sorry for this.'

'Go your hardest,' Bowler said. 'In the meantime, say goodbye to your wife. You're coming with me.'

'That cow. She'd probably be pleased to see the last of me.'

'Muir, how can you say that!' Sheba twisted her hands. 'Mr Brown, are you sure?'

'Sure enough,' Bowler said.

So Hugh Morgan caught the early train and arrived at lunchtime next day. The evening before, at her boarding-house, he had taken Margot's statement and now, in the course of the afternoon, he and Bowler drove out to take statements first from Alan Pedler, and then from Colly Gordon. The old man became agitated with their first questions, almost as though they took his breath away.

'All Silas told me,' Colly gasped, 'was that — he saw Muir — on a train — where he wasn't — supposed to be.' His speech was punctuated with wheezy inhalations.

'What did you think he meant?' Hugh glanced at the old man's daughter-in-law. Although she was frowning, she nodded permission to continue.

'Thought — he meant — Muir was — in Kularook — the night the house — burnt down.'

'Bloody hell,' Bowler said, 'why didn't you tell anyone?'

'None of my — business — Silas said — shut up — I'm afraid — of Silas.'

'Silas wasn't the murderer.'

'Dangerous — all the same.'

Back at the police station Hugh said, 'What time have you arranged with the JPs? Have I got time to have a go at Kenrick? Half an hour? Good. Can you get him up from the lockup?'

'He nearly swiped my head off last time I opened the door. You come too. And bring the handcuffs.'

Muir continued to rant and bluster. He conceded nothing. So they hauled him in front of the Justices, got him remanded, and shut him up again until train time.

Nursing his arm — which Em, a trained nurse, had restitched and declared not infected — Bowler sat on a corner of his desk because Hugh had usurped his chair. Papers and statements were spread around them.

'Though there's no doubt in my mind what really happened we won't be able to charge him with the first murders,' Bowler said. 'There's nobody left who could give us the sort of evidence to put before a court. Colly Gordon's statement doesn't prove anything: it's only hearsay.'

'Confirms some of what the Jennings woman told us, though. Still, if we can't prove the first murders, all we've got on this one are the statements of Tillerman and the Pedler youth.' Hugh flipped a page in his notebook. 'We're only guessing at the meaning of what else the Jennings woman overheard. This business about a train — any ideas about that?'

'The fire started at night, when Muir, his wife, and his parents were supposed to be in Adelaide. So I'm willing to bet he caught the Melbourne express in the early evening in Adelaide, got here just before midnight, then caught the Adelaide express back at three thirty. Three and a half hours between trains. He could have got to the farm and back, easily, even on foot. He'd probably left a horse handy, anyway. And he'd be away from the city for just one night.'

'Easy enough to find an excuse for that. Missed the last tram, had to sleep at a mate's place — all sorts of reasons.'

'Somehow Silas must have seen him on the train and realised he had no alibi for the night of the fire.'

Hugh nodded. 'And told his father, Old James or whatever they called him, to shut him up when he got abusive about how Silas had treated his daughter. Then didn't tell Muir until their cars collided.'

'Stick with the identification,' Bowler said. 'He's still blustering everyone has made a mistake, it must have been Diggory they saw, but Alan and Tillerman will be hard to shake. Mind you, if I was on a jury and had to decide who was telling the truth between uncle and nephew I know who I'd believe.'

Hugh bared his teeth. 'Feeling cocky, aren't you, you bastard. All right, I was wrong about young Kenrick.'

Bowler shook his head. 'I live here. Easier, when you know the locals a bit.'

'Do you think Muir will ever admit what he did?'

'I wouldn't be surprised. Although we're still only guessing part of it, he doesn't have to know that. If we confront him, I think in the end he'll fold.'

'Huh.' Hugh started shuffling pages together. 'No sign of it yet, unfortunately.'

Muir objected violently to being put on the train, and they had to manhandle him into the guard's van of the Adelaide express at three thirty the following morning.

'Enjoy your trip, Hugh,' Bowler said.

100

That all happened on Tuesday.

On Friday afternoon Johnson, plentifully smeared with the good earth, was on her knees grubbing up weeds round some daisy bushes she had discovered in the dense growth of wild oats overrunning the ruined garden beside Diggory's farmhouse. When she heard a car she lifted her head to see Bowler Brown's Chrysler tourer drive up.

Diggory got out. He was dressed in obviously new sports coat and slacks. He put a Gladstone bag on the ground by his feet and stood for a moment looking around, almost to the four points of the compass, while he dragged off his tie. Then he strode over, pulled her to her feet, and hugged her hard, dirt and all.

Johnson, her heart thumping, hugged him back.

Taking his time, Bowler emerged from the car. 'Miss Johns, if you like to collect up your things I can take you back to Kularook now. Em says you're welcome to stay in her back room again.'

Miss Martine Johns, aka Johnson, sometimes answering to Full Stop, had been giving a great deal of thought to what she wanted to do, and even more thought to the small matter of her relations with her cousin — half cousin — Diggory Kenrick. She realised that the high drama of the murder and all that followed had pushed them together more quickly than would have occurred in normal circumstances.

That didn't mean their burgeoning affection for each other was false. She had made her decisions.

She had no one to please but herself.

'Thank you, Mr Brown.' She glanced at Diggory, who was fondling an ecstatic Magnus. 'Thank you, only I am going to stay here now.'

That got the attention of both men.

'You can't,' Bowler said. 'Not now he's back.'

Diggory swung round and gripped both her arms while he studied her face intently. 'Do you mean that?'

Crossly she said, 'No, of course I don't. I always say what I don't mean.'

He let her go and spun away, whirling himself around, spinning faster and faster. '*Yoweee!*' he whooped, arms flailing, feet gripping and turning. '*Yeeaaay!*' He crashed into her, grabbed her into his arms, and kissed her.

She pushed him off. 'Let me breathe, dammit.'

'Don't be difficult. You can do all the breathing you like later,' he said and kissed her again. He held her off, looking into her eyes. 'You won't regret it, I swear.'

Bowler regarded them, chewing his lip. 'Oh, well, I know when I'm not needed,' he said. He didn't think they heard.

He got in his car, reversed, turned, and drove back to Kularook.

ABOUT THE AUTHOR

Alison Manthorpe grew up on a farm with horses. School was correspondence lessons on the end of the kitchen table. She worked as a physiotherapist in Australia and in London, and returned to marry a master mariner, raise a family, and accompany him to sea in yachts. She is also a published poet.

Also by

A M MANTHORPE

The Fifth Bullet

January, 1931.

Mounted Constable Bowler Brown, ex-light-horseman from the Great War, is stationed in Kularook, a small South Australian town. Then Agatha, who two years before ran away from her stifling marriage to Lew Benson, returns to him.

As the summer heats up Bowler tries to keep the peace between factious locals while Agatha, on the isolated farm, struggles to retain her sanity in the face of Lew and his family's hostility. An old friend tries to help, but instead raises tensions to dangerous levels.

When tragedy strikes, Bowler has to find out what really happened. Was it murder-plus-suicide? Were four shots fired from Lew Benson's rifle? Or were there five?

And who is trying to kill Agatha?

Available at Amazon.com
ISBN: 9780992531850

Read on for a sample of

The Fifth Bullet

1

Two years after she left — left the farm, left her husband — Agatha Benson returned. She alighted from the Melbourne Express at the Kularook railway station in the middle of one hot January night in 1931 with a large suitcase in one hand and a baby, wrapped in a white knitted shawl, cradled in her other arm.

Mounted Constable William Brown, propped half asleep against the shelter-shed in the middle of the platform, had woken only when the Pacific engine, clanking like St George and breathing fire like the dragon, rolled past him. The couplings creaked. The carriages came to a smooth stop. Away to his left the engine hissed steam into the profound country silence. He heaved his shoulders away from the corrugated-iron wall and opened his eyes.

In the light from the carriage windows he caught sight of Agatha Benson. Intrigued, he would have stopped to see who was meeting her but a small man in a navy uniform was leaning from the door of the next carriage making hurry-up gestures.

Duty first. MC Brown, more commonly known as Bowler, was there to take an obstreperous passenger off the train. According to the message from further up the line the man was a heavyweight and fighting drunk, and as the train thundered south he had been holding several sleeping-car attendants at bay with a lump of wood wrenched from the arm of a seat.

As he boarded the train Bowler nearly tripped over another uniformed figure huddled on the floor, who was rocking himself and nursing a wrist dented to an odd shape. He stepped over the man.

The senior guard who had beckoned waved a hand. 'He's all yours.'

In the central aisle of the second class carriage, between the two rows of double seats, a hulking figure in shabby clothes filled most of the space. Half crouching, his head thrust forward on a thick bull neck, he was snarling obscenities and sweeping his improvised waddy in wild scything swings at two more guards, who kept backing and advancing in front of him. The carriage was otherwise empty.

'What set him off?'

'We threatened to put him off the train at Branden Corner and he quietened down for a bit. But he's got a bottle of whisky in his coat and he's been getting worse, abusing the other passengers, offending the women, offering to fight anyone who tried to shut him up. Then he went berserk when we tried to nick his bottle.'

'Anyway, you've got the other passengers out of the way. Makes it easier.'

'They got themselves, as soon as we had him bailed up.'

Bowler edged past the guard. 'G'day, sport. What's your problem?'

'Fight the lotta you,' the drunk yelled. He swiped his waddy across and back. 'Thieving bastards!'

Bowler was younger, fitter, and sober; he judged his moment. He blocked, forearm to forearm, a blow aimed at his head. Then he moved inside the man's reach, clamped a hand on his wrist, and while he was still off balance yanked him round until he could shove the arm up his back. The man doubled over, roaring.

The guards looked almost as surprised as the drunk at the speed of events. Bowler smiled on them complacently, exchanged names and details with the senior guard, and told his prisoner to shut up and behave himself.

'I don't play Queensberry rules either,' he said with cheerful menace. He glanced down at the injured man. 'Better take him on to Edgerton,' he advised the others. 'No doctor here.'

Duty done, he pushed his prisoner onto the platform, grabbed the other wrist, and clicked on handcuffs. The man reeled, seeming all at once to be much more drunken. Bowler gripped his arm and held him upright.

Agatha Benson, as though to make herself more easily seen, now stood in the lighted circle under the hurricane lantern that hung inside the shelter shed.

'Stay there,' Bowler told his prisoner, and turned to speak to her.

The drunk took a few unsteady steps in the other direction. Bowler stuck out his foot and watched with detachment as the man crashed forward and lay winded on the gravel.

'Told you,' he said. He walked back to Mrs Benson.

He couldn't imagine what extraordinary turn in her fortunes had brought her back. After her scandalous departure with Monty Whatsit nobody in Kularook had expected to see her again. Was she actually returning to her lawful husband?

But Bowler always had a soft spot for long-legged independent girls — after all, he'd married one — so he raised his hand to tip his hat, remembered he was bareheaded, and smiled instead. 'Mrs Benson? Is someone meeting you?'

She turned from watching the drunk's unavailing efforts to sit up and studied Bowler in the uncertain light from the lantern. 'Mr Brown, is it?'

'I haven't seen Lew anywhere about tonight,' he said.

The carriages began to move past them; the engine huffs gathered speed and dwindled into the south.

'He was supposed to meet the day train, but I missed it.' She sounded angry.

He wasn't certain whether her anger was against herself or her husband, to whom, it seemed, she was returning. Did she ask Lew or did Lew ask her?

Bowler took a sardonic interest in the excesses of those he

referred to as his 'parishioners', and so was well aware of the stir this would cause among the district's numerous wowsers. Scandalised when she left, they wouldn't forgive her now, poor girl. That baby was none of Lew's getting.

All the same, he counted himself on her side. 'What are you going to do now?' he said.

She glanced into the shelter shed. 'Wait until daylight, I suppose, and then find someone to take me out to the farm.' She smiled, a quick softening of her taut, tired face. 'Don't worry, we'll be all right. It's a warm night.'

'You can't do that. I'll take you to the pub, wake Trotter Musgrave, get him to find you a bed. My car's just over there.'

'Sorry. I have no money.'

'Dammit, Lew can pay. Think of your baby.' Though if the child wasn't Lew's he might not be too complaisant about money spent on its welfare: he had a reputation as a mean bugger. Anyway, even if he didn't pay it wouldn't make any difference to the Musgraves, who would take her in for nothing if Bowler asked them. Em Musgrave must be the softest touch this side of the Dog Fence.

Agatha turned her face and rubbed her cheek against the baby's head; then she shrugged. 'All right. He won't like it but he can't kill me, after all.'

Bowler lifted the suitcase, using his other hand to haul his drunk to his feet. 'Sorry about this,' he said to Agatha. 'He has to come too. But he's harmless. Aren't you, sport?'

The man was hunched over, snivelling quietly, and made no answer; Bowler pushed him into the back seat of his Chrysler tourer. When he trod on the self-starter the stationmaster's dog at the nearest railway cottage started a frenzied barking, and set off most of the other dogs in the town.

The dogs had fallen quiet and silence blanketed the sleeping town when Bowler put his thumb on the night bell and heard a tinny ring somewhere deep inside the pub. He opened the never-locked front door. The pitch-dark hall smelled of old carpets and cigarette smoke, with a yeasty overlay of beer. A glow appeared in a passage to the left.

Not Trotter Musgrave but his wife Em trudged into view, a tall thin woman carrying a lighted candle and yawning to crack her jaws. Her feet were bare but otherwise she was fully dressed. Her iron-grey curls stuck up like a cocky's crest.

Bowler closed the door behind Agatha. 'Hullo, Em. Trotter poling on you, is he?'

She lifted her candle to see them better. 'Bowler? What the devil do you want at this time of night? And keep your damn voice down. Customers are sleeping.'

'Sorry. Em, can you rustle up a bed for Mrs Benson?'

'Come down to the kitchen.'

They followed her candle down a passage towards the back of the building. Shadows swirled in the big kitchen, still overheated from a day's cooking although the fire in the stove was out. A ticking clock on the mantelpiece underlined the silence.

Em turned. 'I was on my way to bed — a heavy night,' she said, and yawned again. 'I've been at Thompsons', Jeannette had her baby. Don't know why bloody babies can't keep office hours.'

Bowler said, 'Lew was expecting Mrs Benson on the day train, but she missed it and it seems he's gone home. She needs somewhere to sleep.'

'Yes of course, Mrs Benson,' Em said, as though she'd been trying to remember. 'Lew and his brother were in the bar around lunchtime. Looked a bit sour.' She studied the young woman with open curiosity.

'They would be,' Agatha said.

She stood parade-ground straight, both arms round her sleeping baby as though to protect it from their gaze. She must know Em's reputation as one of Kularook's most dedicated gossips. Bowler saw her strained expression, her attempted mask of indifference, and admired her fortitude.

Em smiled with a warmth that lifted Bowler's spirits too. 'Welcome back. There's a room over here,' she said, and crossed the passage to open a door on the other side.

'Thank you, Mrs Musgrave.' Agatha sounded stiff rather than grateful, as though she resented having to accept favours. 'I wouldn't be here if I had anywhere else to go.'

Bowler wondered whether she meant anywhere else that would give her a bed for the night, or anywhere else but back in Kularook, waiting for her lawful husband.

When Em came back she shoved aside the plates stacked ready for breakfast to make room on the table for the candle, then took a small spirit stove from a cupboard and put on a kettle. The smell of burning meths flooded over the odours of cooked mutton and wood ashes.

Bowler stood for a moment where the candle created a small island of light in the shadowed room, watching her make tea. 'No, none for me,' he said. 'Em, if Lew doesn't turn up tell Mrs Benson I'll run her out after breakfast. Thanks for taking her in.'

'What were you doing, meeting the express in the middle of the night?'

'Collecting a drunk. He's sleeping it off in the lockup.'

'Blasted drunks,' Em said, with the tolerance of a woman who earned part of her income selling intoxicating liquors. She glanced at the open door and lowered her voice. 'Do you suppose Lew knows about the baby? It can't be his.'

'No idea.'

'She looks at the end of her tether, poor girl.' When Bowler merely grunted she continued, 'She's pretty brave to come back.'

'Yes.'

'I was never surprised that she left, mind you. Those Bensons are a strange lot. I can't imagine why she married Lew in the first place.'

Bowler wasn't about to speculate on the workings of the female heart. Nor was he going to stand around gossiping with Em Musgrave in the middle of the night.

'See you tomorrow,' he said. He let himself out the back door and crossed the side street to his house.

www.ingramcontent.com/pod-product-compliance
Lightning Source LLC
Chambersburg PA
CBHW061923130726
47909CB00012B/202